A KISS FROM A PRINCESS

"So, let *me* be perfectly clear, your lordship," she said, jabbing a finger in his direction. "You are not my brother, my father, or anything else that gives you the right to command me. I am a woman grown and I have proven time and again that I am more than capable of making sensible and rational decisions. And given the extremely precarious position in which my grandmother and I find ourselves, my plan is without a doubt the most sensible course of action." She gave her head a dramatic toss. "You, Lord Lendale, have nothing to say about it."

Her disdainful tone and her rejection of their relationship set off a little explosion in Jack's head. He marched around the desk and planted himself in front of her, his legs spread and his hands propped on his hips. It forced Lia to tilt her head back to meet his gaze, glare for glare.

"As much as it pains me to speak so bluntly—" he started.

"Ha! I doubt that."

"The circumstances demand that I must do so," he said, ignoring her jibe. "You are no more an actress than a courtesan. You are no more a Notorious Kincaid than I am. What you are is an innocent and nice young lady who was raised in the country. And that is exactly where you will remain until I figure out how to deal with this situation."

Her eyes blazed with icy blue fire. "I beg to differ, my lord. If I put my mind to it, I'm quite sure I can be just as notorious as the other women in my family."

Then she reached up and clamped his face between her palms. She went up on her toes and planted her mouth on his, kissing him with a fury that almost knocked him off his feet . . .

Books by Vanessa Kelly

MASTERING THE MARQUESS

SEX AND THE SINGLE EARL

MY FAVORITE COUNTESS

HIS MISTLETOE BRIDE

The Renegade Royals

SECRETS FOR SEDUCING A ROYAL BODYGUARD

CONFESSIONS OF A ROYAL BRIDEGROOM

HOW TO PLAN A WEDDING FOR A ROYAL SPY

HOW TO MARRY A ROYAL HIGHLANDER

The Improper Princesses

MY FAIR PRINCESS

THREE WEEKS WITH A PRINCESS

AN INVITATION TO SIN
(with Jo Beverley, Sally MacKenzie,
and Kaitlin O'Riley)

Published by Kensington Publishing Corporation

THREE WEEKS with A PRINCESS

VANESSA KELLY

ZEBRA BOOKS
KENSINGTON PUBLISHING CORP.
http://www.kensingtonbooks.com

ZEBRA BOOKS are published by

Kensington Publishing Corp.
119 West 40th Street
New York, NY 10018

First Printing: July 2017
ISBN-13: 978-1-4201-4111-5
ISBN-10: 1-4201-4111-2

eISBN-13: 978-1-4201-4112-2
eISBN-10: 1-4201-4112-0

10 9 8 7 6 5 4 3 2 1

Printed in the United States of America

Prologue

Lia Kincaid adored Stonefell Hall during the Christmas season, despite the fact that it was the time of year she was most likely to be barred from the place she considered home. As she gazed down at the baronial splendor of the great entrance hall, now festively adorned with swags of evergreens and bay leaves, she couldn't help glowing with a sense of pride and, yes, ownership.

But Stonefell wasn't home. Home for her was a short walk down a country lane to Bluebell Cottage. Bluebell was undeniably charming, except when the roof leaked or the chimneys smoked during an east wind. Still, one learned to live with pans strategically scattered around the house to catch drips and windows could be opened if a parlor grew too smoky.

Of course, Lia had no choice but to live with leaks and other little annoyances. Her grandmother would never complain to the cottage's owner, the Marquess of Lendale, about something as mundane as a leaky roof because his lordship had other things on his mind when calling on

Granny. The two of them lived in a romantic bubble when they were together, leaving the boring details to Lia to handle.

And speaking of leaks, her boots were getting as aerated as the cottage roof. Lia wriggled her damp feet to restore some warmth to her toes, but her cramped position behind a wooden screen made it difficult to move. Maintaining her crouch, she inched her way across the long gallery that overlooked the hall. At the opposite end, she was finally able to stand and partly hide herself behind a stone column. It was colder now because she was farther from the roaring blaze of the hall's stone fireplace, but at least she could hop around and send blood flowing back to her limbs.

Her position offered her an excellent view of Lord John Easton, along with his daughter, Lady Anne, and his wife, Lady John Easton—Elizabeth to her family and close friends.

Neither Lia nor Granny could count Lady John as either family or friend.

The Eastons, who were spending the holiday with the Marquess of Lendale, Lord John's older brother, were the reason for Lia's temporary banishment from Stonefell Hall, when she normally had the run of the place. If Lady John caught sight of either Lia or her grandmother, fire and brimstone would rain down from the skies.

Lady John blamed Lia's grandmother for bringing disgrace to the Lendale good name, and her hatred for the notorious Rebecca Kincaid ran deep. It didn't matter that the marquess had installed Granny on the estate over ten years ago, or that he continued to openly support both her and Lia with the clear intention of doing so for the rest of his life. In Lady John's eyes, Granny was the harlot and enchantress who'd caused Lendale to lose both his wits and his sterling reputation.

But it was mostly because of Anne that Lia was ordered

to remain hidden. Lady John was adamant that her daughter not be exposed to the *moral pollution* of any one of the Kincaids.

Lia propped her shoulder against the column and studied the elegant, beautiful girl. Anne was dressed in a white velvet gown trimmed with spangles that made her shimmer like a Christmas bauble under the flickering lights of the massive chandelier hanging over the hall. She was destined for great things on the marriage mart according to the gossip in the kitchens. And she was certainly popular tonight, with a bevy of callow bachelors trailing along in her wake.

Despite her proud demeanor, Anne had a charming smile and a cheerful laugh that made Lia think they could be chums if given half a chance.

But, of course, they never would be. It would be wildly inappropriate for such a fine young lady to suffer the insult of Lia's presence. After all, not only was she the grand-daughter of Lendale's mistress, she was the daughter of a famous actress *and* illegitimate to boot. Lia had often wondered what would happen if Lady John discovered she and Anne had accidentally run into each other a few times. Total mayhem would most likely ensue, or at least a great deal of screeching and possibly even a decorous faint.

Nothing good came from the visits of Lord John and his family. Nothing good at all.

With one gloriously earth-shattering exception. Jack Easton, eldest child and only son of Lord John and Lady John, would be visiting, too. That fact made up for all the inconveniences and slights a thousand times over.

Unfortunately, Lia's chances of spending any significant amount of time with Jack seemed remote; he was staying in Yorkshire for less than a week and his blasted family was doing their best to monopolize his attention. Not that she could blame them; monopolizing his time was precisely what *she* had been longing for since he'd arrived.

She'd lost sight of Jack about ten minutes earlier because the hall was filled to bursting with the local gentry, all come to partake of the festive hospitality of the Marquess of Lendale. Jack had looked ridiculously handsome and dashing in his new regimentals and, not surprisingly, a horde of country girls had trailed behind him like a gigantic, multihued scarf of fluttering, flirtatious butterflies.

Lia only saw Jack three times a year—at Christmas and two other school holidays, when he came by himself to visit. Because of that, she couldn't help resenting the fashionable, well-bred girls who could speak to him, flirt with him, and dance with him whenever they pleased. It was a luxury she longed for with all her heart.

You nitwit. As if Jack Easton could ever—would ever—fall in love with you.

How could he? Lia was one of the Notorious Kincaids, though the description was ridiculous when applied to her. Skinny, with freckles, and as flat as a board, she could no more follow in the famous footsteps of her mother and grandmother than conjure a mug of wassail from thin air. Despite her scandalous parentage, Lia was as ordinary a country girl as one could imagine.

Still, being ordinary didn't make her acceptable, as least not for the likes of Jack Easton, who was destined to be the Marquess of Lendale one day.

"Lurking in the shadows again, are we? I swear you'd make a splendid spy in Wellington's army."

As Lia jerked around, her foot caught on the sodden hem of her gown. She squeaked as she fell back against the banister rail, frantically pinwheeling her arms to regain her balance. Jack shot out a hand and snatched her from danger.

"Confound it, Lia," he gasped. "Be careful."

After casting a glance into the hall, Jack drew her into the shadows at the back of the gallery.

"I'm sorry," she said. "That was very silly of me." Compared to the elegant young ladies he'd been dancing with earlier, she must seem like a foolish bumpkin.

Jack gave her a brief, fierce hug before holding her at arm's length to inspect her. "Pet, don't apologize. I'm the one who snuck up and startled you. I'm just thankful I caught you before you toppled over the side."

"Jack, I'm not *that* clumsy."

Laughter crept into his dark gaze. "Of course you aren't. I don't know how I could remotely suggest such a thing."

She sighed. "I suppose because you've saved my life any number of times over the years?"

"Well, I *have* pulled you out of the pond at least twice. And then there was that time you knocked down the wasp's nest, and the time you almost fell out of the tree, and the time you knocked over that heavy bookshelf in the library—"

"At least two of those incidents were your fault in the first place. But I will concede that you've rescued me more than a few times. And you're an absolute beast to point that out, by the way."

"I am, aren't I? But whatever would you do without me around?"

He was joking, of course, but it still made her chest go tight with sorrow. Soon she *would* have to do without him. Jack was a man now, and a soldier. In just a matter of weeks, he would be embarking on a life of adventure. God only knew when she would see him again.

"I expect I'll rub along just fine without you," she said, forcing a light tone. She refused to ruin the few moments they had together with high-flown dramatics. He had to put up with enough of that from his mother.

"It was very nice of you to come up here to see me," she added.

"I spotted you crouching behind the screen. That red pelisse of yours was a dead giveaway. Not that I hadn't already guessed you'd be up here."

Lia's heart thundered into a gallop. "No one else saw me, did they?"

Lord Lendale would be angry if he knew she was spying on his guests. She wasn't even supposed to be in the house, much less lurking about the gallery, where she risked discovery.

"No one else saw you," he said. "Except for Richard. He sees everything."

She heaved a relieved sigh. "That's all right, then. He'll scold me, but he won't rat on me to his lordship." Richard was the head footman and one of Lia's biggest supporters at Stonefell Hall. He'd been only a kitchen boy when she'd arrived all those years ago. They'd all but grown up together.

"Fortunately, I managed to distract Debbins before he got a glimpse of you," he said.

Unlike most of the servants, who treated her with indulgence, the butler was offended by her very presence. "Thank you for saving me," she said wryly. "Again."

Jack frowned. "Debbins doesn't mistreat you, does he?"

"Of course not. Lord Lendale would never allow that."

"But he's not very nice to you, is he?"

She shrugged. "It doesn't bother me very much."

His frown deepened to a scowl. "I'll have a word—"

"No. That won't help at all."

"Lia—"

"Why are we talking about that old rusty guts anyway? We've not had a moment to chat and I expect you have to go back down soon before you're missed." She smiled up into his dear, handsome face. "How are you? Are you enjoying your duties in the Horse Guards? I must say you look simply wonderful in your uniform."

He grinned, his evident pride making him seem boyish again. "It's even better than I expected. I've been assigned to Northumberland's staff, so I'll be heading out for the Peninsula within the next few months, I expect."

The very idea of him anywhere near the war terrified her, but she refused to let him see it. Jack had always longed for a military career, and thanks to his uncle's willingness to buy him a commission, he'd finally gotten his greatest wish. As a true friend, she *must* be happy for him.

"That's splendid," she said. "I hope you'll find the chance now and again to write to us here in boring old Yorkshire. It's beastly quiet, you know. Your letters are always a welcome distraction for me and Granny."

"I will, whenever I get the chance."

"You promise you won't forget?" she asked, unable to help herself.

His dark eyes went soft and warm. "I could never forget you, Lia. You know that."

She tried to smile. Of course he would forget her. After all, she was simply a girl, not yet even sixteen. There would be no reason for him to retain more than the occasional vaguely affectionate memory of her.

But to Lia, Jack was the entire world.

When the small orchestra launched into a new set of dances, they both glanced toward the party below.

"You'd best go down before you're missed," she said softly.

"I've a few more minutes and you've not yet told me how *you* are." His gaze traveled over her form. "The hem of your pelisse is soaked." He reached out and took her hand. "And your fingers are freezing."

Though she was indeed freezing, she didn't care. Not when she could spend time with Jack. "I'm fine."

"Did you cut through the back garden?"

"It's the best way to get here without being seen." It meant she'd had to tramp through a foot of snow before she could sneak into the house through his lordship's library.

He gave a disapproving shake of his head. "We've got to get you warm before you go back or you'll catch a chill."

"Really, Jack, it's—"

He forestalled her objection by practically dragging her over to the staircase at the other end of the gallery.

"What are you doing? Someone will see us," she hissed.

"Only if you keep making so much noise, you goose."

Lia huffed a bit, pretending to be offended by his high-handed manner. But, actually, she loved it. She'd follow Jack Easton across the River Styx if he asked her.

They crept down the narrow, winding staircase to the corridor below. It ran from the great hall to the east wing, where the library, the breakfast room, and one of the smaller drawing rooms were located. Because no one would be in those rooms at this time of night, the corridor was deserted.

But Richard popped up before them, making Lia gasp.

"Oh, there you are," Jack said in an easy tone. "Miss Lia rather soaked her pelisse on the way to the house, so I'm taking her to the library to warm up before she returns to the cottage."

"Very good, sir. I took the liberty of lighting a fire a few minutes ago, so the room should be nice and warm by now."

Lia wrinkled her nose at the young footman, who carried himself with a dignity beyond his years. "How did you know?"

"Did we not previously agree that Richard always knows?" Jack said. "Now, come along before you catch your death of cold."

As he hauled her along the corridor, Lia cast a thank-you smile over her shoulder. The footman shook his head with disapproval. Richard was another one who worried about her getting into trouble, although she couldn't imagine what sort of trouble she was supposed to get into with Jack. In his company, she was always safe.

They slipped into the library, their footfalls muffled by the thick Axminster carpet that insulated them from the chill of the old stone floors.

Jack led her to the fireplace and pushed her down onto the thickly padded seat of a club chair. With a sigh of pleasure, she stretched her feet toward the merrily leaping flames, luxuriating in the heat that washed over her.

"Good Lord," he said, crouching down before her.

"What is it?"

He felt her foot. "Your boots are soaked through." His hand moved up to her ankle. "And so are your stockings."

His warm fingers marked her like a brand, even through her thick woolen stockings. Cheeks flaming, Lia jerked away and tucked her feet under herself on the chair. Jack muttered an oath and tugged them back out, propping them against the firedogs.

He inspected her boots with disfavor. "When was the last time you had a new pair?"

Now even more embarrassed, Lia simply shrugged. The boots, hand-me-downs from her grandmother, were perfectly fine for puttering around in dry lanes in mild weather, but the soles had lately sprung a leak. Even lining them with scraps of wool and linen had failed to keep the moisture out.

Jack let out a sigh as he came to his feet, his broad shoulders and long, muscular legs backlit by the fire. She swore he'd grown two inches since she'd last seen him and had certainly filled out very nicely.

"When was the last time you had a new pair of boots?" he insistently repeated.

She waved a vague hand. "Oh, these are just one of my older pairs. I didn't want to ruin the good ones in the snow."

His snort indicated how little he believed that Banbury tale, but Lia chose not to argue. Money had been a bit scarcer of late, although she wasn't sure why. Lord Lendale provided Granny and her with whatever they needed. But he'd recently been forgetful, neglecting details like new boots for her or Granny's favorite gunpowder tea, sent special from London.

Far worse, he'd neglected repairs to their increasingly leaky roof, which was certainly not a luxury.

"I'll speak to my uncle," Jack said. "He'll see to it that you get a new pair."

She shot upright in her seat. "No, please don't."

"Don't be silly, Lia."

"Jack, I'm serious. Don't make a fuss."

"Whyever not? Uncle Arthur would be very unhappy to know you're going about with wet feet."

"Because Granny hates fussing at Lord Lendale, that's why. Or make him feel guilty, which is even worse. He's been so good to us, and we have absolutely no right to complain."

Because his back was to the fire, Jack's face was mostly in shadow. But Lia could see the annoyed set to his shoulders. "Jack, please let it go, for my sake."

"He should take better care of you," he replied in a hard voice.

"Lord Lendale takes excellent care of us, I assure you." She patted the arm of the chair next to her. "Please sit down, at least for a minute. You're like some giant looming over me. I feel quite intimidated."

"That's a laugh," he said, sitting down. "Listen to me, Lia. I'm taking you into the village before I leave and buying you a new pair of boots." He cut off her objections with an imperious hand. "Think of it as my Christmas present to you."

Jack was loyal to a fault, and she knew he worried about her and her grandmother. More than anyone, he understood their precarious position as dependents on Lord Lendale's support. Lia had formed the impression over the years that Jack didn't think his uncle had treated Rebecca Kincaid as well as he should. She half agreed with that opinion, although it seemed utterly disloyal to the man who'd, in many ways, stood in as a father to her.

"Thank you," she said, giving him a warm smile. "But that would be much too generous."

"I can't go waltzing off to the Peninsula knowing you're freezing your feet off up here in Yorkshire. I'd worry so much about you that I'd likely fall into a horrible decline."

She laughed. "Now you're just being silly."

He turned his head to smile at her. "I am, but you should know that I'd already planned to take you shopping for a present before I left for London."

She ignored the stab of pain that pierced her whenever she thought of him going so far away. "I've got a Christmas present for you, too."

"Pet, that was sweet of you, but I don't want you spending money on me." His deep voice curled around her, bringing warmth and peace.

"Then you'll be happy to know I didn't spend a farthing," she replied with a cheeky grin.

He snorted. "Brat. What did you get me?"

She fished under her pelisse and extracted a square of fabric from the inside pocket of her gown. Carefully, she unfolded it to show him the small object contained within.

"Good Lord," he breathed as he took it from her. "Where did you find it?"

"At the ruins of the abbey outside Ripon. Your uncle took Granny and me there last August."

While her grandmother and his lordship had sat on a blanket, talking softly and making sheep's eyes at each other, Lia had gone off exploring the ruins. It had been the luckiest chance when, climbing over a tumbledown wall, her foot had slipped, sending her down on her bottom into the grass. She hadn't hurt herself, but she had dislodged some of the crumbling stone. Lying in the dirt beside her had been an old Roman coin.

Lia had known instantly what she would do with her find. Jack had a passion for history and had spent many a holiday rummaging around various ruins. Roman, Saxon, Norman: He loved them all. Granny had even allowed Lia to go with him a few times, once to the very ruins where she'd found the coin.

"That's where I took you when you were just a little girl," he said as he held the coin up to the light.

"Not so little," she protested.

"You were only nine," he said with a wry smile.

"I suppose you're right," she grumbled. He probably still thought of her as a little girl.

"And a rather grubby one, as I recall," he joked.

"Now you sound like Granny," she said.

He reached over and tugged one of the curls that hung limply by her cheek. "I'm just teasing. Seriously, Lia, this coin is in excellent condition. Are you sure you want to give it to me?"

"Of course," she said, stung that he would even consider refusing it. "I told you, it's your Christmas present."

As he studied her, she felt strangely awkward, as if he saw something new in her.

"Thank you, sweet girl." He tucked the coin inside his coat pocket. "I'll keep it with me always as a good-luck charm."

"And it will help you to remember me when you're far away."

"Goose. As if I could ever forget you."

If only she could believe he would not. "Truly?"

"Of course. You are my dear little friend."

She swallowed a sigh.

When the mantel clock quietly bonged out the quarter hour, Jack grimaced.

"You have to go," she said.

"Yes. I'm sorry. Forgive me."

Lia stood. "Don't be silly. You'll get in trouble if you stay away any longer."

He took her hand and led her to the French doors that opened to the terrace and back garden. From there, she could cut through to the path that led to Bluebell Cottage.

"Go straight home," he said as he opened the doors. "No hanging about and trying to catch a glimpse of the festivities, understand? You'll get too cold again."

"Yes, Jack," she said dutifully. "You don't have to worry about me." She could take care of herself, but his concern warmed her more than any fire could.

"I promise I'll come down in a day or so to visit you and your grandmother," he said.

She smiled up at him before slipping through the door. Then she paused for a moment. "They're singing carols," she said quietly.

He stepped outside and stood with her on the wide terrace, where the stones had been swept clean of snow. When he put a casual arm around her shoulders and tucked her against his side, Lia's throat went tight with emotion.

An enthusiastic if slightly off-key rendition of "Joy to the World" drifted out from the great hall. Lia glanced up at the sky, an inky vault with a bright spangle of stars flung across the void. When she gasped, Jack followed her gaze skyward.

He laughed. "Well, look at that."

It was a shooting star. No, not one, but another and then another, as if fired from the barrel of an enormous gun.

"Quick, Lia. Make a wish," Jack said.

Two wishes came to her instantly. The first was that whatever travels or dangers he faced, Jack would always come safely home. The second was that someday she would stand again on this terrace with him, but as a grown woman. Then she would finally tell him that she loved him with all her heart.

"Did you make a wish, too?" she whispered.

"I did."

"Are you going to tell me what it was?"

He pressed a brief kiss to the top of her head before letting go. "No, because if I told you, it wouldn't come true. Besides, it might annoy you," he added in a teasing tone.

She poked him in the side. "You are so irritating, Jack Easton."

He smiled at her, looking impossibly handsome. "I know, but I'll make it up to you when I next visit."

"Promise?"

"I promise."

"I'll see you later, then," she said, starting for the terrace steps.

"Lia."

She looked over her shoulder. "Yes?"

"Merry Christmas, my dearest girl," he called softly.

Again her throat went so tight she couldn't force out a single word. So she simply raised a hand before slipping off into the dark winter night.

Chapter One

Yorkshire
July 1816

"How the hell did he let it become such a disaster?" Jack said, pushing aside the ledger. Every time he'd looked at the bloody thing he'd held out a faint hope that circumstances weren't as bad as they appeared. And every time he was wrong.

The large, leather-clad account book was one of several piled haphazardly before him on the library desk. On the other side of that pile sat Atticus Lindsey, the longtime estate manager at Stonefell and a truly estimable man. He had to be, because he'd put up with years of financial messes and managed to ameliorate some of the worst effects. But even Lindsey's business acumen and dedication to the family could no longer stave off the inevitable.

Thanks to Jack's uncle, the previous marquess, Stonefell Hall stood on the brink of ruin, and the Easton family fortunes weren't far behind.

His estate manager struggled to articulate some positive news—and failed.

"It's all right, Lindsey," Jack finally said. "I know we're

teetering on the edge of the abyss. The only question now is how to walk ourselves back from it."

The middle-aged widower, whose kind face and gentle manner were combined with a whip-smart mind, pulled a grimace. "There are a few things we can try, my lord. We can take down the remaining viable timber in the home wood, for one. The income from that would stave off the creditors till the next quarter."

Jack hated that idea. So many noble trees had already been lost. Stonefell's woods had once been the finest in this part of Yorkshire, but they were now a pale imitation of their former glory.

"We'll do that only as a last resort," he said. "I'm hoping the harvest will be better this year. The revenues from that should take us well into next year."

Lindsey eyed him. "Of course, sir."

In other words, *good luck with that, you bloody fool*.

He certainly wouldn't have blamed Lindsey if he'd said those words out loud. Jack had rarely involved himself in estate business, even though he'd known for two years that the Lendale title would fall directly to him. That was when Jack's father, heir to his older brother, had died of apoplexy, brought on by a life of drinking and excess. His father had evaded responsibility whenever possible. Even in death he'd run true to form and had left Jack to pick up the pieces of a family all but in ruins.

As for the recently deceased marquess . . . well, Uncle Arthur had been a kind man, loyal to family and friend alike. And he'd been more than generous to Jack, always providing him with a safe haven from his warring parents and helping him achieve a military career by purchasing his commission.

But as a man of business and a caretaker of the family fortune and legacy, the third Marquess of Lendale had been an absolute disaster.

"I'm sorry, my lord," Lindsey said in a tone warm with sympathy. "I wish I had better news to impart, but the tenant farmers are barely holding on as it is. We'll need years of good harvests to make up for the ground we've lost."

Jack repressed the impulse to bang his head on the pile of ledgers. Maybe if he did that long enough the figures would somehow untangle themselves. He'd spent so many late nights pouring over the damn numbers, searching for even a thread of good news, he could barely see straight.

For years he'd tried to escape all the family drama by focusing his energies on his military career. He'd worked his arse off, climbing up the chain of command until serving directly under Wellington himself. And even though the fortunes of war were often bleak, he'd loved his work. If fate had decreed otherwise, he'd still be in the army.

But fate *had* decreed otherwise, and now he was someone he'd never wanted to be—the Marquess of Lendale. The title had been shared by a disreputable group of aristocrats more known for their spendthrift, rakish lifestyles than for nurturing the blessings graced by God and king.

Well, he'd be damned if he was the one to bring the estate crashing down around his mother and sister. They deserved more than that, as did the tenants and staff who worked at Stonefell and in the mansion in London.

And he could never forget Lia and Rebecca, who were as much his responsibility as anyone else under his care.

"What about that idea you floated in your letter to me a few weeks back, when I was in Lincolnshire?" he asked Lindsey.

He'd been there for the wedding of his closest friend, the Duke of Leverton, to the unconventional Miss Gillian Dryden. It had been a welcome respite from his problems, although their marriage had raised a tricky issue he had yet to work out.

Lindsey brightened. "You mean Stonefell's potential for ore and coal mining? The surveys have yielded some very positive results, but in order to proceed, we need . . ."

"Additional investments," Jack said grimly.

"Yes, sir, for more surveys and preliminary explorations. And to go ahead with any sort of comprehensive venture at this point, we would need a substantial investment."

"Would selling the rest of the timber in the home wood be enough to get us started?" Jack loathed the very notion, but he'd be willing to make the sacrifice. A productive mining operation would not only provide jobs for his struggling tenants and villagers, it could alleviate the debts encumbering the estate.

"I'm afraid not," Lindsey said with a regretful shake of the head. "There's no doubt we need outside backers to establish a viable operation."

But any investor worth his salt would want to see profits as soon as possible. No one would be inclined to invest if they had to wait several years until Jack restored the estate to health. There was another alternative, of course, but he wasn't particularly thrilled about that one either.

He closed the ledger in front of him with a thud. "I think we've both depressed ourselves enough for one day, Lindsey. I'll be traveling to London in a few weeks. I will speak to my bankers about finding potential—and patient—investors while I'm there."

Lindsey stood up. "Very good, my lord. I can put out feelers to a few private investors when I'm next in Ripon, if you like."

"Do that but quietly. We don't need word getting around that things are as bad as they are."

"As you wish."

After Lindsey collected the ledgers and soft-footed his way out, Jack eyed the remaining work on his desk. It felt as if he'd been confined to the stuffy old room forever.

Normally, his uncle's library—his library now—was a favorite place to while away the time. It had always been a welcoming retreat, with its elegant Queen Anne furniture richly mellowed by age, a collection of books lovingly built up over the generations, and several truly impressive globes his uncle had acquired over the years. The handsome room spoke of the taste, wealth, and power of the Lendale line.

Today it felt more like a prison.

He stood and headed for the French doors, his hand automatically reaching out to spin the largest and oldest of the globes as he passed.

You really ought to sell that, old boy, along with the rest of them.

It just might come to that. Along with the antique volumes on the shelves, the globes would attract a pretty sum from a collector.

Shoving aside that unpleasant thought, he stepped onto the terrace, lifting his face to the late afternoon sun. It had been a cool, rainy summer, so even a hint of sunshine was welcome.

He gazed out over this little piece of his domain. The flower gardens behind the house had always been a pleasing mix of roses, flowering shrubs, and hedges. And although the roses still bloomed thick and full, and the ivy and honeysuckle twined lushly along the stone balustrades of the terrace, the garden was no longer up to its previous immaculate standards. The hedges looked a bit ragged, the roses verged on running wild, and the lawn was just a little too long. Old Merton, the head gardener, was doing his best, but Lindsey had been forced to let some outside staff go last year. Only the kitchen gardens were still in top shape, and that was thanks to Lia. According to the housekeeper, she diligently helped Merton tend the extensive herb and vegetable gardens that kept the house abundantly supplied.

Lia, what am I going to do with you?

Though he'd only returned to Stonefell two days before, he'd been avoiding her, which was a new and unwelcome development. Jack had loved the girl almost from the moment he'd met her, back when she'd been an engaging, mischief-prone toddler. Lia was family as far as he was concerned.

But she was also his friend, and a very good one. Although she was five years younger, Jack had long trusted her judgment. Lia was both funny and kind, but she also had an enormously practical head on her slim shoulders. After Lindsey, she knew more about the running of the estate than anyone. She'd grown up here, loving it with a fierce devotion that surpassed that of any member of the Easton family.

Unfortunately, that devotion to Stonefell was about to be poorly repaid. Of all the people on the estate, Lia and Rebecca Kincaid were the most vulnerable.

He couldn't put off imparting the grim news any longer. He counted it as ironic that when he could finally see his dear friend as often as he wanted, he was doing everything he could to avoid her.

Using the gate at the bottom of the garden, he strode along the pretty, tree-lined lane that led to Bluebell Cottage. Once a small dower house, Uncle Arthur had converted it into a private abode for his mistress. It was far enough from the main house to be out of sight and out of mind, when necessary, but still close enough for the previous marquess to easily visit the once-notorious Rebecca Kincaid whenever he wished. It had always struck Jack as a medieval arrangement that was manifestly unfair to both Rebecca and her granddaughter. Of course, he'd grown used to the odd situation over the years, as had most in the neighborhood, especially those who depended on the estate for their livelihood. That the marquess had loved his mistress with an abiding passion had never been in doubt, and he'd expected everyone in his circle to accept her presence as an immutable fact of life.

Jack's mother, naturally, had never accepted it. And now that he was the Marquess of Lendale, she expected him to do what she called *the moral thing*.

As he rounded a curve in the lane, the red slate roof of the cottage came into view, its old chimneys poking above the trees. More a small villa than a rustic abode, Bluebell Cottage was built with the sharp angles and pitched roof of the Jacobean era. Set well back from the lane and shaded by ash and sycamore trees, it was surrounded by an old-fashioned flower garden with a spectacular display of rosebushes. But unlike the larger garden at the main house, Bluebell's flower beds were pristinely maintained, flourishing under an expert hand.

Lia's hand. She'd always loved to garden and had never minded getting dirty and wet. As a little girl, she'd been Merton's shadow, imitating his every move. Her enthusiasm and cheery ways had charmed the crusty old gardener, and almost everyone else at Stonefell Hall.

Jack had always believed Lia was the true reason Rebecca had finally been accepted by the estate staff and the locals. Setting up one's mistress in the backyard wasn't generally the done thing, but with Lia's unwitting help, his uncle had pulled it off.

He rapped on the front door. After waiting a few minutes, he hammered again. One of the mullioned windows of the drawing room, to the right of the door, pushed open. Rebecca, her beautifully coiffed, salt-and-pepper hair, topped by a snowy white cap, leaned out.

"Ah, my dear Lord Lendale," she said in an affectionate voice. "I haven't a clue where Sarah is, or Lia, for that matter, and the maid has run down to the village to fetch some headache powders. But the door is open, so do let yourself in."

She retreated with consummate dignity, shutting the window.

Jack couldn't hold back a grin. Leave it to Rebecca to tell the new marquess to walk right in rather than condescend to answer the door herself. Her present position might be precarious but she had been the longtime lover of the Marquess of Lendale and once had been the most sought-after courtesan in London. Although a truly kind and charming woman, she never let the world forget who she was, nor who she once had been.

Not that he blamed her. She didn't have anything else to hang on to now that the man she'd loved for so many years—the man for whom she'd given up so much—was dead.

Jack let himself into the low-ceilinged corridor that ran from the front of the house to the back. A narrow staircase halfway down the hall climbed up to the first floor, with its bedrooms and a private sitting room. It was a lovely old house, with intricate woodwork and paneling, as well as some truly fine plasterwork.

But it was in dire need of repair, especially the roof and chimneys.

He knocked briefly on the drawing room door, which was rather silly because Rebecca was expecting him. But she drew comfort from the formalities, and Jack wished her to know that she still had his respect and friendship, even if she had lost all else.

She moved to greet him. Now in her early sixties, she remained an extremely handsome woman, with a plump, comfortable figure and a welcoming manner. But despite her genuinely pleased smile, he saw sadness in her gaze and weariness in the faint web of wrinkles fanning out from her blue eyes. It had been over three months since his uncle's passing, but Rebecca clearly still grieved. The poor woman had been, for all intents and purposes, the man's wife. And yet she'd been denied even the solace of attending the church services or receiving the sympathy of family and friends.

"Aunt Rebecca, it's good to see you," Jack said, bending to brush a kiss against her cheek. He'd referred to her that way in private for years, which had always pleased his uncle.

"Dear boy, it is so good of you to call," she said, waving him to the settee across from her high-backed chair. "Lia and I were beginning to quite despair of seeing you."

"I apologize for not coming down yesterday. I find myself swamped in paperwork and an endless stream of . . . business." He'd been about to say *disasters*.

"I'm sure you have a great deal of work to attend to, settling the estate and becoming familiar with your new responsibilities. If you need help, you must be sure to ask Lia. Sometimes I think she knows Stonefell as well as Mr. Lindsey."

"She does," he said with a smile. "By the by, where is she?"

Rebecca glanced at the watch pinned to her waist. "I'm surprised you didn't run into her in the lane; she said she'd be home by now. She ran up to the stables to speak to the stableman about her mare. I think Dorcas may be in need of new shoes." She hesitated. "If it's not too much of a bother, that is."

Jack's uncle had always let Lia ride any horse she chose, even picking one out for her special use.

"You needn't even ask."

"Thank you," she said, sounding relieved. "We hate to impose, but you know Lia wouldn't ask if it wasn't necessary."

"Please don't worry, Aunt Rebecca. Now, tell me how you've been. I hope you're well."

As they chatted for a few minutes about the usual mundane things like the weather, Rebecca was clearly making an effort to be cheerful. But Jack could tell it was a strain. His uncle had been the touchstone of her increasingly narrow and circumscribed life. Without him, she must feel her future uncertain.

"And how was your trip to Lincolnshire?" she asked. "I presume the Duke of Leverton's wedding went off without a hitch." Her carefully neutral tone didn't fool Jack in the slightest.

"It was a small, private affair but very happy nonetheless. And I'm glad Lia's not back yet because I wanted to talk to you about that."

"Yes, I expect you do," she said with a rueful smile. "You want to know whether you should tell Lia that Gillian Dryden—the new Duchess of Leverton—is her cousin."

He'd been struggling with that question for some weeks. Leverton was his closest friend, which meant Gillian would now be part of Jack's life. She was the illegitimate daughter of the Duke of Cumberland, the fifth son of King George and brother to the Prince Regent. Because Lia was the illegitimate daughter of the Duke of York, the second son of the king, she and Gillian were cousins.

"Yes," he said. "Naturally I knew I had to discuss the situation with you first. But you must understand there may come a point when Leverton and his duchess will visit Stonefell."

Though dismay flashed across Rebecca's features, her impressive discipline soon reasserted itself. "That's to be expected, naturally. As you know, your uncle rarely entertained due to his health." She forced a smile. "But such

THREE WEEKS WITH A PRINCESS   25

will not be the case with you, I'm sure. You will wish to entertain friends, as well as your mother and sister."

Best to leave aside the issue of his family for the moment. "I'm not planning on rounds of large house parties." Especially given how bloody expensive they were. "But we must at least anticipate the possibility."

"I understand. And to set your mind at ease, Lia *is* aware that the royal dukes dispensed their favors rather widely."

Jack almost laughed at the vagueness of her metaphor. Despite being a noted courtesan, Rebecca had always displayed a delicate attitude when it came to discussing scandalous behavior. In fact, she and his uncle had always reminded him of a rather fussy couple who'd been married forever. Emotionally, they certainly had been. Unfortunately, their steadfast devotion had counted for little in the eyes of the world and nothing in the eyes of the law.

For all his kindness, Uncle Arthur had done Rebecca a great disservice. He either should have married her long ago or said farewell, so she could have pursued wealthier patrons. Rebecca could have become a wealthy woman if she'd remained in London, selecting lovers who would have rewarded her with small fortunes. But his uncle had been too selfish to let her go and too weak to fight against his family's opposition to their marriage.

"So Lia is aware that her situation is not unique?" he asked.

"Of course. It would be impossible not to be aware of the Duke of Clarence's children, for instance, particularly because Mrs. Jordon once traveled in the same theatrical circles as my daughter."

Rebecca's mouth had pulled down in a distasteful little grimace, which clearly indicated her opinion of Clarence's long-standing mistress and the mother of his numerous children. But that might also be resentment on her part; Clarence had acknowledged his by-blows and made some attempt to provide for them. Such had not been the case for Lia and her mother.

"But as a rule we do not discuss such matters," she added. "The Duke of York has never even acknowledged Lia. And my daughter has always been loath to expose Lia to the sort of gossip that comes from contact with the royal dukes, preferring her to lead a more sheltered life in the country with me."

For the last ten years, Lia's mother, Marianne Lester, had been married to the manager of a popular acting troupe. They generally performed in the provinces, but Stephen Lester's troupe had recently taken up a contract in London. Lia would love nothing more than to spend time with her mother, but Jack couldn't help but feel relief that she'd remained safely at Stonefell. The theatrical environment was a hive of salacious scandal and gossip, not for an innocent girl like her.

"We're agreed on that," he said. "But it still leaves us with the issue of the Duchess of Leverton. I think we must soon tell Lia that she has a cousin who will wish to meet her, likely within the next few months. If we don't, the duchess will eventually take matters into her own hands."

The only reason Gillian probably wasn't riding hell-bent for leather for Yorkshire at this very moment was because Jack had sworn the duke to a reluctant secrecy on the matter, at least for now. Once Gillian found out, there would be no stopping her.

"I suppose," Rebecca said. "Although I fail to see how the relationship benefits Lia one bit. After all, the Duchess of Leverton, despite her illegitimate origins, is the daughter of aristocrats and royalty and has the bluest blood in the land. Whereas Lia . . ."

"Comes from good English stock and has a mother and grandmother who love her," Jack interjected. Rebecca Kincaid had come from a family of prosperous merchants in London, and she would have made a respectable marriage if fate hadn't set her on a different course.

Her warm smile rewarded him. "Thank you, Jack. You've always been so kind to us. No wonder my granddaughter worships the ground you walk on."

Her observation made him mentally blink. It seemed an odd way to characterize Lia's affection for him.

"Ah, thank you," he said. "So I take it you do not wish to inform Lia about her connection to the Duchess of Leverton, or some of her other relations, at least for the time being?"

She nodded. "Yes. I must ponder the best way to approach the subject with my granddaughter. Lia must not be allowed to make assumptions about a relationship with the duchess, or make any demands on her. That will only lead to heartache for her. She can never travel in such exalted circles, nor should she have any expectation of doing so."

Her assessment was likely correct. Unlike Gillian, Lia could never hope to ascend into the ranks of the aristocracy, or even the country gentry. Rebecca's fondest wish had always been for Lia to make a respectable marriage with a local merchant or prosperous farmer, and Jack had always known that would be the kindest, happiest outcome for her. But even that future was in jeopardy, thanks to his uncle's stupidity.

"Very well," he replied. "I'll defer to your judgment for now. But when the Levertons visit Stonefell, we must tell Lia the truth—if not before."

Rebecca looked relieved, as if she'd been expecting an argument. "Of course, my dear boy. And thank you for trusting me."

They heard a quick footfall out in the hall. A moment later the door opened and Lia rushed in.

"Oh, confound it, Jack," she said. "I had no idea you were here. I ran down from the big house as soon as Merton told me he'd seen you cutting through the gardens." She rested a hand on his arm and stretched up on her toes to give him a soft kiss on the cheek. "It's shocking that I wasn't here to greet you. Please forgive me."

Jack stared down at her, slightly disoriented, as if someone had given him a knock on the brainbox.

He hadn't seen her since his uncle's funeral, when grief and worry had left her pretty face pinched and wan. Enveloped in mourning clothes and heavy shawls to keep out the chill spring rains, Lia had seemed almost like a sad child, sorely in need of a mother's love and comfort.

Today, though, there was nothing childlike about her, and she was more than merely pretty. His Lia was now full-grown and simply beautiful.

She gazed up at him with peacock-blue eyes alight with affection. Her skin glowed with the warmth of the summer sun and the flush of her exertions. Her enchanting face, with its tip-tilted nose and lush pink mouth, was framed by silky dark hair, some of it falling haphazardly from the simple knot on top of her head. As for her figure, her faded green riding habit with its trim bodice showcased a graceful body that held more than its share of pleasing curves.

When the hell had Lia developed breasts that he actually noticed?

His visits to Stonefell had been rare these last three years, given the fact that he'd spent much of that time on the Continent with the army. In the meantime, his little friend had matured into a woman, with results that were rather astonishing.

And alarming.

Her brow creased and her smile slid into one of perplexity. "Jack, you look as if you don't know me," she said with a self-conscious laugh. Then her smile snuffed out completely. "Oh, am I being too familiar?"

She took a quick step back and dipped into a curtsy. "Forgive me, my lord. I let my enthusiasm run away with me."

Her anxious response jolted him back to himself. He pulled her into a bear hug, all too conscious of how delightful her soft breasts felt against his body.

"Goose, of course not," he said, planting a brief kiss on the top of her head before letting go. "I was just a bit surprised to see you, that's all. You're looking very well, I must say."

She wrinkled her nose. "That's a complete plumper. I look a wreck, but I didn't want to take the time to change and risk missing you."

Rebecca ran a critical eye over her granddaughter. "You do look rather disheveled, my love. I wasn't aware you were planning on shoeing the mare yourself, but the soot on the hem of your habit would suggest you were."

Lia burst into laughter, and the light, clear sound of it loosened the tangled knot in Jack's chest that had moved in some weeks ago. He'd forgotten how much he enjoyed her laughter.

"I know," she said. "But poor Markwith is so busy these days. I thought I'd help him by taking Dorcas down to the blacksmith and saving him the trouble of the trip."

Jack mentally grimaced. In the last year his head groom had been forced to let go two stableboys. That Lia was now acting as a stable hand had the knot in his chest twisting tight again.

"I'm sorry, Lia," he said. "You shouldn't have had to do that."

"You know I don't mind," she said as she folded herself onto the footstool at her grandmother's feet. Rebecca reached out to stroke Lia's thick hair. They were so close. With the death of Jack's uncle, the two women truly now had only each other.

And him.

"Next time you need something, just tell me," he said. "I'll take care of it."

Her eyebrows arched up. "I will when you're in residence. But that's not very often."

Rebecca gave her an admonishing tap on the shoulder. "That's no way to speak to his lordship, my love."

Lia's eyes rounded with mock horror. "Oh, I do hope I haven't offended him." She gave him a comical bow, her nose almost touching the floor. "Forgive my impertinence, Lord Lendale, I beg of you."

He shook his head. "Brat."

She grinned. "Sorry, but I can't help teasing. It's just so good to see you." She glanced over her shoulder at Rebecca. "We missed him greatly, did we not, Granny?"

"Indeed we did. But life is much changed these days, which is something we must all accept," her grandmother said in doleful tones.

Might as well get it over with.

"Yes, and along those lines," he said, "there's some business I need to discuss with you."

Rebecca perked up, looking hopeful, which made him feel even worse. He struggled to find words that would soften the blow.

After several fraught seconds, Lia breathed out an exasperated sigh. "Oh, blast. I thought so. It's no surprise, Jack. Just get it out."

"Ah, what exactly are you referring to?" He'd never discussed estate business with her.

"That your uncle left us destitute, of course, and that your mother wants you to kick us out to the lane. Evict us from Bluebell as soon as possible."

When he simply stared at her, his mouth gaping open like a bumpkin's, her eyebrow went up in a knowing, cynical lift.

"Right on both counts, I see," she said. "How unlucky can we get?"

Chapter Two

"Close your mouth, Lord Lendale," Lia said dryly. "You look like the village half-wit."

Jack's lips curved up in a heart-stopping, wry smile that was typical of him. He'd never once spoken to her in anger, even though she'd given him cause more than once over the years. He was the kindest man she'd ever met.

"Lia Beatrice Kincaid," her grandmother exclaimed in a horrified voice, "you will apologize to his lordship this instant. We are here by his grace and generosity, or have you forgotten that?"

Lia sighed. "Oh, very well. I'm sorry, Jack. I was an utter beast to say that. Please accept my sincere apology."

His smile faded as he shook his head. He looked so weary and frustrated. Lia knew better than anyone that Stonefell had fallen on hard times, but his manner suggested it was even worse than she'd thought.

"No, it's I who should apologize to both of you," he said. "Lia is not far off the mark."

Her heart couldn't seem to decide whether to leap into her throat or plummet to her feet. She had to swallow a few times before she could formulate an answer. "We'll need a few weeks to pack up and make arrangements to store our things. Then again, because most of the furniture belongs to you, a week or so should do it, I imagine."

Both Jack and her grandmother were now staring at her with stunned expressions.

"What?" she said. "Your mother obviously wants to transform Bluebell Cottage back into the dower house, which means we'd best be out of here as soon as possible."

"You're not going anywhere," Jack replied through clenched teeth. "Bluebell Cottage is your home for as long as you want it."

She noticed he didn't deny that his mother wanted Bluebell. Not that Lady John would ever think to live here while Jack was still a bachelor. No, she would reside at Stonefell as lady of the manor for as long as she could. Evicting them from the cottage was about ridding the estate of their *noxious presence*, as Lia had once inadvertently overheard her say. Lady John loathed Granny and would see this as her chance to finally get rid of her.

Her ladyship didn't exactly approve of Lia either. In fact, Lady John had always deplored her son's friendship with both the first and third generations of the Notorious Kincaids and probably even saw Lia as a threat to Jack's moral rectitude.

It was a ridiculous notion. First, Jack would never besmirch any woman's good name—not that Lia's family name covered her in glory. Second, and perhaps more germane, Jack would be more likely to succumb to gales of hilarity at the idea of any sort of intimate relationship with her. In fact, she'd wager the thought had never crossed his mind.

She was the one who was hopelessly infatuated, not Jack. And she didn't expect that to change any time soon.

"Thank you, dear boy," Granny said in a grateful tone. "I know we shall always be able to depend on your generosity."

"Just as we know we can't take advantage of it forever,"

Lia interjected with a warning glance at her grandmother. She and Granny had talked about this, trying to plan for the worst. And it seemed as if the worst was finally upon them.

"You are not taking advantage," Jack said firmly. "I count you both as family and always will."

Lia managed a smile. "That's kind of you Jack, but—"

"But what does it actually mean?" The hard, clean angles of his face took on a cynical cast. "You might well ask."

"Then I am asking," she said. Granny was clearly too disturbed to handle the tricky negotiations that seemed about to occur. That was up to Lia. "Naturally, my grandmother had been hoping for some kind of annuity from your uncle, or an inheritance that would give us a measure of independence. It's been weeks now and we've heard nothing about it from the estate's lawyer, or from you."

"Not that we wished to press you," Granny hastily added. "We both know you've been so busy trying to settle things. It's completely understandable that you haven't had a chance to speak with us."

Lia crossed her arms over her chest. "Not that we've actually had the chance to speak with you about it because this is the first time you've been back to Stonefell since Lord Lendale's funeral."

Jack's dark brows snapped together in a bit of a glower, but Lia didn't care. She and Granny had more or less been confined to the cottage during that awful week when the family descended for the funeral. Even though they'd spent more time with the marquess than anyone, and even though she and Granny had truly been his family, they'd been exiled from all official activities. Jack had stopped by a few times but was too harassed to pay them much attention. Then he'd disappeared for over two months, although at least he'd written them during his absence.

Still, it had felt perilously close to neglect. That had

stung—probably more than it should, if she had half a brain in her head.

"Well, I'm here now," he said. "And I promise we'll get everything sorted out."

"Is there an annuity, after all?" Granny asked.

When Jack hesitated, Lia knew what he would say. "No, Gran, I don't think so."

"Lia is unfortunately correct," Jack said in a regretful tone. "My uncle did not leave an annuity for you, Aunt Rebecca. I'm so sorry."

"But he left me *something*, did he not?" Granny asked in a hopeful voice. "Enough to set us up in a small house in the village, perhaps?"

Jack looked as if he'd accidentally ingested something toxic. "I'm afraid not."

Lia flinched. She'd been preparing for the worst but had assumed they'd get some sort of small bequest—something to tide them over until she could think how to support them longer term. Granny's lover had been a marquess, for heaven's sake. Even though the estate was in poor financial health, surely he'd had other income to draw upon.

"And no dowry for me either, I'm sure," she said, trying not to sound bitter.

Or terrified, even though that emotion lurked just below the surface. But without some sort of bequest to serve as a dowry, Lia had no hope of attracting a respectable suitor. Not that she'd been dangling for one, but she knew Granny had been pinning her hopes on that. After all, his lordship had promised years ago that he'd give Lia enough funds to overcome the stigma of her birth.

Now that hope was dying an ignominious death. Without anything from the estate, they would be almost entirely dependent on Jack for support.

"No, I'm sorry to say." He sounded almost as bitter as Lia felt. "He left Aunt Rebecca some personal items and bequeathed a few things to you—mostly books and some prints from his library that you were fond of."

Lia did a quick mental calculation. If they were the items she suspected, the results were not encouraging.

"Goodness," said Granny in a faint voice. "That is discouraging news, I must say."

She looked so pale that Lia was afraid she would faint. Casting an irate glance at Jack—who didn't deserve it— she crossed to the bellpull and yanked on it. "We'll have some tea, Granny. Then we'll figure this out, I promise."

"There's nothing to figure out," Jack said in a clipped voice. "I'm going to take care of you. Both of you."

"Splendid, just like the previous marquess," Lia retorted.

Jack opened his mouth, but Sarah's entrance forestalled his reply. Lia's former nursemaid, who now served the dual roles of housekeeper and cook, threw a sharp glance at her mistress and then a suspicious one at Jack.

Sarah knew all their secrets and hopes, and their worries, too. She'd developed an unwavering loyalty to Rebecca Kincaid years ago, happily abandoning an unsuccessful acting career to take up Lia's care. Sarah had moved north with Rebecca and her granddaughter, devoting her life to them.

If the Kincaids went down, Sarah would go down with them.

"Oh, I was expecting Elsie. I'm sorry to bother you, Sarah," Granny said, clearly attempting to rally. "But his lordship would like some tea. Could you bring up the tray?"

"Yes, ma'am, right away." Sarah bobbed a quick curtsy in Jack's direction. "My lord."

He gave her a kind smile. "It's nice to see you, Sarah. I hope you've been well."

"Well enough, all things considered, my lord," she said in a blighting tone.

Sarah had known Jack since he was a boy. Clearly, she

was no more impressed with the new marquess than she'd been with the grubby lad who'd tracked mud into her kitchen. And Jack's sigh indicated he'd received the house-keeper's message. Lia was almost beginning to feel sorry for him.

Almost.

She stood. "I'll help with the tea tray, Sarah."

The housekeeper looked scandalized. "I should say not. You'll sit here with his lordship and act like the proper young lady you were raised to be."

"Oh, Lord," she sighed, sitting back down.

After another scowling glance in Jack's direction and a few dark mutterings under her breath, Sarah exited the room.

"Sorry," Lia said to Jack. "She's very worried about us."

"She needn't be," he said. "As you said, we'll figure it out."

"Then along those lines," Granny said, "why don't you apprise us of exactly where things stand? I knew Arthur was concerned about some investments he'd made, but he didn't like to discuss such matters with me. He was concerned that I would worry."

Lia had to swallow a snort. The truth was, his lordship had liked to live in a pretty fantasy when he came to Blue-bell Cottage. Financial discussions would have injected an unsavory note into a relationship where both parties worked very hard to maintain a steadfast air of unmarred domestic bliss.

How stupid and shortsighted of them all.

"Yes, no doubt," Jack said dryly. "As to how bad it is, I won't insult you by trying to minimize the situation. The last few harvests have been disappointing, and my uncle did not, perhaps, make some of the best decisions when it came to managing certain aspects of estate business."

"That's obvious," Lia muttered.

It was well known that Lord Lendale had frequently ignored the advice of his cautious and wise estate manager. But when the old marquess had gotten an idea in his head about how to make money, there'd been no talking him out of it.

"None of that, my dear," Granny said in a stern tone. "I will not have you tarnish my Arthur's memory."

"Unfortunately, Lia's assessment is correct," Jack said. "My uncle meant well, but he had a poor head for both estate business and investments."

Over the next few minutes, he outlined how appalling a businessman his uncle had been. By the time he finished, Lia felt almost faint with horror and Granny looked as if she might really faint.

Thankfully, Sarah chose that moment to bring in the tea tray. Lia immediately poured her grandmother a cup and then handed one to Jack. Sarah had piled the tray high with biscuits and cake, but they remained untouched. After Jack's gruesome report, they'd all, apparently, lost their appetites.

With a weary sigh, Granny placed her teacup on the occasional table next to her chair. "I'm truly sorry, Jack. On top of everything else, you have the added burden of two useless women on your hands."

Anger flared like a torch in Lia's chest. *She* didn't consider herself useless, and her grandmother had given up everything, devoting her life to a man who'd left her in an appalling situation. And where had such selfless behavior left poor Granny? Utterly betrayed by the man she'd loved.

While Lia struggled to contain her fury, Jack thankfully stepped into the breach.

"You're not to think that way for a moment, Aunt Rebecca," he said in a kind but firm voice. "You know better than anyone how despair had taken hold of my uncle, even threatened his sanity. You brought him back from the brink and gave him years of happiness. You must never forget that."

The story was a sad one. In a young love match, Jack's uncle had married the daughter of one of his neighbors, a prosperous gentleman with a tidy estate. Lady Lendale had, by all accounts, been a sweet and pretty girl. They'd been deliriously happy for two years before Lady Lendale tragically died after a long and agonizing childbirth. The infant boy had survived, only to die a week later when he caught a fever. Lord Lendale had plunged into a melancholy that lasted for years and all but ruined his health. He'd vowed never to marry again, claiming he'd grieved enough for one lifetime.

While Lord Lendale never remarried, he did fall in love again, with a courtesan so notorious that no respectable man would marry her. Lia couldn't help thinking, with a good deal of cynicism, that it had been the perfect solution for him.

Granny blinked several times before flashing him a grateful smile. "Thank you, dear boy. Your words give me a great deal of comfort."

"You, on the other hand," Jack said to Lia with mock sternness, "are quite useless. I think I'll have to put you to work in the stables to earn your keep. Or set you up as the estate smithy."

Lia snickered and even her grandmother seemed to relax a bit. They all knew she more than earned her keep, helping out in Stonefell's gardens and lending whatever assistance she could to the wives and families of the tenant farmers.

"I might take you up on that offer if you promise to give me a nice set of livery," she said. "But enough silliness. We really have put you in a pickle, Jack. Granny is right about that."

The beginnings of a plan to address the situation had been coalescing in her mind because she'd begun to suspect

Lord Lendale might not have provided for them. But she wasn't quite ready to trot it out; Jack would not approve.

In fact, he would be furious if he knew.

"Not at all," he said. "Things will go on as usual. All your bills are to be sent up to Mr. Lindsey and I will provide you with pin money every month."

Lia scowled at him. "You can't be expected—"

He held up an imperious hand. "What I expect is that you will not make a fuss about it. Things seem dire now, but it won't always be so. Mr. Lindsey and I are working very hard to turn things around, and I'll be discussing the situation with my bankers when next I'm in London. Everything will be fine, I assure you."

"But—"

The look he gave her was surprisingly stern. "No, Lia. For once, I want you to listen to me."

"I always listen to you," she said indignantly.

"Pardon my laughter," he replied.

She was about to tell him what she thought of his response when her grandmother gave her head a little warning shake. Granny obviously had something to say to her and she didn't want to do it in front of Jack.

He glanced at his pocket watch and stood. "Please forgive me, but I've got to get back to the house. I have an appointment with Richard Hughes."

Mr. Hughes held one of the largest tenant farms at Stonefell. And like the other tenants, he'd been struggling to keep up with his rent. Lia was sure the meeting would be unpleasant for both of them.

"Poor Jack," she said, also standing. "What an awful homecoming you've had. You must be wishing yourself back on the Continent, far away from all of us."

His firm mouth curved in a rueful smile that failed to reach his eyes. "I'll admit there are days I'd rather face a line of French bayonets than wade through another stack of bills, but I'm sure I'll get used to it soon enough."

Lia's heart broke for him a little. Even though she was thrilled to have him back home, he'd loved military life. She knew he'd never complain about his new circumstances, other than the occasional joke. He'd take up his responsibilities, even if he truly didn't feel suited to them, and he'd do the absolute best he could. Lia wished she could do more to ease his burden.

That, however, was not her place, nor would it ever be.

Jack leaned down and kissed Granny's cheek. "I'll come visit in the next day or so. We can discuss things in a little more detail then. In the meantime, you're not to worry."

"Thank you, dearest," Granny said with a misty smile.

He swept Lia up in an encompassing hug. "And you stay out of trouble, pet. Understand?"

She hugged him back, briefly pressing her face into the fine wool of his riding jacket. "You must be thinking of some other girl," she said, her voice slightly muffled. "I'm never any trouble at all."

She felt his lips brush across the top of her hair. "No, you're not," he murmured. "In fact, I don't know what we'd do without you."

Her chest tightened with a mix of gratitude, sadness, and regret, but he was out the door a moment later, sparing her the necessity of a reply. Lia stared after him for a moment before turning to her grandmother.

To her surprise, Granny wasn't looking downcast at all. Resigned, yes, but also . . . calculating?

"What?" Lia asked.

Her grandmother's lips parted in a dazzling smile, the one that had apparently been the downfall of many a hardened rake when she'd been in her prime. Lia recognized that smile. It signaled that Granny was about to engage in a bit of ruthless manipulation.

Heaving a sigh, she trudged back to her seat.

"You can moan all you want, child," her grandmother said, "but it's time to face facts and be practical about our situation."

"I've been trying to do just that for weeks," Lia replied. "But you didn't want to hear any of my suggestions."

"Yes, I must admit I allowed myself to hope Arthur had done a better job of things. How foolish." She shook her head. "I'm sorry I failed you, Lia. You have always been my first responsibility. I let my affection for Arthur get in the way of that."

"To be fair, he did support us all these years. Despite the odd hiccup now and again, we've been comfortable. And happy."

Most of the time they had been, and how many people could claim that? She and Granny loved Stonefell, despite the occasional snub from one of the more persnickety locals, or the sense of exclusion they felt on the rare occasions when Lord Lendale's family had visited.

And then there was Jack, of course. He'd made everything seem worthwhile, even the snubs, the exclusions, and the leaky roof.

"My love for Arthur turned me soft," Granny said. "I believed him when he said he'd always take care of us. I would not have made that mistake when I was younger. I should have asked for more as we went along, and insisted he make some kind of provision for you in writing."

This sort of discussion always made Lia feel squeamish. But such arrangements were a simple fact of life for women like her mother and grandmother. She'd been spared that life and counted herself exceedingly fortunate in that respect.

"You, of course," her grandmother continued, "will do better than I did. You have an excellent head for business, and I don't think you'll ever let a man take advantage of you. That will give you a sound basis for negotiations."

Lia had cupped her chin in her hands, but her grandmother's words had her bolting upright. "What are you talking about, Gran?"

Her grandmother folded her hands neatly in her lap and stared her straight in the eye. "When you look for a protector, you will negotiate a clear and detailed agreement for your ongoing support in writing. I'll help you with that."

"My protector?" Lia's voice sounded rather screechy. "Do you mean a . . ."

"A lover? Don't be a ninny, dear. Of course that's what I mean."

Aghast, Lia stared at her grandmother, who seemed in dead earnest. "But . . . but you always wanted me to find a respectable suitor," she stammered. "To get married."

For a moment a hollow, grieving look threw up ghosts in her grandmother's deep blue eyes. But then her gaze shuttered and her chin firmed. "Of course I did, but we know that's no longer possible. Without a dowry, no respectable man will offer for you."

"Well . . . I don't think that's entirely true." Lia felt quite certain the cheesemonger's son would take her, even over his family's objections, and then there was—

"Jimmy Lanstead?" her grandmother asked.

Lia nodded.

"Certainly not. No granddaughter of mine will marry a pig farmer," Granny said in a haughty voice. "Especially one who rents his farm. We may be courtesans and actresses, my dear, but we are also Kincaids. We do have a standard to keep."

Her grandmother could be an awful snob, but Lia couldn't hold back a rush of relief. She had no desire to marry Jimmy Lanstead or anyone else.

Except Jack.

She firmly pushed that idea to the deepest recesses of her mind. It belonged in the dusty bin of broken dreams.

"I agree with you about Jimmy," Lia said, "but trying to set me up as a courtesan is rather drastic. I'm not you or Mama. I'm not a patch on either of you."

"Nonsense. You've grown into a stunning young woman. With a little help from me and some financial support, you could very well take London by storm."

There were so many things wrong with that plan that Lia didn't know where to start. "I have another idea, Gran, and I'm convinced it's the best one we could possibly come up with."

Her grandmother had been reaching to replenish her teacup, but her hand halted in midair. "I'm listening."

"I'll join Mama's acting troupe. They're looking for new company members now that they're in London. Mama said so in her last letter. And I'm sure I could live with Mama and Mr. Lester in their town house in Kensington."

Her grandmother regarded her with a dubious air. "Unfortunately, there are a number of critical drawbacks to that plan."

"Such as?"

"You can't sing, dance, or act."

That was rather a low blow. "I'm not much of a singer, I grant you. But I'm sure I can learn to dance, and you know very well I can act."

Lia had been playacting for as long as she could remember and had often dreamed girlish dreams of following in her mother's famous footsteps. She'd put on any number of recitations for her grandmother and his lordship over the years and had staged skits and little dramas for the servants, often with help from the kitchen maids and footmen. Granny and Lord Lendale had often told her that she was as fine an actress as Mrs. Siddons.

"My darling, the truth is you're a dreadful actress," her grandmother said in a patient tone.

"But you and his lordship were always so enthusiastic about my performances," she protested.

"Because we didn't want to hurt your feelings."

"But what about the amateur theatricals I put on up at the house? The servants all seemed to think I was splendid."

Her grandmother rolled her eyes.

She couldn't help feeling daunted, but she had no intention of conceding—especially if the alternative was to become the next Notorious Kincaid. Lia was convinced she'd make an utter fool of herself as a courtesan, especially because her heart wouldn't be in it.

"I don't care what you say," she said. "I'm writing to Mama tonight and telling her I'm coming to London. I can at least try out the notion on her and Mr. Lester and see what they say."

Her grandmother seemed to waver for a moment, but then she grimaced. "I feel certain your mother will not be amenable to you taking up the theatrical life."

"But she will be amenable to me becoming someone's mistress?" Lia asked with disbelief.

Granny starched up. "It was good enough for me, was it not?"

"Look how well that's turned out."

"I'm sure under certain conditions your mother will agree to this plan," Granny said, clearly determined to ignore Lia's objections.

"And what are those conditions?"

"That won't become entirely clear until I've had a chance to speak with Jack."

Lia's mind blanked for a few moments. "What in heaven's name does Jack have to do with me becoming a courtesan?"

Granny's eyebrows lifted with delicate incredulity.

"Because you're feeling a little squeamish about this plan, I think he should be your first."

Lia got a very bad feeling—which was something, considering how alarming the entire discussion had been thus far. "First what?" she asked, praying she had misunderstood.

"Your first lover, of course. But only if I can persuade him to agree to our terms."

Chapter Three

"Jack, please wait," called the sweetly lilting voice he knew as well as his own.

He turned to see Lia hurrying along the garden path that cut up from the stables. She was dressed in a faded blue day gown with a light scarf around her shoulders. Her lustrous hair was pulled back in a simple knot, as if she'd been in a hurry to dress.

He couldn't help thinking how pretty she looked as she came to meet him—a domestic version of Flora, as fresh as spring and just as wholesome. He'd always found it ironic that the daughter and granddaughter of two exceedingly experienced women glowed with innocence. Lia was the epitome of a fresh-faced country girl destined for a happy life as a wife and mother. He hoped more than anything that he could still give that to her, even if he would never be the lucky man to claim such a prize.

Claim such a prize?

Jack had never thought of Lia in such terms and wouldn't start now. Besides, he couldn't afford to marry a penniless girl. His mother had made that point in yet another anxiety-filled letter just this morning. She'd included a list of the heiresses she'd vetted, each one a more than acceptable candidate for the role of Marchioness of Lendale.

"Good Lord, such a fierce scowl," Lia said when she reached him. "What's put you in such a bad mood this early in the day?"

"I'm not in a bad mood. Just got a bit of dust in my eye." She looked dubious, but he didn't give her a chance to dispute it. "You're out and about rather early. Have you had breakfast yet?"

"No, just a cup of coffee. I wanted to catch you as soon as I could."

"Ah, then it must be important."

She grimaced. "Rather, I'm afraid."

"Come into the library and I'll ring for something to eat. It's never a good idea to discuss important matters on an empty stomach."

She smiled as she fell into step beside him. "I won't say no to a roll and another cup of coffee."

"I think we can do better than that."

"You're up early yourself," she said as they turned the corner of the house and headed along the main path through the ornamental gardens.

The day promised to be fine, with clear blue skies and a light breeze. Swallows flitted through the trees, twittering like mad, and bees darted from one heavily laden rosebush to another. It was the most bucolic scene one could imagine.

"I was awake early, so I thought I'd take a ride across the downs before starting my work day," Jack said. They would be his only moments of peace before once more surrounding himself with ledgers, bills, and aggravating letters from his bankers.

"Yes, I know. I just missed you. I stopped by the stables to check on Dorcas."

He cast a quick glance down at her lovely face. Lia had

always had the run of the entire estate and countryside. Her roaming about so freely had never bothered him—until now. "You seem to be spending quite a bit of time in the stables. I know you like to assist Markwith, but it's not appropriate."

Her elegant brows winged up in an almost comical slant. "What in heaven's name are you talking about? I've been helping out at the stables since I was a little girl."

"But you're no longer a little girl. You're a grown woman, Lia. And you seem to wander around a great deal without a chaperone."

She stared at him with complete incredulity. "It's my home, Jack. Everyone knows me. And it's the country, after all. I'm perfectly safe."

He found her naïveté appalling. "Still, it's not a good idea for you to be hanging about the stables. If you want to ride, simply send your maid up with a note to Markwith. He'll have your mare saddled and ready for you."

Lia stopped in the middle of the gravel path and regarded him with an expression that suggested she thought him dicked in the nob. "In case you haven't noticed, I don't have my own maid. We have one young girl who helps Sarah, and the poor thing is run off her feet as it is. Goodness, Jack, what's got into you this morning?"

As he struggled to find an answer that wouldn't offend, a surprisingly cynical expression transformed her features. He'd seen that look on her face a few times yesterday afternoon during that gruesome talk at Bluebell Cottage. He didn't like it.

"Afraid I'll be dallying with the stableboys, are we?" she asked sardonically. "Dear me, Lord Lendale, such a vulgar assumption to make about your old friend."

"For God's sake, Lia, of course I'm not making such a ridiculous assumption," he said, quickly becoming exasperated.

"Then what is the problem?"

"I don't want anyone treating you with disrespect or making assumptions about your character. You're safe on the estate, but the countryside is changing, especially with so many men coming home from the war. The world is a rough place, Lia. I won't have you exposing yourself to unnecessary danger."

When she started to roll her eyes, he scowled at her. "I mean it," he said. "You're more vulnerable than you know."

"I'm not a peagoose, Jack. I know that Granny and I have very few resources at our disposal. I know how vulnerable we are." She grimaced. "It's a wretched situation, I'm afraid."

"Sweetheart, there's no need for drama. You and Aunt Rebecca have a home here at Stonefell for as long as you desire."

She crossed her arms and regarded him with a thoughtful air. "Really? And what happens when you get married, Jack? I wonder how your wife will feel about having a former courtesan and her bastard granddaughter living in the dower house."

Bloody hell. He'd had more than one tussle with his mother about Lia and Rebecca and what to do with them. But he hadn't yet contemplated how a wife would react to them living on the estate.

"I'm not planning on getting married any time soon, so it's not a problem," he hedged.

"But you will eventually marry, and I'm sure the average aristocratic miss will look askance at the notion of having the Notorious Kincaids living just down the lane. You think people talk now? Just wait until you pitch a gently bred young lady into the middle of that mess."

A footfall on the gravel had them turning to see old Merton coming along the path, trundling a wheelbarrow full of gardening tools.

"We are not discussing this for any Tom, Dick, or Harry to overhear." Jack took her by the elbow and started to propel her toward the terrace.

"Stop making such a fuss." She resisted his efforts to get her moving. "Merton, you should check the rosebushes by the arbor. They're showing signs of blight."

The old man gave her a fond smile. "I'll do that, miss, ye can be sure."

"Thank you. I'll come see you once I'm finished with Lord Lendale. I'd like to talk to you about some ideas I have for the kitchen garden, too."

"Aye, Miss Lia, I'll wait for ye."

Jack cursed under his breath as she finally let him march her up onto the stone terrace.

"And now what have I done to annoy his lordship?" she asked.

"It seems to have escaped your notice that you don't actually work here at Stonefell. There's no need for you to be running about instructing the staff. They're quite capable of doing their jobs without direction from you."

She yanked her arm away, coming to a halt in the middle of the terrace. "Yes, they are. But, again, in case *you've* failed to notice, Stonefell is severely understaffed and the servants are quite overworked." She glanced away and blinked several times, as if she'd gotten a speck in her eye.

"I'm only trying to help," she added in a tight voice.

Jack breathed out an irritated sigh. He had no damn business taking his frustrations out on her, especially when she did everything she could to make his life easier. "I don't seem to be able to keep my blasted foot out of my mouth this morning, do I? You might as well give me a kick in the backside and get it over with. I certainly deserve it."

Her startled gaze flew back to him.

"I'm sorry, sweetheart," he said. "I didn't mean to insult

you. But you're not a servant here at Stonefell. I don't ever want you to feel you have to earn your keep."

She gave him a quizzical smile. "Stonefell is my home, and your people are the closest thing Granny and I have to family. If I can help them, I'm happy to do so." Her shoulders lifted in a practical little shrug. "And although I wouldn't quite phrase it as *earning my keep*, we do owe the Lendales a great deal. Your uncle supported us for almost twenty years, and now you've pledged to do the same. And you, I might add, get nothing out of the deal, unlike the previous lord."

He found her cynical assessment unnerving. "That's a rather hard-hearted way to look at it."

"But it's the truth, isn't it?"

He shoved a hand through his hair, hating the discussion. He'd always done his best to shelter Lia from the more unpleasant facts of life, but she'd grown into a woman who had a decidedly unvarnished view of the world. He realized now that he'd been a fool to think he could protect her from the realities of immutable circumstance.

When she was a little girl, they'd all pretended there was nothing out of the ordinary in her upbringing, or in his uncle's relationship with Rebecca. Selfish and stupid was what they'd all been, and poor Lia would pay the price.

She placed a gentle hand on his arm. "Jack, we can't go on pretending nothing's changed, or that nothing's going to change. That's why I came up to the house so early. I need to talk to you before Granny does."

"What does Rebecca want?"

She nudged him toward the open French doors of his library. "Trust me, you do *not* want to have this particular conversation with her."

The morning sun cast bands of light across the library carpet and gently highlighted the faded shades of blue, cream, and rose. Lia wound her way between the scattered chairs and low tables of the comfortable room, then flopped into one of the creaky leather club chairs in front of his desk. Even when she flopped she managed to look graceful, although Rebecca would surely read her a lecture for reclining so casually, with her booted feet propped up against one of the desk legs.

Those boots looked familiar.

"Lia, are those the boots I bought for you when you were sixteen?"

She gave him a sheepish smile. "I suppose they are."

"They're practically falling off your feet. When was the last time you got a new pair?"

She glanced down negligently. "I just wear these when I work in the garden. Now, would you please stop worrying about such silly things and sit down? You can be such an old biddy sometimes."

He snorted. "Well, that's a first. Nobody's ever called me an old biddy before."

She grinned. "They don't know you as I do."

"You mean you think you know me. Now, would you like me to ring for something to eat?"

She shifted and sat up in her chair. "Thank you, but I think not. I don't have much of an appetite, as it turns out."

He studied her face, noticing the shadows under her eyes and the tight set to a mouth that was normally generous, lush, and tilted up in a smile. She looked worried and nervous. But Lia had never been nervous with him—not once that he could remember. It sent a faint chill of warning up his spine.

"That bad, is it?" he said, forcing a light tone.

"You have no idea," she said with a sigh.

"Then I suppose there's no point in putting it off, is there?" He took his seat.

It seemed odd to be sitting across from her like this—

the all-powerful lord of the manor at his desk. It still felt awkward, and he wondered if the feeling would ever fade.

Lia was staring down at the floor, her arms resting on her knees and her hands clasped in a tight knot. "I don't know where to start, Jack."

"You know I will always do anything I can to help you, my dear."

She flashed him a rueful smile. "Like that time you rescued me from the chimney?"

When she was six years old, she'd taken it into her head to become a chimney sweep. She'd wedged herself into the flue in her grandmother's bedroom and gotten stuck. Jack had been terrified that she'd hurt herself, but she'd begged him not to tell her grandmother or run for help. He'd finally managed to extract her with only a few scrapes and bruises, but she'd emerged covered with soot and her clothes more or less in tatters. She'd simply giggled uproariously, chalking the whole episode up as a grand adventure.

Lia nodded. "I know. You've always been my best friend. No one could ask for a better one."

Her words set off a pang in his chest. Other than the servants on the estate, Lia had no friends, and no confidants besides her grandmother and him. In so many ways, she'd existed in an odd sort of isolation—not alone, but without the relationships any normal girl in a country village should have.

He forced aside the weight of guilt that pressed down on him. No matter what it took, he would do right by her. Lia could never be just an obligation to him. Yes, he'd rather neglected her these last several years, but she mattered to him in a way that few people in his life ever had.

"Good," he said. "Now that we've agreed that I'm a perfectly splendid fellow, why don't you tell me what Aunt Rebecca is worried about?"

"It's not that she's worried exactly. It's something she, er, wants you to do."

It wasn't like Lia to hedge. "Pet, we haven't got all day. Just spit it out."

She sighed. "Very well. But please do remember that it wasn't my idea."

"I give you my word."

Sitting up straight, she met his gaze. "Granny wants you to become my protector."

That was a puzzling choice of words. "Of course I'll protect you. Didn't I make that clear yesterday?"

"Yes, but not my protector in a general way. She means protector in a rather specific way."

The vague conversation began to frustrate him. "I'm not sure what else I can do to address her concerns, other than to say that I will provide for anything you need."

She looked over at the window, shaking her head and muttering under her breath.

"Perhaps you could clarify what she means by *specific*," Jack suggested.

Lia finally looked at him, her cheeks blazing as red as apples. "Granny wants me to be your mistress, you nodnock. She wants you to be my lover. Is that clear enough for you?"

Jack probably looked like a fish who'd landed on a bank, stunned and gasping for breath. And the entire time he stared at her, Lia glared back at him, looking furious and embarrassed. And anything but loverlike.

He finally marshaled the few wits that hadn't been stunned into insensibility. "Clear? It's insane. Take you as my mistress? How your grandmother could come up with such a ridiculous notion is beyond me. It's simply laughable."

He felt as if someone had knocked him on the head with a brick. And even more appalling, now that she'd put the idea into his head, some part of his brain—well, not his brain actually—thought there was some merit to the notion. How could it not, when she looked as she did now, her cheeks flushed, her gorgeous eyes snapping with fury, and her pretty breasts pushing up over the simple trim of her bodice with each indignant and huffy breath.

Get a handle, you idiot. He would no more take Lia as his mistress than he would don minstrel's garb and caper about in Hyde Park.

When she crossed her arms under her chest, the movement pushed the plump white mounds up even higher over her bodice. Her scarf had slipped aside, and Jack fancied he might even see the edge of one nipple peeking out from behind the narrow band of lace. That lascivious hint sent a bolt of lust thrumming through his body to settle in his groin.

Argh. He'd never thought of Lia in that way and he was utterly horrified by his reaction.

He forced his gaze up to her face. The fury and hurt he saw in her eyes immediately dampened any misplaced ardor on his part.

"I'm sorry you find the notion so repugnant," she said tightly. "Of course I realize I can't hold a candle to all the fine ladies you're accustomed to consorting with in London."

"Good God. I don't consort with fine ladies," he exclaimed. "What sort of man do you take me for?"

"The regular kind. And don't pretend you're a virgin, Jack, or that you've never had an affair or slept with, well, you know." She paused, suddenly looking uncertain. "You aren't a virgin, are you?"

He dropped his forehead into his hand. "Lia, this is an entirely demented conversation."

She let out a horrified gasp. "You *are* a virgin. Oh, dear.

I'm so sorry, Jack. This must be thoroughly embarrassing for you. Please forgive me."

He looked up with a scowl. "It is embarrassing, but not because I'm a virgin. I am not, by the way, though that is beside the point."

"The point seems to be that you find the notion of me as your mistress hideous beyond imagining," she said with irritation. "Well, let me tell *you* that I'm not exactly thrilled by the notion, Jack Easton."

"Why the hell not?" he asked before he could stop himself. "Never mind, don't answer that. And just to be clear I don't find you repugnant in the least. Quite the opposite, in fact."

She blinked. "Then there is a chance you *would* consider taking me as your mistress?"

"Christ, no!"

Lia tucked her chin down and winced. "There's no need to yell, Jack. I'm not deaf."

He gripped the edge of his desk and took several deep breaths, trying to steady himself. Then he pushed himself out of his chair and stalked over to the drinks cart. He poured a splash of whiskey into a crystal tumbler and tossed it back. The burn hit his stomach like a gunshot, but the jolt of heat cleared his head.

"I could use one of those," Lia said.

"I am not giving you whiskey before you've had anything to eat," Jack growled. He refused to look at her before he got himself under some semblance of control. He felt as if he'd fallen asleep and woken up in a madhouse.

"Spoilsport," she muttered.

He tugged at the hem of his waistcoat and then turned around to face her. Lia was now twisted around in her chair, arms crossed and shoulders hunched in a sulky pose. But because she never sulked, he suspected it was a defensive posture to cover up the pain of his unintentional insult.

Whoever would have thought that refusing to take Lia as his mistress would count as an insult?

"Now, let us start over again and try to speak to each other like rational human beings," he said.

"I'm perfectly rational. You're the one who's acting like an escapee from Bedlam."

He reached for his patience, now thin as a gossamer thread. While he rummaged his brain for something sensible to say that would lower the temperature in the room, Lia sighed and pushed herself to her feet.

"I'm sorry, Jack. That was rude of me. And I don't mean it, of course. It's just that—"

"I hurt your feelings," he said gently.

She gave him a sad smile that made his heart cramp. "You did, rather. I know that makes me sound like a coxcomb, and it's not as if I truly want to be your mistress. But you made it sound like the most ridiculous thing one could imagine—as if I'm utterly repugnant, despite your claims that I'm not."

"Don't be silly," he said gruffly. "It's just that I don't think of you that way."

She tilted her head like an inquisitive puppy. "Just how do you think of me, Jack?"

His mind blanked again. This should *not* be a difficult question to answer. "Almost like a little sister, I suppose. Someone I grew up with."

Her eyes narrowed, as if the answer didn't please her. "I'm not your sister, Jack."

"I'm well aware of that, Lia."

"I am not in any way related to you."

"Yes, I know." He was going to crack one of his back

molars if he didn't stop clenching his teeth. "What is your point?"

She reached a hand up to rub the center of her forehead, as if she was developing a headache. He knew the feeling because he was beginning to think someone had dropped an anvil on his head. The whiskey, in retrospect, might have been a mistake.

"I seemed to have lost it, actually," she said. "Perhaps you might try looking for it."

"Gladly." He went to her and placed a hand on her shoulder, gently nudging her down into her chair. Then he went round the desk to his. "Why don't we start over? I understand Rebecca's concerns about the future, but how did she come up with this scheme in the first place? On a practical level alone, it doesn't make a lot of sense because I'm not exactly flush with funds. Taking on a mistress is not on my list of priorities."

"I told her that," she said in a gloomy voice. "But she says if you're willing to keep supporting us at Bluebell Cottage, there's no reason you can't take me on as your mistress. Formalize the relationship, as it were."

He shook his head. "I don't understand."

"Draw up a contract outlining terms."

"Again, that makes no sense. I'm willing to do that without imposing . . ."

"Conditions?" she finished dryly.

"For lack of a better term, yes."

"It's merely a guarantee against what will happen in the future, Jack. A form of protection for us, at least financially," she said in a tone that suggested he wasn't very bright.

Not that he could blame her. He was feeling remarkably fuzzy at the moment, and not from the whiskey. "What's going to happen in the future?"

"You're going to get married of course," she said in a flat tone. "If I have a formal contract of, er—"

"Conditions?"

She nodded. "Then you can't throw us out, willy-nilly. Or at least your wife can't anyway."

Jack wanted to thump his head down on the desk. That would probably hurt less than the headache roaring behind his temples. "As I explained a few moments ago, I have no immediate plans to take a wife."

His mother would have something to say about that as, strictly speaking, it would be the easiest way out of their financial mess. But as far as he was concerned, that was a weapon of last resort. Jack had no desire to rush into a marriage that wasn't grounded in genuine affection and respect. His parents' battling had taught him that lesson.

"What a disaster," he murmured.

"I'm sorry, Jack. What was that?"

"I said, I have no intention of getting married any time soon."

"Yes, but you will someday," she said patiently. "And when you do, you can hardly expect the Marchioness of Lendale to tolerate a pair of scandalous females in residence just down the lane."

He started to protest, but she held up a restraining hand. "It's ridiculous to assume otherwise and you know it."

"I would never abandon you or Rebecca," he said.

"I know you wouldn't want to, but you might not have much choice."

It felt as if she'd just jabbed a long, cold needle into his heart. Did she truly have so little faith in him?

"Let's set that aside for now," he said. "But let us be clear on two things. The first is that you will remain at Bluebell Cottage for the indefinite future and the second is that I will *not* be taking you as my mistress."

She nodded. "I assumed as much of course."

He waved his arms with exasperation. "Then why the hell are we having this conversation in the first place?"

She rounded her eyes at him. "Because otherwise Granny would have. And she'll probably still try to speak with you about it."

"And I'll tell her exactly what I just told you."

"She'll simply present you with another idea if you shoot down her first plan."

"Which I already have," he said through clenched teeth.

"I'm not an idiot," she said. "You don't have to keep beating me over the head with your rejection."

"I'm not beating you . . . oh, never mind. Do you know what this other plan is likely to be?"

She shifted in her chair, looking a bit squeamish. "Granny thinks that since you're so well-placed in the Ton, you're bound to know lots of important, rich men. So, if you can't be my patron, she wants you to help me find a suitable candidate for the position. Sponsor me, as it were."

Once again he could feel his eyes bugging out. "You're joking."

"Yes, ha-ha. That is exactly the kind of thing I like to joke about," she said sarcastically.

Jack placed his palms flat on his desk and came slowly to his feet. He glared down at her, as if trying to impress her with the full weight of his authority. Lia simply stretched out her legs, crossing them at the ankles, then propped her interlaced fingers on her stomach. She ticked up a decidedly unimpressed eyebrow, waiting for him to speak.

"Let me be very clear on one thing," he started.

"Just one?"

"Lia . . ." he said in a warning voice.

She wrinkled her nose at him. "Sorry. It's just that I'm

not used to you going lord-of-the-manor on me. It will take some getting used to."

"Then you'd better get started, because I want you to hear *very* clearly what I'm about to say. You are not embarking on a career as any man's mistress or becoming a courtesan."

"Well, of course I'm not, Jack. Do you really think I want to follow in my grandmother's footsteps?"

He was trying very hard not to lose his temper. "Truthfully, I don't know what you think at this point. I assume you made your grandmother aware of your position?"

"I did, for all the good it accomplished. Because, as Granny so cogently pointed out, the original problem remains, which is that we can't rely on you to support us indefinitely. So *I've* come up with another plan, one I feel confident will work."

How many mad schemes had she and Rebecca conjured up? "Which is?" he warily asked.

"I'm going to London to join my mother's acting troupe," she said triumphantly. "That way, I can support both myself and Granny. And I'll be with my mother and her husband. It's exceedingly respectable, so even you can't object."

He fought the impulse to tear around the desk, haul her up, and shake some sense into her head. Either that or pull her into his arms and keep her safely there forever, protecting her from all the dangers that seemed to be springing up in her path like weeds. While he didn't have the right to claim her like that, he'd be damned if he stood idly by while she rushed out into the world to ruin herself.

"Absolutely not," he said, struggling to keep his voice calm. "You know as well as I do that actresses are viewed in much the same way as courtesans. Your family history should serve to confirm that."

Lia pulled herself up, her back ramrod straight. She

regarded him with a degree of haughtiness that would do a princess proud.

"If you're referring to my mother, she has been respectably married for ten years. My stepfather is a well-regarded businessman whose conduct is above reproach."

"In the theatrical world, yes. But society still looks askance on those engaged in that particular business and you know it."

"But—"

"And let's not forget that your mother came rather late to domestic respectability," he continued. "We both know she was considered as notorious as your grandmother in her day. For you to join her company as an actress, even under the protection of your stepfather's good name, would invite exactly the type of attention from exactly the type of men you're trying to avoid. I absolutely forbid it."

That brought Lia to her feet in a flash. "You forbid it? May I remind you, sir, that you have no right in that regard?"

"Legally, perhaps not. But I'm responsible for you nonetheless. Aside from your grandmother, I'm the closest thing to family you have—which you just pointed out only a few moments ago."

"You seem to be forgetting that I do have a mother—and a stepfather," she said with a lethal glare. "And I said you *were* my best friend. I'm starting to doubt that particular relationship at the moment, given your wretchedly selfish behavior."

"Good God, Lia, my behavior is anything but—"

"So, let *me* be perfectly clear, your lordship," she said, jabbing a finger in his direction. "You are not my brother, my father, or anything else that gives you the right to command me. I am a woman grown and I have proven time and again that I am more than capable of making sensible and rational decisions. And given the extremely precarious position in which my grandmother and I find ourselves, my plan is without a doubt the most sensible course of action." She gave her head a dramatic toss. "You, Lord Lendale, have nothing to say about it."

Her disdainful tone and her rejection of their relationship set off a little explosion in Jack's head. He marched around the desk and planted himself in front of her, his legs spread and his hands propped on his hips. It forced Lia to tilt her head back to meet his gaze, glare for glare.

"As much as it pains me to speak so bluntly . . ." he started.

"Ha! I doubt that."

"The circumstances demand that I must do so," he said, ignoring her jibe. "You are no more an actress than a courtesan. You are no more a Notorious Kincaid than I am. What you are is an innocent and nice young lady who was raised in the country. And that is exactly where you will remain until I figure out how to deal with this situation."

Her eyes blazed with icy blue fire. "I beg to differ, my lord. If I put my mind to it, I'm quite sure I can be just as notorious as the other women in my family."

Then she reached up and clamped his face between her palms. She went up on her toes and planted her mouth on his, kissing him with a fury that almost knocked him off his feet.

It wasn't the first time she'd kissed him, but those had been chaste pecks on the cheek. This clumsy kiss took him like a storm, blasting amazement through his veins. Instinctively, his arms started to wrap around her to pull her close.

But she shoved him away, leaving him slack-jawed and gasping for breath. The color was high on her cheekbones and her lush, pink mouth was dewy. Like him, she was panting, but from the look on her face he suspected it had more to do with rage than passion.

"Let that be a lesson to you, Jack Easton. You don't know me as well as you think you do."

Then she turned on her heel and marched to the French doors. Spinning around, she once more jabbed a minatory finger in his direction. "And don't *ever* try to tell me what I can and cannot do."

With that daunting remark, she disappeared into the bright morning sunlight, leaving Jack with the unnerving sensation that he'd just lost control of everything.

Chapter Four

"I'm truly sorry, dearest," Lia's mother said as she lounged gracefully on a yellow velvet chaise in her drawing room. She looked as beautiful and stylish as always, completely at home in the elegantly decorated town house her husband had recently rented on a quiet street in Kensington.

Lia sighed and briefly pressed her palms to her tired eyes. If one more person said she lacked acting talent, she might just scream. "But Mama, you've seen me act only once and I was just twelve years old at the time."

She remembered the occasion with ringing clarity, because she and Granny had staged the performance in honor of one of Mama's rare visits to Yorkshire. With help from the servants, they'd put on a very abbreviated version of *Richard III*, with Lia playing most of the roles.

Her mother gave a slight shudder. "It was not an occasion one would forget. Although I do give you full marks for such a bold venture."

"I'm sure it was much better than you remember, my love," said Stephen Lester, casting a worried look Lia's way. "After all, one's memory does grow dim over the years."

"There is nothing wrong with my memory," Mama huffed. "I've memorized dozens of roles over the years and not forgotten a single line."

Mama did have a spectacular memory and she was a very good actress, so her unflinching assessment was likely correct. Still, Lia wasn't yet ready to give up the fight.

Along with Sarah Rogers, who'd served as her chaperone, Lia had arrived in London late last night. The days-long trip from Yorkshire had been rather gruesome, as they were crammed into an overcrowded, hot, and rather smelly public coach. She'd spent much of the trip trying to control a queasy stomach and struggling not to second-guess her decision.

Despite the inconvenience, the trip had provided an entertaining and often unvarnished display of humanity. When one cheeky fellow tried to corner Lia on the landing of a narrow staircase, Sarah had dispatched the idiot with a few good whacks of her umbrella. And although that encounter had been distasteful, Lia told herself it was useful fodder for a budding actress. The more she knew about her fellow man, the more skillful her performance on the stage was likely to be.

"I truly wish you'd written to me earlier, Lia," Mama said in a plaintive voice. "We'd only just received your grandmother's letter and there you were on our doorstep."

Lia tried for a doleful expression. "I'm so sorry, but there really wasn't any time. Matters have reached a crisis point."

It had been Granny's idea to avoid giving the Lesters too much notice. Lia had been quite sure her mother would welcome her with open arms, but it turned out Rebecca Kincaid knew her daughter better than Lia knew her mother. It now seemed clear that Mama would have refused to allow Lia to stay with her if she'd only had the opportunity to do so.

The most charitable interpretation was that the former Marianne Kincaid had spent years trying to put her reputation behind her, refashioning herself as the respectable—if rather dashing—wife of a well-regarded theater manager and playwright. The accomplished Mrs. Lester likely had no wish to be reminded of the old scandals she'd done her best to overcome. In that sense, her daughter's sudden appearance in London was bound to be an unsettling reminder.

But what choice did Lia have but to ask for her mother's help? Leaving her entire future in Jack's hands was no option, as their ridiculous last meeting had made clear. She cringed every time her memory dredged up the appalled expression on his face when she'd revealed Granny's scheme. It had been the most humiliating moment of her life.

Even worse, she was now an object of pity to Jack and a source of embarrassment. And if she made him that uncomfortable, he would be much less inclined to fight for her and Granny when he did finally marry and his future wife set about evicting them from Bluebell Cottage.

"Oh dear, I simply don't know what to do," Mama said, fluttering a handkerchief at her husband. Mr. Lester, sitting next to her on the chaise, patted her knee.

Personally, Lia thought her mother's melodramatic pose was a bit much, but she had to admit she did it well. Mama was lovely, with big, expressive eyes, an enchanting manner, and a figure as slim and elegant as in her youth. Even her black hair remained untouched by gray markers of time, although Lia suspected a bit of artful assistance in that regard.

That no one would ever deduce that Marianne Lester had a twenty-two-year-old daughter was probably another reason she didn't want Lia hanging about. It was hard to maintain the fiction of youth when one had a child full-grown.

"Tut-tut, my dear," Mr. Lester said in a bracing tone.

"We'll think of something. And if nothing else, it's quite lovely to have dear Lia for a visit. Why, the girl hasn't been in London since she was a toddler. Think of all the fun we'll have taking her out and about, visiting all the sights."

Lia gave him a grateful smile. She was very fond of her stepfather, a middle-aged, ordinary-looking fellow with a receding hairline. He seemed more like a shopkeeper than a proficient playwright and a successful theater manager. Mr. Lester had spent years toiling in the provinces, building up his name and company and carefully accumulating funds and backers. Recently, he'd been able to lease a theater in London—in Holborn—and move his wife into a charming town house nearby.

On top of all those estimable qualities, he adored Marianne and clearly never held her past against her, including her bastard daughter. He'd always treated Lia with affection and respect, remembering her at Christmas and on her birthday, sending her packages of books and exceedingly kind letters full of news of the company and her mother's successes.

"If you say so," Mama said. Then she frowned at Lia. "But I'm not sure I understand your sense of urgency, dearest. Is Jack not paying your bills? Is he allowing that awful mother of his to kick up a fuss?"

Lia shook her head. "He's been very kind and generous. But his uncle left him in a ghastly financial bind. He simply can't go on supporting us like this for much longer."

"But Lord Lendale did it for years. Is it truly so dire now?"

"Yes. And Lendale left us without a farthing to call our own," Lia said. "I know he loved Granny, but he ended up leaving her high and dry."

Her mother winced. "That is most distressing. I wouldn't have thought he could be so careless."

"That's one way to put it," Mr. Lester said gloomily. "I

must agree with Lia's assessment of the situation. Neither she nor your mother can rely on the new Lord Lendale."

"Thank you," Lia said, perhaps too emphatically.

"How dreary," her mother said with a sigh. "But what does Jack think about this plan of yours? For such a kind man, he *is* rather a high stickler when it comes to female behavior—much like his mother in that regard, I'm afraid. He most certainly didn't get it from his father," she added with a knowing wink.

Jack's father, Lord John Easton, had been almost as notorious as the Kincaid women because of his numerous, brazen affairs. Lia could only hope her mother's analysis of Lord John was not based on personal experience. That simply didn't bear thinking about.

"No point in digging up old stories about departed friends," Mr. Lester hastily interjected. "But I must confess I'm curious about the current Lord Lendale's reaction. Did he approve of your trip to London?"

"He was fine with it," Lia said with an airy wave. "After all, my absence leaves him with one less problem to deal with."

"I wish he'd dealt with it enough to hire you a chaise or lend you a carriage," he said in a disapproving tone. "I can't think what he was doing to allow you and Sarah to come by mail coach."

Lia shrugged. "I suppose it just didn't occur to him. Besides, it's not really any of his business, is it? Jack is a friend, nothing more."

Her mother and stepfather exchanged a dubious glance. Lia prayed they would let that particular detail drop; Jack would be furious if he learned she'd traveled to London on the mail coach.

Which was precisely why she hadn't told him.

She hadn't even told him she was going, instead leaving that bit up to Granny. There was little doubt that the annoyingly overprotective Lord Lendale would have done his best to stop her, and she couldn't afford that. Jack would get over her departure soon enough and realize this was best for both of them.

"I do hope you're not getting the sniffles," her mother said, studying her with concern. "One can pick up such nasty infections on public conveyances."

Lia blinked hard against incipient tears. "It's just a little dust in my eye. Now, let's get back to the problem at hand."

Mama pouted. "Must we? Can't we just pretend you're in London for a little visit and leave it at that?"

Lia struggled against a wave of disappointment. For so long, she'd dreamed of being reunited with her mother; it was bitter medicine to realize her parent didn't feel the same way. Still, she'd known for years that Mama, while charming and good-natured, was quite selfish. There was no point in lamenting her character at this stage or letting it get in the way of necessary plans.

"I'm afraid we cannot, Mama," she said firmly. "Although if you find the discussion too taxing, perhaps I can just work things out with my stepfather."

"Please call me Stephen, my dear," he said. "We don't stand on ceremony in this household."

"And perhaps you can call me Marianne instead of Mama," her mother added in a hopeful voice. "That doesn't sound nearly as frumpish."

Lia tried not to roll her eyes. "No one could ever be so silly as to call you frumpy, Mama. I mean, Marianne."

When her mother beamed at her, Lia had to swallow a laugh. Flattery was clearly the right tack.

"Well, let's discuss what you might be able to do and what roles you might be able to play," Stephen said. "Can you sing or dance?"

"Um, no," Lia said. "But is that necessary? Don't you primarily focus on spoken drama and the classics?"

"We do when we're touring the provinces," her mother said. "But only the licensed theaters are allowed to perform spoken drama in London. Your stepfather is very good at getting around the restrictions with his burlettas and musical interludes, but we still must abide by the law."

"Oh," Lia said. "I'd forgotten about that. So, does everyone in the company sing and dance?"

"Mostly," replied Stephen. "We do have some speaking parts set to music, of course, and we have the pantomimes. There are always the occasional walk-ons, as well. We might be able to squeeze you into that sort of role."

"But darling, we already have a full slate of actresses," Mama said. "They won't be happy if we elevate Lia in their place."

"I'm sure we can find something for her to do without ruffling feathers," Stephen said. "Besides, this is *my* company, and if I want to cast my stepdaughter in a part I shall certainly do so."

Lia almost fell off her chair in her eagerness. "I'll do anything, and I promise I'll study very hard. I have a wonderful memory and I can help out around the theater, too. I can take notes for you or work on the costumes. I've become very good with the needle."

Her mother perked up. "We are rather shorthanded backstage. We lost one of our seamstresses last week and dear Stephen hasn't yet had a chance to replace her."

"Actually I've been trying to economize," he said with a sigh. "London is proving more expensive than I anticipated."

"I'm happy to work for nothing, at least in the beginning," Lia said. "Until I prove myself and get established." Though she'd hoped to start making money as quickly as possible, she knew she had to win her mother's approval first.

"It's not right to take advantage of you that way," Stephen said with a frown.

"Nonsense," Mama said briskly. "After all, she'll be staying with us, so we'll be providing her room and board."

Stephen nodded. "True, and I could provide a weekly stipend to pay for all the little things a young lady needs from day to day."

Lia clasped her hands tightly, almost afraid to hope. "So you'll let me stay?"

Her mother cocked an eyebrow at her husband, who gave her a nod and a smile.

"Very well, my dear," her mother said. "We will give you a try and see how it goes."

Lia jumped up and rushed over, bending down to hug her mother with fervor. "Thank you. I promise you won't be disappointed."

"We'll see," her mother said, awkwardly patting Lia on the back before gently disengaging herself. "We can't make any promises for the long-term."

Lia refused to be discouraged. It wasn't much, but it was a start, and a start was all she needed. With a little luck, within the next few months her career on the stage should be firmly launched.

Chapter Five

Jack stalked into the foyer of Boodle's, silently handing the footman his hat. He'd been in a foul mood for days because he had yet to run Lia to ground, even though he'd been in the city since Monday.

The blasted girl had given him the slip. Sadly, he'd believed the doleful tale that she'd been laid up with a severe cold, unable to receive visitors. He'd even ordered pots of beef broth, bowls of fruit, and baskets of the best pastries and treats from his kitchens to tempt the invalid's supposedly delicate appetite. By the time Rebecca told him the truth—Lia had left for London on the mail coach three days before—it had been too late for him to have any hope of catching her.

Jack's first panicked thought had been that she'd gone haring off on her own, and it had almost given him a heart attack on the spot. But Sarah Rogers—apparently the only member of the household with a whit of common sense—had insisted on accompanying the girl to London, and he had every confidence that the redoubtable housekeeper would hold even the most impertinent fellow at bay.

It had been some days before he could follow her because he'd been forced to deal with pressing business in

Yorkshire, including a number of increasingly hostile creditors. Fortunately, his estate manager had created enough breathing room to keep things in order until Jack returned to Stonefell—hopefully with a new line of credit from his bankers. There was also his mother to deal with, along with a London set of creditors—also increasingly hostile. According to his mother, they were all but banging on the front door of the mansion in Bedford Square.

But his most pressing concern was Lia. He might not have much control over his life at the moment, but he knew one thing with absolute certainty: Lia would be going home to Bluebell Cottage within the next forty-eight hours if he had to lock her into his traveling coach and drive it north himself.

He swallowed a sigh as he made his way to the reading room of the exclusive club. He'd already twice left his card at her stepfather's surprisingly elegant town house, stating that he'd keep calling until she was at home. Their relationship had clearly undergone an unfortunate change. In the past, Lia had always anticipated his visits with great eagerness. Sometimes she'd raced up to the main house at Stonefell before his bags were even unpacked.

Those days were obviously long gone. Their last meeting had been so catastrophic that he couldn't blame her for wanting to avoid him; he'd obviously wounded her deeply.

And then there was that earth-shattering moment when Lia's fiery kiss had all but stunned him senseless. Ever since, Jack had been wrestling with a regrettably strong desire for her to engage in yet more shocking behavior with him. The idea of taking her as his mistress horrified him, but it also enticed him much more than he cared to admit.

He spotted his quarry in a quiet corner and stalked over to join him. Charles Valentine Penley, Duke of Leverton, glanced up from his paper, his surprise registering in the elegant uptick of his eyebrows.

"Good God, what are you doing back in Town?" Charles asked.

"It's delightful to see you, too," Jack said. "I do hope I'm not disturbing your cogitations on important affairs of state, Your Grace."

His best friend cut him a grin. "I'm reading the on-dits. They are generally more entertaining than your company, especially when you're glowering at me. Suffering from a little dyspepsia, are we?"

"Ah, the gossip columns. Is the duchess making an appearance in them this week? She does have a tendency to liven things up, and London is so quiet at this time of year."

"That's a delicate way to characterize my wife's adventures. We've not had any incidents in some weeks, so I suppose we're due for one." Charles breathed out a dramatic sigh.

Jack laughed. "Your wife is utterly charming and you adore her—as you should, by the way. I tried to steal her for myself, but for some demented reason she chose you over me, no doubt because you're a duke *and* disgustingly wealthy."

He winced as soon as the words were out of his mouth. He'd meant it as a joke, but more than a little bitterness had leeched into his tone.

His friend simply gave him a smile, rising politely to his feet. "No, it's because my manners are so distinguished. Or so Gillian assures me. And you know what a stickler she is for polite behavior."

The absurd comment made Jack laugh and lightened the moment. The Duchess of Leverton was the opposite of a high stickler. She was also one of the kindest, most intelligent young women Jack had ever met.

"You're a lucky man, you blighter," he said. "I hope you give her all the appreciation she deserves."

"She is the light of my life," Charles said quietly. "I don't know how I got along without her."

"And don't forget that Her Grace is very handy when it comes to dealing with ruthless brigands or, even worse, jug-bitten aristocrats."

"Don't I know it," his friend replied with a rueful smile.

To say that the former Gillian Dryden was an unconventional woman was perhaps the understatement of the decade. Still, there was no doubting that the duke and his new duchess were deeply in love and, in their own odd way, a perfect match.

"I am truly happy for you and Gillian," Jack said, turning serious. "You both deserve it."

His friend gave him a shrewd perusal. "Thank you, Jack. You, however, seem to be weighed down these days. Care to have a brandy with me and unburden yourself?"

"I'll join you in a brandy, although I'm sure you have no wish to hear about the sorry state of my affairs. They're both mundane and dreary, I assure you."

"Don't be an idiot. I will happily listen to any number of your sad tales. God knows you did it for me in my callow youth." Charles glanced past him. "But Lord Stalworth is glaring daggers at us for disturbing the peace. I suggest we repair to the club room where we can talk more freely."

Jack followed his friend, flashing the elderly viscount an apologetic smile. Stalworth, the very picture of decrepitude, rustled his paper in disapproval. Boodle's was known for its genteel atmosphere, and the distinguished and mostly elderly members tended to frown on any behavior that disturbed the tranquil atmosphere.

Jack's membership in London's clubs was of recent vintage, after he'd assumed the title. He could certainly see their value; a great deal of business was conducted over brandy or port or at a hand of cards. But the hard truth was that he couldn't afford the lifestyle that came with club privilege—the gambling and wagering on things from the arcane to the idiotic. He avoided the tables and never made wagers on any of the other *sure bets* that were so much a part of the masculine life of the Ton.

As far as he was concerned, he'd won the ultimate wager by escaping the battlefields of Spain and Belgium with only a few minor wounds. To risk his livelihood—and the security of all those who depended on him—by gambling would be tempting fate to a reckless degree.

Jack's father had brought his family to the brink of ruin more than once at the tables of London's elite clubs. Uncle Arthur had rescued them from debt more than once, at great cost to his own purse.

But Uncle Arthur had squandered great sums of money as well until ill health and Rebecca Kincaid persuaded him to retreat to Stonefell. Jack had no intention of adhering to the family tradition of losing one's shirt, nor would he ever keep a mistress. Uncle Arthur had at least had the decency to fall in love with his, but Jack's father had traded in expensive women as easily as he'd entered a wager in the betting book at White's or tossed down a hand of cards in a gaming hell.

He and Charles found two seats in a relatively secluded alcove, keeping away from a group of men boisterously gossiping about the Prince Regent and his latest rumored mistress. It was another unwelcome reminder that Lia might also become an object of such gossip. The by-blow of a prince taking to the stage and following in her mother's scandalous footsteps was as salacious a picture as one could imagine.

After ordering brandies from a passing footman, Charles stretched out his long, booted legs. While his friend looked the picture of contentment, Jack felt as if he had a swarm of wasps buzzing around in his brain.

Charles eyed him. "Why are you scowling at that lot over there? They're just engaging in the usual idiocy."

"God knows Prinny and his loutish relations provide them with enough fodder. Doesn't it bother you?"

"Why? Because my wife's father is the Duke of Cumberland, the absolute worst of the lot?"

Jack cut him a wry smile.

Charles shrugged. "He's so disreputable that Gillian wants nothing to do with him. We make a point of not discussing him and avoid him whenever possible."

"Does that actually work? The royals are all over the place, now that the war has ended."

"Gillian hasn't been in London that long, so there haven't been many opportunities to run into them. And most of them are out of Town a great deal, either at their estates or in Brighton with the Regent. So far, our luck has held."

"But when the Season begins, it'll be next to impossible to avoid them completely. What will you do then?"

"Are you asking out of genuine concern for Gillian?" Charles shrewdly asked. "Or is there another motive at play here?"

Jack supposed it was obvious he was worried about what might happen to Lia if she stayed in London. "For now, let's go with the former."

"As you wish. Gillian and I have decided that we will treat the majority of her royal relations with the accepted standard of respect and courtesy, but we will not acknowledge any familial relations, especially with her father. Gillian has said that she'll walk right over Cumberland if she has to. She'll refuse to acknowledge he even exists."

"That's bound to go down well," Jack said dryly.

"You forget a pertinent fact—her half brother is Griffin Steele, who, as you know, is also one of Cumberland's by-blows."

"Are you telling me that he threatened Cumberland?" Jack had only recently met the former crime lord, now a semi-respectable member of the Ton. No sane person would ever wish to cross Griffin Steele, and that would presumably include his royal father.

"That would be most unseemly. But he did remind his esteemed parent that he was still in debt to him for quite a large sum, left over from the days when Steele ran his gaming hells."

"Good Lord, do you mean to tell me Cumberland actually borrowed money from his bastard son?"

"Does that really surprise you? Most of the princes did the same thing. Steele has quite a lot of influence within the royal family, as you can imagine."

Jack couldn't help laughing. "God, what a pack of buffoons, all of them. So Steele warned Cumberland away from his sister?"

"Suggested, more like it. But my brother-in-law would do anything to protect her."

"As would you," Jack said quietly. He wished he had that kind of power and influence, when it came to him.

"Naturally, but let's talk about your royal problem," Charles said. "Gillian is quite eager to meet her cousin. I am less so, but if I don't support my wife she's bound to do something drastic, and that would hardly help Miss Kincaid. So, what can we do to assist her now that she's in Town?"

Jack stiffened. "How did you know Lia was in London? She arrived less than a week ago and she's not announced herself in any way."

"Let's just say I have my sources," Charles said with a negligent wave of his hand.

"You mean Gillian's been gossiping with your servants again."

Charles sighed. "I can't seem to break her of the habit. But this time we heard it from Steele, who knows everything that happens in this blasted Town. He came calling the other day with the happy news that Gillian has a cousin living only a short carriage ride away. Needless to say, my wife was more than a bit peeved that I hadn't already provided her with that information."

"And knowing the duchess, I imagine she wanted to run right over to meet Lia."

"I was only able to stop her by explaining that Lia might not yet be aware of her existence, and that the responsibility for imparting such news rested with the Kincaid family or with you."

When Jack relaxed back in his chair, Charles lifted a sardonic eyebrow.

"So, I take it from your reaction that you have not yet told Lia about her kinship with Gillian, or any of her other relations?" His friend's tone was austere and disapproving.

"I wanted to, but I was overruled. Her grandmother feels it wouldn't be helpful or fair to allow Lia to associate with a cousin who is . . ."

"So far above her?" he finished as the footman returned with their brandies. When the man retreated, Charles continued. "Jack, you know we don't care about that sort of thing."

"Believe me, I share your frustration, although I understand Rebecca's concerns. She feels certain that Lia and Gillian will never move in the same circles. After all, Lia is the granddaughter of an infamous courtesan and the daughter of an actress who was once equally notorious.

Gillian's family lines, on the other hand, are impeccable, and she was raised as an aristocrat. She truly belongs where she is—as your duchess."

"And where do you think Lia Kincaid belongs?"

Jack drank his brandy as he struggled with the question, not liking the answers that sprang to mind. "Not on a bloody stage, that's for damn sure."

Charles's eyebrows shot up. "Is that what she wants to do? Join her mother on the stage?"

"Yes, I'm sorry to say."

"That is a most unfortunate development. Even though Mr. Lester's troupe is considered respectable, Lia's appearance on the stage certainly will not help her reputation. Is she pretty?"

"Very," Jack said, feeling gloomier by the minute. His friend's reaction was confirming his fears.

"Then she'll be a target for every damn rake in London. Did she discuss this course of action with you?"

"She did, along with some other alarming potential career choices. I told her that none of them were remotely acceptable for a gently bred girl such as herself."

Charles stared blankly at him for a moment before understanding took hold. "Are you suggesting she is considering a life in the demi-monde?"

Jack waggled a hand. "That was more her grandmother's notion. Lia's the one who wants to perform on the stage. Unfortunately, before we could discuss either issue to any degree of satisfaction, she gave me the slip and came here."

"That was very enterprising of her—and explains your precipitous return to London."

"Lia is exceedingly resourceful. When she puts her mind to something, she generally makes it happen." While that was fine when it came to managing Stonefell's gardens or helping the tenant farmers, her current misadventure had all the hallmarks of a disaster.

"And are you going to let this particular enterprise happen?" his friend asked gently.

"Don't be an idiot, Charles. As soon as I get my hands on her, I'm taking her back to Stonefell, where she belongs. It's the only place she'll ever be safe."

"Are you in love with the girl, Jack?"

Jack almost dropped his glass. "Are you out of your bloody mind?"

An unfortunate lull in the conversation on the other side of the room brought a number of heads whipping around to observe them. Charles gave the assembled men his chilliest ducal stare, which had its usual and desired effect.

He turned back to the discussion. "A little less heat, Jack, or we'll be the ones to instigate the gossip about poor Miss Kincaid."

Jack was already mentally kicking himself for revealing so much. "Sorry. As to your question, of course I love Lia. And of course I feel responsible for her and Rebecca. My uncle left them in a terrible fix and it's up to me to make it right."

Charles turned an elegant hand palm up. "So, your feelings for Miss Lia are . . ."

"Are those of a brother," he said firmly. "And even if they weren't, there's not a damn thing I can do about it, for a dozen reasons."

"Everyone said the same about me and Gillian, and yet here we are, the Duke and Duchess of Leverton."

"The extremely wealthy and powerful Duke and Duchess of Leverton. Unfortunately, I possess neither power nor wealth."

Charles frowned. "Jack, I'm more than willing to help with your financial situation. I can easily lend—"

"I appreciate your generosity, but that is the fastest way to ruin a friendship. I won't risk it."

If he were able to secure some significant backing for the proposed mining venture, Jack might then approach Charles with a proposal to invest. But until that point, he refused to be indebted to his friend any more than he already was. Charles had helped him out of more than one sticky patch during the war, when Uncle Arthur couldn't afford to send along his usual quarterly allowance. He wouldn't impose on his friend again.

"I understand," said Charles with a sympathetic grimace. "But where does that leave you in terms of Stonefell's current financial situation?"

"If my bankers won't help me, then I'll be on the lookout for a willing heiress," Jack said with a sigh. "My mother and sister are already compiling lists of candidates."

Charles eyed him for a moment before nodding. "Very sensible. I'm sure they'll find you a most pleasing group of young ladies from which to choose."

Whether they would want to choose him, simply another penniless aristocrat up to his ears in debt, was a different question.

"That leaves us with one more concern," Charles added. "What do we do about Gillian's desire to meet her newly discovered cousin? I will not be able to hold her back for long, as you can well imagine."

"All too well. And I will talk to Lia as soon as it's convenient." Jack gave his friend a determined stare. "She needs to hear it from me. It's bound to upset her one way or another, and she'll want to talk it through with someone she's close to." At least he hoped so. She might throw him out onto the street instead.

Charles nodded. "I can get Gillian to agree to that, if she only has to wait a few days. Let me know when you've discussed the issue with Miss Lia and we'll talk about the best way for the ladies to meet each other."

"Very privately," Jack said wryly. One never quite knew how Gillian would react in situations like this. With a boisterous degree of enthusiasm, he suspected.

Charles's eyes glinted. "I agree with that assessment. Very well, we will look forward to speaking more about Miss Kincaid in the near future."

Now all Jack had to do was run the infuriating girl to ground.

Chapter Six

"Lendale, a moment of your time, please."

Jack had almost escaped, but fortune was not with him today. In fact, although Lady Luck had been with him for many a long year during the war, the fickle beauty had clearly abandoned him once he'd returned home to England's verdant shores.

As he transferred his hat back to the footman who waited by the front door, the fellow gave him a slight, sympathetic grimace. Lady John had all the servants hopping these days, now that she'd finally gotten herself established in the Bedford Square mansion. It had been his mother's fondest dream for as long as Jack could remember, and although her dream had finally come true, it presented enough challenges to daunt even his strong-willed parent.

"There's no need to address me so formally, Mother," he said to the dignified woman waiting for him in the door of the library. "Jack served quite well for my entire life."

Her narrow, clever eyebrows pulled together in a slight show of disapproval, but she refrained from answering until the footman closed the doors of the library behind them. His mother crossed to one of the slender, Hepplewhite-style chairs grouped around a table that looked much too delicate

for the masculine décor of the library. The furniture grouping
was new, as were the gold window hangings. They were not
to his personal taste, but he had no doubt his mother's
choices were bang up to the mark and expensive.

She took a seat, nodding for him to do the same. Jack
waved a hand, preferring to remain on his feet in the hope
that she would receive the unspoken message that he was
pressed for time.

"Now that you are master of this house," she said, "it
would be inappropriate for me to address you with so negligent a degree of respect. What would the servants think?"

"That you're my mother and that I'm your son?"

He heard her breathe out a tiny sigh. "My son, as much
as I esteemed the previous marquess—"

"That would be my uncle and your brother-in-law, I
believe."

"Really, Jack, must you keep interrupting me?"

He laughed. "I'm sorry, Mother, but sometimes you are
remarkably easy to tease. And I did get you to call me Jack,
which I count as a small victory."

The corners of her mouth tipped up, albeit reluctantly.
When she forgot her worries—or her pride—she transformed into the good-humored woman he remembered
from his childhood. Too many cares and too much bitterness had made that woman increasingly hard to find as the
calendar turned one year to the next.

"Touché," she said. "But my point remains. As fond as I
was of your uncle, he was too lax in his domestic affairs,
and that led to a degree of vulgarity in the tone of his
household. For your sake, that state of affairs must not be
allowed to continue. We may address each other informally when we're alone, but it's important to maintain the
appropriate decorum in front of the household staff."

Jack knew there was little point in arguing with her;
she would do as she wished regardless. And he *had* given

the running of Lendale House over to her because he had more than enough on his plate dealing with Stonefell.

"I bow to your superior judgment in such domestic matters," he said.

She studied him with a disconcertingly acute regard. "I know all these rules and restrictions are not to your liking, but the servants gossip, you know. And that talk never stays within the household because they all have friends and acquaintances working in other London establishments. You may think your secrets are safe, my dear, but they are not."

Jack raised his eyebrows. "Mother, I have no secrets worthy of salacious gossip. And even if I did have something of interest to hide, I would not share it with any of the staff, including my valet. I know you think me guilty of a low sense of informality, but I am not a stupid man."

Her slight flinch represented uncharacteristic vulnerability and immediately made him feel guilty. When it came to his mother, guilt was a constant companion. As much as he cared for her—for his entire family—that unpleasant emotion was one of the reasons he'd been happy to remain on the Continent. Life had been easier when he was Major Jack Easton. Then his only problem had been French soldiers, and sometimes he thought he'd understood those adversaries better than he did his own family.

"I apologize," he said quietly. "You must know how grateful I am for all your help. It certainly hasn't been easy for you these last several years."

Her answering smile was warm but tinged with sadness. "And you must know that I would do anything for you, my son. I realize that I must seem like the worst sort of stickler, but for too long our family has been an object of mockery. It will take a lot of work to restore the appropriate sense of dignity to the Easton and Lendale names."

He thought she overstated the case, but she wasn't entirely wrong, given how both his father and uncle had misbehaved. No wonder his mother, who with quiet grace had suffered years of humiliation, longed to see the family's reputation restored.

"I understand completely. Now, what did you wish to speak to me about?" He hoped to God she wasn't about to hand him an unexpected set of bills. He'd given her a free hand to reorder the household, trusting in her good sense not to spend beyond their means. Unfortunately, he may have underestimated her eagerness to restore Lendale House to its former glory. To his mother, the family's dignity was just as bound up in external appearance as it was in the appropriate forms of address.

"I was thinking it past time for us to host a proper dinner party," she said. "It's been some years since your sister has been to Town, and we should hold one to honor her visit."

Jack's sister had married a prosperous country squire with significant holdings in Somerset. Richard Kendall was a thoroughly decent man who adored his wife and children but abhorred city living. Although happy to indulge Anne, he put his foot down when it came to anything but short visits to London. Now that Jack was marquess, Kendall had finally agreed to let his wife come for an extended stay. She was due tomorrow and would remain with them at Lendale House for over a month.

"I'm sure Anne would like that very much," he said. "And I suppose we've got to start entertaining sooner or later."

The idea didn't thrill him, but looking like paupers might scare away wealthy members of the Ton who were potential investors in his mining scheme.

"Your sister will be delighted. Poor Anne has been rusticating for so long, I wonder if she remembers what a proper party looks like."

"Surely you exaggerate," Jack said. "Kendall is a very

wealthy and generous fellow. And he seems to dote on her, from what I can tell."

His mother flicked an impatient hand. "Yes, but he's a country squire, my dear." Her jaw worked for a moment. "You're well aware of the hopes we had for your sister when she came out."

Anne had been considered a diamond of the first water, a beautiful girl with a kind nature and quick wit. By all rights, she should have made a splendid match. Unfortunately, she was virtually lacking a dowry, thanks to the spendthrift ways of her father and uncle.

After three years on the marriage mart, Anne had been verging on spinsterhood. Only Richard Kendall, in London visiting aristocratic relations, had proposed. Since it was clear she'd never receive a better offer, she'd accepted. She'd done it with good grace, too, unlike her mother, who still hadn't overcome the cruel disappointment of her beautiful daughter being forced to marry into the country gentry.

"How could I forget?" he said dryly.

"You know the sacrifices your sister made on behalf of our family," his mother said tartly. "And how generous she's been in helping us through many a difficulty."

"Kendall, too," Jack said. "He's never once voiced a word of complaint over the years. He certainly had every right to, given how many times he's pulled us out of the River Tick. We'd probably be in debtor's prison without his help."

His mother blushed. "I've never denied Richard's better qualities, but I do not believe we must resort to vulgar cant to acknowledge them. You're a marquess now, my son, not a soldier on the battlefield. You must act accordingly."

Jack was tempted to point out that he'd known many a common soldier with better manners than the average male aristocrat but refrained. "Point taken. As to the party, I'll leave all the details in your capable hands. How many do you expect to invite?"

"At least forty, I should think."

That made him blink. "That many?"

She nodded. "It will be a splendid opportunity for you to meet some of the Ton's most eligible young ladies and their parents. You can't put it off much longer, Jack. You need a wife and a helpmate."

His stomach turned sour, but he forced a smile. "Why? I've got you taking care of everything for me."

"Jack—"

"Very well. I'll inspect as many heiresses as you care to trot out. But right now I must be off. I have a fairly urgent matter to attend to."

He bent to press a quick kiss to her cheek but drew back when she frowned. "Now what?" he asked.

"You're going to visit her, aren't you?"

Christ. "It's nothing to concern yourself about, Mother."

"I thought so. You're going to see that Kincaid girl." Though she didn't raise her voice, her tone was heavy with disapproval.

"I am," he said tersely. Though Jack never discussed the Kincaids with his mother, he'd been forced to tell her why he'd unexpectedly returned to London. They'd already had one argument about Lia.

"I don't know why you bother," she replied in a cold voice. "You told me that she's staying with her mother and stepfather. It's their responsibility to take care of the girl, not yours."

"If I had any confidence that Mrs. Lester would exercise her parental responsibility, I might agree with you. But because she's never shown any inclination to safeguard her own child, I'm not hopeful. Besides, as I already explained, the Lester household is not an appropriate place for Lia."

"I would think the opposite is true. Miss Kincaid is now

at her level, instead of pretending to be something she isn't," his mother said with a curl of her lip.

Jack had to swallow the impulse to snap back at her. "Despite Lia's unfortunate parentage, she's been raised in a genteel fashion in the country."

"Yes, so genteel that she's taken the first opportunity to run away to London to become an actress," his mother said sarcastically. "The foolish girl seems determined to follow in her mother's disreputable footsteps."

Jack shook his head. There was a yawning chasm between them on the issue of the Kincaids. "Mother, I realize it's difficult for you to understand, but I have a deep responsibility toward Lia. And whether you believe it or not, she has no idea what she's gotten herself in to. She's a country girl through and through, and the type of life she's contemplating—through a ridiculously romantic haze, I might add—will destroy her. As her friend, I will not allow that to happen. Now, if you'll excuse me, I'll see you at dinner."

He started to turn away, but her desperate voice stopped him. "Jack, wait."

Turning, his heart sank when he took in the pain in her gaze and the lines of bitterness scored so deeply around her mouth.

"You've forgotten what it was like," she said. "You were able to escape to school and then to the army, so you didn't have to live with it as your sister and I did. The humiliations your father inflicted. The mistresses I turned a blind eye to." Her hands fisted into her skirts. "Your father spent so much on them, giving them jewels and fine clothes while I struggled to pay the bills. And the money he squandered on horses, the gambling . . ." Her voice quavered before she stopped, trying to regain her self-control.

Jack's heart ached for her. He'd loved his father—they all had, including his mother. Lord John had been a handsome, witty man, with an affectionate manner and a gregarious personality that charmed all who knew him. The hell of it was, his father had genuinely loved them back. But he'd loved himself more. Like generations of Easton men preceding him, he'd been too spoiled and arrogant to control his baser appetites.

"I know what you suffered," he said in a quiet voice. "I'm sorry I couldn't do more to help you."

She gave him a sad smile. "You did try, more than once. But nothing ever worked, did it?"

A few times, when it was especially bad, Jack had even come to blows with him. Invariably, his father apologized, shedding tears and promising to reform what he called his *sad character*. But his resolve only held until another beautiful woman or a cracking great horse crossed his path.

"No, but we weren't entirely left to our own resources. Uncle Arthur always did what he could. He was very generous to me."

Her ladylike snort signaled what she thought of that line of argument. His mother had hated the time he'd spent at Stonefell, fearing he would be corrupted by his uncle's lax morals. She'd hated even more that Uncle Arthur had paid for his commission in the Horse Guards because she'd lost her staunchest ally in the fight against her husband's reckless ways.

"Yes, and for you to pursue your dream," his mother said, "Anne and I were forced to make many sacrifices."

"I understand that, and I will do everything in my power to secure our family's future and ensure that you never have to suffer again."

"I'm sure that is your intention, but such is not the case. In fact, I think you are in danger of making the same mistake your uncle did—a mistake that will destroy everything I have fought to achieve for you and this family."

Jack stared at her silently until clarity dawned. "You think I'm having an affair with Lia? That's ridiculous."

"Is it?" she asked in a haughty voice.

"You know it is."

"Regardless of what I think, others might not find it so."

"Others can mind their own damn business. I will not apologize for helping one of my oldest friends."

His mother rose hastily to her feet. "Jack, you *must* make a good marriage. What respectable girl would wish to betroth herself to man openly involved with an actress, especially one with that particular name? No young woman of breeding, nor her parents, would even contemplate it."

"For the last time, I am not involved with Lia," he gritted out. "And she's not an actress."

His mother waved her arms. "Jack, it only matters what people think. And they *will* think you are just like your father—a rakehell of the first order. Someone who cares only for his own animal appetites."

Disbelief and anger surged through him. "I am nothing like my father—or my uncle, for that matter. You know that."

"Then give up this foolish notion that you owe anything to this creature or her family," she pleaded. "She's at her level and you are at yours. They cannot and will not ever meet."

"Her name is Lia," Jack said quietly. "And she's a kind and decent young woman who's never done anything to wrong any of us."

"I know her name," his mother said bitterly. "It's Kincaid. And like every woman in that family, she wrongs us by her very existence. For God's sake, let us be done with them before they ruin us yet again."

She turned on her heel and swept from the room.

Chapter Seven

"Stand still, Amy," Lia said around the pin in her mouth, "or I might stick you."

The dancer looked over her shoulder, her eyes bright with laughter. "You've already done that once, and right in my arse, too. If you keep poking holes in me I might spring a leak."

Lia pulled the pin from between her teeth and carefully inserted it along the back seam of the girl's bodice. "That's because you wriggle around like a fish on a hook. I can't get you to stand still for a minute."

"I'm a dancer, love. That's what we do—we move."

"Well, don't move while I'm checking the fit or this seam will be crooked." Lia fiddled with her pins some more, then gave a satisfied nod. "That should do it. Now step back and let me look at you."

Amy obediently retreated to the center of the Pan Theater's green room, which doubled as a dressing and fitting room before performances. The graceful girl spun, spreading her arms wide in a theatrical pose. She was tall and shapely, with a doelike gaze and a sensual mouth that belied her youthful, almost innocent air.

Though Lia had grown quite fond of Amy over the past

week, the girl was anything but innocent. As the Lester Troupe's most popular dancer, Amy had garnered a legion of admirers bent on luring her to bestow her favors on them. Not a day went by that some little gift or carton of sweets or small posy didn't arrive from one of her swains. Not that Amy was the only recipient of such largesse. Most of the female performers regularly received gifts from their admirers. And Lia was under no illusions that some of those men were not intimately rewarded for their generosity. Amy, the most popular girl, was currently being courted by a viscount, a baronet, a bachelor magistrate, and a prosperous haberdasher who kept her well supplied with stockings and lace.

"Will I do?" Amy smoothed down the bodice of her costume. "Or will you need to stick me some more?"

She was dressed as a nymph for the upcoming production of *The Queen of Mount Olympus*, which would star Lia's mother and open in a few days. Amy looked more like a naughty milkmaid than a classical nymph, given the cut of the costume and the stays that pushed up her décolletage. When Lia pointed out to her mother that the outfits were historically inaccurate, Mama had simply laughed and said that no one in the audience, especially the men, gave a fig about sartorial accuracy when it came to dancers.

Lia had found it disconcerting to discover that some pieces in the theatrical program were quite unsophisticated and even ribald. She'd known, of course, that the licensing laws prohibited the company from performing spoken drama and the classics. And while she didn't expect Shakespeare, she'd hoped to be given something more challenging—not to mention tasteful—than a nonspeaking role in the unfortunately named burletta *A Surprise for the Publican's Wife*.

"We're done for now," she said to Amy after inspecting

her work. "Just let me unpin you, and then I'll go ahead and finish stitching up the repair. Your costume will be ready for opening night, I promise."

Amy breathed out a relieved sigh. "You're a dear, Miss Lia. When it ripped at rehearsal, I was afraid I'd have to repair it myself, and I'm all thumbs when it comes to needlework. Never been much good at all that domestic nonsense." She gave Lia a knowing wink. "Not that I have to be, thank God."

"Indeed not," Lia said dryly.

Apparently Amy was very particular when it came to her lovers. They had to be handsome, rich, and willing to spend to keep her in style. Lia couldn't help feeling a bit squeamish about the hard-nosed way some of the company actresses and dancers discussed their current or prospective lovers, as if they were horses at auction at Tattersalls or investments on the Exchange.

Not that she blamed them; the theatrical profession was uncertain at best. It was no wonder female performers often supplemented their incomes with gifts or financial support from lovers or patrons.

Thankfully, Lia would never find herself in such a vulnerable position. With her mother and stepfather's patronage, she should be able to establish a successful acting career that would enable her to support herself and Granny. In the meantime, her stepfather had made it perfectly clear that she was welcome to stay with them for as long as she wanted, despite her mother's obvious reluctance to go along with that plan.

The final niggle—and a fairly large one at that—went by the title of the Marquess of Lendale. Lia had been dodging him for almost a week. She knew she wouldn't be able to get away with that much longer, though; Jack was an exceedingly determined man. She did miss him terribly, except when the image of that humiliating scene in the library sprang into her mind. Then she told herself she never wanted to see him again.

"Hallo, Miss Lia," Amy said, waving a hand in her face. "Are you in there?"

Lia startled. "I'm sorry. What were you saying?"

Amy peered at her. "You're not coming down with the beastly cold that tackled Mrs. Andrews, are you? You look flushed as anything."

"No, I'm perfectly fine, thank goodness, although I can't say the same for poor Mrs. Andrews. It was bad enough that her assistant seamstress decided to run off and get married. Then to come down with that awful cold, and with less than a week before the opening, too."

"That was bad luck," Amy said as she struggled to get out of her costume. "But you're almost as good with the needle as she is." She wrinkled her nose. "Still, it don't seem quite right that you had to take on the job of wardrobe mistress, you being Mrs. Lester's daughter and all."

Lia moved behind Amy to help her. "Most of the work was already done, and I did promise Mama I would assist in any way I could."

"Yes, and they've got you copying out the cue lines and speeches for the actors when Mr. Lester makes changes to the script. If you ask me, they're taking advantage of you, love."

Lia couldn't hold back a sigh. "You're very kind to say so, but I truly don't mind. Although I had been hoping for more than just a walk-on part in one little scene."

"I think it's because your mother's jealous of you. Anybody can see you're a younger version of her, and it can't be easy to have that thrown in your face every day. She won't want you stealing her thunder on that stage, I guarantee it."

Lia stilled for a moment. "Mama just wants to make sure I don't rush into anything or get in over my head."

Amy snorted. "I don't think so, love, but you tell yourself that if it makes you feel better."

"Don't worry about me." Lia's hands were a bit clumsy and she snagged a pin in the strap of Amy's stays. When she tugged it out, it pulled the strap down, exposing the girl's shoulder and upper back.

"Goodness," she said with a frown. "How did you get that awful bruise?"

Amy hastily stepped away. She yanked off the bodice and handed it to Lia, then pulled her strap back over her shoulder. "I don't even know. I suppose I was clumsy and bumped into something."

That didn't make sense because Amy was the most graceful person Lia had ever met. She practically floated, both on and off the stage.

"You should put some cool cloths on it, or perhaps some arnica. I'd be happy to go to the apothecary and get some for you."

"Don't fuss, Miss Lia," Amy said sharply. "It's fine."

"All right, if you're certain." It was the first time Lia had known Amy to snap at anyone.

The dancer grimaced. "Just listen to me, biting your nose off like that. Sorry, love. I always get a little peevish before opening night. It's nerves, that's all."

"You have nothing to be nervous about. Everyone will adore you. Now, give me your skirt and I'll finish this all up by tomorrow."

Amy obediently untied her skirt and stepped out of it, leaving her clad only in her shift, stockings, and stays.

"Where's your wrapper?" Lia asked. "You'll catch a chill if you wander around dressed like that."

"Bloody hell, I left it in my dressing room. I'd better

fetch it before Mr. Lester sees me going about half-naked. He's a bit of a prude, which is odd considering his missus. Not that Mrs. Lester hasn't gone right respectable since she married him," Amy added hastily, flapping an apologetic hand.

The comment was another reminder that her mother's past was not yet forgotten. Though Lia had kept mostly to the Lester town house and the theater, gossip had already started to circulate about the arrival of a new Notorious Kincaid. Needless to say, Mama was not pleased. When Mr. Lester had tried to console his wife by pointing out that Lia's addition to the company would likely boost ticket sales, that argumentation had gone over as well as could be expected—which was to say, not well at all.

As Amy hurried out the door, she collided, bosom first, with a tall, broad-shouldered man wearing a deadly scowl on his handsome face.

Hell and damnation.

Jack's hands shot out and grasped Amy by her bare shoulders. The dancer wobbled dramatically and clutched at his waistcoat, as if she would fall flat on her backside without his support. Because Lia knew Amy could balance on the toes of one foot with no trouble at all, she had to swallow a snort.

"Oh, la, thank you, kind sir," Amy trilled. "I would have taken quite the tumble if you hadn't caught me."

Jack blinked down at her, looking befuddled. Then the scowl returned, and it grew even more severe as he took in Amy's generously displayed charms.

"I'm happy I prevented so unfortunate an occurrence." His tone suggested the opposite as he tried to extract himself from Amy's deathlike grip.

"And who might you be, sir?" the dancer asked with a flirtatious smile. "A new patron for our little company or a member of our illustrious board? I do hope so." She gave his waistcoat a little stroke, as if checking out the goods. "You would make a fine addition, I'm sure."

Because Jack was now directing his scowl in Lia's direction, she was tempted to leave him to his fate. Still, he *was* Jack, and he'd come to her rescue numerous times over the years. "He's a friend of mine, Amy. A good friend," she added pointedly.

The girl cast a shrewd glance at her, then relinquished her grip. "So that's how it is, eh? Forgive me, love. I didn't know you had a *special* beau."

Jack's expression had now become an interesting combination of outrage and alarm. Lia started mentally bracing herself for the forthcoming scold. It was sure to be a ripper.

"He's not a special beau," she said, trying to minimize the damage.

Amy's eyebrows went up in an incredulous lift.

"Never mind," Lia said with a sigh. Trying to explain her relationship with Jack wasn't worth the bother; Amy wouldn't believe it anyway. "This is the Marquess of Lendale. Lord Lendale, allow me to introduce Miss Amy Baxter, a member of my stepfather's company."

"A pleasure," Jack replied in a tone so clipped Lia was tempted to smack him.

"Don't look very pleasurable to me," Amy said with her usual fatal candor. "But I'm sure our Lia can find a way to sweeten your mood." She finished up that bon mot by giving Jack an exaggerated wink.

"Oy, Amy, my love," came a welcome interruption from out in the hall. "Are you in the green room?"

"In here, Bertie," Amy yelled back.

A moment later one of the musicians stuck his head through the doorway. "A few of us are popping out to the pub for a bite before rehearsal. Fancy joining us?"

"Yes, please," Amy replied.

Bertie was not the least bit nonplussed by Amy's half-naked appearance. Most of the members of the company were used to seeing each other in various states of undress and never blinked an eye. It had taken Lia a few days to get used to it, but she now realized that the men in the company were fiercely protective of all the women, even if morals on occasion did tend to get a bit wobbly.

One glance at Jack's face, however, signaled that she had work to do when it came to explaining how tame her new life was, despite appearances to the contrary.

Amy disappeared with Bertie, leaving Lia with the ignoble urge to slink out after her friend. Unfortunately, Jack was blocking the doorway with his tall, muscular frame.

Might as well bull through it, old girl.

"You're looking well, Jack," she said brightly. "It's lovely to see you."

"Really? You've been assiduously avoiding me for a week now."

Drat. She *had* been avoiding him, and not simply because she didn't want to reprise their argument. Their disastrous kiss in the library at Stonefell had been the most mortifying moment of her life. How could they ever get back on the old footing with something like that hanging between them?

"I've been very busy," she explained. "The theater will open with a new program in only two days. It's been a madhouse."

"So I see," he said, casting a dark look around the room.

Some of the plasterwork was a little worse for wear and the paint was a bit faded, but it was in better shape than some of the shuttered rooms at Stonefell. Her stepfather had plans to renovate the entire backstage area, but that would have to wait until they were making a profit. So far, all his efforts had gone into refreshing the galleries, boxes, and public areas of the theater. The Pan was now almost as elegant as the big theaters in Drury Lane.

"Now that I've finally got a moment of your time," Jack said with gentle sarcasm as his gaze returned to her, "may I comment that your behavior has been nothing short of reckless? First you lied to me by feigning illness, then you ran off to London on the mail coach, of all things. What in God's name prompted such foolishness, especially after I told you that I would take care of you?"

Lia carefully folded the costume and placed it in her workbasket. Then she crossed her arms over her chest and stared at him. "You can't think of one thing that would make me bolt?"

He flushed a bit. "You were the one who kissed me, not the other way around. It wasn't as if I had designs on your virtue, pet—quite the opposite, in fact."

"Yes, you made that abundantly clear," she said coolly.

He slapped a hand to the back of his neck, rubbing it as if it pained him. In the process, he knocked off his hat.

"Dammit," he muttered as he stooped to retrieve it. "All right, let's leave aside the issue that you apparently resent the fact that I refuse to take advantage of you. And let's also defer for now any discussion of your precipitous, nay, insane departure from Stonefell."

"Thank you, my lord," she said with sugary sweetness. "I'm ever so grateful."

Jack looked as if he might have to pry his jaw open to continue. "I understand that you might wish to visit your mother, but working in a theater? Did I not already point out the risks of such a venture to a girl in your position? You might as well send out invitations to every rakehell in Town." He swept another disdainful glance around the room. "This place is barely one step up from a brothel."

She scoffed at the exaggeration. "The Pan is nothing of

the sort. My stepfather is a well-regarded theater manager and this is a legitimate, respectable establishment."

"So respectable that the females in the company apparently scamper about in an advanced state of undress."

"Not at all. I was simply fitting Amy's costume. It is a common occurrence in a theatrical troupe and no one thinks twice about it. Goodness, Jack, when did you turn into such an old miss?"

He shook his head. "I'm the furthest thing from an old miss one can imagine. But I know very well how men think about actresses."

"You have no cause to worry. For one thing, I'm the theater manager's stepdaughter and the leading lady's daughter. And I've found the men in the company to be very protective of the women. A theatrical troupe is much like a family, especially when they have an excellent manager like Stephen Lester. I couldn't be safer than if I was in my own bedroom in Bluebell Cottage."

As Jack set his hat down on the large worktable beside the bits and pieces of costumes and a stack of programs for opening night, Lia let her gaze slide quickly over his body. He had always been a handsome man, but now he was something more—he was a marquess, and he carried himself with an understated but formidable masculine power. Although never a dandy, his clothes were beautifully tailored and had an air of elegance that befitted his new status. As Marquess of Lendale, Jack might have his financial challenges, but no one could doubt for a second that he belonged in the rarified atmosphere of the beau monde.

Suddenly, she was painfully aware of her plain round gown, now several years out of fashion. It was good enough to work in but certainly not good enough to attract the notice of a man like him. What a fool she'd been to think she could.

"I do worry because you are far from safe," he said. "This building is a maze of poorly lit corridors and grimy little rooms, as far as I can tell. Anything could happen to a young woman wandering around so ramshackle an establishment. Especially at night."

"Did you tour the building on the way to see me?" she asked sarcastically.

"Because the front door was locked, I was forced to come around to the back through that exceedingly dank alley. Which, by the way, I forbid you ever to go into by yourself."

Despite her irritation, Jack's concern warmed Lia enough to smile. "Surely you must have seen that we have a man at all times at the stage door. He doesn't let just anyone in, you know. My stepfather is very strict about that."

"He let me in," he replied.

"No doubt because you obviously told him that we know each other."

"Yes, and he thought I was your lover," he said with disapproval. "When I disabused him of that notion, he then made the assumption that I was 'sniffing around Miss Lia's skirts.' He made a feeble attempt to prevent my passage, but I was able to bribe my way in."

Lia felt her shoulders go up around her ears. "I'll have to speak to my stepfather about that." She'd had her doubts about the fellow who manned the stage door during the day. He was a rather disreputable-looking character who tended to leer at the dancers and actresses.

"And while you're at it, why don't you also tell your stepfather that you're going to give up this mad scheme and return to Stonefell, where you belong?"

Lia pulled out one of the chairs from the worktable and wearily subsided into it, ignoring the alarming creak of the old spindles. "And what has changed that would make such a thing possible? Have you discovered some previously overlooked annuity or a forgotten inheritance? Perhaps one fell out of a secret drawer in your desk or a priest's hole in the wall?"

"Even though we're in a theater, we're not living in the pages of a melodrama, Lia," he said quietly.

He grabbed the back of another chair, swinging it around to face her. "I wish I had unearthed a cache of gold coins," he said ruefully as he sat. When he pulled off a glove and took her hand, Lia had to resist the impulse to clutch at the familiar warmth and strength of his long fingers and callused palm. "But even though such is not the case, I promised to take care of you and Rebecca, and I shall."

She made herself gently withdraw her hand. "I don't doubt that is your wish, but life often gets in the way of giving us what we wish for, does it not?"

He shook his head. "My sweet girl, don't you realize that I would—"

"Hush." She briefly pressed her fingers over one of his hands, now clenched on his knee. "No more promises, Jack. You are my dearest friend and I love you more than I can say for wanting to help us."

He flinched and sat back, as if she'd pushed him.

She'd all but confessed her true feelings for him and that was his reaction? Lia swallowed the pain and continued. "But we are not your responsibility and you've done more than enough."

"I haven't done a damn thing," he said through clenched teeth.

Ah, it seemed guilt was at the root of this. If so, that would poison what little friendship they had left.

"I do have a family," she said, forcing a cool tone. "It is their responsibility to help me. And might I add that given the differences in our social standing, if you were to help me it would only cause more salacious gossip."

Instead of being offended, he flashed her a wry smile. "Now you sound like my mother. And I cannot believe I just said that."

She briefly smiled. "I suspect you'll never have cause to say so again. Now, if you'll excuse me, I must get back to work. There's a great deal to be done before opening night."

His improved mood vanished in an instant. Jack had been an incredibly good-natured boy and was now a man with an easygoing, laughing manner. These days, however, he more closely resembled a bear with a sore paw.

She came to her feet, prompting him to stand as well. "Will you come see the play? Mama is simply splendid in her role."

"If you mean *A Surprise for the Publican's Wife*, dare I ask what the surprise is?" he asked in a dour voice.

Drat. He must have glimpsed the program on the worktable. "No, that's the comic burletta. Mama is starring in *The Queen of Mount Olympus*. I truly think it's one of my stepfather's finest works."

"I see. And are you appearing in either performance?"

Lia had to resist the impulse to look down at her feet. "As a matter of fact, I'm in the burletta. It's just a bit part, though," she added hastily, taking in his expression. "Not even a speaking role."

That qualification didn't assuage him. "Lia Kincaid, if you think I'm going to allow you to make a spec—"

"Lia, darling, are you in there?" trilled a voice, cutting off Jack's incipient tirade.

Breathing a prayer of thanks, Lia slipped around her fuming companion. "Yes, Mama."

Her mother glided through the door. Her costume vaguely resembled a toga—although one hardly imagined togas with gold spangles and gauze—and she carried a helmet. "There you are. I was hoping—" She broke off, seeing the stranger in the green room. After running a quick, assessing gaze over Jack's form, she flicked an enquiring glance at Lia.

"It's Jack, Mama," Lia said with a mental sigh. "Lord Lendale, that is."

Her mother flashed him a dazzling smile and dropped into a graceful and extravagant curtsy, helmet notwithstanding. "Goodness, how could I not have recognized you? You're looking well, your lordship. *Extremely* well."

Jack executed a polite bow. "There would be no reason for you to recall me, Mrs. Lester. It's been years since we last met. Allow me to say that you're also looking very well."

Despite her irritation, Lia couldn't help but be touched by his courtesy. Jack had never acted the snob with her family, which was a sign of his kind nature.

"You flatter me, my lord," Mama trilled in a pretty voice. "Lia, why didn't you tell me that Lord Lendale had grown up to be such a distinguished man?"

Lia's cheeks burned. "I suppose there wasn't any reason to discuss it." She did her best to ignore Jack's ironic gaze.

"Well, never mind. You've obviously come to visit Lia, which is splendid," Mama said, placing her helmet on the table. "I hope you will be sure to take in the program on opening night. And you must certainly visit my darling daughter afterward in the green room."

With a sinking heart, Lia realized her mother and grandmother had probably written to each other on the subject of reeling Jack into the role of her first protector.

"Actually, I've come to persuade Lia to return to Stonefell, where she belongs," he said with something of a growl. "It's time for her London adventure to conclude."

Lia's mother threw her a triumphant glance. "I entirely concur, my lord. Lia would be much more comfortable set up quietly in the country. It would be more private that way, too."

Jack peered at Mama for a moment, but then his features transformed into a horrified understanding.

Lia pulled in a deep breath, fighting the anger that was sucking the air from her lungs. She couldn't decide which of them she'd rather murder first.

"Lord Lendale's intent is not what you think, Mama. He simply wants me to return home to live with Granny. In genteel poverty, I have no doubt," she couldn't help adding sarcastically. "His finances are a complete disaster. I'd probably end up in a hovel if he somehow *did* become my protector."

"There's no need to be rude about it," Jack said.

"You're much ruder than I am," Lia said. As a retort it was exceedingly lacking, but her head felt like it was about to explode from a combination of humiliation and fury.

Mama cast Jack a doubtful glance. "He doesn't look like his pockets are let. Quite the opposite, in fact."

Jack drew himself up and gazed at Mama with masculine dignity. "I am indeed well able to take care of Lia and her grandmother. As one helps members of one's family."

Lia waved a disdainful hand. "You can't. Not with Stonefell in such a horrible mess."

Her mother crinkled her nose. "How very dreary. Your grandmother had such high hopes for his lordship. Oh, well, we'll just carry on until something more fortuitous presents itself."

Jack blinked several times, as if he were trying to reset something that had gone awry in his brain. "She will do nothing of the sort," he finally said. "Lia will be returning to Yorkshire immediately."

As embarrassed as Lia was by her mother's nakedly

avaricious behavior, Jack's high-handed manner seemed worse.

"*She* will do nothing of the sort," Lia snapped, echoing him. "I am not going back to Yorkshire with you, Jack Easton. And the sooner you get that through your thick-headed skull, the better."

She pushed past him and stalked from the room.

Chapter Eight

"Jack, I don't know why you made us sneak up that dingy back stairway instead of going through the lobby," commented the Duchess of Leverton. "That's hardly an exciting way to start the evening."

"I thought you enjoyed sneaking up dingy stairways and along gloomy corridors," Jack said as he handed Gillian to her seat. "Especially in pursuit of bloodthirsty brigands."

Charles rolled his eyes before addressing his wife. "Gillian, it's not a dingy back stairway. It's a *private* stairway for patrons who've reserved a *private* box. That way we can reach our seats without jostling our way through crowds in a lobby full of pickpockets and other disreputable sorts."

"A private stairway for the snobs, you mean," said the duchess. "God forbid the aristocracy should ever mingle with ordinary folk."

Jack cast a glance over the rail of their box to the pit below. "I don't think you'll need to worry about that. There will be plenty of mingling between the gentlemen of the Ton and the ordinary folk before the night is out."

"Ah, you mean they will soon be availing themselves of the company of the ladybirds who frequent the pit and galleries." Gillian stood to peer over the rail, leaning out to take a good look. "I must say it does look like quite a lot of fun down there."

Charles reached out and snagged the velvet sash around her waist. "Please sit down, my dear, before you fall out and land on some poor fellow's head."

Gillian subsided into her seat, scoffing at her husband's request. "As if I would ever be so clumsy. You just don't want me making a spectacle of myself and you know it."

"I do apologize for being so tiresome," he said in a regretful tone. "But if you make a spectacle of yourself, no one will watch the evening's entertainment. You're much more interesting and prettier than any of the actresses performing tonight."

Her sherry-colored eyes danced with laughter. "Well done, Charles, turning a scold into a compliment. Then again, you are the most polished man in London."

"I try, but you do present a challenge, even for my vaunted skills," her husband said dryly.

"Wretch," his wife replied. "I intend to ignore you for the rest of the evening."

That was unlikely; Charles and Gillian couldn't go five minutes without making sheep's eyes at each other or slipping off to a corner for a stolen kiss. In society's view, their recent marriage was scandalous and the gossip surrounding them had yet to die down, but anyone with sense could see they were madly in love and surprisingly well-matched. He gentled her fire and tempered her brash behavior, while she brought a joy and spontaneity to his life.

As if to make good on her word, Gillian gave her husband a shoulder and turned her attention to Jack.

"I'm sure Charles is wrong about me being prettier than all the women in the acting company," she said. "I've heard

Mrs. Lester is a great beauty and I have no doubt my cousin is very pretty if she intends to have a career on the stage."

"Over my dead body," Jack muttered.

Since his disastrous encounter with Lia the other day, he'd been kicking himself for making such a hash of things. In his defense, he'd been stunned to see her in such an environment, keeping company with someone like Amy Baxter. As the stepdaughter of the troupe's manager, Lia might be afforded some measure of protection, but she was still at risk. Anyone with a brain should understand that.

Worse yet, Lia's mother seemed absolutely fine with the notion of her only child following in her footsteps. Mrs. Lester had even made another stab at it after Lia stormed out of the green room, once more quizzing him on his relationship with her daughter. Jack had replied in an icy voice that Lia was like a sister to him. That Mrs. Lester was disappointed by that characterization was all too evident.

Not that he was actually thinking of Lia in those terms, but he intended to keep that fact strictly to himself.

Gillian's gloved hand came to rest on his, pulling him out of his dark thoughts.

"You were right to come to us," she said in a gentle voice. "We'll think of some way to help my cousin."

Jack forced a smile. It was a mark of how concerned he was that he'd asked the Levertons for help in persuading Lia to return home to Stonefell. And it was bound to be tricky, at least initially, because he hadn't yet had the chance to tell her about Gillian—much less that her cousin was a duchess.

"Thank you," he said. "I'm sure we'll be able to talk some sense into her."

"She doesn't seem inclined to take anyone's advice so far," Charles said.

"She's still entranced with the dream of making a life for

herself on the stage. But she'll listen to reason eventually. She always has."

"You mean she always listened to *you*," Gillian said in a wry tone. "But that was in the past. And as much as you want to help her, you're not her family. The Lesters are." She gave him a meaningful look. "As am I, I might add."

"She's got you there, old son," Charles said. "Hard to argue with blood."

"Her blood relations are utterly hopeless in protecting her," Jack said caustically. "Besides, with the exception of her grandmother, nobody knows her better than I do. And what I know is that a life on the stage—or as a courtesan, God forbid—is not for Lia. She belongs back at Stonefell."

With me.

Gillian leaned forward again and gazed at the pit, which had grown exceedingly lively. "Yes, but I must admit I see the appeal. I think we should buy a box for the season, Charles. Then we can come see my cousin whenever we want."

"I think not," her husband said in a pained tone.

"Don't be such an old biddy. It's very jolly."

"*Vulgar* is the term that comes to my mind," Charles said. "Besides, you'll send Jack into fits if you encourage Miss Kincaid. We're supposed to be getting her out of the theatrical life, remember?"

Gillian wrinkled her nose. "I know, but it does seem rather dashing of her. And theatrical pieces can be very edifying, especially Shakespearean dramas or the classics."

"There is nothing remotely Shakespearean about the Pan Theater," Jack said, glancing down at the playbill in his hand.

The program was the usual nonsense and started off with a pantomime and a musical piece with a recitation by Mrs. Lester. The main attraction of the evening, the absurdly named *The Queen of Mount Olympus*, was followed by the burletta in which Lia was to appear. *A Surprise for the Publican's Wife* filled Jack with a sense of dread.

"When does my cousin appear?" Gillian asked.

"Not until the burletta at the end," Jack replied.

Charles let out a groan. "Splendid. We must endure an entire evening of horrifically bad acting and even worse singing—not to mention an audience full of scoundrels, pickpockets, and drunkards. We'll be lucky to escape with our lives."

"I'll protect you, darling," Gillian said with a grin. "Besides, it can't be that bad. Lord and Lady Montgomery are just a few boxes over from us." She leaned out and waved enthusiastically at the startled pair of elderly aristocrats before her husband pulled her back in.

Jack tried to assess the theater with a dispassionate eye. "It actually isn't," he finally said.

For one thing, the crowd in the pit and the galleries seemed no worse than in any other theater in London. They were comprised of a mix of nobility and various sorts of respectable shopkeepers and their families, along with the usual disreputable elements. The public rooms were also better than expected, tastefully done up in soothing greens and pale yellows, accented by gilt molding. Though the backstage areas were a dark and dingy nightmare, as he'd discovered to his dismay, Stephen Lester had clearly put some money into creating a venue that could compete with the licensed theaters of Drury Lane.

"The musicians are taking their places," said Gillian.

After settling in the small pit in front of the stage, the musicians led the assemblage in "God Save the King." Once the audience was seated again, the curtain went up and the evening's performance began.

Jack immediately winced at the skimpy costumes worn by the dancers, especially the buxom Amy, but he soon found that the performers were talented and the choreography entertaining. And Marianne Lester was a revelation. She not only had a fine speaking and singing voice, she possessed an arresting sense of drama. Within seconds of stepping onto the stage, she had the enthusiastic audience eating out of her hand. Despite his expectation, Jack enjoyed the recitations, which had been written by her husband and showed a deft turn of mind.

After a short musical interlude, the main performance began. *The Queen of Mount Olympus* was a ridiculous pastiche of classical myth and Greek history that featured chanted recitations and several musical numbers. The queen, Mrs. Lester, took center stage, cutting an impressive figure in a spangled toga, gilt breastplate, and plumed helmet. The audience loved her, cheering loudly every time she launched into her recitations, which she chanted dramatically in a singsong manner.

The real spectacle began when the first battle scene commenced to loud whistles and cheers. Players garbed as soldiers in short tunics and breeches launched into a mock battle, enthusiastically whacking at each other with painted wooden swords.

"This is much more fun than Drury Lane," Gillian said, almost doubling over with laughter. "Even if it's completely absurd."

"With emphasis on the absurd," Charles said.

Jack, however, felt as if a very large sword had just whacked *him* on the back of the head, because unless his eyesight had rapidly begun to fail him, one soldier looked very familiar.

"Goodness," Gillian said. "I think that soldier standing by the proscenium is a female."

Jack squeezed his eyes shut for a moment, hoping they

were deceiving him. That hope was dashed when he cracked
his eyelids open again.

"I'm afraid so," he said, barely able to choke out the
words.

Both Gillian and Charles looked at him. "What's wrong?"
she asked.

Charles looked back at the stage. "Good God, is that
Miss Kincaid?"

"It most certainly is," Jack ground out.

Gillian leaned forward to get a better look. "That's Lia?
Well, I must say she looks *very* dashing in that outfit. Don't
you think so, Charles?"

"That's one way of putting it," he replied in a faint voice.

Jack stared until he thought his eyes would pop out of
his head. Lia's costume was scandalously revealing. The
form-fitting tunic revealed the lovely swell of her bosom,
before nipping in to showcase her trim waist. It barely
reached midthigh, which meant her shapely legs, clad in
breeches that unfortunately fit her snuggly, were on full
display.

The only saving grace was that she was not front and
center on the stage. Because it was a crowded scene with
frenetic activity, her identity as a woman might go unno-
ticed. Jack clutched at that faint hope as if it were a rope
tossed to a drowning man.

"You didn't tell me she was playing a breeches role,"
Charles said, his consternation clear. It wasn't uncommon
for certain actresses to don breeches and play a male part,
but those roles were notorious for attracting all sorts of
salacious attention from male audience members.

"Because I didn't know," Jack said. "That blasted girl
doesn't tell me anything anymore."

Gillian shot him an irritated look. "I shouldn't wonder,
if you speak to her in that tone of voice."

Charles shook his head. "Under the circumstances,

Jack's dismay is quite understandable, my love. This sort of thing won't help Miss Kincaid's reputation at all."

She shrugged. "I don't see why. I wear breeches myself on occasion."

Her husband stared at her in disbelief. "Only in the country when riding, and very discreetly. You certainly don't go parading around in front of half of London."

Lia had retreated and was now partially concealed by the proscenium. Jack couldn't understand why she was in the scene at all because she didn't seem to be doing much of anything.

"This theater is not half of London," Gillian pointed out. "Besides, she's entirely covered, so I don't see what you and Jack are fussing about."

"No, I suppose you wouldn't," Charles said in a long-suffering tone.

He alluded to his wife's unconventional upbringing in Sicily and her sometimes equally unconventional behavior. But unlike Lia, Gillian's powerful relatives could and did protect her from both malicious gossip and ill-intentioned men.

Lia's family didn't even care to try.

"I'm not sure anyone's yet noticed that this particular soldier is a woman," Charles said, craning forward to peruse the audience. "With a little luck—ah, she's disappeared backstage."

"Thank God," Jack muttered. He and his friend exchanged a relieved glance. "I think we dodged a pistol ball on that one."

"Look! There she is again," Gillian said. "Now what is she doing?"

Appalled, Jack saw that Lia had quickly reappeared, accompanied by one of the other soldiers. They carried a large piece of fabric to the front of the stage and unrolled it.

"That's called a scroll," Charles said. "It details the

narrative that can't be explained by the recitations or songs." He sounded like someone was strangling him.

Jack understood exactly how he felt. Everyone in the pit was now discovering that one of the soldiers was indeed a woman, and a very comely one at that. They were reacting as he'd expected, with a rising tide of loud, ribald comments, a few of which he could make out over the din.

"That's odd," Gillian said. "Why don't they just act it out or present it in a speech, like a Greek chorus?"

"This is how theaters like the Pan get around the legal restrictions on spoken drama," Charles said.

"You two are missing the point," Jack growled. "Lia is now front and center in a breeches role, and every damn rake in this blasted theater has taken note of it."

Gillian grimaced. "That is rather bad."

"We'll have to do what we can to minimize the damage," Charles said. "But it's not going to be easy."

"At least she's off the stage again," Jack said, relieved that the piece was finally drawing to a close.

The curtain came down, signaling the interval. Jack stood, almost knocking his chair over in his haste. He needed to get downstairs to gauge people's reactions concerning Lia. If no one realized she was Marianne's daughter, they might still scrape by.

"I'll meet you down in the saloon," he said.

"Jack, wait," Gillian called out.

He didn't. A sense of urgency pushed him forward, one that seemed eerily like the sensations he'd felt on the eve of a battle. He knew it was a ridiculous comparison because, after all, no one's life would be lost. But Lia's life could be changed forever by what had transpired tonight, in ways that could forever demolish her peace.

He forged his way through the crush in the hall and on the stairs, ignoring both the calls of acquaintances and the entreaties from prostitutes trolling for business. He could never blame those poor creatures for their way of life—after all, the vast majority of them had no other choice. But the hard, grasping look he saw in the eyes of the older ones served as a grim reminder of a future that loomed like an approaching storm in Lia's innocent path.

Eventually, he jostled his way through to the back of the crowded saloon, where liveried footmen served refreshments. He gave Lester credit for creating an elegant atmosphere that had obviously attracted a fair number of nobility and other prosperous folk to the opening. Right now, though, he was tempted to throttle the man for throwing his stepdaughter to the wolves.

He secured a glass of port and bolted it down in one shot. It seared its way down his throat and exploded in his stomach, but it did the trick of blunting the edge of his fury. Taking a deep breath, he began prowling the room, exchanging the occasional word with a friend but always moving.

And listening.

Although most of the discussion was about the leading lady and the plays, he overheard a number of the men talking about Lia in the most vulgar terms. Two particularly repugnant fellows were graphically parsing her figure, each vowing to seek her out in the green room after the performance. Jack was considering the best way to warn them off without exposing Lia's identity when a voice blared right next to his ear.

"I say, Lendale, I didn't expect to see you here tonight. Theater ain't usually your style, you know."

Sighing, Jack turned to greet Viscount Medford, a generally harmless rattle with an unfortunate tendency to gossip. He normally tried to avoid him, but Medford's mother was bosom bows with Jack's mother, so in all good conscience he couldn't snub the poor fellow.

"No, it isn't," he said tersely.

Medford, never the sharpest of pins, peered at him with a puzzled expression. "Then what the devil are you doing here?"

"I came with friends." Jack caught sight of the Levertons making their way over. "If you'll excuse me, I see them—"

"Certainly, certainly," Medford interrupted. "But before you dash off, I was wondering if you could do me a favor."

"If I can."

"Splendid. I was hoping you could introduce me to Mrs. Lester's daughter after the performance. You must know her, of course, because she lived on your uncle's estate all those years, did she not? Ah, perhaps that explains your presence. You've come to see your little friend. She'll no doubt be very popular after tonight, eh? Let's hope she's as lively as her dear mama once was."

A series of small explosions reverberated through Jack's skull.

"I say," the viscount said as consternation descended on his amiable features, "is she already your light o' love? If so, didn't mean to steal a march on you, old man. I was just hoping you could slip me ahead of the line. You know, before the other fellows got to her."

Before the top of Jack's head could blow off—or he could smash in Medford's vapid face—a slender gloved hand clamped onto the viscount's arm and Gillian spun him around to face her. Medford gaped, obviously surprised by the strength contained in the slim body of the young woman standing before him.

"I suggest you put that thought completely out of your mind," she said in a voice that all but resembled a snarl.

"How-do, Your Grace," Medford said in a weak voice. "Um, what thought would that be again?"

"Engaging in any kind of nasty thoughts, much less conduct, with my cousin," she said.

"Your Grace," Jack warned, appalled that Gillian would so brashly allude to Lia's parentage.

When she held up an imperious hand, he bit back a curse. In that moment, she looked entirely like a woman with the blood of princes running through her veins. He cast a glance around the room. Where the hell was her husband?

Jack spotted Charles across the room with Sir Dominic Hunter, a magistrate with close connections to the royal family—and to Lia's family as well. The two appeared to be speaking earnestly.

"Your cousin?" Medford repeated, peering at Gillian with all the comprehension of a plate of boiled potatoes. Then his brow cleared. "Yes, of course, Lia Kincaid is your cousin! You're both royal bas—"

"Careful, Medford," Jack interrupted in a lethal voice.

"Yes, of . . . of course," Medford stammered, taking in Jack's glare. "And I understand completely, Your Grace. No need to worry about a thing."

"There'd better not be," Gillian said. "Now, please be off before I decide to become unpleasant."

Since Gillian's version of unpleasantness could be an uppercut to the jaw or worse, Medford gave a fumbling bow and retreated, almost running into Charles.

"That was not very wise of you, my love," the duke said in disapproving tones.

"What?" She rounded her eyes in a completely unconvincing assumption of innocence.

"You know very well. Announcing to the world that Miss Kincaid is your cousin."

"You have the most disgustingly acute hearing," she complained. "I was barely speaking above a whisper."

"Trust me, you weren't," Jack said, eyeing the people

around them. Several had obviously heard the exchange with Medford and would no doubt be spreading the most interesting on-dit to hit Town in ages.

Gillian shrugged. "It's not as if people don't know who our fathers are. They'd make the connection soon enough. I simply refuse to stand by and let people insult the poor girl."

"I understand, but I'd prefer that we not draw the picture for them until we have a chance to come up with a strategy to deal with the situation," Charles said.

Jack shook his head. "Too late for that now. We might as well go back to our seats and see what other disasters are in store for us."

Gillian grimaced. "I'm sorry, Jack. I didn't mean to cause more problems."

He briefly pressed her shoulder. "None of this is your fault. It's mine for making such a hash of things with Lia."

"Perhaps we can save the self-flagellation for after this gruesome evening has concluded," Charles said dryly. "For now, I'd like to return to our box and pretend that I'm not in the middle of yet another spectacular scandal."

"But I never cause scandals anymore," Gillian protested.

Her husband scoffed as he took her hand and led her out of the rapidly emptying saloon.

As they made their way in silence back to their box, Charles made a point of directing his most killing glare at anyone who stared at his wife or dared to start to comment. Because Jack did the same, they cleared their path like a hot knife slicing through butter.

The curtain rose on *A Surprise for the Publican's Wife* and, as its unfortunate title suggested, it was a bawdy romp that soon had the audience roaring with laughter. Fortunately, Mrs. Lester was not in the production; she rarely played comic roles. Jack could only imagine the glee that would result if Lia and her mother appeared on the stage together.

As Jack waited for Lia to appear, it felt like the Sword of Damocles was poised over their heads. When she finally walked onto the stage, carrying a large pitcher on a tray, he took in her costume and barely held back a groan.

"That's not good," said Gillian in a massive understatement.

Playing a tavern girl, Lia wore a simple blouse tucked into a skirt that displayed her shapely legs well above her ankles. Her blouse was cut so low that the top of her stays peeked above the neckline, over which her breasts swelled in tempting mounds. Her hair was pulled back from her face to fall in an extravagant tumble around her shoulders. With her cheeks flushed, she looked madly delectable, as the whoops and cheers from the male members of the audience made all too clear.

"Oh, God." Charles sighed. "This is a complete disaster. I have no idea how we're going to fix this."

"We're going to—" Jack broke off and leaned forward, frowning.

Balancing her tray, Lia walked carefully across the stage, where the leading lady and other actors were gathered around a table singing a ridiculous drinking song. Clearly, her role was to replenish their mugs. It seemed a simple enough task, but Lia had the oddest look on her face. Jack swore he could see her nose twitching.

Because he'd spent a lifetime getting to know her, he knew for a fact something was very wrong now.

The lead actress held up her mug to be refilled, not missing a beat of the song. When Lia froze, the woman waggled her mug and shot her a quick, fierce scowl. Pressing her lips together, Lia reached for the pitcher.

Before her hand touched it, she let out an enormous

sneeze. It was so violent that the tray flew from her hands and the contents of the pitcher tipped onto the head of the leading lady. To the utter delight of the audience, the drenched and furious actress leaped up from her chair and commenced screeching in a voice loud enough to wake the dead.

Chapter Nine

"Mama, it truly wasn't that bad," Lia said after blowing her nose for possibly the hundredth time since she'd come offstage. All week she'd staved off the cold that had swept through the company, but her luck, alas, had finally run out.

"And although my little mishap wasn't very nice for either Miss Parker or Mr. Thompson," she added, "no one was really hurt."

Her mother, pacing back and forth across her dressing room, stopped to wave her arms. "Not hurt? Reggie has a lump on his head the size of a goose egg."

"That's because that confounded tray is so heavy," Lia said. "Besides, Mr. Thompson was very nice and said he didn't blame me at all."

"Unfortunately, Serena does blame you. She was completely humiliated."

Lia winced. "Yes, but she did overreact, you must admit. It wasn't my fault she slipped and fell."

Serena Parker had kicked up an enormous fuss after Lia spilled the ale, flailing around with such vigor that she'd fallen on her backside. The actress's screeching had reached operatic levels at that point. Lia's ears were still ringing.

"I don't think the audience minded," she added. "In fact, they found it rather hilarious."

So hilarious that the gentlemen in the pit had given Lia a standing ovation. Yes, it was awkward, but they *were* performing a comedy, after all. Her blunder clearly had added to the popularity of the piece.

Her mother flopped down at her dressing table and began rubbing her temples. Lia understood exactly how she felt as she subsided into the old, cane-backed chair tucked next to the costume rack. Her head ached and she felt utterly miserable. All she wanted to do was to crawl into bed and stay under the covers, perhaps permanently.

"Serena certainly did not find it hilarious," Mama said. "She's threatening to quit and go to another company after *so profound a humiliation*, as she called it."

"That's unfortunate."

After her mother, Miss Parker was the most popular actress in the company. She brought in the crowds, which meant she had power. "I'll be happy to apologize to her, Mama. I tried to do so immediately after the performance, but she stormed away from me. I can go right to the green room this instant and tell her how very sorry I am."

It was customary at the end of the evening for the performers to remain in costume and congregate in the green room, meeting the wealthier members of the audience there. It was an important part of the night, where a theatrical manager could find potential investors or patrons willing to purchase an expensive box for the season.

Her mother bolted upright. "Please do not even *think* about doing so. Serena would cause a scene, and you need to learn, my dear, that a leading actress in a snit is something to be avoided at all costs."

Lia eyed her mother, who could have been describing herself. Naturally, she refrained from making that observation.

"Besides," Mama continued, "it would draw a great deal of inappropriate attention to you. That is something we also wish to avoid."

"If that's the case, then I shouldn't appear in any more breeches roles," Lia said, stating the obvious. She'd done her best to carry it off, but she'd hated every moment of that particular theatrical experience. Feeling exposed and half-naked, she'd cringed at the leering gazes and ribald comments after the audience discovered she was a female.

"Half the company has been felled by that awful infection, which left us short of actors," her mother said in a plaintive voice. "How was I to know you would succumb as well?"

"Please just tell me what I must do to correct the situation with Miss Parker. I'm willing to do anything."

"Well, that's just it, darling. I'm afraid there is only one thing you can do. You must not perform anymore."

Lia had been fighting another sneeze, but that announcement knocked the ticklish feeling right out of her head. "You cannot be serious!"

Her mother's chin went up in a stubborn tilt. "I'm sorry, Lia, but Miss Parker told your stepfather right after the performance that she will quit the company if you continue to perform in any capacity. Even in walk-on roles."

"But that's so unfair. It was an accident and she knows it."

"I do realize that, but Serena feels your departure from the company is necessary for her to recoup her dignity. She's deeply concerned she will become an object of ridicule."

"And is that how you see it?" Lia didn't have the energy to conceal the pain that her own mother would fail to defend her.

Mama hesitated, as if weighing the question. But then

one side of her mouth lifted in a grimace. "I'm sorry, dearest, but it can be fatal for an actress to become the object of mockery, even a comic actress. Serena is too sensitive, but I understand her concern."

Clearly, Marianne Lester sympathized more with her fellow actress than she did with her own daughter. That ugly little morsel of truth was a hard swallow.

"But what am I to do?" Lia felt so miserable and desperate that her chest hurt. "You know better than anyone how limited my choices are. I can't become a governess or a companion to a wealthy invalid—no one would have me." In any case, those professions were akin to indentured servitude as far as she was concerned.

Her mother folded her hands in her lap and adopted a perfectly calibrated expression of maternal regret. If only she truly were that maternal instead of playacting at motherhood.

"My dearest daughter, it grieves me to the soul to be the one to bring about the ruination of your fondest dream."

When she heaved a dramatic sigh, fluttering a hand up to her heart, Lia had to work hard not to roll her eyes.

"But I fear I must," her mother continued. "To be blunt, you are not meant for a career on the stage. You are most welcome to remain with us in London for a spell. Your stepfather and I quite value your help backstage. But that is only a temporary solution. Sooner or later, I think you must return to Stonefell. I'm sure Lord Lendale will come up with some solution to your problem if you give him half a chance."

She shook her head. "That's not a helpful suggestion, Mama. You know Jack can't afford to support us. If you won't let me continue with you, I will have to try another acting company. Perhaps you could put in a good word for me with some of the other company managers?"

Her mother practically toppled off her stool. "I will do

nothing of the sort. Can you imagine the gossip if we were to compete against each other in different theaters? I would be utterly humiliated—not to mention roundly criticized for not supporting my daughter in my own company."

It dawned on Lia that her mother's refusal to help must be based at least partly on jealousy. Though Marianne Lester was incredibly popular and still very beautiful, the slightest hint of competition seemed too horrifying to contemplate, even if it meant depriving her daughter of the opportunity to make her way in the world.

As Lia struggled to absorb the pain of that betrayal, a knock on the door interrupted them. Her stepfather cautiously opened the door. "I hate to interrupt, my love, but you and Lia have some visitors most eager to see you."

His wife fluttered her handkerchief in a distracted manner. "Stephen, I simply cannot bear the green room tonight. And Lia will certainly not be going out in public. You must make our excuses."

"They're not in the green room, they're—"

Stephen bit off his words as the door jerked fully open and Jack elbowed him aside. Lia let out a quiet moan; it wanted only this to complete her humiliation. She'd seen Jack up in the boxes, of course, but she'd been certain he'd be too appalled by her performance to want anything to do with her.

"Sweetheart, are you all right?" he asked, crouching down and taking her hands. "You didn't get hurt in all that commotion, did you?"

Actually, one of the other actors had trod very hard on her foot and her toes would be bruised for days. But that hardly seemed worth mentioning at the moment.

She tried to tug her hands away, fighting an absurd desire to collapse into his arms and burst into tears. "I'm fine. There's really no need to make such a fuss."

His fingers tightened in a gentle but determined grip. "You're not fine. You look whey-faced and sickly."

"Thank you for that gracious assessment. Perhaps you'd better leave before you catch my cold."

"You know I never get sick," he said, ignoring her sarcastic tone.

He finally let go of one of her hands, rising to loom over her. He pressed his palm to her forehead, then her cheek. Lia suffered it with a sigh, hating that he was treating her like a child.

"Right," he said. "You have a fever. I'm taking you to your mother's house and putting you to bed straightaway."

Lia blinked at the image that evoked—she and Jack in a heated tangle under crisp sheets. The notion was surprisingly enticing, especially considering how wretched she felt.

He frowned. "Now you've gone flushed. Clearly, the London air and this theatrical environment have damaged your health. The sooner we get you well and back to Stonefell, the better."

He punctuated that comment by scowling at Lia's mother, who bristled like a hedgehog, albeit one dressed as a Greek goddess.

"You needn't lecture me, my lord," Mama said. "I've been telling her to go back to Yorkshire for days."

"Good, then we're all in agreement," Jack said.

Lia finally yanked her hand away and stood up. When she tried to edge away from him, she found herself half-immersed in the pile of frothy, elaborate costumes hanging from the rack behind her. Impatiently, she batted away feathers from a large purple ruff that insisted on poking her in the face.

"I am *not* going back to Stonefell," she said. "Jack, it's none of your business where I go or what I do. My stepfather said I could stay in London as long as I wanted. Isn't that right, sir?"

Stephen's bushy eyebrows tilted up in a comically distressed slant as he cast his wife an alarmed glance. "Er, of course, my dear. For as long as you . . ." He stuttered to a stop when he took in Jack's basilisk gaze.

"Stop trying to intimidate my stepfather," Lia said.

"Stop trying to ignore the truth of your situation," Jack retorted. "After tonight's debacle, there is an even greater necessity for you to rusticate, and as soon as possible."

"Again, thank you for such kind words," she said caustically. "There's no need for me to flee like a thief in the night. I didn't do anything wrong. It was just a slight mishap and not worth the fuss you're *all* making."

"A slight mishap? Are you completely mad? Your performance gave London its most delicious piece of gossip in months. *And* you've now attracted a legion of scoundrels and rakes." He shook his head, looking disgusted. "I cannot believe you or anyone else thought it appropriate to play a breeches role."

"I say, that's not fair," Stephen piped up. "Lots of actresses do so, including my wife."

"Well, *this* particular actress isn't doing it anymore," Jack said. "In fact, her acting days are over."

Lia was considering running her dearest friend through with her mother's prop spear when a woman shoved Stephen aside to enter the room.

"Confound it," her stepfather said. "No need to push, young lady."

The newcomer ignored him. "Do stop badgering the poor girl," she said, glowering at Jack. "She's correct—she didn't do anything wrong."

"You're as bad as she is." Jack shot a disgusted look at the tall, elegant man who'd crowded into the room behind the young woman. "Can't you keep her under some semblance of control?"

"You know the answer to that question as well as I do," the man said sardonically.

"My husband is much too intelligent to hinder me when he knows I'm right," the woman said.

Feeling muddled by her headache and the commotion, Lia shook her head. "Excuse me. I don't mean to be rude, but who are you?"

The woman gave her a dazzling smile. "You couldn't possibly be ruder than I am, as my husband would be thrilled to tell you. My name is Gillian and I am your cousin."

That announcement stunned the entire room into silence, although Lia fancied she heard a weary sigh from Jack. She stared at the tall, lovely young woman dressed in the first style and decked out in a set of obviously expensive diamonds. Everything about her and her husband shouted of membership in the upper tiers of the nobility.

Instinctively, her gaze flew to Jack, whose expression comingled resignation and annoyance. "She's my cousin?" she managed in a thin voice.

He nodded. "You have many cousins, pet, as you know. And aunts and uncles, for that matter."

"Not that any of them would have anything to do with us," her mother said with an offended little sniff. "The nobs love looking down on our sort."

"You'll be happy to know that I'm not the least bit snobby, Aunt Marianne," Lia's newfound cousin said in a cheery tone.

Even Mama looked shocked by the informal address.

Gillian stepped forward and extended her hand. "But allow me to properly introduce myself, dear cousin. I'm Gillian Dryden Penley, Duchess of Leverton. And that distinguished fellow in the doorway is my husband, the Duke of Leverton. In truth, he *is* a bit of a snob. But because he's also an exceedingly nice man, I hope you'll overlook that little flaw."

To his credit, the duke simply lifted an ironic eyebrow in response to his wife's summary of him.

Lia weakly extended her hand to the duchess, who clasped it in a no-nonsense grip. Part of her wanted to laugh at the young woman's forthright manner, but she couldn't seem to process the astounding turn of events. Jack not only knew the duchess was Lia's cousin, he was apparently quite friendly with her. That he had withheld such knowledge from her grew more annoying with every passing second.

Mama, never one to miss a golden opportunity, leaped to her feet, then swanned into a deep and graceful curtsy. "Your Graces, we had no idea you were in the audience tonight. This is such a great honor. We do hope you enjoyed the performance."

"It was . . . illuminating," the duke said. He glanced at Lia. "In more ways than one."

She fancied she caught a note of disapproval in his smooth tones, which didn't improve her rising temper. Even worse, her head was pounding like a blacksmith's hammer. As much as she wanted to stay and speak with Gillian Penley, she was desperate to flee the confusion and noise and collapse into a warm bed.

"Jack, why didn't you tell me the duchess wished to meet me? She's obviously a friend of yours," she said, focusing on the part that bothered her most.

He grimaced. "I was trying to figure out the best way to break the news. It's rather tricky, as you must admit."

"By telling me straight out, I would think," she said. "'Lia, you have a cousin and she seems very nice.'"

The duchess beamed. "Thank you, my dear. If it's worth anything, I thought Jack should have told you weeks ago."

"Yes, so did I." Jack looked at Lia, his dark eyes shadowed

with regret. "But your grandmother asked me to hold back. She wished you to find out at what she felt was the appropriate time."

Now it was her turn to sigh. "I suppose she didn't want me to get any ideas above my station."

Although Granny certainly had her pride, she also had very definite ideas about the social order. It was understandable, given that she'd built her entire life around settling for something considerably less than what she deserved.

Jack waggled a hand. "I wouldn't put it quite that way. But she did fear that such a relationship would ultimately lead to rejection. She didn't want to see you hurt."

"As if I would ever do something so shabby," the duchess indignantly said.

Lia gave her a wobbly smile before returning her focus to Jack. "I understand that you wanted to respect Granny's wishes, but I still wish you'd told me about Her Grace, *especially* after I came down to London."

"Have you forgotten you've been avoiding me?" he asked. "And when I did finally see you the other day, you stormed out before I could tell you. You keep cutting me off at the damn knees, Lia."

"Lendale, you know I'm very fond of you," the duchess said, in what Lia could only describe as a threatening tone. "But I must insist that you address my cousin with respect or I'll be forced to knock your—"

"Gillian," the duke interjected sharply.

"Er, I'll be forced to speak very sternly to you," she amended.

Jack snorted in disbelief.

The duchess directed an apologetic grimace at Lia. "Please call me Gillian," she said. "And to be fair, Lendale only met me a few months ago. At the time I wasn't yet married and wasn't even sure if I was staying in England. It didn't make sense to tell you if we were never to meet."

Lia nodded, feeling slightly mollified. Absently, she rubbed her aching head, pondering the best response to the fraught situation.

"Lia, please sit down before you fall down." Jack pressed her down onto her mother's dressing stool before stroking her cheek. "You need to rest, sweetheart, or you'll fall into a bad state."

Her anger dissipated another notch, but he ruined it a moment later by shooting an irritated glance at her mother. "She needs to go home, Mrs. Lester. And no more of this acting nonsense."

"Of course, my lord," Mama said instantly. "Lia can rest up with us before she returns home to Yorkshire. There's no need to rush, but I'm sure the city doesn't agree with her at all. No wonder she fell so ill."

"I caught a cold," Lia said through gritted teeth. "As did half the people in the company. And I have no intention of returning to Stonefell, so you can both stop nagging me about it."

"Of course she's not going back to Yorkshire," Gillian said. "She's staying right here in London with us, at Leverton House." She shot her husband a winning smile. "Isn't that right, sir?"

The duke, who'd been leaning against the doorjamb watching their little scene with a mostly lofty sort of disinterest, moved closer and suddenly looked uncomfortable. "My love, I don't think that's the best idea, either for you or Miss Kincaid."

"Why not?" his wife asked. "She'll receive the best of care, and we can also get to know each other."

"You know why," her husband said in a firm voice.

"Are you truly going to worry about gossip at a time like

this?" Gillian demanded. "You know I don't care about that sort of nonsense."

"I'm afraid you do need to care about this," the duke said.

"I simply ignore the opinions of idiots," she said, "and you should, too. God knows we've done enough of that in the past few months. Our marriage was supposed to be the biggest scandal of the decade and yet everything's fine. Besides, you're going to make poor Lia feel unwelcome and that's perfectly awful of you."

"It is not that simple. Not this time," Leverton said. Then he gave Lia a kind but regretful smile. "I have no intention of making you feel unwelcome, Miss Kincaid. In fact, I look forward to getting to know you better."

Lia wondered if that was the case, although he sounded sincere. "I understand, Your Grace. I'm not offended in the least."

"But I am, confound it," Gillian said. "Why in heaven's name can't my cousin stay with us?"

"It is a lovely and generous offer, Your Grace," Mama piped in. "I'm sure Gillian would be thrilled to spend some time with you. Wouldn't you, my love?"

Now Lia wanted to crawl completely behind the costume rack—or, better yet, flee the room. Of course Mama would wish her daughter to cozy up to a rich and powerful duke and his duchess, especially if they were near relations. Lia had no doubt her mother planned to exploit that connection to the troupe's advantage, likely by asking them to become investors. But she'd rather go back to Yorkshire than allow anyone to impose on the generosity of the kind young woman who seemed so eager to help.

"You see, Charles?" Gillian said in a triumphant tone. "If Lia's mother approves, what is the problem?"

"The problem is that two royal side-slips staying under

one roof would be manna from heaven for the gossips," Jack said bluntly. "It would wash right off you because you're a duchess and married to a powerful man. But such would not be the case for Lia. Moving to Leverton House would focus a great deal more attention on her, which is exactly what we don't want right now."

Gillian let out an endearing little growl. "Blast! I simply hate the Ton and their small-minded ways. I'd like to set fire to them all."

"Small-minded but dangerous, at least for Miss Kincaid," said the duke. "Lendale is right, I'm sorry to say."

"We have to do something," Gillian said, waving her arms so wildly she almost knocked the plumes out of her coiffure. "I won't let her be shipped off to Yorkshire if she doesn't want to go."

"I believe I have the solution to this particular problem," said a deep voice from the hall.

Lia looked up to see yet another stranger in the doorway. Like Jack and the Duke of Leverton, he was tall, broad-shouldered, and elegantly dressed, but he was some years older, probably in his forties. He had a rugged face with a great deal of character and carried himself with an air of powerful authority.

"There you are, Hunter," said Leverton. "Finally."

The newcomer gave a slight smile. "I wished to get the measure of the situation before I intruded."

"So, you were eavesdropping on us, Sir Dominic?" Gillian asked.

The man raised his eyebrows in polite inquiry. "Isn't that exactly what you would do, Your Grace?"

Her mouth twitched in a smile. "Yes, but how dreadful of you to point that out. Well, you'd best come in while we try to sort out this mess."

"Indeed," he said, easing in beside the duke. The room

was now so crammed that Lia's stepfather all but climbed up onto Mama's dressing table to avoid being trampled.

Lia pressed the tips of her fingers to her temples, suddenly overwhelmed by the heat and by absorbing too many surprises in so short a space of time. With the appearance of the mysterious Sir Dominic Hunter, she suspected yet more revelations in the offing.

He smiled at Lia and managed a very credible bow, considering the tight quarters. "I am Sir Dominic Hunter, Miss Kincaid, and it is a pleasure to meet you. I come on behalf of your half brother, Captain William Endicott, who wishes me to extend his best wishes and his protection on your behalf. In short, Captain Endicott has made it clear that he desires you to come home with me."

Chapter Ten

"Don't tire yourself out, Lia," Chloe, Lady Hunter said. "You're still convalescing, so the last thing you need is a rambunctious baby to manage."

Lia settled little Dom on her lap, smiling at the lovely woman who'd so kindly taken care of her during her illness. "I'm feeling much better now, thank you. I still can't believe I was so ill."

This was the first day she'd come down to the drawing room since moving into the Hunters' lovely town house on Upper Wimpole Street. Far from contracting just a little cold, she'd been felled by a nasty infection that had left her as weak as a half-drowned kitten.

Chloe rummaged in the sewing basket by her chair. "It was no doubt from all the hard work and excitement leading up to opening night, combined with a jarring transition from the country to the city." She glanced out the pretty bow window onto the quiet street. "I've always found the country to be a healthier environment, and certainly more peaceful."

While it was true the Hunters' town house was tucked away in one of the quieter neighborhoods of the city, Lia had discovered they generally lived quite out of the way at their manor house in the country village of Camberwell. Their primary home also doubled as a charitable establishment for unwed pregnant girls and young women, providing shelter for those cast aside by their families.

Most members of the Ton had already decamped to their country estates, and Lia suspected Chloe and Sir Dominic would have done the same had she not been so precipitously thrust into their care.

"You are not to be considering yourself as any sort of burden," Chloe said, clearly reading her expression. "We're thrilled to have you stay with us for as long as you like."

When Lia bounced Dom on her knee, the baby chortled and waved his chubby fists in the air, then made a grab for the ribbons that trimmed the waist of her dress. "You're very generous, but I'm sure you'd both prefer to be in the country."

"Indeed, no. My husband has a number of interests in Town. There is always something to keep him occupied while we are in residence here."

"And you? Don't you miss your home and your charity work in Camberwell?"

A soft smile curved Chloe's mouth. "I do, but my true home is wherever my husband and little Dominic are. I can ask for nothing more. Besides, while I do miss my work, my son and his wife are staying at our villa, looking out for my girls. Justine is close to one of the children under my care, and she never misses the opportunity to spend time with him."

"And your son? Does he enjoy it?" Lia couldn't help asking with a hint of mischief. From everything she'd heard about Griffin Steele, she found it hard to believe that the former gaming hell owner was the sort of man to enjoy spending time in a house full of women and babies.

Chloe laughed. "Griffin is less enthusiastic but surprisingly good at keeping order and generating a calm atmosphere in a sometimes exceedingly lively household. In any case, he goes wherever Justine goes, especially now that she's with child."

"I'm very much looking forward to meeting the Steeles. It's still amazing to me that I have a real family beyond my mother and grandmother."

While Lia had always counted Jack and Lord Lendale as family, now she was discovering she had a *real* family, bonded by blood and apparently eager to accept her. She'd barely gotten over the shock of meeting Gillian when Sir Dominic had marched into the room and announced she also had a half brother. Captain William Endicott was the natural son of the Duke of York and had been raised by his aunt and uncle, respectable members of the country gentry. Privately acknowledged by his father, Will had gone on to have a successful military career and marry the daughter of a viscount. He was now stationed in Vienna as part of the British diplomatic delegation.

Another shock had followed when Sir Dominic further revealed that he was married to Lia's aunt, who was the mother of Griffin Steele. Griffin was Gillian's half brother and yet another thread in the tangled web of relations Lia had recently acquired.

Remarkably, none of her newly found relatives seemed at all bothered by her dubious lineage, even though it included two notorious courtesans, one of whom still made her living on the stage. But while her half brother and cousins also carried the stain of illegitimacy, they came from good families on their maternal sides—even from among the aristocracy, in some cases. Because of that, they'd been able to establish lives within the Ton and find spouses with impeccable backgrounds. It was a feat Lia could never hope to equal.

"You have quite a large family now, my dear," Chloe

said, "and we're all happy that you have joined our ranks. We're quite a loyal lot, as you will find out soon enough."

"You're all very kind, but I cannot impose upon you forever. That would be utterly selfish of me."

"Nonsense. William and his wife have made it clear that they would prefer you to remain with us until they return from Vienna. That is, of course, unless you'd prefer to join them instead. They will defer to your wishes, but I know they would be delighted if you went over to the Continent." Chloe gave her another warm smile. "But Dominic and I would be thrilled if you stayed with us. It's been a joy for me to have such a lovely niece to pamper. Gillian won't let me coddle her at all, she's so fiercely independent."

Lia's throat went tight with emotion. From the moment she'd walked through the door, Chloe had welcomed her with genuine affection and gone out of her way to make her feel wanted.

It was a startling contrast to her mother's behavior. Mama's tepid welcome had been bad enough; Lia could put that down to surprise and consternation over what to do with her. But when Sir Dominic proposed taking her home to his wife, Mama had leaped at the opportunity with an almost embarrassing enthusiasm. After all, not only did it resolve the problem of Lia's immediate future, it removed her from the acting troupe and the ire of the other performers.

And then there was Jack. She'd not seen him since the night of her humiliating debut. He'd called in Upper Wimpole Street three times, but at first she'd been too sick to see him and then simply too mortified to face him. He was bound to be annoyed, if not downright angry with her.

Chloe put her needlework aside and crossed the room to join Lia and the baby on the chaise. Dom gurgled happily at his mother, enthusiastically grabbing at her.

"I know it's a lot to take in," she said, letting her son grasp her finger. "Having a ready-made family thrust upon you can be unnerving. But I promise we're not so scary once you get used to us."

"No, you've all been splendid." Lia shifted the baby so he could get close enough to grab Chloe with both hands. "It's just . . ."

"Overwhelming? Believe me, I understand. I was in a similar position when Griffin and Dominic first came back into my life. After years of seclusion in the country and no contact with my family, I struggled with the change. A new life does take getting used to." She laughed. "Especially with our large and ridiculously interfering family."

"It's certainly different. It's always been just Granny and me. Well, there was Jack, too, of course, and Lord Lendale before he died." Lia shook her head. "But I don't know where Jack fits in anymore. He wants to take care of us, but that's not possible. Not in the long term anyway."

Nor was it his responsibility. It was Lia's, and she'd spent most of the last week in bed thinking of little else. How *was* she to support Granny?

Acting was now out of the question. Nor could she reasonably expect her half brother, William—a man she'd never met—to take up supporting her *and* her grandmother. Lia simply refused to put herself into the position of a poor relation, entirely dependent on the goodwill of others. As she and Granny had already discovered, that rarely ended well.

Charity and kindness were all to the good; control over one's fate was even better.

"I can see that living at Stonefell would not be appropriate in the long term," Chloe said. "But that doesn't mean Lord Lendale can't be of assistance. We can chat with him about that when he stops by this afternoon."

The prospect of seeing Jack again set Lia's heart on a

gallop around her chest. She couldn't decide whether the reaction was evoked by anticipation or dread.

"You can't avoid him forever," Chloe said, again reading her expression. "Dominic had to all but sit on his lordship to prevent him from barging up to your room the other day."

"Jack's not used to me avoiding him. But I don't know how I'm going to face him after everything that's happened. I suspect he's quite angry with me."

Not that he had any right to be. If anything, she should be furious with him for throwing obstacles in her path every time she tried to move forward.

"Lord Lendale is worried about you," Chloe said. "Now, I think it's time my little boy went back to his nurse for a bath and a nap." She leaned over her son and sniffed. "Oh yes. He definitely needs to go back to his nurse."

Lia reluctantly relinquished the little dear, instantly missing his comforting weight. Holding a baby always made the world feel like a happier place. "I hate to give him up. He's so sweet."

"Sweet is not the word I would use to describe him just now," Chloe said, hoisting her son into her arms. Dom was a robust, squirming bundle, almost too big for his mother to lift. Chloe's delicate beauty made her appear almost frail, but Lia had discovered she was anything but. She had a quiet strength and supervised everyone in her orbit— including her powerful husband—with calm determination.

"You're very good with babies," Chloe said, rising to her feet. "Dom already adores you."

"I love children. I always spent quite a lot of time with the tenants' little ones at Stonefell. Their poor mothers are frequently in need of help." Lia mentally blinked as a thought darted into her head.

Could she possibly ask it of her aunt? "I don't suppose

you could use a nursemaid or helper at your establishment in Camberwell, could you?"

Chloe paused on her way to the door, glancing back with a startled look on her face. When she didn't come right out and say no, Lia took heart.

"I could bring Granny down to stay with me," she said, warming to the idea. "We wouldn't need much—just a few rooms in the village. I promise I would work very hard, and we wouldn't be a burden to you at all."

Chloe shook her head. "My dear, I think we can do much better than that."

"But—"

"No, Lia. It's out of the question."

Before she could ask for an explanation, the door opened and Sir Dominic strolled into the room. As always, his craggy features lit up when he saw his wife. The transformation from somber magistrate to besotted husband was both startling and moving. Chloe and Sir Dominic had been married for less than two years, but their steadfast devotion to each other shone through in every word, look, and gesture. She didn't know much about their history other than it had been full of grief and extended separation. That they'd overcome so many obstacles and found a second chance later in life dared Lia to hope she, too, might find a similar happiness one day.

Almost.

"Good afternoon, my love," he said, bending slightly to kiss his wife. "I hope you ladies are having a pleasant day."

It was surprising perhaps that the dignified Sir Dominic should act so informally in front of a near stranger, but he'd accepted Lia with a warm welcome, just like his wife. She could easily get used to life in their serene and cheerful household. That was a clear warning that she needed to stop lolling about and come up with a plan for her future.

"And how's my boy?" he asked, gently cradling his son's head.

"In desperate need of a change," Chloe said.

"Yes, I see that. Or, rather, I smell that. It always amazes me that so small a creature can emit an odor that forcefully reminds one of a barnyard."

His wife gave him an affectionate swat on the shoulder. "What a dreadful thing to say. Lia will think you don't love your son."

"From the look on her face, I think Lia agrees with me," Dominic said with a twinkle. "Give me the rascal and I will transport him to Nurse."

When he cuddled his son against his chest, Dom grabbed onto his father's starched linen, demolishing the elegant folds.

"Oh dear," Chloe said. "Another cravat ruined."

"I'll change it before dinner. God forbid I should offend your fashion sense, my lady wife," he said on his way out.

Chloe scrunched her nose at Lia. "I'm the last person to keep up with the current styles, as Dominic knows. If I had my way, I'd spend most of my days in an old round gown, taking care of babies or tending to my garden."

"It's been quite a change from your former life, hasn't it?" Lia asked. "You and Sir Dominic seem to be in great demand throughout the Ton."

"My husband certainly is," Chloe said. "I'm generally not fond of socializing in large groups. When we were first married, Ton parties made me so nervous I would break into hives. But I eventually got used to them, and so will you. In fact, you might even come to like parties. After all, you are a beautiful, vibrant young woman and deserve to have a bit of fun."

Lia carefully smoothed out the faint web of wrinkles

Dominic's fat little body had pressed into her cambric skirt. "I'm sure I won't have the opportunity."

"I've instructed Smithwell to bring up the tea tray," Dominic said as he reentered the room. "It's early, but I profess to being famished after an exceedingly boring afternoon at Whitehall. And we must continue to build up our guest's appetite, too." He ran a quick, practiced eye over Lia. "You seem much better, but you're still rather pale."

"I'm feeling quite robust, sir, thank you. You and Aunt Chloe have taken such good care of me. If you continue to spoil me like this, I shall never wish to leave."

"You are welcome to stay as long as you like," Dominic said as he settled into one of the wingback chairs across from the chaise. "Is she not, my dear?"

"So I have told her, repeatedly." Chloe took the chair next to her husband. "But I don't think the message is penetrating."

"Please don't think I'm ungrateful," Lia said apologetically. "In fact, your invitation was so fortuitous that I was tempted to believe you had conspired with Jack to remove me from my mother's house."

She caught the quick glance between husband and wife.

"You didn't, did . . . did you?" she stammered. "I mean, beyond simply telling me my half brother wished to help me?"

"Of course not," Dominic said calmly. "As you say, it was all quite fortuitous."

Lia studied him without a hope of cracking that impervious façade. "As grateful as I am, I cannot stay here forever. And although I do appreciate Captain Endicott's offer to join him in Vienna, I cannot possibly abandon my grandmother. It will be difficult enough for her to leave Stonefell, and moving to the Continent would be out of the question. Nor can I imagine Captain and Mrs. Endicott would truly wish it. Surely they are both very busy with the duties that must come with their diplomatic position."

"I'm sure you'd find that Will and Evie would like nothing better," Chloe said. "But I do understand your concerns about your grandmother."

"Perhaps you should tell us what *you'd* like to do," Dominic said. "I suspect you've been giving it a great deal of thought while in your sick bed."

"You would be right, sir. I must find some kind of position because my mother made it clear she will not countenance any further attempts to establish a theatrical career."

Mama had made that clear when she visited yesterday. Her lack of support had wounded Lia more than she wanted to admit. She could almost believe her mother would prefer her to become a courtesan rather than have a flourishing career on the stage.

"Perhaps she wishes for a more settled life for her daughter," Chloe said gently. "One better suited to her nature."

"I'm not sure of her reasoning," Lia said, trying not to sound bitter. "In any case, while I cannot be a governess, I do have experience dealing with children. Sir Dominic, I just suggested to Aunt Chloe that she consider taking me on as a nursemaid or companion to the children in her establishment."

"I think we can do better than that," Dominic said, strangely echoing his wife. Lia was just as irritated the second time she heard it.

"Yes, I will not have Lia thinking she needs to go into service," Chloe said.

"There's nothing wrong with going into service in a good household," Lia protested.

"I agree," Chloe said, "and I have a great deal of respect for those who do so. But that is not what your family wishes for you. Nor, might I add, have you been raised to lead such a life. I suspect you would find it difficult."

"I'm not afraid of hard work."

"I'm sure you're not, but Will Endicott would have my head if I allowed his sister to go into service," Dominic said. "Even into our service."

Lia flopped her hands into the air. "Then what in heaven's name am I to do? I must take care of my grandmother."

"Then you'll be happy to hear we do have a plan for that. Along with the Duke and Duchess of Leverton, we're going to introduce you into society," Chloe said, sounding as if she were giving Lia a wonderful treat. "Given our unique positions and personal histories, we're all very well aware of the obstacles facing you. And we know how to overcome them."

It took Lia a few seconds to find her voice. Chloe and Dominic waited patiently, making no attempt to rush her.

"Why would you want to introduce me into society?" she finally managed.

"Why wouldn't we?" Dominic answered with maddening calm.

Lia could think of a hundred reasons, but a knock on the front door interrupted the discussion.

"Ah, that will be Jack," Dominic said, "arriving just in time for the tea tray."

As if on cue, the door opened and a footman carried in a large tray. A few moments later, Smithwell, the butler, ushered Jack into the room.

Dominic rose, as did Lia, who pinned a smile on her face even though she felt almost light-headed with nerves. She wasn't used to feeling rattled in Jack's company and she found the sensation both irritating and alarming.

"Don't get up, Lia," Jack said. Taking her arm, he gently steered her back to the chaise. The warmth of his large hand through the thin fabric of her sleeve made her clumsy and she stumbled slightly.

"I'm fine really," she said, sinking down.

"You seem rather wobbly to me." He shot Dominic a scowl. "Should she even be out of bed? Has she seen the doctor today?"

Lia rolled her eyes. "Good Lord, you're worse than Granny."

His gaze shot back to her. "Someone has to take care of you; you seem incapable of doing it yourself."

She sighed. The bear with the sore paw had obviously resurfaced. "If you're going to be such a scold, you can leave right now."

"I assure you, Lia is on the mend," Chloe said. "The doctor saw her yesterday and pronounced her free of infection."

"There, you see?" Lia said. "Now, stop fussing like a nervous bachelor and sit down, please."

He seemed inclined to argue, but then his strong mouth curved into a rueful smile. It made her heart catch with a staccato rhythm that almost hurt.

"My apologies," he said, "but you were quite sick, pet, and you never get sick. I was worried about you."

"I know, and I'm sorry for that, but everything's fine." She patted the cushion beside her. "Why don't you sit with me and we'll have a nice cup of tea and a cozy chat."

"Now you're just humoring me like I'm some sort of half-wit."

"Is it working?"

"Apparently," he said, sitting down.

Smithwell and the footman arranged the tea things on the low table in front of them. After they withdrew, Chloe poured everyone a cup.

"You were all looking quite serious when I came into

the room," Jack said with a smile. "What were you talking about?"

"What *were* we talking about?" Chloe said, casting her husband a wide-eyed glance that didn't fool Lia a bit.

"You remember, my love," Dominic replied. "We were discussing the best way to introduce Lia to the marriage mart."

Chapter Eleven

Jack looked momentarily stunned; then a fierce glower descended on his features. Lia couldn't blame him. After all, introducing her into polite society to find a husband was even more demented than Granny's idea to make her over into a courtesan.

"I beg your pardon?" he said in a frosty voice to Dominic.

The magistrate gave him a genial smile. "I'd be happy to repeat it if you didn't hear me the first time."

Jack set his teacup down with a decided clunk. The amber brew sloshed from the cup into the dish beneath it. "I heard. I merely couldn't believe my ears." His narrowed gaze shifted to Lia. "This mad scheme wasn't your idea, was it?"

His dismissive attitude sent her already volatile emotions careening in the opposite direction. "I suppose you can't imagine any respectable man wishing to marry me," she said tartly. "It's obviously entirely outside the realm of human possibility, given my background *and* my lurid stage debut." She crossed her arms over her chest and glared back at him.

When Jack's gaze flickered down to her bodice, she hastily uncrossed her arms and pressed her fists in her lap.

When he looked back up, there was a slight flush glazing his high cheekbones.

"Don't be silly, Lia," he said in a milder tone. "Your stage appearance was ill-advised and a bit provocative, but there was nothing truly lurid about it."

"You didn't seem to think that the other night at the theater."

He blew out a long breath, as if trying to find patience in some deep well and pull it to the surface. "I'll grant you I was upset, but it wasn't your fault. Your mother and stepfather should have known better than to expose you so publicly."

"They didn't force me, Jack. I did it willingly." That wasn't quite true, at least when it came to the breeches role. But she had done what was necessary and she refused to regret it. "Besides, a dedicated actress must be willing to make sacrifices for her art."

"Good God, is that what you call it? Now get this through your head right this minute, my girl," he said, looming close. "Your acting days are over, and that's that."

She whipped up a finger and jabbed it toward his nose. "Now, you listen to me, Jack Easton—"

He grabbed her hand. "I would be most grateful if you would cease jabbing me in the nose, the chest, or anywhere else."

She wrenched her finger from his grip. "I can think of a certain portion of your anatomy I'd like to give a good poke right at this moment."

Jack's mouth dropped open and Chloe let out a startled squeak. Dominic's eyebrows lifted in mild shock.

"For heaven's sake, I meant his backside," Lia said as her face heated.

It wouldn't be the first time she'd given him a boot in the posterior. That had been when she was thirteen. Granny had finally allowed her to let her skirts down and put her hair up, mostly because Lia had been pestering her for weeks. Jack had come to take her fishing in the pond at Stonefell, and he'd teased her rather mercilessly about her new, ostensibly grown-up appearance. Though it had all been in fun, she'd been devastated that he still saw her as a little girl. After one flourishing bow too many, she'd dashed behind him, planted her foot, and given him a good shove.

Jack had gone flying into the pond, fishing tackle and all. He'd surfaced a few seconds later, spluttering and stunned. Lia was stunned, too, and horrified that she'd lost her temper. When she started babbling an apology, extending a hand to help pull him out, Jack had burst into laughter. He'd then taken her hand and pulled *her* into the pond. Lia had been torn between outrage over the destruction of her new coiffure and amusement over the silliness of it all. One look at Jack's gleeful, sopping face and laughter had won out. They'd dripped their way back to Bluebell Cottage, once more the best of friends.

Jack's dark eyes sparked with reluctant humor. "It wouldn't be the first time, would it, old girl? Please accept my abject apology, Lia. I obviously lost my manners."

She wasn't sure she was ready to forgive him. "You certainly did," she grumbled.

"But he seems to have recovered them quite nicely," Dominic said. "So perhaps we might discuss the situation with just a little less heat."

"And fewer threats," Chloe added.

"I'm frequently forced to threaten Jack," Lia said. "He won't listen to me unless I do."

"I do listen to you," he said, his voice now gone almost somber. "I may not always agree with what you have to say, but I do listen."

"Blast," she said. "Now you're just trying to make me

feel like a wretch. It's too bad of you, Jack. I have enough to worry about without you heaping guilt on my poor head."

"If I didn't make you feel guilty, you'd never listen to *me*."

"Nicely done," she said with reluctant admiration. "I think you've won this round."

"It's not a boxing match," he said, "and I have no desire to win anything. I simply want you to return to Stonefell to your grandmother. I promise all will be well if you do."

She took in the stubborn expression on his handsome face and struggled for patience. He meant well, but she suspected his blasted male pride was now involved, too. It was difficult for him to accept that he couldn't afford to take care of her. "That's no solution, Jack. You know the reason for that better than anyone."

"I don't," Dominic said. "Perhaps you could explain it to me."

Lia had all but forgotten that Dominic and Chloe were in the room. "Well, it's a bit difficult to explain." It was also embarrassing.

Jack grimaced. "It's a rather private conversation, best discussed only with family."

"But we are Lia's family now, my lord," Chloe pointed out. "Or have you forgotten that?"

He gave his hostess a rueful smile. "I walked right into that one. But it doesn't make me any less responsible for Lia's welfare."

"Jack," Lia said quietly, hating to point out the obvious, "you are my dearest friend, but you are not family."

"Thank you for the reminder," he said. "But in every way that matters, I *am* your family. I cannot believe you would think otherwise."

He hid it well, but she caught the whisper of hurt in his dry tone. She wrinkled her nose in a silent apology. Still, it was time Jack realized once and for all that he was no longer responsible for her future.

"Lia's brother now has a greater claim to protecting her," Dominic said. "Although it's to your credit that you wish to do so."

"Captain Endicott is not here, so I hardly think that applies," Jack said. "The fact remains that the best course of action for Lia is to return to Stonefell, where everything will remain as it always has been."

"No, no, and no," Lia said through gritted teeth.

Chloe's puzzled expression cleared. "You're worried about what will happen when Lord Lendale brings home a wife, aren't you?"

Lia nodded, relieved that her aunt had guessed it. "It would be rather awkward, you must admit."

"Indeed it would," Chloe said. "The future Lady Lendale would have to be exceedingly tolerant. To have not one but two Notorious Kincaids living down the lane would test any newly married young woman."

"To repeat, there is nothing at all notorious about Lia," Jack said, clearly annoyed by Chloe's blunt assessment. "And Rebecca is in her sixties. Her past is ancient history."

"That's not exactly true," Dominic said. "No one can deny that your uncle installed Rebecca Kincaid as his mistress on his estate. Because of your close association with the family, it seemed natural to you. But no one else will think so, especially not the parents of any respectable young lady you should wish to marry."

"With someone as pretty as Lia in residence," Chloe added, "no wife in her right mind would put up with such a state of affairs. She would be bound to think she was your mistress."

"I've been telling Jack that for weeks," Lia said. "But he refuses to admit to the realities of the situation."

The high color on Jack's cheekbones signaled how embarrassed—and annoyed—he was by the frank conversation. "It's nobody's business who I allow to live on my estate. And it's your *home*, Lia."

She reached over and took his hand, wriggling her fingers between his. He resisted for a moment, but finally returned her clasp. "Jack, you are the soul of generosity, but you know how important it is for you to marry well, especially given Stonefell's wretched finances. You can't afford to have me hanging about like an old piece of fish that's gone bad. All of the tenant farmers and most of the villagers are depending on you."

The idea of Jack wed to someone else made her feel positively ill, but she refused to be selfish. He needed to make a good marriage and she could not be an impediment to him achieving that.

He snatched his hand away. "May I just say that this is one of the most awkward conversations I've ever had?"

"You may," Dominic said. "But it is informative for all that. I was aware that your uncle was rather lax in his financial affairs, but I hadn't realized matters had grown desperate."

"I'm sure I'll be able to turn things around in no time," Jack said stiffly.

Lia nodded. "Certainly, *if* you find a rich wife. You should be spending your time courting eligible girls on the marriage mart, not worrying about me. I'll be fine."

"And that brings us back to our original discussion," Dominic said. "Our plan to introduce Lia into society. The best thing for her is to find a suitable husband who will value her many fine qualities and—"

"Overlook my many flaws?" Lia finished in a wry tone.

"You have no flaws, my love," Chloe said. "Only a few minor obstacles to overcome."

Jack's eyes all but popped out of his skull. "You're even more unrealistic than I am if you think Lia can waltz into a ballroom and not be ripped to shreds by the gossips. All the rakes and scoundrels will hunt her like jackals after wounded prey. I will not allow you to subject her to so ugly a fate."

Lia had been about to object to the scheme on exactly the same horrid grounds before Jack had knocked her off course with his overbearing intervention.

"Do you truly think I would allow my wife's niece to be ripped to shreds?" Dominic asked, staring Jack down. "Or that I would allow anyone less than respectable to even talk to her?"

"Of course not," Jack said tightly. "But you can't be with her twenty-four hours a day. And even you can't stop the gossips, Sir Dominic. Not even the king is that powerful."

"Sadly true," Chloe said with a sigh. "In fact, the king's sons generate some of the most salacious gossip in Town, as we are all painfully aware. As much as I hate to admit it, his lordship is not wrong to point out the challenges involved in finding Lia an acceptable husband. It won't be easy."

"Especially after my rather unfortunate theatrical debut," Lia said.

"That regrettable incident aside, I'm confident we can rehabilitate your good name," Dominic said. "In all other respects, you've led an unexceptional life in the country. No gossip has attached to you personally and your mother has been married these past ten years to a good man who is both respectable and well-regarded." He smiled at Lia. "Your mother is very popular, my dear. Your relationship with her isn't all a black mark."

"It's not exactly a ringing endorsement either," Jack

said. "You may be able to rehabilitate Lia, though that word should not apply because she doesn't need rehabilitating."

She squeezed his hand, silently communicating her gratitude. He flashed her a brief smile.

"But you're all demented if you think she's going to catch a wealthy aristocrat or member of the gentry," he continued. "The chances of a nobleman marrying her—or allowing his heir to marry her—are all but nil. And there would be absolutely no incentive for a younger son to do so either because she has neither a fortune nor a good name to bring to the relationship."

Lia's warmer feelings for him disappeared like smoke up a chimney. Unfortunately, she couldn't argue with his blunt logic.

"Not every man in the Ton needs a wealthy wife," Chloe pointed out.

"They may not need one, but they usually want one," Jack bluntly replied. "And they invariably want their wives to come from impeccable backgrounds, usually even better than theirs. We're all a fat lot of snobs and you know it."

"Not all of us, but I take your point," Dominic said. "Lia may do better with the country gentry, especially because she is a country girl herself."

"Really?" Lia said doubtfully. All the country gentry she knew liked money and status just as much as their counterparts in London.

"Hmm," Chloe said, resting her chin on the tips of her folded hands. "There are other possibilities we could consider. We know some perfectly respectable families who've done very well in trade or made fortunes in India. Who is to say that a wealthy nabob wouldn't make a fine husband for Lia?"

"You talk about her as if she's a commodity to be bought and sold," Jack said in a disgusted tone. "I will not allow

Lia to be sold off to the highest bidder like a piece of horseflesh."

"That's rather a good description of how the women in my family operate," Lia said. "We generally have been in the business of buying and selling ourselves."

Jack looked appalled. "I forbid you to say anything like that ever again, do you hear me? It's utter nonsense."

"We're just exploring options," Chloe smoothly interjected. "No one will try to force Lia to do anything. We only wish for her happiness."

"It's not that I don't appreciate what you're trying to do," Lia said. "In fact, you're all incredibly kind. But I must agree with Jack on this."

He looked at her with exaggerated surprise. "Wait, I must mark this special occasion in my daybook. Lia Kincaid finally agrees with me."

"Idiot," she muttered.

Dominic studied her for a few moments with an uncomfortably penetrating gaze. "I feel confident we can overcome any obstacles of significance, my dear. But only if you truly wish to succeed."

And that was the crux of the matter. Lia knew enough about the marriage mart to see what a gruesome exercise it would likely be. "I . . . I'm not sure," she said, hedging. "It sounds as if it won't be very pleasant, to be honest. I'm not sure I want to bother."

"Right," Jack said. "You will return to Stonefell—at least until your brother is back in England," he added, anticipating her objection. "Then you can decide what you wish to do."

She chewed that over for a few seconds before glancing at Dominic. "Do you know when Captain Endicott will be returning?"

"It's rather up in the air, given the situation in Vienna," he said regretfully. "Probably not for some months."

Drat. Their proposed solutions contained too many unknown variables. Besides, there was Granny to think of. It would be too much to ask a half brother she'd never met to take on supporting both of them for months, if not years.

The discussion brought her back to the one place she hadn't wanted to go—the place that now began to seem ordained. She finally let out the weary sigh that had been building up behind her breastbone, seemingly for days. "There is still one other option. It is probably the most realistic one, under the circumstances."

"And that is?" Dominic asked with a pleasant smile.

"I could start looking for a protector."

Dominic's face went blank.

Lia shrugged. "It is the family business, after all. Both Granny and my mother think I might have better success at it than anything else."

Jack clamped a large hand around her arm. "We have been over this already and I believe I expressly forbade you to raise the issue again," he gritted out.

She yanked her arm away, increasingly irritated with his tendency to order her about. "I will do exactly what I want, when I want. And if I wish to take a protector, I will bloody well do it."

His gaze practically scorched her. "Don't push me, Lia. I assure you the result will not be pretty."

Too annoyed to be rational, she did the one thing that used to drive him around the twist when they were children. She stuck her tongue out at him.

He stared at her in disbelief. A moment later, his features went hard with masculine determination. "Right," he said, standing up. "You and I are going somewhere private to sort this out, and then you'll be packing your bags for Stonefell."

"No, I will not."

"Nor will she be embarking on a mad scheme to become a courtesan," Dominic said, giving her an intimidating glower. "There will be no more nonsense of that sort from you, niece. I absolutely forbid it."

Lia gaped at him, surprised at the change in his normally calm behavior.

Chloe put down her teacup and rose, regarding her husband with gentle disappointment. "I forbid you to raise your voice to Lia, my dear. Really, Dominic, what can you be thinking?"

He winced a little. "I didn't mean to raise my voice, but you must admit—"

"I admit nothing of the sort." His wife ruthlessly turned her back on him to face Jack. "As for you, Lord Lendale, I expected better from you. Badgering Lia is unacceptable. Why, look how flushed she is. You've obviously upset her greatly and I only hope she doesn't suffer a relapse."

Lia wouldn't relapse, though she appreciated her aunt's tactics.

"Well, confound it, Lady Hunter," Jack said, looking shamefaced, "someone's got to talk sense into the girl."

"Chloe, perhaps you can explain to Lia why her idea is so foolhardy?" Dominic said.

She took Lia's arm and drew her up. "I will do no such thing. In fact, I think Lia's idea has a great deal of merit."

That shocked everyone into silence for several seconds, the men clearly stupefied by Chloe's assertion.

"Ah, you do?" Lia finally managed.

Her aunt nodded. "As you said, you don't have many options, so we might as well explore all of them. Why don't you and I go up to your room and have a nice, rational discussion without any more nonsensical interference from the men?"

She didn't resist when Chloe led her toward the door, although she threw a glance over her shoulder at Jack. He looked as if someone had dropped a cannonball on his head.

Once they'd left the room and started up the stairs, Lia cleared her throat. "You don't really believe I should become a courtesan, do you?"

Chloe grinned. "Of course not. Nor will it be necessary."

"Then why did you say it was a good idea?"

Her aunt stopped on the landing, one step above her. "Because it's clear to me that Jack Easton is in love with you. It's also clear he has yet to realize it, the poor man. So we've got to make him figure it out, and then we can proceed from there."

For an alarming moment the stairs seemed to tilt under Lia's feet and she found herself clutching the banister with both hands.

Jack Easton, in love with me?

How in God's name had Chloe arrived at such a bizarre conclusion? The notion that Jack might be in love with her was the most ridiculous thing she'd ever heard. After all, he'd all but fainted when she'd kissed him in the library at Stonefell, and he'd been an absolute crab with her ever since arriving in London. His actions certainly didn't strike her as those of a man in the throes of love or even passion— quite the opposite, in fact.

As Lia marshaled her scattered wits, her aunt regarded her with inimitable calm. One could almost imagine she'd just delivered a casual comment about the latest fashion in bonnets instead of turning the world on its head.

She finally found her voice. "I don't believe that's true, Aunt Chloe. Jack's very fond of me and of course he's protective, but—"

"He's in love with you," Chloe said firmly. She took Lia's hand and pulled her the rest of the way up the stairs. "But as I said, he's not fully aware of it yet. So we've got to give him a nudge."

Lia drifted down the hall after her aunt, too dazed to feel the floorboards under her feet. "And pretending to become a courtesan will make Jack realize he's, ah, in love with me?"

Chloe flashed a brilliant smile as she opened the door to Lia's room. "We've got to start somewhere, dear, don't we?"

Chapter Twelve

"It's about time you showed up," the Duke of Leverton said to Jack as he passed the previous guest over to his wife. "The evening is half over."

"Don't be an idiot. Besides, I got here ages ago. It took me forever to get into the house and up the blasted stairs." He glanced down at the front door of Leverton House, where the butler and three footmen were taking wraps and directing eager guests. "I thought this was supposed to be a private ball, but it's more crowded than Vauxhall Gardens."

He'd decided to walk over from his club after spending a gloomy hour brooding over the potential disasters looming before them. When he'd reached Grosvenor Square, he'd been dismayed to see the long line of carriages. Given the time of year, the event should have been of fairly modest proportions, not a mad crush that rivaled some of the largest public balls held during the Season.

"Wait until you see the ballroom," Leverton said. "It'll be a miracle if the floor doesn't collapse and send us crashing down into the kitchen."

Faint strains of music drifted out over the din of loud conversation, but there were too many guests blocking the hall to see into the ballroom. "This was a bad idea, Charles. It puts too much pressure on Lia to be introduced in such an environment. Not to mention you seem to have lost control of the guest list."

His host snorted. "Lost control? I suspect half the people currently trampling my carpets and bolting down my best champagne weren't even invited."

"Splendid," Jack said sardonically. "What a disaster in the making."

"Stop worrying. We've got everyone out in force tonight. Sir Dominic is watching over Lia with a hawklike regard that even you would approve and Gillian has promised to stab anyone who gets too familiar with her cousin or insults her."

"Yes, murdering guests will certainly help keep gossip in check."

His friend grinned. "I recall you laughing at my predicament when I was trying to introduce Gillian into society. I can't tell you how delighted I am to see you in this position."

Jack could vaguely remember a time when he'd been a happy man—even a cheerful one. Now, as problems piled up with alarming regularity, he could feel his sense of humor and charitable view of the world fading away.

"Gillian didn't have near as many obstacles to overcome as Lia," he said.

"No? My wife punched an earl in the middle of a ball, which even you will admit was a steep challenge to my skills. Lia certainly will not engage in that sort of behavior."

"Really, Charles," Gillian said, turning to her husband. "When will you stop holding that silly little incident over my head?"

"My love, the sheer horror of that moment will remain engraved in my memory for all eternity."

The duchess laughed. "What nonsense. Now, you and

Jack have been complaining and holding up the line for long enough. Poor Lady Cardwell will end up with bunions if you keep her standing there any longer."

Jack turned to see the lady in question regarding him with a scowl, her gray ringlets and mauve turban all but quivering with displeasure. He murmured an apology even as he mentally frowned. Lady Cardwell was both an intolerable gossip and a starched-up, disapproving biddy. Her presence tonight signaled nothing good.

"What in God's name is she doing here?" he murmured to Gillian. "She's a dragon."

"Believe me, I know. She gives me the cut direct every chance she gets. But she's a dear friend of Charles's mother, who insisted on inviting her." She cast a disgusted look toward the ballroom. "Along with half the other people who are here tonight."

"I didn't know your mother-in-law was in Town." He couldn't hide his dismay.

"She arrived at the beginning of the week, and with only a few days' notice," Gillian said in a gloomy tone. "It was too late to cancel the ball because most of the invitations had already gone out. And then she insisted on inviting even more people."

That was not a positive development in more ways than he could count.

Though the Dowager Duchess of Leverton was a genuinely good woman, she was remarkably high in the instep. And while she'd apparently accepted her son's marriage to Gillian Dryden, her support for Lia was likely to be much less robust.

"I suppose it could be worse," he said cautiously. "If Leverton's mother has agreed to lend her countenance this evening, she must approve of Lia's presentation to the Ton."

"Yes, let's all pretend that, shall we?" Gillian said brightly.

"And where is your sainted mother-in-law? I thought she'd be in the receiving line."

"She's right behind you, unfortunately," Gillian muttered.

Jack had to bite the inside of his lip to keep from laughing as he turned to greet Leverton's mother.

"Lord Lendale, how nice of you to finally grace us with your presence," said the dowager, a short, stout woman who, despite the fact that she walked with a cane, carried herself with great dignity and a ramrod posture. "I began to think you would never arrive."

"Your Grace, it's a great pleasure to see you," he said, bowing over her hand. "You're looking in fine trim, as always."

"None of that frippery, young man. It's something I especially abhor."

Jack saw a twinkle in the old girl's eye. She might not always approve of him—which she'd told him any number of times over the years—but she'd grown used to him, almost seeing him as a second son.

"You look very nice tonight, Mother," Gillian said politely. "That color is most becoming on you."

Even Jack had trouble swallowing that one; the dowager was dressed in a particularly violent shade of purple.

The dowager duchess ignored the compliment. "Gillian, stand up straight. Your posture is simply ghastly."

Gillian's posture was anything but ghastly, but she rolled her eyes and pulled her shoulders up as her mother-in-law inserted herself into the receiving line next to her son.

"She loves to boss me around," she said in a stage whisper to Jack. "It gives her something to do."

"And cease that whispering, both of you," the dowager added. "It is most unseemly."

"Ears like a bat, too," Gillian added.

"You're incorrigible," Jack said.

"So my dear mother-in-law tells me on an hourly basis. Now, stop holding up the receiving line and go find Lia."

"I suppose I can't put it off any longer, can I? I just hope to God we don't get in another fight."

She patted his arm. "Nonsense. She's very eager to see you, I'm sure."

"When did she get here?"

"About a half hour ago, with very little fanfare and only a minimum of gossip. That should please you."

She knew he was still chafing that he hadn't been part of Lia's escort. He'd naturally assumed he would be, charged with warding off any rakes or bounders who might have the nerve to approach her. Given her insane plan to start looking for a protector, it had seemed an essential and sensible precaution. After all, if there was one thing he knew how to do, it was keep an eye out for Lia Kincaid.

Sir Dominic had not agreed with him, nor had Lia, saying it would only draw attention to his unusual connection with her family. In fact, Jack and Lia had exchanged a few choice words on the matter, which led to her storming out of the Hunters' drawing room and leaving him with his mouth hanging open—again.

All he could do at this point was get as close as she would allow and do his best to protect her.

"All right, I'm going," he said. "By the way, I do generally understand things once they're explained to me a few times—preferably in one-syllable words."

Gillian laughed. "I think you're quite trainable, my lord. In fact, I'm sure we'll be advancing to two- and even three-syllable words in no time."

"That was an insult worthy of your husband, Your Grace."

"I will take that as a compliment."

"I wouldn't."

She gave him a cheeky smile before turning to speak with Lady Cardwell, who'd finally moved on from the dowager.

It took Jack several minutes to elbow his way into the ballroom, as he ran into friends and answered inquiries after his mother. A few older ladies archly expressed surprise at her absence, even though they knew Lady John would rather shoot herself than come within a hundred feet of a Kincaid. Their veiled remarks were another warning of the dangers that lurked right there in the ballroom.

He paused by one of the Corinthian columns inside the entrance and scanned the room. There was hardly a spare inch around the perimeter of the dance floor, where a crowded swirl of colorful gowns and glittering jewels was offset by dark, masculine garb. Fortunately, he was taller than most of the men, so he was able to locate his target quickly.

Good to his word, Dominic Hunter loomed right behind Lia and Chloe, looking his most forbidding. Unfortunately, even Sir Dominic's frightening scowl didn't seem to be doing the trick of keeping an enthusiastic group of young and not-so-young bucks away from Lia.

While most of them, thank God, were entirely respectable, others were not. Jack recognized the members of that second group, both by name and by type. Despite their impeccable manners and polished regard, he knew their purpose as well as he knew the distressing state of his purse. They were trolling for a new conquest and they'd set their sights on Lia.

The competition to win her favor—and complete her ruin—had already begun.

Over my dead body.

Impatient to reach her, he started to push his way through the crowd. He was still several feet away and had yet to get a good look at her when the crowd suddenly parted as a new set began on the dance floor. Several of the gentlemen moved away, presumably to find their partners. Jack all but tripped over his feet, stumbling to a halt as his mind grappled with the vision before him.

He'd always realized Lia was a pretty girl. Her sweet, generous smile won her allies wherever she went. She was a veritable pattern card of the English country lass—fresh-faced, unadorned, and dressed in a way that befitted a quiet life revolving around the work and seasons of an out-of-the-way estate in Yorkshire.

The simple, fresh-faced girl was tonight replaced by a sophisticated young goddess, one garbed in a cream and gold-spangled gown that made her skin glow and clung to curves that seemed considerably more ample when displayed by a low-cut bodice. Glossy chestnut hair was piled in intricate curls on her head, with delicate strands drifting enticingly down her long, graceful neck. Her smooth, straight shoulders were mostly bare and her dainty cap sleeves gave the impression that they might slip down her arms any second, exposing all the bounties inadequately hidden by her clinging gown.

Good God.

He breathed heavily through his nostrils—rather like an enraged bull, he couldn't help thinking. He had to fight the urge to rip the scarf off the shoulders of the matron next to him and fling it over Lia's naked shoulders. The blasted girl had put herself on display as the next Notorious Kincaid. If she'd placed an advertisement in the papers, she couldn't have made a better job of it.

As he started forward, a restraining hand clamped down on his shoulder. "Jack, hold up," Charles said, tugging him behind a marble column. "We need to talk."

"I don't have time," he snapped. "I've got to get to Lia before she does something foolish."

"She's fine. Sir Dominic and Lady Hunter are keeping an eye on her."

"Have you seen the way she's dressed?"

Charles frowned. "Of course. She looks lovely."

"She looks like a blasted courtesan putting her wares on display."

His friend's eyebrows shot up at the description. "Hardly. Her dress is entirely appropriate for a young woman not in her first or even second season. Gillian helped her pick it out."

"Has every woman in this family lost her bloody mind?" Jack asked.

"I have no idea what you're talking about. But that's not important right now because we've got a problem. Or, I should say, you've got a problem, and so does Lia. I'm afraid it's a rather big one, too."

Jack sighed. "What now?"

Charles glanced over his shoulder toward the ballroom door. Then he looked back at Jack, his features set and grim. "Your mother and sister just arrived and they're headed this way."

"There, Miss Kincaid, now you can catch your breath," said Sebastian Sinclair. "That was quite the mob milling about you." He flashed a charming smile, his teeth gleaming white in his tan face. "Fortunately for me, all your would-be swains were engaged for the next set of dances. I now have you all to myself."

Lia politely smiled as she resisted the urge to swipe at the perspiration that trickled down the back of her neck. What she wouldn't give for a breath of Stonefell's crisp country air.

She glanced around the room, still surprised by how many

men seemed eager to meet her. But it was obvious from a few veiled references that at least some of the gentlemen had seen her performance at the Pan. That made her an object of interest—and, she suspected, a challenge.

"It's very close, isn't it?" she replied. "You, however, don't seem at all discomposed, Mr. Sinclair."

A few minutes ago she'd felt positively woozy from the heat and the odors of perfume, bay rum, candle wax, floral arrangements—heavy on the lilies and roses—and at least three hundred bodies packed into the confined space of a few rooms. She swore she could almost see a scented miasma floating over the dance floor.

"I spent most of the last ten years in India," Sinclair answered. "As bad as it is, this ballroom cannot begin to compare to Bombay during the monsoon season. There it's hard to draw a fresh breath for months at a time."

"I'd love to hear about your adventures in India," Lia said. "It seems like such a fascinating country, albeit one with challenging weather."

Of all the men she'd met tonight, she liked Sinclair the best. According to Aunt Chloe, he was the youngest son of an impecunious baronet. He had been shipped off to India when all but a boy and had made his fortune there. He was tall and handsome, with wheat-colored hair, startling green eyes, and a friendly manner that seemed entirely natural. Unlike some of the other men, he didn't appear to regard her as a tempting morsel just waiting to be gobbled up. He spoke like a sensible, well-educated man, and listened with interest whenever she ventured an opinion.

He shrugged. "One gets used to it." Something in his tone suggested he hadn't had much choice in the matter.

"I envy your fortitude, Mr. Sinclair," Chloe said, vigorously fanning her face. "I'm all but ready to expire. I'm amazed Gillian found so many people left in Town, given that the Season is long over. Perhaps too many, to tell the truth."

"I suspect not all of them are actually on the guest list," Dominic said sarcastically.

Lia frowned. "You mean people came without an invitation? Why would they do that?"

Chloe and Dominic exchanged glances.

"I suppose they came to gawk at the latest Notorious Kincaid." Lia grimaced. "How very rude to inflict themselves on the Levertons with such annoying disregard."

"One can never go wrong in anticipating bad behavior in the Ton," Dominic said. "In fact, it's generally better to expect it, so one can be pleasantly surprised when the opposite occasionally occurs."

"That's certainly squares with my experience," Sinclair said. "Since my return to London a few months ago, I've been treated to the most impertinent questions about everything from my encounters with the exotic women of India to the size of my fortune."

"That's awful," Lia said. "How do you stand it?"

He winked at her. "By inventing the biggest whoppers I can think of, especially regarding the state of my wallet."

Lia and Chloe laughed, and even Dominic cracked a smile.

It was the first sign of good humor he'd displayed all evening. Her uncle-in-law had thus far spent his time scowling at the men who'd spoken with her, doing his best to frighten them off. Chloe finally had to remind him that the entire point of the exercise was for Lia to meet eligible suitors. Dominic had replied rather tartly that he was only scaring away the ineligible ones, of which there seemed to be an inordinate number.

That such was the case illustrated Lia's belief that it was a fool's errand to introduce her into society. Only a few respectable bachelors had asked her to dance, and that probably had more to do with the mothers than the gentlemen themselves. She'd been introduced to a number of aristocratic ladies, and although none had snubbed her outright, they'd made no attempt to converse with her beyond a few coolly polite words. To expect that they would wish their sons to court someone like her was too much to ask.

"That's an excellent tactic, Mr. Sinclair, but I don't think telling whoppers will work in my case," Lia said. "My background is shocking enough as it is."

"Nonsense, my dear," Chloe said. "You are a kind, beautifully mannered girl with a great deal of common sense. There is nothing at all shocking about you."

"Tell that to the guests," Lia said wryly. "I don't think most of them would agree with you."

"Is that because you appeared on the stage last week or because your mother and grandmother were courtesans?" Sinclair asked.

Lia blinked, surprised by his forthright manner.

Sinclair gave them all an apologetic smile. "Forgive me for speaking so bluntly. Living rather roughly these last ten years has obviously had a deleterious effect on my manners."

Lia smiled at him. "It's so much easier when people speak plainly instead of twisting their meaning up with pretty, flowery phrases—especially the snubs."

Chloe nodded. "How true. I can't tell you how many times I've been insulted at a social event and didn't even realize it until some hours later."

"The next time that happens, I want you to tell me," Dominic all but snarled. "I won't have anyone insulting my wife and getting away with it."

She patted his arm. "You're a darling, but I can't have

you frightening people half to death over a little snub every now and again."

"I don't see why not," Dominic said. "What's the use of having influence if you can't use it to scare people into good behavior?"

"Or bad behavior, as the case may be," said Sinclair with a grin.

"According to my family, I've engaged in quite enough bad behavior," Lia said. "I'm to be a pattern card of rectitude from now on."

"That would be a nice change," Dominic said with a wry smile.

"Miss Kincaid's stage appearance didn't sound all that scandalous," Sinclair said. "But rather more like a fun adventure. And it was your stepfather's company, was it not? Truly, it sounds quite tame when one knows the details."

Lia wrinkled her nose. "I suppose you didn't hear about my breeches role."

He shook his head, looking slightly mystified.

"We don't need to discuss that now," Dominic said in a firm tone. "Or ever, in fact."

"I suppose you're right," she said. "Mr. Sinclair, forget I even mentioned it."

"Well, that's no fun," he said with mock complaint. "Because I am a gentleman, however, I will manfully wrestle my curiosity under control—but only if you agree to allow me to call on you one day soon, Miss Kincaid. And Lady Hunter, of course."

Lia caught the quick glance her aunt flicked at Dominic, who gave an almost imperceptible nod back. Apparently, Mr. Sinclair had passed muster.

"I am sure both Lia and I would be delighted to see you, sir," Chloe said. She gave Lia an encouraging smile.

"Yes, that would be very nice," added Lia politely.

Because Sinclair seemed like a genuinely nice man, she couldn't imagine why he'd waste his time on her. With his looks, background, and wealth, he would be considered a prime catch on the marriage mart. She suspected he was simply being polite, likely because his father was friendly with Dominic.

His eyes glittered with emerald sparks of amusement. "You are too kind, Miss Kincaid. I will do my best to entertain you and Lady Hunter with appropriately thrilling stories of my travels through India."

Many of the gentlemen Lia had met tonight had struck her as little better than strutting peacocks, preening in front of the females, waiting for—and expecting—their full approval. Sinclair, while obviously a confident man, didn't appear to take himself too seriously.

Perhaps she wouldn't mind spending time with him, after all. If nothing else, he might take her mind off Jack. She'd had yet another fight with him only a few days before and it had left her feeling gloomy and hollowed out. They'd once been the best of friends, but now they'd somehow lost the ability to talk to each other, much less understand how the other felt.

If Jack truly was in love with her, as Chloe had suggested, that shouldn't be the case, as far as Lia was concerned. If anything, their relationship seemed to be fracturing under the weight of disagreements and misunderstandings, driving them further apart every day.

She was afraid it was feeling rather hopeless.

Then stop moping and do something else instead.

"That would be simply splendid," she said, giving Sinclair a bright smile. "I will look forward to your call."

His eyebrows ticked up at her marked increase in enthusiasm. Socially adept she was not, as she'd tried to tell Aunt Chloe and Gillian a thousand times. Jack had agreed with her on that point, which, while honest, wasn't very flattering.

Sinclair briefly bowed over her gloved hand. "Thank you, Miss Kincaid. I will be sure to—"

Suddenly appearing out of the crowd, Gillian ruthlessly elbowed Sinclair in the ribs to move him aside. "Lia, there you are. I've been looking all over for you, but this bloody ballroom—er, this ridiculous ballroom is so crowded that one can barely find one's hand."

"Forgive me, Your Grace," Sinclair said in a dry tone. "I didn't realize I was in your way."

Gillian gave an exaggerated start as she met his gaze. "Mr. Sinclair, is that you? I do apologize. I didn't notice you."

He was well over six feet tall and Gillian was an exceedingly observant person, so that didn't seem likely. "I hope I didn't step on your foot and injure you," the duchess added, almost as an afterthought.

"No indeed, madam, my *foot* was not injured in the least."

Gillian gave him a reluctant smile. "You're very nice. Under other circumstances, I would quite like you."

That threw him for a few seconds, but he recovered with a quick smile. "Thank you—I think."

"Your Grace, is there something you need from Lia?" Dominic prompted, sounding a bit long-suffering. Gillian tended to elicit that response in her family and friends. The duchess was even more unconventional than she was and had immediately taken Lia under her wing with a fierce and unquestioning loyalty. Lia had already come to adore her.

"Yes. It's very important that I speak with Lia, you, and Aunt Chloe." Gillian slid an impatient glance at Sinclair. "Now."

He took the hint, excusing himself with a quiet murmur

before slipping into the crowd. For such a large man, he moved with a prowling grace that was quite entrancing. If not for Jack . . .

She clamped down on that thought. "Is something wrong, Gillian?"

"You have no idea." Gillian glanced over her shoulder, then moved closer and lowered her voice. "Jack's mother and sister just entered the ballroom. He and Leverton are trying to keep them to that side of the room, but I don't think they can manage it for very long."

Chloe gasped and put a hand to her lips. Dominic let out a salty oath.

"My feelings exactly, Sir Dominic," Gillian said. "There's nothing to be done, however, except manage it as best we can. Keep Lia under wraps, as it were."

"That poses a challenge," he replied with some asperity, "because this is Lia's introduction to society. It would hardly be appropriate for the guest of honor to suddenly disappear."

"Lia, dear, are you all right?" Chloe asked, placing a hand on her arm.

Lia forced her muddled brain back into some semblance of rational thought. "I don't understand. Lady John and Lady Anne were not invited, were they?"

"Good God, no," Gillian said. "Normally, we would be happy to invite any member of Jack's family to a party, but under the circumstances, it would be a disaster if the three of you were to meet."

That was putting it mildly. Lady John had always resented Granny's presence at Stonefell with every particle of her being, and she loathed her son's friendship with Lia. About four years earlier, on one of the rare occasions when the entire Easton family had come to visit, Lia had overhead Jack and his mother having a crashing row out in the gardens. Lia had been the subject of their argument, and she could recall with perfect clarity the humiliating names Lady John had called her. Even now, the memory made her stomach tighten into a painful knot.

"I was under the impression that Lady John made a point of avoiding the Kincaids," Chloe said. "So this makes no sense."

"Normally she avoids us like the plague," Lia said, trying not to sound as miserable as she felt.

Despite Dominic's assertion, retreat seemed the best way to avoid an ugly confrontation. As distressing as such a scene would be for her, it would be worse for Jack. He was devoted to his mother and sister. To have his loyalty split in such a way, and so publicly, was something she couldn't bear.

"Charles says she's taking a stand," Gillian said. "Whatever that means."

"I know exactly what it means," Lia said. Lady John had spent decades believing she and her daughter had been shunted aside from their proper places in the family, displaced by the Kincaids. "I do think I should leave, Sir Dominic. I suspect she wants to make a scene, and that will devastate Jack."

"It won't help you very much either," Chloe said grimly.

Gillian slipped her arm around Lia's waist. "I won't have Lia driven away," she said in a challenging voice to Dominic.

He glanced around, distaste marking his features. Although they were speaking in low tones, people nearby were starting to take note of their intense conversation. Some of the other guests were bound to have seen the new arrivals and were no doubt already gleefully spreading gossip—and anticipating an explosion.

"It's fine, Gillian," Lia said. "I'm ready to go."

Dominic shook his head. "No, sneaking away like a thief isn't the answer." He glanced at his wife. "My dear, please take Lia to the supper room and find a quiet corner. I'll join you there shortly."

"What are you going to do?" his wife asked.

"I'm going to intercept Lady John and see if I can talk some sense into her."

"Oh blast," muttered Gillian. "It's too late."

The crowd in front of them rippled like the tops of wheat stalks in a late summer breeze and then parted. Into the gap sailed Lady John, followed by her daughter. Jack and Leverton were right behind them, both looking utterly frustrated.

Actually, Jack looked ready to murder someone— probably even Lia for pitching everyone into the middle of such a disaster.

Gillian gave Lia's waist another quick squeeze and then stepped forward. "Lady John, what a surprise. We hadn't expected to see you at our little affair."

Lia blinked. Her cousin, the most natural and unaffected person she'd ever met, had instantly transformed into the epitome of a duchess—and a very regal one at that.

Jack's mother was not to be intimidated. "I expect not," she said in a haughty voice, "because we were not invited." Her hostile glance slid over Gillian.

Dominic moved forward and gave her ladyship a clipped bow. "Lady John, may I escort you and your daughter to the supper room for some refreshment? It's much quieter and cooler there, so we can have a comfortable chat."

If a curtsy could be labeled begrudging, Lady John's certainly was. "Thank you, Sir Dominic, but neither my daughter nor I are in the mood for refreshments. I have business to attend to that will not wait."

An anticipatory murmur whispered through the gathering throng. Even though the orchestra still played and some of the sets continued to dance, the people closest to the tawdry drama had stopped pretending they were doing anything but watching with avid attention.

Jack moved up to join his mother, his expression frozen into a stonelike mask. Still, his touch on her arm was so gentle, his demeanor so protective, that Lia's heart broke for him.

"Mother, please go with Sir Dominic," he said quietly. "You will simply cause yourself more anguish if you insist on doing this."

When she angrily jerked her arm away from him, Jack made an impatient noise and glanced at his sister. "Anne, this is madness."

His sister cut a quick, troubled look between them, then lifted her shoulders in a shrug that indicated she wouldn't interfere.

"Lady John," the Duke of Leverton began.

She flung up an imperious hand, cutting him off. Her gaze finally skated past Gillian to Lia. Jack had gotten his dark, laughing eyes from his mother, but there was no laughter or kindness or love in her ladyship's gaze as it latched onto Lia now. There was only loathing and contempt.

"You," she said in a throbbing voice, pointing a dramatic finger. "Why must you bedevil my family? Why can you not leave my son alone? Your family is like a blight we cannot be rid of no matter how hard we try."

A collective gasp, at once both delighted and appalled, went up from the assembled guests.

"Good God," Gillian said with disgust.

Lia had to repress a wildly inappropriate impulse to laugh at Lady John's melodramatic language and pose. Under other circumstances, Mama might even have offered her ladyship a position in the troupe.

"My lady, it is neither my desire nor my intention to trouble you or your family," Lia said, forcing a calm tone.

"And I barely see Jack these days, so you needn't worry about that either. There is nothing between us but a child-hood friendship."

As soon as the words escaped her mouth, she knew she'd made a fatal mistake.

Lady John seemed to grow inches taller in her righteous indignation. "How dare you speak of my son with such casual regard, as if you were equals! Do not think for a moment that I will allow you to drive a wedge between us, or drive me away from my rightful place in society. *You* are the one who doesn't belong here."

The woman would be surprised to know how much Lia agreed with her.

Jack's hand landed on his mother's shoulder. "That's enough, Mother. You've said your piece and now we're leaving."

She ignored him, once again jabbing her finger at Lia's nose. "I know you to be a whore, Lia Kincaid, just like your mother. And if you don't stay away from my family, I will make you regret it for the rest of your life."

As everyone absorbed that exploding squib, Gillian shoved her ladyship's arm out of the way and stepped in front of Lia. "Right, that's enough out of you," she snapped.

Lia tried to pull her back. "Gillian, it's all right. She can't hurt me." Not anymore than she already had anyway. A lifetime of hatred had seen to that.

"I won't allow her to insult you," Gillian replied, keeping her gaze squarely on Lady John. "Madam, allow me to tell you that you are nothing but a nasty, crabbed-up old biddy. And if you don't get out of my house this instant, I'll toss you out on your backside myself."

Lady John's eyes went wide with shock. A moment later she hauled back and slapped Gillian across the face.

Chapter Thirteen

"Please stop apologizing," Gillian said in a voice muffled by the cold cloth she held to her cheek. She patted Lia's arm with her free hand. "It wasn't your fault."

"Yes, it was," Lia replied miserably. "I wasn't strong enough to say no to this terribly misguided notion of introducing me into society. And now I've landed you all in the worst sort of scandal."

Although the party was still going full force downstairs, they'd retreated to a private sitting room at the back of the house. Lia sat next to her cousin on a chaise while Dominic and Chloe were across from them in comfortably overstuffed chairs. Both looked concerned but remarkably calm under the circumstances.

Leverton, however, prowled like an annoyed lion from one end of the room to the other, working off the fury of Lady John's insults to both his wife and Lia. Thanks to Jack's mother, what little had been left of Lia's reputation was now thoroughly shredded.

Predictably, Dominic recovered first. "It's a setback, I admit," he said to Lia, "but no rational person could blame you. You did nothing to provoke Lady John's unfortunate reaction."

The duke stopped in midstride and scowled at the older man. "Unfortunate reaction? Demented and mean-spirited would be a better description. The woman is a lunatic."

Chloe cast him a troubled glance before directing a comforting smile at Lia. "My love, you're still looking very pale. Let me give you some tea and perhaps a bit to eat. Gillian's housekeeper brought some lovely treats with the tea."

"Actually, I'd rather have a brandy," Lia said.

"That's an excellent idea," Gillian said. "Charles, will you do the honors?"

Leverton headed to a chinoiserie sideboard that held a number of decanters and a collection of delicate crystal goblets. He splashed brandy into two of the glasses and stalked back to the chaise, silently giving one to his wife and the other to Lia.

Lia forced herself to meet his gaze, which still burned with anger and frustration. "Your Grace, I'm so sorry I embarrassed your family. I wish there was some way I could go back and redo this entire miserable night."

"Yes, it's unfortunate that we cannot," he said in a clipped tone.

"For God's sake, stop acting like such a discourteous grump," Gillian said, scowling at her husband. "You'd think you were the one who'd been slapped instead of me."

He drew in a breath. "I wish it had been me, my love. That harpy actually left a mark on your cheek."

Gillian removed the cloth and carefully worked her jaw. "Lady John has quite a good arm. Now, apologize to Lia for being such a brute."

Lia jumped as if someone had jabbed her with a pin. "Please don't. Lord knows you have nothing to apologize for."

Leverton unbent a bit more, giving her a rueful smile.

"My wife is quite right, Lia. None of this is your fault. Events unfolded in a way no sane person could have predicted."

"It was rather exciting, you must admit," Gillian said with surprising good cheer. "And I honestly don't think it was all that bad. Yes, there will be gossip, but lots of people in the Ton behave badly on a regular basis. It was just one little slap."

Lia was rather stunned by her cousin's assessment. Then again, Gillian had punched an earl at her debut, all but causing a riot in the ballroom. Perhaps by that standard, tonight's events seemed a pale imitation.

"You're taking this rather well," Leverton said, eyeing his wife with a puzzled look.

"I suppose you expected me to pull a knife from under my gown and stab her," Gillian said with some asperity.

Her husband's raised eyebrows supplied the answer.

"Really, Charles, I would never stab Jack's mother, no matter how much she might deserve it. He would be very displeased if I did."

Lia had to choke back a giggle. The entire evening had turned into a domestic farce that would probably have been hilarious if it involved someone other than her and Jack.

"I agree it could have been much worse," Dominic said, smiling at Gillian. "And that's mostly due to you, my dear. Your reaction was eminently sane and generous."

"And unexpected," Leverton said with a glimmer of humor. "I was convinced I'd be breaking my wife out of Bridewell before the evening was over."

"I am capable of self-discipline when the occasion calls for it," his wife said dryly. "Even if sometimes a little late."

The assembled guests had been stunned into silence by Lady John's resounding slap. They'd stood frozen in horror, waiting for the Duchess of Leverton, well known for her volatile temper, to respond to the insult. Jack's mother had refused to back down one inch, meeting Gillian's dagger-filled glare with one equally fierce.

Jack and Leverton had immediately started to move to intervene between the combatants, but Gillian had stopped them dead in their tracks by giving Lady John a rueful smile as she extended her hand.

"That was a nice, flush hit, my lady," she'd said. "I commend you. Now, why don't we shake on it and call it an evening, man to man."

Lady John had stared at Gillian with utter consternation, but she'd clearly been so stunned by the gesture that she'd weakly extended a hand. Gillian gave it a brisk shake.

As if a spell had been broken, the ballroom had whirled back to life. Everyone started talking at once and the orchestra, by a miracle of timing, struck up a waltz. After Jack exchanged a glance with his sister, they'd taken their mother by the arm and led her swiftly away. Dominic and Aunt Chloe had done the same for Lia, removing her through a side door and taking her upstairs.

Lia gave her cousin's hand a squeeze. "You were absolutely splendid, Gillian. I don't know how you managed it."

"I'm quite good in a crisis." Gillian's eyes twinkled as she glanced at her husband. "As Charles can tell you."

Leverton snorted, but his smile was warm and approving. A man of great presence and authority, he obviously adored his exceedingly unconventional wife. While Lia was thrilled for Gillian, she couldn't repress a twinge of envy. To be so completely accepted by the man you loved, warts and all, seemed like the stuff of dreams.

"Speaking of managing a crisis," Gillian said, putting down her glass, "I suppose we'd best get back down there and assess the extent of the damage."

"There's no need to rush," Leverton said. "My mother and your grandmother are keeping an eye on the situation.

Between the two of them, I'm sure they have everything under control."

Lia had met the dowager duchess and Lady Marbury, Gillian's grandmother, before the party started. They were both impressively dignified women. But while the dowager had looked down her nose at Lia, Lady Marbury had been friendly and apparently willing to accept her into the family.

After tonight's events, however, that was likely to change.

Gillian grinned at her husband. "You don't want to go down because you're afraid of facing your mother."

"Can you blame me?" Leverton asked.

"I don't," said Lia. "She's terrifying."

Gillian wrinkled her nose. "She is rather, isn't she?"

"I think we'd best remain up here until Lord Lendale returns," Dominic said. "We need to discuss with him how we're going to manage the reaction to our little incident—and manage his mother."

Leverton started pacing again. "Little incident? Ha."

Dominic looked the soul of patience. "As far as I can tell, no one was killed, blackmailed, kidnapped, robbed, or found in a compromising position. By our family's standards, tonight's events were decidedly mild."

"That is certainly true." Gillian pointed a warning finger at her husband. "And I absolutely forbid you to be rude to Jack. It's not his fault his mother is so dreary."

Leverton wasn't the only one who didn't want to see Jack. Lia was so mortified that she wished she could open a window and slide down the drainpipe before he arrived.

Of course, after tonight it would probably be a moot point. Jack would never wish to see her again after such a total humiliation. He'd been right about everything all along and they should have listened to him.

She should have listened to him.

"Lady John is not a bad person," she said. "She's had an

unhappy and difficult life in many respects and I can't fault her desire to protect her family."

"She has a rather odd way of doing it," Gillian said. "Causing a major scene at a ball is more likely to add to one's troubles rather than diminish them. Trust me on that point."

"She must be feeling desperate," Lia said.

"Lady John sees you as a threat to her son," Dominic said quietly.

She nodded. "Exactly. I believe she wanted to trigger a scandal to force Jack to make a choice. He is so loyal to his mother and sister, he would not want to subject them to more gossip and ugliness because of me."

"That's rich," Gillian said. "She triggered the blasted scandal and yet you're the one who has to face the consequences. I should have thrown her out on her ear before she got anywhere near you."

Chloe grimaced. "There's a horrible sort of logic to her actions. We're trying to put the best face on it, but most people will see Lady John as the injured party. I fear the effect on Lia could be quite profound."

Dominic reached over and took her hand. "We've faced worse odds, my dear."

"Indeed we have," Gillian said stoutly. "Just look at me."

"Yes, but your family lineage is impeccable," Lia said.

Dominic shook his head. "Nonetheless, I think—"

Chloe interrupted by placing a gently restraining hand on his arm. "Why don't we allow Lia to tell us what she wants? We've not given her much chance to do so, have we?"

"Ugh, we're an awful lot, aren't we?" said Gillian. "Sorry, Cuz. My family used to order me about all the time and I hated it."

"It turned out fairly well for you," Leverton said with some exasperation.

"Yes, but not because I listened to all of you but because eventually you all listened to *me*," she retorted.

He looked disgruntled but didn't contradict her.

"You've all been lovely," Lia said, giving her cousin a reassuring pat on the knee. "It's just that . . ."

"It's just that we've not been listening to you," Dominic finished wryly. "Even worse, we've been ordering you about."

"Not me," Leverton said. "I never tell anyone what to do."

"That's a joke," Gillian said with a hoot. "You're an absolute dictator."

Lia couldn't help but smile at their affectionate banter, even though another ache wove itself into the one that seemed permanently attached to the center of her chest. She'd only just found her new family and they were all so wonderful. But too soon she'd have to bid them good-bye. Where she planned to go, they couldn't possibly follow.

"Very well, cousin," Leverton said, smiling down at Lia. "Please tell us how you wish us to deal with this regrettable situation."

"There's only one thing to do," she said, bracing for their reaction. "I must leave."

Chloe frowned. "London? Surely you don't want to return to Stonefell, especially now."

"No, that's not possible," Lia said. After she put her plan into effect, she could never go home either.

It's not your home, remember?

"Do you wish to return to your mother's house?" Dominic asked.

"Perhaps for a bit," she hedged.

They stared at her, clearly puzzled. A moment later Dominic got it. "No," he rapped out. "Absolutely not."

"What other choice do I have?" Lia said. "You must see how impossible it is for me to recover from Lady John's insults, not that there was much chance of the beau monde accepting me to begin with. After tonight, that chance is all but nonexistent."

"Would you two care to explain what you're talking about or must we guess?" Leverton asked.

Before Lia could answer, there was a tap on the door and Jack brushed past the butler. He paused for a moment, taking everyone in. He looked utterly weary, with worry lines scored deep around his mouth. Jack had always been so lighthearted, with a ready wit and a kind, generous nature. Now he looked as if he'd aged ten years in only a few months.

She steeled herself, knowing she couldn't let him go on like this, continually torn between conflicting loyalties. The Kincaids were part of his past and that was where they belonged. It was time for all vestiges of her family to be wiped from his life, once and for all.

Jack headed toward the chaise until Leverton intercepted him. They stared at each other for a long, tense moment, their faces set and stony. Then Jack grimaced and shook his head, letting out a sigh. Apparently, the duke was satisfied with that tersely masculine communication because he nodded and stepped aside. Everyone in the room seemed to breathe out relief and the tight feeling in Lia's chest eased a bit. Leverton was Jack's best friend and she'd been terrified that tonight's events might have destroyed their relationship.

Jack stopped in front of Gillian and gave her a formal bow. "Your Grace, I cannot begin to apologize for my mother's outrageous behavior. On behalf of my family, please know how deeply regretful I am, and also know that I will do everything in my power to ameliorate any ill effects of her actions."

Gillian jumped to her feet with a funny little growl. She punched Jack in the shoulder, then threw her arms around him and gave him a fierce hug. After a moment's hesitation, one of his hands stole up to awkwardly rest on her back.

"Don't be such an idiot," she said, her voice muffled against his coat. "No one in their right mind could have predicted that ridiculous scene." She pulled back and cut him a grin. "And here I thought I was the only one who went around pummeling aristocrats in ballrooms. Now I might have to cede my title to your mother."

He gave her a faltering smile. "It's kind of you to make light of it, but I know how upsetting this was for all of you. And especially for Lia."

When his gaze touched her, he couldn't seem to hold it, and Lia's heart sank even more. Not that it mattered, because she was going to free him from the anchor around his neck.

"And it *is* my fault," he added. "I knew how upset my mother was. I should never have come to the ball in the first place."

Everyone started talking at once, protesting his statement. But when Lia stood, they all fell silent.

"No, Jack," she said. "The very last person at fault is you. In fact, you were the one most opposed to this scheme. We should have listened to you."

He finally held her gaze and she saw how ashamed he was. She *hated* that. Jack was the finest man she knew and he didn't deserve this.

"Lia, I am so sorry you had to be exposed to her . . . her madness on this." He rolled his lips together, as if in pain. "My mother is not herself. She's not thinking rationally just now."

"Lady John has been forced to endure too many indignities in her life," Lia said. "I'm sure your uncle never meant to humiliate her, but he did, as did your father. Tonight must have seemed like the final straw."

He huffed out a bitter laugh. "That's essentially what she said, believe it or not."

"I believe it because it's the truth."

"None of which makes it your fault," he said. "You are entirely blameless in this, Lia."

"Not in your mother's eyes," she said quietly.

How strange to be defending the woman who had always treated her with contempt and believed her nothing but a whore. Unfortunately, Lady John's view was now likely shared by most of the Ton.

"My mother is wrong," he said firmly.

Now he was beginning to look annoyed, which was at least an improvement over grim and hollowed out. It also made it easier for her to say what needed to be said.

"Jack, for too long you've been pulled between Granny and me and your real family. Before you inherited the title, there was little you could do about it. But now there is. And you should do what's best for you and for your good name."

"I reject that as a false equivalency," he said stubbornly. "I can be loyal to all of you."

She pinched the edge of her nose for a second, praying for patience. "No, you cannot, because your family and society will not allow it. It's tearing you apart and it's tearing me apart, too. So it has to stop."

He flinched but recovered quickly. "Sweetheart, don't you think you're being a bit melodramatic?"

Her patience finally unraveled. "Splendid, more insults. I may be overly dramatic, Jack Easton, but you are entirely pigheaded. Everything would have been fine if you hadn't come racing down to London after me instead of attending to your business at Stonefell. You've probably left things back there in a complete mess, by the way."

"Fine? Really?" he said, ignoring her gratuitous shot. "You think that debacle at the Pan was *fine*?"

"Perhaps we might resume our seats and chat about this

less heatedly," Dominic interjected. "I do not believe the situation is nearly as dire as it might first appear."

"That is a capital idea," Gillian said. She reached out a hand. "Come, Lia, sit back down with me."

Lia was about to do so when Jack's fingers wrapped around her wrist. He hauled her back to the chaise and then plunked down beside her, taking Gillian's seat. He crowded Lia against the upholstered arm, as if protecting her from the others in the room.

"Well, aren't you the masterful one?" the duchess said, regarding him with an amused air.

Jack simply shrugged and looked stubborn. Clearly, he was going to be difficult to reason with. She'd have to manage things very carefully because her tolerance for any more scenes had evaporated.

He blew out a long, calming breath and finally settled against the back of the chaise. He kept her hand in his lap, stroking it, as if to soothe her. But, in fact, it wound her up, making it harder to think.

"All right, pet?" he murmured.

She managed a nod. He was always trying to take care of her, but one of these days he needed to realize that she had to make her own decisions.

"Good."

Jack then made a credible attempt at smiling at Dominic, who was regarding them with an expression that sent a frisson down her spine. The magistrate was plotting, moving the various pieces on the gameboard around in his head. Lia was obviously one of those pieces, as was Jack.

"Why don't you catch me up on what you've been discussing?" Jack said. "I'm sure Sir Dominic has some sort of plan, and I have a few ideas I'd like to share, too."

Gillian had remained standing, calmly regarding Lia and Jack sitting side by side. She didn't trust the glint in her cousin's eyes.

"We've been talking about Lia's plan to address her situation," Gillian said. "Or we were about to before you came in."

Confound it.

Jack gave Lia a wary look. "And what plan is that?"

Her tongue seemed to freeze to the top of her mouth. "Um, well, I'm still working on the details . . . oh, maybe we should hear what Sir Dominic has to say first." For some horrible reason, she simply couldn't bring herself to say the words.

"What is your plan, Lia?" Jack said through clenched teeth.

"She's going to become a courtesan," Gillian said brightly. "And I'd wager she'll become the most popular one in London."

The stunned silence that followed her unfortunate announcement lasted several long seconds. When the yelling commenced—courtesy of the men, naturally—Lia covered her eyes, wishing she were miles away.

Too bad she hadn't slipped out the window and down that blasted drainpipe when still she'd had the chance.

Chapter Fourteen

"Isn't everything just lovely?" Amy Baxter enthused. "I don't know when I've ever been to such a bang-up party or a more elegant house."

Lia was wedged against a huge marble column ostentatiously painted with a great deal of gilt. It matched the rest of the Great Russell Street mansion, which was dripping with gold molding, painted friezes, gigantic chandeliers, and what seemed like endless gilt-covered columns. To her mind, the décor was more overpowering than elegant or lovely.

She'd never thought purple a particularly felicitous color, but Mr. Welby, a wealthy merchant and the host of the party, clearly liked it a lot. All the draperies and furniture fabrics were in various shades of that unfortunate color, as were many of the floral arrangements that graced the various tabletops. Even the marble under her feet had veins of purple running through it. She guessed Welby's aim was to impart a sense of royal elegance. Instead, it seemed rather like a gigantic vat of grape juice had exploded all over the ballroom.

Barbara Carson, a pretty young actress from the Pan troupe, snorted in response to Amy's comment. "This is the first mansion you've ever been in, so I guess it would be the most elegant one you've seen."

"How do you know where I've been and haven't?" Amy said. "I'll have you know that my lord takes me out and about to many a fine party. And it's not as if your beau ever takes you any place special."

"You needn't get in a twist over it," Barbara said defensively. "Anyway, you're wrong. Why, just last week my Anthony took me to a ball at Vauxhall that was just as splendid as this. And a great deal cooler, mind you, because it was outside. I'm about to expire from the bloody heat in here."

"If you don't like it, you can just leave," Amy said tartly. "We only took both of you along tonight as a favor."

"It was very kind of you and Sir Nathan," Lia said hastily. "Barbara and I are very grateful, are we not?"

Barbara dug a friendly elbow into Amy's side. "Lord, of course I am. I was just teasing you a bit. But you have to admit it's roasting in here."

Lia peered around the ballroom. "I don't know how anyone can move, much less dance." Apparently, balls held by the demi-monde were just as uncomfortable as those of the Ton. She began to wonder if it was possible to have fun at a London party.

Barbara vigorously flapped a large fan at her face, causing the curls around her temples to blow straight back. "At least you're not dressed as the bloody Virgin Queen. This blasted Elizabethan choker is all but choking *me*."

The enormous ruffled collar appeared both heavy and scratchy, but it did little to cover Barbara's breasts, which were almost popping out of the low-cut, square bodice of the period. All one had to do was lean in a bit to see the tops of the girl's nipples.

"Perhaps if you fan your, er, chest you'll feel a bit cooler," Lia suggested.

"God knows there's enough of it on display," Amy said with a grin. "Maybe you could find a nice gent to put some ice down there and cool you off. Then you could ask him to go looking for it—if it doesn't melt first."

When the girls burst into laughter, Lia could only manage a weak smile. By the evening's ribald standards, it was certainly a mild jest. Still, it was enough to embarrass her, which was not an encouraging sign given her mission tonight.

"Are you all right, Lia?" Amy asked, peering at her. "You've gone red as a radish. Hang on, because Sir Nathan will be back soon with our drinks."

"I'm just hot," she said. "But you made a very good choice, Amy. You look very fetching and quite cool."

Ventilated would be a better description. Amy preened, smoothing down the wispy and revealing skirts of her nymph's costume. It was the perfect selection for this masked ball. There were no sedate black dominoes or respectable ball gowns at this gathering. No, this was a riotously scandalous affair, frequented by demireps, light-skirts, and, it seemed, every young buck and rake in London. It was the sort of masquerade that no decent woman would ever set foot in, even if escorted by her husband.

And it also was the perfect opportunity for Lia to make her first tentative foray into the world of the demi-monde, beginning a discreet search for a potential protector.

Discretion was essential; her family would go into collective fits if they found out what she was doing. As far as they knew, she was home in bed with a headache, excused from a night at the opera with the Hunters and the Levertons. A worried Chloe had tucked her into bed with a cold cloth and a tepid cup of chamomile tea. Lia had waited in the dark for half an hour before making her escape. She'd had to steal out through the French doors in Chloe's sitting room, then climb over the terrace railing and down into the back garden. She'd then hailed a hackney to take her to the Pan, where she met up with Amy and Barbara. The theater was dark that night, so they were able to raid the costume closet. After they dressed, Sir Nathan Prudhoe, Amy's lover, had picked them up in his carriage.

"And you look very pretty, too, love," Amy said with an encouraging smile. "Although I wish you'd let me dress you as something more exotic than a simple old milkmaid. I swear I've seen at least ten other milkmaids already."

Lia absently tugged up her bodice. Amy had laced her in very tightly, causing her breasts to all but pop up over the top. A sartorial disaster was only one deep breath away, although with all the breasts on display tonight, hers would hardly stand out.

Still, she breathed a silent prayer that her elaborate lace mask would serve as an effective disguise. Her bosom might be exposed for the world to see, but none of the guests would know her identity.

She had no intention of removing her mask or making an effort to speak to anyone but her friends. She was here to shop the goods, so to speak, not make a purchase. That would come at some time still vaguely in the future, when she'd had a chance to review appropriate candidates for the role of protector—and, more importantly, to figure out how to make a final selection. She had yet to come up with a list of qualifications for the position except for the obvious two—he must be rich and he must not entirely disgust her.

As for the logistics of putting her plan into action . . . that mostly eluded her right now, too.

If only Granny were here to advise her. Lia had tried broaching the subject with her mother a few days earlier, but it hadn't gone well. Mama now seemed convinced that Lia's new and wealthy relations could take care of her, and that trying to find a protector risked offending both the Hunters and the Levertons.

Her mother's newfound squeamishness would be laughable if it weren't so annoying and unhelpful.

Mentally glowering at all the obstacles in the way of her plan, Lia tugged again on her bodice. Amy reached over and slapped her hands away.

"Now, stop that, Miss Lia," she said. "You're covering up your best assets."

"Aside from your face, that is," Barbara added. "But nobody can see that."

Lia grimaced. "I'm not very good at this, am I?"

"It just takes a little getting used to," Amy said. "You'll be fine."

"Especially once you've had your first lover. Then you'll start to have some fun with it," Barbara added.

Lia managed to dredge up a weak smile. There wasn't one thing about any of this that struck her as fun.

Amy studied her with a thoughtful expression. "How about asking that lovely bloke who came to see you at the theater? Lord Lendale, was it?"

"He'd be the last person I could ask to be my protector," she said in a gloomy tone.

"Turn you down, would he?" Amy asked sympathetically.

"He doesn't approve of this sort of thing. He's very respectable and he'd kill me if he knew what I was doing tonight."

Lia hadn't seen Jack for some days, not since that dreadful night at Leverton House. Dominic had all but forbidden contact between them on the grounds that it would only exacerbate gossip. Jack had objected but had eventually— if reluctantly—agreed that it was necessary to safeguard what little reputation she had left. Though it was an eminently sensible decision, Lia couldn't help missing him with an ache now permanently lodged in her heart.

Still, if it helped usher Jack from her life, so much the better for him.

"You don't seem very enthusiastic about finding a lover," Barbara said. "Are you sure you want to go through with this?"

Lia winced. "I was hoping it wasn't so obvious. But, yes, I do want to go through with this. And I'm ever so grateful that you two agreed to help me."

Approaching Amy for help had been the only idea Lia was able to come up with. Dubious at first, the young woman had eventually come around.

"I just hope Mrs. Lester doesn't throw my arse out onto the street for bringing you here," Amy said. "I don't understand why your own ma won't help you. After all, it's how she got her start."

"Her reasons don't matter," Lia said firmly. "And I promise she'll never find out you helped me."

"And the rest of your family? What about them?" Barbara asked.

"My grandmother will be fine. As for the others, it's not up to them."

Lia simply refused to become a poor relation dependent on someone else for every morsel of bread she put in her mouth. Besides, it was far too late to change course. In the eyes of polite society, she was already a whore, just like her mother and grandmother. Perception was very little different from reality for a woman like her, no matter how many times Dominic or Chloe tried to persuade her differently.

That perception—cemented by that scene with Jack's mother—had sealed Lia's fate. All that was left was to exert as much control over the future as she could.

"You're a lovely, sweet girl, so you'll find yourself a rich one," Amy said. "If you stop trying to pull up your damn bodice."

Sir Nathan finally strolled up, but without a footman bearing drinks.

"I apologize for abandoning you for so long, my dears," he drawled. "I was detained."

"Not by the line at the refreshment table, apparently," Amy said in a teasing voice. "La, sir, we're positively parched by the heat."

Sir Nathan's unmasked gaze flickered with irritation. "Perhaps you can fetch the drinks next time, my sweet. I'm sure you could find any number of admirers happy to assist you."

Amy clearly heard the implied threat. She waved an airy hand and laughed, saying she'd merely been bored without him because he was the only interesting man in the room.

Sir Nathan Prudhoe was both wealthy and handsome, and securing him as her protector had been a coup for Amy. Lia, however, found him cold, with a brusque and dismissive manner. She'd instantly disliked him, despite Amy's assurances that he was the perfect person to give her entry into the world of the demi-monde. Sir Nathan knew all the wealthiest men in the Ton, including those who might be interested in finding a new mistress.

The notion of being indebted to a man like him, however, made her skin crawl. Nor did she appreciate the way his gaze had flickered over her body with an avid, impersonal lust. Thank God she'd thought to don her mask and had insisted that Amy introduce her to him and to every other man they met tonight as Miss Smith.

For now, and until she was ready to make that final step, she would keep her identity a closely guarded secret. The last thing she needed was word filtering back to Dominic or, even worse, Jack. They would do everything they could to squash her plans.

"I don't know about you, but I need something to drink," Barbara grumbled. "If Sir Nathan won't fetch us refreshments, I suppose we'll have to go do it ourselves."

"I'm sure a footman will pass by any minute," Lia said hastily when she saw temper stamp an ugly scowl on Sir Nathan's arrogant features. She remembered the bruise on Amy's shoulder and her uneasiness grew. "After all, our host is obviously most generous and attentive to his guests, and this is such a wonderful party. I can't thank you enough for allowing me to join you and Amy tonight, Sir Nathan. So very kind of you."

She sounded like a prattling twit, but Prudhoe seemed like a man who would take fawning as his just due.

He leveled a suspicious stare for a few moments, but then smiled and gave Lia a mocking little bow. "It was my pleasure, Miss Smith. Welby is always happy to invite unattached ladies to his events, as I'm sure you've been able to deduce." He punctuated his remark with a leer that made Lia feel nauseated.

"Oh, yes, Mr. Welby," Amy said brightly, obviously happy for the change in subject. "Will we meet our host at some point this evening?"

Prudhoe shrugged. "Perhaps. He frequently throws this sort of affair but only rarely attends them. The man's as odd as the devil, but what can you expect from a cit?"

"Still, it would be nice to meet him," Lia said.

"Because he's so rich, my avaricious little dove?" he asked with a cynical smile.

"No, I'd simply like to thank him for his hospitality," she said, swallowing the impulse to snap at him. It would be a miracle if she didn't smash a vase over Prudhoe's head before the night was out.

"He wouldn't care. Besides, you and Miss Carson should have ample opportunity to meet admirers tonight. I would suggest, however, that you begin circulating. No one will be able to sample your many charms if you continue to hide yourself away in a corner."

When his gaze dropped to her chest and stayed there, Lia's gaze strayed to a large crystal vase with lilies and purple irises on a nearby sideboard.

"Come on, love," Barbara said, taking her arm. "Why don't we fetch something to drink, and then we can stroll about the room." She gave Amy a nod. "We'll find you later, shall we?"

"Yes, be sure to find us at midnight for the unmasking," Prudhoe drawled. "I'm most eager to see Amy's little friend without her disguise."

That would never happen. And from the look on Amy's face, she wasn't too keen on the idea either. She already seemed to be having trouble affixing her lover's interest, which wasn't a bad thing as far as Lia was concerned. The man was a complete lout.

"What a right bastard that fellow is," Barbara said as they skirted the dance floor. "Even if he is a rich nob."

"He's certainly not very kind," Lia said. She thought that kindness in a protector was the first thing she should look for. All the money in the world couldn't make up for a brutish man.

Perhaps the best thing to do tonight was compile a list of attributes she would wish for in a protector. Given the number of men at the ball—men who engaged in all sorts of bad behavior, she couldn't help noticing—she would have plenty of material to work with.

As they squeezed past a crowd of young bucks, Barbara let out a squawk. When she spun around and glared at one of the men, he flashed her a leering grin.

"You keep your hands to yourself, you jackass," she said. "Or I'll show you what for, I will."

"I'd like to see that," the man said with a drunken laugh. "Why don't you and your pretty friend join us? Then you can show us whatever you want, starting with your pretty boobies."

"Not bloody likely," Barbara snapped. "You're nothing but a—"

"Thank you, sir, but no," Lia interrupted. "Don't get in an argument with them," she hissed at Barbara as she dragged her in the direction of the refreshment saloon. "We don't have anyone to protect us if things get ugly."

"But he groped me right on the arse. My Anthony would take him apart if he saw me being treated like that."

"Good Lord, Barbara, what are you doing here?" Lia asked, exasperated. "You already have a beau who sounds devoted to you."

Her companion started to reply, but a heavily rouged vestal virgin and her male escort, garbed as one of the more flamboyant Stuart kings, separated them. Barbara ruthlessly elbowed them out of the way, ignoring the protests from the offended monarch.

"He is very devoted," she said. "But his pa owns a cartage business and they've got a job transporting goods up to Glasgow. He knows I like to go to parties and entertainments and he don't have a problem with that." She winked at Lia, her generous mouth curving into a smile beneath her pretty feathered mask. "Besides, there's nothing wrong with a girl making a little extra on the side, is there? This is just the sort of place to do it, what with all the gents around. My Anthony will be happy with the extra blunt when we set up housekeeping for ourselves."

It was hard to believe that any man could be so tolerant and forgiving. Then again, Barbara did seem the practical sort, and perhaps her beau was as well. Lia had to admit that money and status trumped love more frequently than not. Given what had happened to her grandmother, who had allowed herself to be seduced by affection rather than commerce, perhaps it was better to be practical.

"The man who squeezed your backside was eager to spend time with you and he looked very well-heeled. Why not spend time with him?"

"I choose who I spend time with, love. Not the other way around. That's Amy's problem. She's not choosy enough, if you ask me."

Lia added that bit of wisdom to her list of things to remember when choosing a protector.

They eventually made their way forward with the colorfully garbed crowd to the refreshment tables at the end of the spacious ballroom. Beyond the tables, a wide set of doors led into another drawing room, one set up for supper. But rather than tables and chairs, the space was filled with chaises and settees, with low tables scattered among them. That arrangement was obviously intended to allow the guests to recline at their leisure, eating and drinking and engaging in . . . certain other activities.

From what Lia could tell, those activities seemed more prevalent than enjoying a light repast. She saw one man nestle a plump strawberry in the even plumper décolletage of his companion. The effect was rendered more licentious by the fact that the pair had dressed as a bishop and a nun, although the lady's religious habit featured an extremely low-cut bodice and skirts that fell open to reveal her garters and stockings. When the bishop leaned over to gobble the strawberry up from between his companion's breasts, Lia had to swallow a dismayed squeak.

That display, however, was tame compared to the activities of a couple on an adjoining chaise. The gentleman—and she used the term loosely—had a giggling and quite buxom lady who was dressed in the manner of a young schoolgirl perched on his lap. He tugged on her bodice until one of her breasts popped out like a pastry freshly baked from the oven. After pouring his champagne over her chest, he bent to suck her nipple into his mouth with what could only be described as a marked display of enthusiasm.

Mortified, Lia yanked her attention away to stare desperately at the back of the tall gentleman in front of her. Heat flushed through her body and perspiration began to trickle down her spine. Sucking in several deep breaths, she tried to calm herself even as she cursed her naïveté. She'd stumbled into the middle of an orgy and she had only herself to blame.

Barbara had begun a lively chat with a dandyish fellow dressed as a cavalier, so Lia had plenty of time to stew about her decision to attend the masquerade. Although she was well aware that a Cyprians' ball was likely to involve inappropriate behavior, she hadn't expected to stumble across outright nudity in the supper room. Surely there must be ways to find a protector that didn't involve dipping one's nipples in champagne or getting one's backside groped by strangers.

When fingers brushed against *her* backside a moment later, she jumped and let out a squawk. She stumbled into the man in front of her, slapping her palms on his broad back to regain her balance. He whipped around and peered down at her, a scowl on his unmasked features. His gaze seemed to snag on her mouth, then slowly traveled down over her figure as horrified recognition dawned in his eyes.

Damn, damn, damn.

Lia's heart began thudding like a hammer against an anvil and for a dreadful moment she was afraid she might swoon. The blasted man had seen through her disguise.

"Good God," exclaimed Sebastian Sinclair. "What in hell's name are you doing here, Miss—"

She slapped a gloved hand to his lips. "Miss Smith. My name is Miss Smith."

Looking stupefied, he slowly removed her hand from

his mouth. Lia briefly thought about dropping to her knees and crawling away into the crowd.

"Everything all right, love?" Barbara asked in a sharp voice. She planted herself by Lia's side, regarding Sinclair with thinly veiled hostility. He, in turn, studied the actress with obvious disapproval.

"Yes," Lia said weakly. "I know this gentleman. I think he's just a little surprised to see me here."

"Utterly astounded would be a better description," he growled. "Why *are* you here, Miss Kin—er, Smith? Who are you with?"

She grimaced. "It's rather complicated to explain."

"Not that she has to explain herself to the likes of you," Barbara said.

"And who the bloody hell are you anyway?" Sinclair shot back.

"I'm her friend. And who the bloody hell are you?"

"I'm her friend, too, and a better one than you if it was your idea to bring Miss *Smith* to such an affair as this."

Barbara propped her fists on her hips. "Now see here," she said belligerently, "you've got no business lecturing me or her. Especially since I don't have a bloody clue who you are."

Barbara's cavalier gallantly but unfortunately decided to intervene. "Sir, I do hope you're not disturbing these ladies. I shall be quite perturbed if you are."

Sinclair, who towered over the man by several inches, let out a derisive snort. "How terrifying. I suggest you mind your own damn business before I take you by the collar of that absurd costume and throw you out the nearest window."

As the cavalier began to bluster, Barbara crowded forward, practically stepping on Sinclair's toes.

"You listen to me, you sauce box," she began, waving a finger in his face.

Lia grabbed her arm. "Don't," she murmured. "We're attracting too much notice."

Sinclair cast a quick glance around and let out a low curse. "You're right. We can't talk here. Are you truly without an escort to this damnable affair?"

Barbara started to bristle, but Lia kept a restraining hand on her arm. "We came with another friend and her gentleman, but I believe they're off dancing."

"By gentleman, I don't suppose you mean Sir Dominic, Lord Lendale, or the Duke of Leverton," he said dryly.

She couldn't help a laugh. "You must be joking."

"Right, then you shouldn't be here. I'm taking you home this instant."

"No, you are not," she said, starting to get annoyed. "If you want an explanation, I'm happy to give you one, but that is all."

He cast another stony glance around and nodded tersely. He took her by the elbow to steer her out of the line.

Barbara shot a hand out to stop them. "You don't have to go with him if you don't want to, miss. We'll find Sir Nathan if you want this gent to leave you alone."

"Sir Nathan Prudhoe? He's your escort?" Sinclair looked even more incredulous.

Lia thought it best to ignore his question. "Thank you, Barbara, but this gentleman is truly a friend. I'll talk to him for a bit and then come look for you. Where shall I find you?"

Barbara eyed Sinclair with a dubious expression, but finally gave a shrug. "I'll meet you in the corridor outside the ballroom. We'll snaffle some champagne and victuals and wait for you on the benches."

Lia nodded. "I'll join you soon."

"And make sure you treat miss with respect," Barbara said, glaring at Sinclair. "Or you'll have me to answer to. I promise you won't like it."

"If she wanted to be treated with respect, she wouldn't have come to a blasted Cyprians' ball," Sinclair said.

He wrapped his hand around Lia's elbow and began hauling her through the crowd. Because they were wading in the opposite direction of the flow, it was slow going and would have been slower still but for the fact that Sinclair was all but shoving people out of their way. Unfortunately, he was leaving a chorus of protests in their wake.

"Mr. Sinclair," she finally said with asperity, "if you were trying to draw attention to us, you couldn't do a better job."

He muttered another curse but moderated his pace. "Forgive me, Miss K—"

"Smith."

"Smith," he ground out. "I didn't mean to be quite so rough. You may put it down to the fact that I was stunned out of my senses by running into you at a function of this disreputable nature."

"I was surprised to see you, too," she said. And a little disappointed. Sinclair didn't seem like the type to consort with the demi-monde. "Do you often frequent affairs like this?"

"I certainly don't make a habit of it," he said as they skirted the edge of the dance floor. "I was out for the evening with some friends and found myself here."

"Just as I did," she said, trying to brazen it out. "How funny."

He gave her another incredulous look. "Yes. Hilarious."

Sinclair quickly steered her to a large window alcove, where a column would give them a degree of privacy. He all but shoved her into the shadowed space, turning his back to the crowd to shield her.

"Now, *Miss Smith*, please explain why I shouldn't haul you back to Sir Dominic's house this instant?"

Chapter Fifteen

"Because you have no right to do so, for one thing," Lia said, trying not to glower at Sinclair. She was exceedingly weary of well-intentioned males trying to run her life. "And I hardly think dragging me out of a ballroom under protest will achieve your desired end of shielding me from gossip. Just the opposite, don't you think?"

When he started to argue, she pointedly looked past him to the long French windows that appeared to lead out to a terrace. "Unless, of course, you wish to throw me over your shoulder and spirit me away through the back garden," she added. "I'm sure that wouldn't look the slightest bit suspicious. And think of the fuss my friends would kick up when they discover I'm missing."

Sinclair blew out a disgruntled breath. "I am tempted to haul you out through the back garden, believe me."

"Go right ahead. But you'd better be ready to explain your actions, because I won't go willingly. In fact, it's entirely possible my mask will fall off, and then you'll be stuck. If people see us in such a compromising situation, you might even be forced to declare your hand. Otherwise, you would risk being murdered by one of the men in my very overprotective family, who will no doubt hold you responsible for demolishing what's left of my reputation."

His mouth dropped open to give him a somewhat breathless look. Obviously, that thought hadn't occurred to the poor man.

"I don't think you want to do that, do you?" she asked gently. "Marry me, I mean."

He cleared his throat. "Well, no. I mean, of course, any man would be honored to call you his wife, but that's not . . . oh, bloody hell. You know what I mean," he said with a wince.

"I do. There is another alternative, of course. Would you like me to become your mistress?"

His eyes popped wide with outrage. "Of course not! What kind of loose screw do you take me for? Of all the outrageous suggestions . . . to think I would take advantage of a gently bred lady such as yourself."

Lia nodded. "Then I think we understand each other, sir. Please believe that I know exactly what I'm doing. My friends will see me safely home, so that should set your conscience at ease."

"That doesn't do a damn thing for my conscience," he said tartly. "Not with Sir Nathan as your escort. He doesn't know who you are, does he? As far as I can tell, he's entirely lacking in morals and is an inveterate gossip to boot."

"I'm not a complete idiot, Mr. Sinclair. Of course he doesn't know who I am. As for my two friends, I trust them completely—if for no other reason than my stepfather would probably fire them from his acting troupe if he knew they'd helped me tonight."

He shook his head. "You're not just kicking up larks, are you? You're courting disaster by doing this, you know. It's completely insane."

Lia reminded herself that he was trying to be helpful.

"I'm touched by your concern, but please believe that I know what I'm about."

"If you're on the lookout for a paramour, I must disagree with you."

When his gaze flicked over her body, lingering for a few moments on her bosom, she was grateful she wore a mask to hide her blush. It wasn't pleasant to present oneself as an object of commerce to strangers, but to see herself judged in that context by someone she knew—and liked—was disturbing.

The disapproval in his eyes gave her a taste of the future. The people she loved would feel more than disapproval—they would feel betrayed, probably even disgusted. Jack would want nothing to do with her. He would be infuriated that she had so recklessly disregarded his wishes and would no doubt vow never to see her again.

Which is exactly what you want, is it not?

"What's wrong?" Sinclair asked, his expression transforming into one of concern. "You're looking rather ill just now."

She forced a smile. "I'm laced too tightly into this costume, that's all."

He waved a vaguely imperious finger at her. "What are you supposed to be, a milkmaid? Where's your bucket and stool?"

"I checked them with a footman, obviously." She made a point of perusing his garb. He looked very elegant in discreet black and white, with a black silk evening cloak flung carelessly over his shoulders.

She waved a vague finger back at him. "That's not much of a costume. What are you supposed to be?"

"A bored gentleman of business," he said dryly.

She laughed. "I suppose that fits, then. And I'm afraid I agree that this affair is rather boring, despite its salacious nature."

For a moment Lia considered sounding the retreat and

allowing Sinclair to escort her home. But who knew when she would have another opportunity to scout out potential protectors? She couldn't afford to let this opportunity go to waste.

"Then let me take you home," he said gently, as if reading her thoughts. "You don't need to do this."

Lia shrugged. "Not true. And I suspect you've already heard why I do."

"I have, but that ugly incident wasn't your fault."

"It doesn't matter whose fault it was, the damage is done."

"Your family would not agree."

"My family is wrong."

She thought she saw pity in his gaze. That felt worse than his disapproval; pity was likely the only charitable feeling she could expect from her family and friends. And pity so often turned to scorn.

"If you'll excuse me, sir," she said, desperate now to make her escape. "I must find my—"

"I know what it's like to be an outsider, you know," he interrupted. "To realize that no one can understand you."

She couldn't repress a snort. "I don't mean to be rude, Mr. Sinclair, but you're wealthy and the son of a well-regarded baronet. Short of being a royal, one couldn't be much more of an insider, especially among the beau monde." If he noted the irony in her statement—because royal blood ran through *her* veins—he didn't acknowledge it.

"I don't pretend to understand your particular situation," he said, "but I will say that appearances can be deceiving. My personal history, for instance, involved an exile from my home and everyone I cared for. I was in India for over ten years and it was not by choice."

His somber expression tugged at her sympathies as well as her curiosity. Lia wished she could ask for an explanation, but she'd already spent too much time with him.

Barbara would come looking for her sooner rather than later and she didn't want to risk another scene.

She briefly pressed his forearm. "You're very kind, Mr. Sinclair. Please don't worry about me. I promise to be careful."

When he tried to hold on to her, she evaded his grasp.

"Wait, don't go," he said in a sharp tone.

Lia dodged away from him and onto the dance floor. She heard him curse but didn't look back. Instead, she wove between the groups of dancers, ducking low as she made her way across the wide room to the other side. When she finally cleared the floor, she glanced back and breathed a sigh of relief. Sinclair was lost in the mass of bodies that crowded the room. With any luck, he would respect her wishes and leave her alone for the rest of the evening.

She made her way into a long corridor that appeared to stretch to the back of the mansion. It was dimly lit and much cooler than the ballroom or saloons and she longed to take off her mask and breathe in the fresher air. But that would be a mistake. Despite her almost careless manner with Sinclair, she intended to be very careful. She had no desire to be pitched into the middle of another scandal before she had a plan and the resources to control the outcome.

The occasional servant scurried by, but Lia had the corridor mostly to herself. She did pass a shadowed alcove that contained a couple behaving a bit too amorously for her taste, but Barbara and her new friend were nowhere to be seen.

She found a comfortable bench and was settling in to wait when three gentlemen came out of the ballroom and turned in her direction. Clearly in their cups, they burst into raucous laughter and began to weave down the hall.

As they came closer, Lia's heart lurched. She recognized one of the men from the Levertons' ball. In fact, she'd not only chatted with the man—a middle-aged, widowed viscount—she'd even stood up with him for a set of country dances.

Fighting panic, she debated her best course of action. Dressed as she was, it was unlikely he would recognize her, especially in the dimmer lighting of the hall. She curled up on the corner of the bench, hoping they were too inebriated to pay her notice.

As usual, she wasn't that lucky. The viscount changed direction and weaved to a stop in front of her, a gently puzzled expression marking his pleasant features.

"I say, don't I know you?" he asked, hiccuping a bit.

Lia shot to her feet, dropping a quick curtsy while she glanced past them and calculated a path of escape. "No, milord," she said, affecting a nasal tone. "Never seen you before in my life."

He frowned. "Voice ain't familiar, but your nose and mouth . . . I swear I've seen you before."

One of his companions dug him in the ribs. "Who cares where you saw her? She's here now and a tasty little piece she is." He gave Lia a sloppy leer that made her hand itch with the desire to slap him.

"That she is," said the third man. He was tall and thin and, bizarrely, wore a jester's belled cap with his sober evening attire. When he held up a quizzing glass to inspect her, he was so jug-bitten he almost poked himself in the eye. "Would you like to share a beverage with us, miss?" he asked in a polite tone.

"And then we can take turns sharing *you* afterward," the leering one added.

They erupted into more laughter, the rude one slapping his knee as if he'd just made the cleverest joke.

While they were doubled over, Lia scampered around them and started backing away. "No thank you, sirs. I . . . I've got an assignation with another gent. You'll have to excuse me."

The viscount snapped his fingers. "Ah, I definitely know you. Just give me a minute and I'll figure it out."

Confound it. She'd allowed her accent to waver. Mama was right; she was an utter failure as an actress.

The leering man started after her. "Now, don't run off, my pretty one. I'm sure we can give you much better romps than your mysterious beau."

"And I want to see who's under that mask," said the viscount. He began stumbling after her with stubborn determination.

Lia threw dignity to the winds and bolted down the hall. With her tormenters in hot, if clumsy pursuit, she rounded a corner into another hallway. Flinging open the door to the first room she came to, she looked inside. The small sitting room was thankfully empty.

And it had a key in the lock.

She quickly closed the door and twisted the key. Then she slumped against the wooden panels, struggling to catch her breath. Outside, the viscount and his friends loudly called for her and crashed about like a herd of wild boar. When one of them thumped on the door and rattled the knob, she slapped a hand over her mouth to stifle a startled yelp.

She crept back a few feet, holding her breath. It was highly unlikely they could break in, but they could hunt down a footman to open it for them. Or else they could simply try to wait her out. Lia couldn't help castigating herself for allowing Sinclair to separate her from her friends.

Trying to keep her panic in check, she stole over to the room's only window and hissed out a small sigh of relief. There was a large balustrade that fronted a wall separating the house and a lane. If necessary, she could climb out the window and across the balustrade and then shimmy down the wall. It was a rather high drop to the lane, but she had climbed any number of trees in her youth and fallen off limbs that were higher than the top of that wall. While she'd probably ruin the costume and receive a scolding from her mother that was infinitely preferable to fending off three drunks who'd taken her for a light-skirt.

Of course they did, you ninny.

After all, she'd done everything she could to advertise that very fact. Still, it was infuriating that they hadn't accepted her very polite refusal. No man had the right to force himself on any woman, even if she were a light-skirt.

With a sigh, she dropped into a leather reading chair by the empty fireplace grate, rubbing the corded muscles in the back of her neck. So far, her incipient career as a courtesan had proven as ill-favored and hapless as her acting career.

Her biggest problem at the moment remained the viscount, and the chance that he might identify her. Lia could only hope her drunken admirers would grow bored and wander off, allowing her to slip out and find Barbara. With any luck, she could be home and in bed long before Chloe and Dominic returned from the opera.

Within a few minutes, the ruckus in the hall began to lessen. One man proclaimed his boredom with the search, and soon their voices receded. A blessed silence once more reigned in that part of the house.

Cautiously, she got up and tiptoed to the door, then peered through the keyhole. Seeing nothing, she turned the key and cracked the door open, peeking out but ready to slam it at the first sign of trouble. Fortunately, the shadowed hall was disturbed only by the sound of music echoing faintly from the distant ballroom.

She hurried out of the room, untying the long sash at her waist as she went. Wrapping it over her head and across her chest, she tucked the ends into her bodice. Her priority was no longer to flaunt her plumage to attract a male but to disguise herself as much as possible.

When she came to the main corridor, she stopped to peer around the corner. A few guests strolled outside the ballroom or headed toward the terrace, and footmen bearing trays rushed hither and yon. Fortunately, the viscount and his drunken friends were not in sight.

Unfortunately, there was no Barbara in sight either.

Lia was beginning to think she'd have to brave the street and hire a hackney because forging through the mob in the ballroom in search of her friends was a daunting prospect. It had never occurred to her that there would be so many vexing details to confront when attending a Cyprians' ball. Clearly, she needed to pay more attention to the practical aspects of her future career.

While she pondered her next move, she heard the patter of hurried footsteps. She spun around to see Barbara rushing toward her, wide skirts bunched up in her hands. Breathing out a sigh, Lia sagged against the wall, feeling weak with relief.

"There you are," she said as Barbara skidded to a halt. "I was beginning to—"

The girl grabbed her arm. "Where have you been? I've been searching everywhere."

Lia blinked, disconcerted by her sharp tone. "I had to hide from some very persistent gentlemen. One was convinced he knew me from somewhere."

Barbara grimaced. "Did he?"

"Yes, but he was too drunk to puzzle it out and I was able to escape before he got close."

"Thank God." She started to drag Lia back the way she'd come. "We'd have been in an awful mess if he'd recognized you."

"Barbara, what's wrong? Why are we going to the back of the house?"

"Because Amy's in trouble." Her voice was thin with

anxiety. "She and Prudhoe got into a fight and he hit her. Hard."

Lia stumbled. "What? Why?"

Barbara urged her on. "Because he's a bastard, that's why. She wouldn't do something he wanted her to do."

"What did he want her to do?"

Her friend threw her a grim look. "Nothing you need to know, love. Trust me on that."

That sounded awful. "Where are they?"

"There's an orangery at the back of the house. When you didn't show, my gentleman and I took a short stroll and that's where we ended up. Prudhoe and Amy were already there and we heard them fighting."

"Did you go in?"

"Of course I did. He was shaking poor Amy like a rattle, the bastard. I yelled at him to stop, but he told me he'd give it to me next if I didn't watch out. I tried to get my gentleman to help, but he tore out of there like his arse was lit with a rocket. That's when I decided to look for you. Maybe the two of us can get her away from him."

"Should we try to get a footman to help?" Lia asked.

Barbara grimly shook her head. "They won't want to help neither. Not against a lord."

They rounded another corner and halted in front of a set of doors that led into the glass-fronted observatory. Barbara reached for the door, but Lia stopped her. "Barbara, listen. I'll try to talk some sense into Prudhoe and get Amy out of there. But I want you to return to the ballroom to see if you can find my friend, Sinclair. He's a very good man and he'll come to our aid."

The girl's eyes went wide. "I can't leave you alone with that pig. Your ma will kill me if she finds out."

"It's fine, I promise. I can manage it." If worse came to worse, she'd take off her mask and threaten Prudhoe with the wrath of Sir Dominic Hunter. It would expose her to scandal, but it was a risk she had to take.

She gave Barbara a little shove. "Now run."

Her friend lifted her up Elizabethan skirts and took off down the hall.

Lia sucked in a calming breath, ordering her pounding heart to slow down. Then she threw back her shoulders, opened the door, and strode into the room.

She came to an abrupt halt because she could barely see more than a few feet ahead of her. The various potted plants and trees cast heavy shadows and the light seemed filtered and diffused throughout the unusually shaped glass structure. Lia blinked several times, forcing her vision to adjust.

Her hearing was fine, however, and what she heard made her stomach churn. Amy's voice was thick with tears as she pleaded with Prudhoe to stop hurting her. Lia picked up her skirts and rushed up the center aisle of the orangery, following the voices. She rounded a high stand of potted bamboo plants and ground to a halt.

Amy was on the floor, huddled against the side of an ornate marble fountain. The cheerful burble of water flowing from a stone cherub's jug formed a ghastly counterpoint to the girl's wrenching sobs. Her diaphanous gown was torn, exposing most of her breasts. Her hair was badly disheveled, as if someone had dug his fingers into her coiffure and dragged her across the room. Even in the dim light, Lia could make out the bruises on the dancer's face and neck.

The girl was hunched over, her hands wrapped tightly around herself as if to guard her midsection. Prudhoe loomed menacingly above her.

"Don't kick me again," Amy sobbed. "I'll do whatever you want."

"Yes, you will, you whore," the brute said. "And you'll

do it whether I hit you or not." He barked out an ugly laugh. "I do enjoy hitting your sweet, plump flesh, my little Amy. It feels so lovely under my fist or boot."

When he drew back his leg, Lia catapulted forward.

"Stop it, you monster," she yelled, shoving him from behind with all her might.

Prudhoe stumbled hard, cursing as he crashed heavily against the side of the fountain.

Lia braced herself, legs wide. She didn't dare turn her back on him, so she just threw a quick glance over her shoulder at Amy, who'd all but curled up into a shivering ball.

"Can you get up?" Lia asked.

"I . . . I think so."

As Amy laid trembling hands on the rim of the fountain and started to pull herself up, Prudhoe made it up on his knees, his features twisted with pain. His dark eyes blazed with a fury that made Lia's heart pound its way into her throat.

"You goddamn bitch," he snarled. "I'll bloody well kill you both."

"I think not." Lia was rather astonished by her outward sense of control because her insides were trembling like a broken branch in a gale. "In fact, if you don't take yourself off immediately, I will report you to the magistrate myself. I assure you, he'll take this matter very seriously."

Prudhoe finally hauled himself to his feet in an awkward maneuver; his shoulder was clearly damaged. Lia had no regrets about injuring him.

"Really?" he said with a nasty hoot as he planted himself in front of her. "Do you think a magistrate will take the word of two whores over that of a baronet? Hardly, you daft bitch."

"While whores are just as deserving of justice as anyone else, may I point out that we are actresses? Mr. Lester will be livid when he sees how you've abused poor Amy. I'm sure he'll swear out charges."

Prudhoe went still, his head tilted at an odd angle as he studied her. Then his lips peeled back in a vicious smile. Lia silently thanked the saints that she wasn't a woman prone to fainting because the evil intent in his expression was truly unnerving.

"Not when Mr. Lester—and the magistrate, if necessary—learn that you and your little friend tried to rob me."

"Trust me, Sir Nathan, Mr. Lester will not believe you."

"How's this for an idea? Why don't I fetch a constable right now and see what he has to say about it? Or, better yet, why don't we proceed directly to Bow Street? Then we'll see who believes whom."

Amy clutched at Lia's skirts. "Miss, I can't go to Bow Street," she whispered in a shaky voice. "It'll be a huge scandal. Please, let's just get out of here."

"Nobody's going to Bow Street," Lia said firmly. "Except possibly Sir Nathan after we tell Mr. Lester what happened here."

Unfortunately, her threat seemed to have little effect on the dreadful man. He took a menacing step forward. Amy whimpered, sinking down again. She kept a firm grip on Lia's skirts, which would hamper their ability to escape.

"Not another step, Sir Nathan," Lia ordered, holding up an imperious hand. If Barbara didn't return with help soon, she'd have to resort to desperate measures.

Naturally, he ignored her and moved closer. The glint in his eyes told her that he was enjoying himself, despite his injured shoulder.

"What will you do if I don't obey your silly commands?" he drawled. "Will you hit me again? I assure you, the result will not be pleasant if you do. But how I punish you in return will be exceedingly pleasant for me."

If only Gillian were here, she would deliver a smashing

uppercut to the bastard's jaw, or stab him, if necessary. Lia, unfortunately, had never trained in the pugilistic arts, nor did she carry a knife, although she intended to address that oversight in the future.

For now, she could only rely on her wits.

As calmly as she could, she reached behind her head and untied her mask. When she pulled it down, Prudhoe's mouth sagged open.

"Bloody hell," he muttered. "You're the Kincaid girl."

"I am also the cousin of the Duchess of Leverton and, more to the point, the niece of Lady Hunter." Lia gave him a bright, artificial smile. "You do know who my aunt's husband is, do you not? Sir Dominic Hunter is a magistrate, and an extremely powerful one, as I'm sure you've heard."

He stared at her for a few seconds longer, clearly stunned. But then he shrugged it off, as if her words held no more inconvenience than a pesky fly. Her gambit had failed to have the desired effect. It probably didn't help that the man was likely made reckless by intoxication.

"I also know what happened at the Leverton ball," he said. "You were exposed as a whore, just like your mother. And if you were still under the protection of Dominic Hunter, you wouldn't be cavorting with whores at a Cyprians' ball."

"I'm simply enjoying an evening out with friends," she said.

He ignored that bit of errant nonsense. "I'd also wager you're looking for a protector, aren't you?" he mused. "What other choice do you have? No decent man would have you, naturally. You're soiled goods."

Blast. He might be drunk, but he wasn't stupid. Lia had now effectively put her fate into the hands of the worst sort of person and there would be no recovering from it.

He patted his chest. "Well, I'm happy to inform you that you've found your new protector. Your little friend Amy has grown most dreary; it's time to replace her with someone fresh. In fact, I've a mind to have a little taste right now. Shall we see what's between those sweet thighs of yours?"

Desperately, Lia tried to pull Amy to her feet. "If you touch me, I'll kill you," she said through clenched teeth.

"I'm going to do more than touch you," Prudhoe snarled.

His hand shot out so quickly that he caught her off guard. His fingers curled into her bodice, slipping inside her stays. Lia tried to pull away, but he easily yanked her against him. His strength was frightening.

"Let me go, you bastard," she growled. His other arm went around her, his fingers digging into her side. Still she managed to dodge his wet, openmouthed kiss as he bobbed down.

"Let her go," Amy shrieked, trying to shove at Prudhoe's legs while still holding on to Lia.

She appreciated the effort, but Amy's weight was throwing her off balance. Lia clamped her lips shut for what she knew would be a slobbering, disgusting kiss. But perhaps when Prudhoe was occupied with that nasty business, she'd be able to get enough purchase to give him a knee to the groin.

Then she felt a rush of movement from behind her and something as hard as stone butted against her back— something warm and blessedly familiar. The clean, masculine scent of him, the shape of his muscular frame—she knew it all instantly, as well as she knew herself.

Prudhoe's hold on her bodice loosened and he went slack-jawed with surprise. He took two quick steps back.

"You'd best listen to the girl," Jack said in a voice that promised death. When she shivered at his icy tone, his hands curled protectively over her hips. "Because if you ever touch her again, I will bloody well tear you apart. Or maybe I'll just do that anyway, for the fun of it."

Chapter Sixteen

Prudhoe snatched his hand away. Despite the alarm flaring in his gaze, he managed a credible sneer. "No need for threats, Lendale. How was I to know the girl was yours? Besides, I barely touched her."

Yes, she's mine.

The words rang like a clarion bell in Jack's head.

"That's the only reason you're not lying in a mangled heap on the floor." He glanced down at Amy Baxter, who was huddled against Lia's leg. The dancer sported nasty bruises on her cheek and jaw and her lip was cut. She wiped a shaking hand across her tearstained face, smearing blood and makeup in a ghastly trail of red.

"Then again," Jack said softly, "maybe I'll beat you to a pulp anyway."

He pulled Lia more snuggly against him. Her sweet bottom pressed against his groin and her lush hips curved under his fingertips. Dressed as she was, she was a fantasy and a dream unfulfilled—*his* dream. He'd been resisting that realization for weeks, but seeing Prudhoe's filthy hands all over Lia's body had brought the lesson home with thundering clarity—and horrific timing.

"Certainly no one could blame you," Lia said in a crisp

voice. "But the better course of action would be to call the constable. Sir Nathan should be arrested immediately."

She twisted in Jack's arms to look at him. Her color was high and her sky-blue eyes glittered with residual fury, but she didn't seem frightened or cowed.

Although he was enormously grateful the bastard hadn't injured her, Jack had to bite down on the impulse to thunder out an epic scold. Never had he seen a situation more out of control, for a dozen reasons he intended to outline once he got Lia alone. She'd gone entirely beyond the pale this time. It would be a miracle if he managed to salvage the tattered remnants of her reputation.

She gave him an encouraging smile. "Shall I ask a footman or the butler to fetch the constable, or shall we take Sir Nathan to Bow Street ourselves?"

Amy tugged on Lia's skirts. "Miss, please don't."

Lia pulled out of Jack's loose embrace to crouch beside her friend, gently brushing the girl's hair away from her bruised face as she murmured a soothing endearment. Old memories flooded through his brain, catching him off guard. Kindness and compassion were Lia's greatest gifts, always freely given. When he thought of the love and generosity she'd shown him over the years, his heart ached with something perilously close to regret.

"Dearest, he beat you. He should be punished," Lia said in a low, urgent voice.

"You'd be wise to listen to Amy, Miss Kincaid," Prudhoe said. "Gossip can be such a nasty thing, don't you know?" He glanced at Jack, a sly smile playing around the corners of his mouth. "I'm sure you agree, Lendale."

Jack's fists balled up with an urgent need to rearrange the coward's features, both for what Prudhoe had done and because his assessment was unfortunately correct.

"I don't care about that," Lia said, throwing Prudhoe a

contemptuous glance. "You shouldn't be allowed to get away with this." She looked up at Jack. "Isn't that right?"

He tried not to wince. "Lia, I would like nothing better than to haul Prudhoe down to Bow Street, but that might not be the best choice for either Miss Baxter or you."

She slowly rose to her feet, although she kept a hand on Amy's shoulder. "What are you talking about? Sir Nathan beat her terribly. No one should be allowed to get away with that."

The pleading look in her eyes begged him to agree and he wished like hell he could. Just thinking about what Prudhoe had done to Amy and what he might have done to Lia made Jack's blood boil. And yet there was very little he could do about it, at least at the moment.

He had his own ideas about how to punish the baronet, but it would take time and discretion to put them into effect.

Prudhoe lifted a mocking eyebrow and then extracted a snuffbox from his waistcoat and flipped it open for a pinch. "Lendale, perhaps you could explain to Miss Kincaid why making a fuss would be a bad idea for both her and for you. Or, should I say, for your dear mother and sister. Imagine their distress when the details of this unpleasant event filter back to them."

"Don't threaten me, Prudhoe," Jack said in a hard voice. "I guarantee you won't enjoy the results."

The baronet's hand wavered, causing him to spill snuff down the front of his waistcoat.

Lia helped Amy to get up and sit on the edge of the fountain. "Jack, please do something," she said in an irritated tone. "We need to get Amy some help."

Prudhoe flicked the snuff off his waistcoat. "I don't care what you do, but I'm leaving."

Jack shot out a hand to stop him. "I'm not done with you."

The baronet flushed an angry red. "Are you going to

challenge me to a duel over a pair of whores? And here I thought you were a sensible man, Lendale."

"You lout," Lia snapped, taking a quick step forward and raising her hand as if to slap him. Jack grabbed her by the arm and hauled her back.

"That's not helping, Lia," he said through clenched teeth.

"Neither are you," she said.

They heard a rush of footsteps and Lia's other companion appeared, closely followed by Sebastian Sinclair.

"Ah, good," Jack said, "I see you found him, Miss . . ."

"Carson, your lordship." The young woman plunked down on the edge of the fountain and wrapped a protective arm around Amy's shoulders.

When Miss Carson came running toward him outside the ballroom, skirts up to her knees and her ridiculous starched collar bouncing in front of her face, Jack had been skating along on the edge of panic. He'd arrived at Welby's only minutes before, and a quick perusal of the ballroom had not yielded any sign of Lia. Fortunately, the young actress had recognized him from his visits to the theater and hadn't hesitated. She'd dragged him into a window alcove and blurted out what had happened, telling him she'd been searching for Sinclair to ask for his help.

Surprised that Sinclair was aware of Lia's presence at the ball—something he intended to get to the bottom of—he'd sent Miss Carson off to find the man. Jack didn't know what role Sinclair was playing in tonight's events, but he was relatively sure he could count on him to lend a helping hand, if necessary, and keep his mouth shut about Lia.

Sinclair wore a rather stunned expression, but it quickly transformed into one of fury when he took in Amy's bruised face. "What the hell is going on here?"

Prudhoe heaved a dramatic sigh. "Really, why don't we

just invite the entire party in to witness our little farce? I'm sure the guests would be vastly amused."

"Another word out of you and I'll kill you myself," Jack said. "And since I'm more soldier than gentleman, be assured that I'll not bother with the absurd formalities of a duel."

The baronet's gaze flared with rage, but he was smart enough not to give voice to thought.

Sinclair bent down to inspect Amy's face. "Sir Nathan did this?"

The girl nodded miserably. "But I don't want any trouble, sir. Please."

He slowly straightened and turned to Prudhoe. His odd green eyes took on a deadly cast. "You're a brave one, beating a defenseless woman."

"She tried to rob me," Prudhoe said. "What was I supposed to do?"

All three women protested at once. "That's a lie," Lia said. "You wanted her to do something she didn't want to do and you beat her when she refused."

Sinclair frowned. "What did he want her to do?"

When Lia cast Amy a grimace, Jack intervened. "It doesn't matter. What matters is getting these women safely home."

"And hauling Sir Nathan in front of the magistrate," Lia said, planting stubborn fists on her hips. Her expression defied Jack to challenge her.

Sinclair looked at Jack. "I can do that, if you wish."

While Prudhoe sputtered an outraged protest, Lia gave Sinclair a dazzling smile. "That would be wonderful, sir. Lord Lendale seems reluctant to do so."

Her approval of Sinclair and her very evident disapproval of him did nothing to sweeten Jack's mood.

"What's the problem, Lendale?" Sinclair asked.

"You were at the Leverton ball last week, were you

not?" He pointedly shifted his gaze to Lia, who scowled back at him.

The other man grimaced. "Right. Of course."

"I don't care about any of that," Lia said. "My reputation is already ruined."

"No, it's not," said Jack, "No thanks to you, I might add."

"Please, I don't want to go to Bow Street," Amy tearfully interjected. "It'll cause an awful fuss and I'll come off the worse for it." She sniffed and took Lia's hand. "And it won't do *you* any good either, Miss Lia, so just let it drop."

"Lia, I'll take care of this," Jack said quietly. "I'll make sure that Prudhoe won't hurt Miss Baxter again, I promise."

She opened her mouth, clearly wanting to object, but Amy tugged on her hand. "Please, I just want to go home."

Lia gave her an odd grimace but then nodded. "Of course, dear. Whatever you want."

"What can I do to help?" Sinclair asked Jack.

"If you could take Miss Carson and Miss Baxter home, I would be grateful. I'll handle Prudhoe and Miss Kincaid."

"You do not need to *handle me*, Jack Easton," Lia grumbled.

Sinclair cast a concerned glance between Jack and Lia. "Is that agreeable to you, Miss Kincaid? I'm certainly happy to take you home if you wish it."

"I'm grateful for your help this evening, Sinclair, but let me make one thing clear," Jack said before Lia could answer. "Miss Kincaid is my business, not yours."

The nabob's eyes went hard as malachite. "I don't take orders from you, Lendale."

"For God's sake," Lia said with disgust. "It's fine, Mr. Sinclair. Please take Amy and Barbara home. Believe me, I have a few things I'd like to discuss with his lordship."

"You're sure?" Sinclair asked.

Lia went up on her toes and pressed a quick kiss to his cheek, causing Sinclair to blink with surprise—and causing

Jack to want to toss the man into the fountain. He began to wonder if he was losing his mind.

"You've been wonderful, sir," Lia said. "Thank you for all your help."

"It's my honor, Miss Kincaid. And I hope to see you very soon."

"Looks like you've got some competition, old boy," Prudhoe drawled to Jack. The idiot clearly had little regard for his own safety.

"Prudhoe, empty your pocket," Jack said as Sinclair wrapped his domino around Amy and then helped her to her feet.

"Pardon?" the baronet said.

Jack gave him a lethal stare and held out his hand.

Grumbling, Prudhoe extracted a small leather purse and handed it over. Jack took out several pound notes before tossing the purse at Prudhoe's feet, eliciting a string of vile curses.

"Make sure you get her a surgeon," he said to Sinclair as he pressed the notes into Amy's hand.

"Thank you, sir, for everything," Amy whispered, giving him a trembling smile.

"I'll come see you tomorrow," Lia said to the girl. "We'll talk about what to tell my mother."

Amy cast her a grateful smile before she limped out, with Sinclair carefully supporting her. Miss Carson dropped a curtsy to Jack, shot a scowl at Prudhoe, and hurried after them.

"Have we addressed everything to your satisfaction, Lord Lendale?" Prudhoe asked sarcastically. "Might I now be released from one of the most dreary episodes of my life?"

"You be quiet, you awful man," Lia snapped. "And, no, we're not done with you."

Swallowing a curse, Jack took her by the arm and

steered her to the fountain, plopping her down on the edge. "For God's sake, please just sit for a moment and allow me to deal with this."

Her chin went up at a mulish tilt. After a moment she rolled her eyes and waved a hand as if to say *get on with it*. He'd seen that disgruntled expression a thousand times when they were young, whenever he'd tried to safeguard her from some little adventure he thought too risky for her. Under other circumstances, he might have been tempted to laugh at seeing it again.

"You've got your work cut out with that one," Prudhoe said. "But you could always let Sinclair take on the job if you don't want it."

Jack crowded him, almost stepping on his toes. "Another comment like that and I'll throttle you on the spot, and no one would give a damn if I did. Now, shut your bloody mouth and listen carefully."

Hatred sparked in the man's gaze, but he retreated a few steps and nodded sullenly.

"You are not to breathe a word about Miss Kincaid's presence here," Jack said. "As far as you're concerned, you have no knowledge of the identity of Miss Baxter's friends. Are we clear on that point?"

The baronet affected a careless shrug.

"Not good enough," Jack said. "I want your sworn word."

"Ha," Lia said. "As if anyone could trust *his* word."

"What would a stupid whore know about a gentleman's word?" Prudhoe shot back.

Jack grabbed the man's throat and slammed him onto an enormous stoneware pot holding an orange tree. When the baronet thrashed, Jack simply leaned into him and shoved the bastard's face against the bark of the trunk.

"Don't ever speak to Lia Kincaid again," he gritted out.

"In fact, don't even look at her. If I ever hear that you've troubled her by so much as a glance, I *will* destroy you."

Prudhoe started to go purple as he struggled, clawing ineffectually at Jack's hand around his throat.

"Do I have your word that you will *never* mention Miss Kincaid's presence here tonight?"

"I don't think he can answer," Lia piped up from her perch on the fountain. "What with you strangling him, as it were."

"I suppose you have a point." He loosened his grip to let the baronet draw in some air. "Do I have your word?"

"Yes, damn you," Prudhoe managed in a gasping voice.

When Jack released him, the baronet stumbled, clutching at the rim of the pot to keep his feet under him.

"You filthy scum," he spat out as he tugged frantically to loosen his cravat. He'd flushed crimson and sweat poured down his face. "Have a care, Lendale. You're not as powerful as you think you are. Your bloody pockets are to let, from what I hear."

"You hear wrong. And you forget that Miss Kincaid also enjoys the protection of the Duke of Leverton and Sir Dominic Hunter, an exceedingly influential magistrate. He'd be most distressed to hear of these events. He might well want to take some sort of action on Miss Baxter's behalf were I to explain matters to him."

"I told Sir Nathan exactly that," Lia said in a triumphant tone. "But he refused to believe me."

"Do you believe it now, Prudhoe?" Jack asked.

The baronet gave another angry nod. "Now are we finished?"

"Yes, you can go."

When he tried to brush by him, Jack grabbed his arm. "And leave Amy Baxter alone as well. My protection extends to her, too."

Prudhoe yanked his arm away. "I wouldn't touch that

whore if you gave me a purse full of gold coins." He stormed away, knocking over a planter as he rounded the corner and disappeared. His pounding footsteps faded, then the door to the orangery slammed shut. A quivering silence settled over the room, broken only by the splash of water falling from the cherub's jug into the fountain.

When Jack turned to face Lia, she regarded him with narrow-eyed disapproval. "Now what's wrong?" he asked.

She jumped to her feet and stalked over. "Aside from the fact that I'm thoroughly sick of men in general?"

"Yes, besides that."

"You let that awful brute off much too lightly."

"In other circumstances, I would agree. But in addition to the fact that Miss Baxter wishes to avoid the notoriety from such a scene, you do realize I'm trying to protect you, do you not?"

She batted that aside with an impatient gesture. "Thank you, but I don't need protecting."

He felt torn between wanting to shake some sense into her and snatching her into his arms and never letting go. "I suppose you didn't need any protection when Prudhoe was molesting you?"

Her shoulders climbed up around her ears. "He wasn't actually molesting me. He was just trying to . . . um . . ."

He crossed his arms over his chest and lifted an eyebrow.

"Oh, blast," she muttered. She absently tugged on her bodice, trying to pull it up. It didn't help. Her breasts were still spilling over the gauzy trim of the absurd costume.

"I'll grant you that he was *trying* to molest me," she said, "but I'm fairly confident I would have been able to fight him off."

"Oh my God," he said, shaking his head.

"But I'm very grateful you appeared when you did." Then she paused to peer at him with a puzzled frown.

"What are you doing here anyway? I was expecting Mr. Sinclair to come to our aid, not you."

"About that; how did he know *you* were here?" He propped his hands on his hips. "And do not tell me you arranged to meet him at a Cyprians' ball. If you did, I'll have to murder him."

"Don't be an idiot, Jack. It was merely an unfortunate happenstance that I ran into him. He recognized me behind the mask, which was quite unnerving." She gave him a rueful smile. "You'll be happy to know that he was very perturbed to see me. In fact, he was quite insistent that I leave and return home."

"Clearly, you didn't listen to him." He took her by the wrist and started hauling her with him along the path.

"Wait one moment, please," she said, tugging back.

Although just as delectable as any pale London beauty, Lia was a sturdy country girl and she was strong enough to slow him down.

"First, tell me how you knew I was here," she said, digging in. She impatiently slapped away a vine trailing down from a hanging pot, which had caught on her filmy sleeve. "More importantly, who else knows?"

The anxiety in her voice was certainly understandable. Her family would fall into fits over this escapade—except for Gillian, who would view it as a corking adventure.

"The Levertons invited me to the opera tonight."

"Along with Sir Dominic and my aunt." She looked disappointed. "You were going to scheme about me, weren't you?"

"Has it slipped your mind that you were to attend the opera as well? Charles thought this might be an acceptable way to introduce me back into your circle of friends without causing too much gossip."

She gave him a weak smile. "Sorry. I didn't know that was the plan."

"I thought you were avoiding me by claiming a headache because you never have headaches."

She sighed and rubbed her forehead. "I might very well be getting one now. And I'm not avoiding you on purpose."

"To quote you, *ha*. In any event, my suspicions were aroused, particularly because Gillian had seen you for tea only a few hours earlier and claimed you were perfectly healthy. I was annoyed until Lady Hunter took me aside at the interval. She said she'd found your behavior these last few days worrying and suspected you were up to something. Not wishing to alarm the others or embarrass you, she asked me to excuse myself to check on you."

Lia winced. "Aunt Chloe is alarmingly perceptive, I must say."

"Indeed she is. At the Hunters' town house, Smithwell informed me that you were abed. After I asked him to check, he returned with the unhappy news that you had absconded from the premises. He was quite stunned by your ability to slip away undetected." He tweaked one of the bedraggled curls tumbling down from her disheveled coiffure. "From what I've heard, no one slips anything past Smithwell. How did you do it?"

"I went from Aunt Chloe's study to the terrace and then over the back wall of the garden. It was easy to cut through the back alley to the street."

"Splendid," he said. "Nothing dangerous about that at all."

"It wasn't anything I haven't done a dozen times before at Stonefell."

"May I note that you're no longer in the country? No respectable woman would go lurking about the city alone. It's insane."

"I didn't lurk. I simply walked a few blocks and caught

a hackney to the theater. It was a completely uneventful journey." She frowned up at him when he muttered a low curse. "I'm sorry, what did you just say?"

"You don't want to know. Anyway, Smithwell guessed that you'd gone to the Pan, so that's where I went. There was a lad watching the stage door—"

"Sammy. He's there on nights when the theater is dark."

"Yes, the lad informed me that you and your companions had raided the costume closet and then met Prudhoe. Fortunately for me, young Sammy made a point of eavesdropping on Miss Baxter and Miss Carson's conversation regarding tonight's outing, which led me here."

She wrinkled her nose. "I didn't think to swear Sammy to secrecy. I suppose that was a flaw in our plans."

"Just one of many."

"You needn't be insulting, Jack," she said, sounding wounded. "Everything would have been fine if not for the fact that Sir Nathan is a monster. I still think we should report him to the magistrate, even if we have to keep Amy's name out of it."

He had to battle the urge to rip out his hair. "I'm trying to keep you from being ruined, you daft woman."

She clapped her hands together and briefly pressed them to her lips. "Jack, you need to get it through your thick skull that I am already ruined."

"Not yet, although you're doing your best to get there. Please tell me that you kept your mask on at all times tonight."

"Of course I kept my mask on. I'm not a complete nincompoop."

"That remains to be seen."

She let out an outraged squeak and tried to push by him.

"Wait," he said, holding her back. "Aside from Prudhoe and Sinclair, you're positive no one else recognized you?"

She started to glare at him, but then her full lips pursed up with uncertainty.

Jack sighed. "What?"

"It's nothing," she finally said, shaking her head. "I was very careful to conceal my identity. I don't want anyone to find out who I am until I'm ready to move ahead with the next step in my plan."

He did his best to keep the frayed threads of his patience intact. "Your plans, which I have no doubt are entirely demented, must remain unfulfilled. I will not allow you to destroy your life this way."

"It's not your choice to make, Lord Lendale," she said, shoving past him. She all but charged along the path to the exit.

"Put on your damn mask," he yelled after her.

He caught up with her at the door as she was struggling to retie her mask. Jack brushed her hands aside and untangled the ribbons. After properly fitting the mask to her face, he secured the ribbons in a sturdy bow at the back of her head. Every second he gazed at the tender curve where her neck met her shoulder, he was tormented by an insane urge to bite that very spot.

One moment he was roaring mad at her and the next he wanted to drag her behind a potted plant, fling up her silly, frothy skirts, and have his way with her. She was turning him into a lunatic.

"Thank you," Lia said in a crisp tone. She flung open the door and stalked into the hall. Jack was right on her heels, but a moment later she skidded to a halt. He crashed into her, and only by luck did he manage to keep them both from going down in a farcical heap on the floor.

"Oh no," she said, staring straight ahead.

"My little dove, there you are!" cried a man. "I've been looking everywhere for you."

Jack peered down the hall. "Is that—"

"I'm afraid so," she muttered.

Viscount Stanley, obviously jug-bitten, stumbled toward them with great enthusiasm, arms open wide and a foolish grin on his face.

"He seems quite happy to see you," Jack said.

"Yes," she said with a sigh. "And he's brought his friends along, too."

Chapter Seventeen

Jack shielded Lia as Stanley and two other men drunkenly wove their way toward them. Should he drag her back to the orangery? That would leave them with no exit and far from help. He likely could handle all three men, given their inebriated state, but that would still place Lia in danger.

"And how do you know these gentlemen?" he asked.

"I don't, except for the viscount," she grumbled. "When I ran into them earlier in the evening, he thought I seemed familiar. Fortunately, I managed to evade them."

"You seem to have had quite a lot of bad luck this evening."

She sighed and briefly rested her forehead on his back. "I am painfully aware of that."

"Lendale, what a pleasant surprise," Stanley said as he staggered to a halt in front of them. "Don't usually see you kicking up larks at a Cyprians' ball."

"And you hopefully won't in the future," Jack replied in a blighting tone.

A befuddled expression crossed Stanley's genial features. "Not a fan of light-skirts and orgies, are you? Then what the devil are you doing here in the first place?"

One of his companions, a tall, cadaverously thin fellow who looked vaguely familiar, cranked sideways to give Lia an oily smile. "His lordship's reasons are obvious, given his pretty little companion. Seems like you're following in your esteemed father's footsteps, after all, Lendale, and bravo, I say. The man had a good eye for the ladies."

He followed up that bon mot by digging an elbow into the side of the man who made up the third leg of their jug-bitten stool. His friend giggled but was too incapacitated to do much more than blow sloppy kisses in Lia's direction.

"Lord Lendale is nothing like his father," she huffed. "And you . . ." She jabbed her finger at the man blowing kisses. "Stop making those noises. It's revolting."

Jack swallowed a groan. He appreciated her show of support, but the blasted girl never seemed to know when to hold her fire.

"Golly, I was just trying to express my appreciation," the fellow slurred, his expression more sad-eyed beagle than pink of the Ton. "No need to bite a man's head off."

Jack reached behind and grabbed Lia's hand. "Indeed. Now, if you'll excuse us, gentlemen, we must be off."

"Wait, what's the rush?" the viscount said, blocking them. His friends shuffled with him in drunken tandem. "The evening's young, ain't it? Besides, we've spent almost an hour looking for you, my little dove. It was cruel of you to run away, just when we were starting to have fun."

"Fun?" Jack jerked his head around to look at Lia. A fiery blush crept out from beneath her mask. "Did they touch you?"

She shook her head but kept her focus on the viscount.

"I already explained," she said, adopting a hideously nasal tone to disguise her voice, "I didn't have time to kick up larks with someone else. You'll have to find some other girls to make sport with because I ain't available."

Obviously, they'd tried to persuade her to join their

sexual adventures so persistently she'd been forced to run and hide. When he thought of all the ways tonight's events might have damaged her, fury leached like poison through his body.

He glared at the sorry specimens of humanity blocking their way and wished he could throttle all of them. Apparently, it showed, because Stanley's eyes went wide with dismay, while his friends shared an uneasy glance.

"What sort of gentleman pursues a woman who wishes to be left alone?" Jack asked. "Rest assured, if not for my duty to this lady's safety, I would happily illustrate exactly how I deal with cowards like you."

"No need to be insulting." Stanley's expression was a nice mix of wounded dignity and fear. "We had no idea the girl was yours, Lendale. We'd have left her alone if she'd only told us so."

"I tried," said Lia, "but you wouldn't listen."

"You didn't say it was *Lendale*," protested the owlish one who'd made the kissing noises.

"And that would have made a difference? My saying no wasn't enough?"

She was so outraged that she'd left off her atrocious faux accent. Lia's melodic voice, with its hint of a Yorkshire accent, was distinctive. The more she spoke, the more likely Stanley would finally be able to place her.

"Let me handle this," Jack said. "And stop talking."

He leveled his most lethal stare at Stanley and his friends. "Let me explain in a way simpletons such as yourselves can understand. When a woman asks to be left alone, you comply. An affair such as this is no excuse to force yourself on any female."

"Such delicate sensibilities, my lord," sneered the one who resembled an animated corpse. "But very well. There are dozens of amenable whores floating around tonight and one's just as good as the other. No point in wasting time on a chit that's already bought and sold." His gaze shifted to Lia's bosom and lingered there. "Although I still wouldn't mind getting a taste of what his lordship is shagging. I'd wager she's as juicy and sweet as a ripe little peach."

Jack sensed Lia's temper shredding completely, so he tightened his hold on her wrist.

"You see here, you disgusting lout," she growled, charging forward before Jack reeled her in and clamped her against his side. She snapped her head up to glare at him. "Let me go this instant." She was in such a rage she'd lost all sense of caution.

"That voice!" exclaimed the viscount. "I've almost got it. Say something else, my dove. Better yet, take off that silly mask and let me see who you really are."

When Stanley made a lunge for Lia's face, Jack yanked her back just in time, wrapping an arm around her waist and lifting her off her feet. Ignoring her protests, he trotted down the hall until he came to the nearest door. He flung it open, carried her inside, and then slammed it shut. Thankfully, there was a key, so he quickly locked the door, cocking an ear for sounds of pursuit.

"I am not a sack of grain to be hauled from one place to the next," Lia said in a frosty tone. "Please put me down."

He set her down but kept his attention on the noises in the hall. He heard lumbering footsteps and incoherent protests; Stanley and his fellow buffoons were still out there.

"I'm sure they'll grow bored and leave in a minute," Lia said. "Although I wish I could give them a piece of my mind. Their behavior has been nothing short of disgusting."

"They deserve it, but that would be an exceedingly bad idea. Viscount Stanley seems fixated on you and he was close to figuring out who you are."

"I suppose you're right." She glanced around the small room and grimaced. It was little more than an antechamber, although a comfortably appointed one. "Oh splendid. Here we go again."

"What was that?"

"I had to hide in this room when the viscount and his friends were chasing me."

The image of those immoral louts pursuing her sent his temper spiking and made him want nothing more than to toss them into a large heap of horse dung in the street. Because he was to be denied that pleasure, he intended to use the time to battle it out with Lia once and for all. She was a captive audience; for once she wouldn't be able to dodge him.

The trick would be getting her to see reason, which he sincerely hoped she would because his patience was at its end. He was even starting to formulate ridiculous ideas about abducting her, spiriting her away from London. Unfortunately, that fantasy usually veered off in a direction that involved secluded country cottages and Lia tied to a bed with his cravats, wearing nothing more than her stockings and garters.

He grappled with that enticing image, finally shoving it to the back of his brain. Now was hardly the time to be indulging in lewd fantasies. He could never have Lia, and the sooner he got that through his thick skull, the better.

She wandered over to plop into the leather club chair in front of the empty grate. Sighing, she pushed up her mask and then leaned forward to rub one of her ankles, as if it pained her. The pose gave Jack an almost unimpeded view down the front of her bodice. In fact, if he moved forward just a wee bit, he would no doubt be able to see her entire—

"What a total disaster this evening has been," she grumbled, derailing his thought. "It's incredibly annoying, given all the trouble I had to go through to attend."

Jack leaned back against the door, forcing himself not to

look at her chest. He would *not* be like the Stanleys of the world, hounding women. He had vowed long ago never to follow in his father's disreputable footsteps.

"You have a talent for understatement, pet," he said. "And although I'm truly sorry you had to suffer insults from swinish men tonight, coming here was an incredibly foolhardy thing to do. You don't belong in this world and you know it."

When she took off her shoe to rub her toes he was momentarily transfixed by the delicate arch of her foot and her pretty ankle. The sharp tone of her voice, however, yanked him back to the conversation.

"Does any woman belong in a place like this? Most of what I saw tonight was, well, shocking, frankly."

"Of course it was shocking. It's meant to be shocking."

She made a disgusted little snort and went to work on her other foot. "Truly, I don't know how these poor women can bear to be touched with such lewd intent."

He couldn't help a rueful smile at her naïveté. "There are some women who are quite amenable, although I'm sure most would prefer not to be viewed as a commodity. But a number of the ladies—not all of them prostitutes, I might add—generally enjoy the evening's activities as much as the men do."

She dropped her shoe. "Really? Scampering about in public half-naked and letting men . . ." She waved a vague hand. "Well, I'm sure you know. The financial compensation hardly seems worth it."

"For some it is. I think you already know that, given your family's history."

She shot upright, giving him an offended stare. "I can hardly imagine Granny or my mother participating in orgies. They have too much dignity."

Jack had heard enough about Lia's mother to know she'd

probably taken part in more than one Cyprians' ball in her younger years. That tidbit, however, he would keep to himself. "If you think it's so bloody awful, what the hell are you doing here, Lia? What was the point of this misadventure?"

"We've discussed it a million times," she said impatiently, "and I'm not getting into it again. Suffice it to say that I don't have a choice in the matter."

He dug his fingertips into the door's wood panels. "You know very well you do have choices; we've discussed those a million times, too."

Her full lips pursed, forming a pretty rosebud that nonetheless suggested a scolding was imminent. But then she blinked twice and her mouth rounded into a silent *oh*, as if something—an image or an idea—had surprised her.

Oh hell. He knew *that* look, too.

She folded her hands neatly in her lap and demurely tucked her feet under her skirts—or tried to; the bloody dress stopped several inches above her ankles. Still she made a game effort at looking as ladylike as she could under the circumstances.

His sweet girl was getting ready to pull something over on him.

"Of course you're absolutely right," she said in a cheerful tone.

"That you have choices?" he asked cautiously. "I'm glad you agree."

She gave him a smile so indulgent it raised the hairs on the back of his neck. "Not that, silly. You're right about not wanting me to sneak around the demi-monde searching for a protector. Not only is it a disgusting exercise, it's not a very efficient way of achieving my ends."

"That's not what I was talking about at—"

She held up a hand. "Please don't interrupt, Jack. Whether you like it or not, this is happening. And instead of putting obstacles in my way, I would be most grateful if you decided to help me. That is what a true friend would do."

He felt sure his eyeballs had just popped out to the end of their stalks. "Help you become a whore? Are you mad?"

Her smile wobbled a bit. "There's no need to be rude. I don't want you to help me become a whore. I want you to help me find a protector."

"It amounts to the same thing," he said incredulously.

"I do not agree. A prostitute has very little control over her circumstances and life. But if I can find a suitable protector, one who is both respectful and trustworthy, I believe I can negotiate an arrangement suitable to both of us. That will allow a degree of independence and control in my life that has been missing—as well as allow me to comfortably support Granny."

"You want to find someone who is both respectful *and* trustworthy? Given what I know about most of the men in the Ton who keep mistresses, I'd say you have your work cut out for you," he said sarcastically.

"Exactly my point. I never thought of you as dense, Jack, but I'm beginning to wonder."

"Lia, what the hell do you want from me?"

"I would like your assistance in identifying potential candidates and establishing qualifications, pointing out what characteristics I should be looking for. Of course, I need to find someone who's plump in the purse—"

"Which rules me out, of course," he snapped before he could stop himself.

She looked taken aback. "You rejected me, remember?"

"I'm just trying to make a point," he said, trying to recover his footing.

"Which is?"

It was no longer a question of him possibly losing his mind. He was now convinced it had gone permanently missing. "I'm not going to waste my time trying to explain something that should be perfectly obvious."

Her scoff indicated she was well aware of his profound mental lapse.

She studied him for a few moments with a skeptical twist to her mouth. "Jack, do you truly want me trolling events such as this one?" she finally asked. "Because that's the only alternative I can think of at the moment."

He jabbed a hand at her. "No, but I am not helping you find a protector."

She jumped to her feet and stalked over to him, her lovely breasts jiggling with the force of her stride. "Then how in God's name am I to support myself and Granny? Every other suitable avenue has been closed to me, thanks to my mother and *yours*."

He winced. "Yes, I know. And I am sorry about that, which I'm sure you realize."

"I don't want you to be sorry. I want you to help me achieve the necessary ends." She shook her head, looking somber. "I'm the child and grandchild of courtesans, Jack. My course in life was marked out long ago. All I want now is do the best I can in a situation I can no longer avoid."

He dragged his hands through his hair, tugging on the ends. It was that or he might drag Lia across his knee and spank her for putting him in so untenable a position. "You really expect me to do that, as a sign of friendship?"

Studying him, she crossed her arms. God, he wished she'd stop doing that. Every time she did, he had to wrestle with the unholy temptation to yank down her bodice and feast on her gorgeous breasts.

Lia unleashed a smile that could coax angels down from the heavens. "All I ask is that you assist me in drawing up a list of qualifications and perhaps identify a few suitable candidates. You must know one or two gentlemen who would be willing to consider me. In fact . . ."

She stopped and frowned, as if already reviewing a mental lineup of potential protectors. The very notion set off a series of rapid-fire explosions in his brain.

"In fact, what?" he asked.

"Nothing," she said with an airy wave.

"Do you already have someone under consideration? Someone like Sebastian Sinclair?" he ground out. He'd seen the way the bastard looked at her.

She blew an exasperated breath out one side of her mouth. "He's already turned me down. It's a bit of a shame because he's a very nice man. Too nice to take a mistress, I suppose."

The sizzling explosions in his head coalesced into a fire-ball that seemed to blow the top right off. He grabbed her by the shoulders and pulled her straight onto her toes, her mouth level with his.

"You want to learn how to be a courtesan? How to seduce and control a man?" he growled.

She let out a squawk. "Jack, what are you doing?"

"Let's start with this and see how you like it." He tugged her mask fully off, then clamped his lips over hers in a hard, desperate kiss that breached his walls and lay him open to his worst enemy.

Himself.

Chapter Eighteen

Lia clung to Jack's shoulders, her eyelids instinctively fluttering shut. One minute they'd been sniping at each other and the next he'd swept her clean off her feet and into a hard embrace. She could barely think or move with his tongue filling her mouth in a hot sweep, his kiss drawing the breath from her lungs. No doubt she would soon faint from lack of air—or from the shock of Jack actually kissing her, and enthusiastically, too.

This was no decorous kiss between friends. This was a tempest, unleashed upon her with the force of a thunderstorm rolling down from the craggy Yorkshire dales. It knocked every sensible thought out of her head.

Digging her fingers into his coat, she tried to find purchase. She needed to push him away, if she wanted to retain a particle of sense in her frazzled brain, because any second now Jack would come to himself and no doubt pull away, horrified and guilt-ridden for losing control.

It felt like passion, the luscious taste of his mouth, the nip—*oh*—of his teeth on her lower lip. But this surprising, impetuous, *scorching* kiss wasn't passion. It was anger and the need to teach her a lesson. It wasn't desire or love or even lust. It was Jack, the most easygoing and patient man on the planet, finally reaching the end of his rope. And once he clambered back up that rope, he would be mortified by what he'd done.

And she would be utterly devastated when he rejected her—again.

Push him away—now.

She breathed a sigh of regret, then flattened her hands on his chest and shoved. It wasn't easy because her toes dangled above the floor and his muscled arms lashed her close with startling strength. Jack seemed reluctant to release her, even though he'd surely made his point. In fact, when she wriggled, trying to put some daylight between them, the growl from his throat sounded more like a feral dog than a man trying to impart a scold. Even more amazing was the feel of one of his hands sliding down her spine to clamp onto her bottom, tucking her tight against him.

Lia froze, completely shocked. She was a maiden but hardly naïve. She knew what happened between men and women and knew that a certain degree of enthusiasm was required to complete the deed, especially on the man's part. To say that Jack had reached such a state of enthusiasm would grossly understate the case; his erection pressed against the softness of her belly with insistence. It also pressed against other parts that no respectable young woman generally thought about.

Of course, that was *all* she could think about at that moment, and it triggered a desire to squirm just a little bit closer and a little bit higher, so that her—

Stop.

She slammed the door to the images flooding her brain and pressed her lips shut against him. It wasn't an easy task when a man was trying to push his tongue deep into one's mouth. Jack sensed her retreat and drew back, his mouth slowly, reluctantly, sliding away. His arms, however, remained locked around her in an intractable hold.

Gasping, Lia gazed up at him, her head swimming as she absorbed the hunger in his glittering, dark eyes and the sensual set to his mouth.

"What's wrong, Lia?" His tone was husky and deep, making her shiver.

"You truly don't want to do this, Jack. Besides, you've amply made your point."

His lips, damp from their torrid kiss, curved up in that wry, familiar smile. "The hell I don't. And if I did have a point when I started this, I've completely forgotten it."

When he started to lower his head again, she locked her wrists to hold him back. "That comment proves my point. You need to stop and think, and in the meantime, please put me down."

As much as she enjoyed his quite arousing strength, she was also getting tired of dangling like a rag doll.

He grimaced, but then eased her down in a deliberate slide that left her gasping. She felt *everything*, and it all felt deliciously . . . hard.

"That wasn't very polite of you," she said as her toes hit the floor. She was forced to keep a tight grip on his forearms until she regained her balance.

Jack leaned down and nuzzled her cheek. "I'm not feeling very polite at the moment."

She shivered. "Ah yes, I couldn't help but notice. But please just stop and think for a minute before something unfortunate comes to pass."

He barked out a short laugh. "I'm done thinking. Besides, I don't think I could if I tried." He tapped a finger to his skull. "At least not with this particular head."

"Good God, Jack. Have you completely lost your senses? You'll only—"

He leaned against the door and pulled her between his braced legs. There wasn't a scrap of space between them and only a few scraps of cloth between body parts that had no business interacting in such a reckless fashion.

"I'll only what?" he asked.

"Ah, I forget." She needed to get the situation under control, but neither her brain nor her body showed the slightest inclination to cooperate.

He flashed her a wicked, seductive smile. "Good, because I'm done talking. All I want do is *feel*—feel you."

She goggled up at him, unable to formulate a sensible response. The way he looked at her—as if he wanted to strip her bare and devour her—made her go positively light-headed.

When his hands stroked down from her waist, cupping her bottom, Lia didn't even try to swallow the moan that rose from her throat. She might even have wriggled a bit, although she wasn't sure because her brain had ceased to function with any reliability. When he nibbled her jaw and then kissed her neck, she found herself craning her head to the side, silently urging him on to the shivery part right behind her ear.

Clearly, she was an idiot.

"Aren't you tired of talking, too?" he whispered. "Don't you want this as much as I do?"

"I . . . I'm just trying to be sensible, Jack. One of us has to be."

His hands came up to her shoulders and he tipped her back a few inches. His gaze ran hungrily over her form. "There's nothing sensible about any of this, love. Especially the way you're dressed," he added, as if he'd just noticed her ridiculous costume.

He ran a finger along her collarbone and then dipped down between her breasts. It felt as if he'd brushed a flame over her skin. When he trailed hard fingertips across the plump swell of her breasts, a sultry heat cascaded through her body to settle low between her thighs. How could such a simple touch evoke so much sensation?

Because it was Jack.

"I want you, Lia," he said in a low, rough voice. "All of you. No more barriers between us, no more being sensible." He leaned down to flick his tongue across her parted lips. "No more saying no," he whispered.

She clung to him as the axis of her feverish, spinning world, the only thing keeping her from collapsing in a quivering heap. He'd been everything she'd ever wanted for as long as she could remember. When she was a little girl, he was a comet shooting through the ordered march of days, flaring brightly through her life a few times a year. And from the moment she'd started to grow into womanhood, she'd yearned for him with an ache that could never be assuaged. That ache now flooded her body, refusing to be denied for one second longer.

"But, don't you think . . ." she quavered, making one last push to save herself.

To save *him*.

He nuzzled her mouth, cutting off her objection and sealing her fate. From the moment he'd come to her rescue tonight, she'd been fighting against this moment of surrender. She'd even asked for his help in finding a protector. It had been her last stand, a gamble to either secure his help or drive him away once and for all.

What she hadn't expected was his rejection of both those scenarios. What she hadn't counted on was Jack laying hands on her and staking his claim.

One of those hands swept down over her chest to cup her breast. He swiped a thumb over the nipple, gently teasing it, and her feeble resistance crumbled into dust.

"Hmm, that's nice." An utterly satisfied smile raised the

corners of his mouth as he flicked his thumb back and forth across the stiffening peak. "Do you think it's nice, Lia?"

"I . . . yes," she whispered. Her voice sounded as wobbly as the muscles behind her knees.

"Good," he growled.

"And you're sure?" she asked, still doubting. "Really sure?"

Because if he later regretted this she would simply die. Whatever else might happen between them in the future, she wanted this moment to be untouched by guilt—or anything that wasn't passion or grace or even good, clean lust between two adults who knew exactly what they were doing and why.

He cradled her face between his palms. "Love, I've never been more sure of anything in my life."

"Oh, I . . . well, that's all right, then."

His quiet laugh was rueful. "Please trust me, Lia. Trust me as you always have. As you know you can."

She let his words sink into her heart, because that was where trust lived. "Always, Jack."

"Thank God." He swept her into his arms, lifting her high against his chest. "Because your costume is driving me insane. I've spent the entire evening trying not to look at your breasts and wanting to murder every man who did look at them."

She hid her face against his shoulder. "I'm sorry I'm such a trial," she said, trying not to laugh.

"Oddly, I don't seem to mind," he said, "at least not at the moment."

That brought her head up. "Because you're going to have your evil way with me?"

"Indeed I am," he said, sounding remarkably cheerful. He looked cheerful, too, albeit in a lustful way. In fact, he seemed much more like his old self than the man who'd spent months struggling under the burden of too many responsibilities and a life he'd never wanted.

He carried her to the large leather club chair, wincing slightly as he settled her on his lap. When she wriggled a bit to get comfortable on his hard thighs, it drew a slow hiss from between his lips. Although she feared she'd hurt him, his expression suggested the opposite. His gaze was heavy-lidded and sensual as one hand cradled the back of her neck and the other settled comfortably under her breasts.

She cocked an eyebrow. "Are we staying here? I'm sure Lord Stanley and his friends are long gone by now."

"Don't remind me of that loutish crew. No, we're staying here because it's private and no one will interrupt us."

She slid her arms around his neck. "That's all right, I suppose." She wasn't quite sure how she was going to lose her virginity sitting up in a chair, but no doubt Jack knew what he was about.

He gave her a sardonic look as he went to work unlacing the crisscrossed ribbons on the front of her bodice. "I'm hardly going to despoil you in a grimy hackney on the way back to Upper Wimpole Street. I cannot imagine a more unromantic setting."

She crinkled her nose. "And you're much too big for me to sneak you up to my bedroom, although we could give it a try."

He pulled the ribbons free and her bodice sagged open, exposing her stays and shift. "The only thing less romantic than making love in a hackney would be doing it with Sir Dominic and Lady Hunter just down the hall."

"Yes, I imagine that would be rather off-putting."

Not to mention exceedingly risky. If anyone got wind of what happened tonight, Jack would be compelled to offer for her hand in marriage. Lia had no intention of ever putting him in that untenable situation. Tonight was a moment out of time, a magical interlude in which they could pretend to meet on equal footing, with no obligations weighing them down and no families to disapprove.

She had to blink back tears, knowing it would likely only be this once. But at least, this first time, it would be him, the man she loved. That was a memory and a blessing she would cherish forever.

"Granny was right," she whispered.

He glanced up, his busy fingers resting on her stays. "Sorry, what?"

She gave him a smile. "Nothing. Carry on, Lord Lendale, and do let me know if there's anything I can do to assist."

His laugh was husky and so delicious it made her want to squirm.

"All I want you to do is enjoy yourself," he said. "This night is entirely for you."

He kissed her lips, briefly parting them for a taste. She sighed into his mouth and let her fingers curl into the silky tips of his hair. Her heart thumped as her mind struggled to grasp that she could touch him as much as she wanted, wherever she wanted.

It was so much more than she'd ever thought she'd have.

He pulled back with an appreciative murmur and went to work on her conveniently front-laced stays.

"That was much too easy," he said, tugging them down. "You're not to wear a garment like this again, is that clear? It gives a man ideas."

"It certainly seems to have worked with you."

"Yes, and all my ideas about you are scandalous," he said as he cupped her breast.

Her nipples were dark and stiff with arousal, pushing against the thin fabric of her shift. He thumbed first one, then the other. The linen rasped across the tight beads with delicious abrasion, sending shivers coursing along her skin.

"Beautiful," he whispered.

Jack held her tight as he slowly lowered his head. His

tongue flicked out, laving her nipples through her shift. Lia wriggled, silently urging him to increase the pressure. He resisted, obviously intent on teasing her. When she tried to arch up into the light pressure, he lifted away from her.

"That's just cruel," she gasped.

"Is it?" he murmured. His entire focus was on her chest, where he'd pulled the damp fabric tightly across the stiff peaks.

"Yes." She needed so much more than gentle play. She needed his hands and his mouth on every part of her, drawing forth the sensations she'd craved for so many long, lonely years. "I don't like being teased and you know it."

He scraped a palm across the tight point. "But it's such fun to tease," he said, his tone full of masculine satisfaction.

Well, two could play at that game.

Giving him a taunting smile, she flexed her hips, pressing down into his lap. His erection pulsed against her bottom and he made a slight, choking sound. Lia ran her index finger down his proud, aristocratic nose, then dragged it across his lips while she wriggled her hips again.

"You were saying, my lord?" she purred.

In retrospect, her form of teasing might have been a bit of a mistake because lust burned hot across Jack's features, searing away any hint of laughter in his eyes. The muscles of his legs went as hard as iron and his arm locked around her shoulder in an unbreakable grip.

"No more games, Lia." His hand curled around her breast, firm and possessive.

"But it's all a game, isn't it?" she whispered. Even as her heart swelled with emotion, she knew that this could never be more than a brief moment of magic. It could never be forever.

"It's much more than that," he said, sounding almost grim. "Because you're mine."

He took her shift and yanked, ripping the top. She gasped as he squeezed a flushed nipple between his fingertips.

"*All* mine," he rasped.

Then his mouth was on her. She cried out and jerked against him, but he held her fast, sucking and laving her breasts until she thought she would faint. Lia had dreamed of this so often, their first time together, and she'd always thought it would be slow and gentle, with tender touches and tentative whisperings. That their lovemaking would be dreamy and soft, in her cozy bed under the eaves of Bluebell Cottage.

But instead this was a hurricane, terrifying in its intensity, and she wanted it so much her heart threatened to beat its way out of her chest. She squirmed, pulling a hand free and clamping it to the back of Jack's head, pushing her breast into the scorching depths of his mouth. Her back curved in a fierce arch, her body offering him everything he wanted.

A few seconds later he eased back—she wanted to scream from frustration—and let his tongue rest flat against one throbbing nipple. Lia moaned and yanked on the thick locks of his hair.

"Ouch," he said, glancing up at her. The laughter was back in his eyes, although heat flickered behind the amusement, like distant summer lightning.

"Why are you stopping?" she panted. Her sex had grown soft and wet, throbbing with the need for release.

"Because I shouldn't be all over you like a slavering beast. At least not our first time together."

First and only time together.

Shoving aside that pang of sorrow, she stretched up to kiss him, nudging his lips open and sucking on his tongue. He groaned deep in his chest as she filled her mouth with him, reveling in the slick exchange. It was hot and delicious, as she'd known it would be. It was a promise of things to come, when he would kiss her like this while slowly thrusting into her, his erection pulsing inside her yielding body.

How shocking it was to think such scandalous thoughts—to want this from a man who could never wed her. Lia supposed that made her just as wicked as her mother and grandmother, and that was probably a good thing. After all, if she intended to embark on a career of having sexual relations with men, it would be terrible to discover she didn't like it.

Unfortunately, she had a sinking feeling that only Jack could ever make her feel this way.

She drew back and had to stifle a smile at the slightly dazed expression on his face. "You're not acting like a beast. Besides, do I look as if I mind?"

His gaze traveled over her face and down her semi-nude body. "No," he said, gently tugging her nipple between his fingertips. "In fact, you look ready for more. Much more."

"Splendid," she whispered, feeling rather dazed herself. Her limbs had never felt like this—practically quivering with energy and yet so heavy and languid at the same time. She wanted to sprawl on his lap all night, letting him play with her for hours on end.

He slowly swept his hand down her body, lingering on her belly before drifting down to her mound. He gently cupped it briefly through her silly, frothy skirts before letting his hand glide down to her thigh.

"You have a gorgeous body, Lia," he murmured as he gently squeezed her thigh. "I never knew how gorgeous because you always wore such plain, practical gowns."

"Yes, because one doesn't generally dress like a tart when weeding the kitchen garden or cleaning out the pantry."

When his hand stilled on her thigh, his fingers digging in slightly, she glanced up to see him glowering at her.

Lia sighed. "Now what?"

"You may have dressed like one tonight, but you are *not* a tart," he said emphatically.

She lifted an ironic brow and glanced down at herself. She was sprawled across him, half-naked, her breasts still damp and flushed from his mouth. "Oh really?"

He leaned in until they were practically nose to nose. "I repeat—you are *not* a tart."

It was terribly sweet of him to be so insistent, but it was also quite absurd. Still, she had no intention of getting into an argument with him on the subject. He'd probably dump her off his lap and then drag her home—maidenhead intact—just to prove his point.

She rested a hand on his cheek. "I know. Thank you, Jack. Now, can we get on with things?"

He let out a reluctant laugh. "You're very impatient, aren't you?"

"For some reason I'm feeling quite restless and irritated. I'm hoping you can do something about that." She began to unbutton his waistcoat.

Jack brushed her fumbling hands away. "I can and I will. You, however, are to do nothing but sit back and enjoy."

"But—"

When he lifted an imperious eyebrow, she subsided on his lap with a grumble.

"Good girl," he said, giving her an approving kiss on the tip of her nose.

"But I don't understand—" Her eyes widened when he slipped a hand under her knee and propped her leg over the arm of the chair, spreading her.

"Oh," she breathed out.

"Oh," he echoed her with a smile.

As he nudged her thighs wider, the air seemed to catch in her lungs. And when he pushed her skirts up to her waist, completely exposing the soft tangle of dark curls at the top of her thighs, she lost her breath completely.

"Look at you," he said in a low, husky murmur, his hand settling low on her belly. "You're so beautiful, my sweet." His fingers drifted down. "So soft."

Lia trembled as she watched him delve into the curls hiding her sex. The erotic sight made her feel wanton. She lay across him, her body completely exposed, a sensual plaything for him to use as he wished. And yet he cradled her with a tenderness that made her eyes start to sting. His gaze held as much reverence as it did heat, making her feel utterly cherished.

What she felt for Jack was too big for her body to contain. It almost seemed like a fatal blow to her heart.

"Lia, are you all right?" He withdrew his hand, a quiet concern marking his brow.

She had to swallow a few times before she could answer. "I will be, once you start touching me again."

There was passion again in his eyes. "Oh, love, I never want to stop touching you."

He took her mouth in a kiss that scorched her. Then his hand, possessive and hard, cupped her sex, claiming her. When he parted her folds, Lia moaned and jerked against him. He held her tightly against his brawny chest, murmuring encouragement as he played with her. His fingertips moved with assurance, slickly spreading her wide. He teased her bud to aching, hard prominence. Lia arched her back, pushing into his hand to increase the delicious pressure.

Oh, and he teased her there, just as he'd teased her nipples, circling and making her strain for his touch. When he finally touched the bud, she cried out as luxurious spasms rippled out from deep inside.

Her skin felt shockingly hot and every muscle seemed to skitter and jump with restless desire. She flung her arm around his neck, digging her fingers into his cravat as she tried to spread her legs even wider.

Jack leaned forward and nuzzled her mouth, sliding his

tongue across her lips. "What do you want, sweetheart? Are you ready to come?"

"Yes, dammit," she choked out. "Do something."

His laugh was wickedness incarnate. He flicked her sex once, twice, and a third time, but it still wasn't enough. She let out a soft wail and arched off his lap.

"Tell me what you want." His voice was so low and hard it seemed almost like a stranger's.

"I want you inside me," she gasped. "Why do you wait?"

He was holding back, damn him, so careful with her that she wanted to scream. Even now he wouldn't take her—at least not all of her—even though she was more than ready to give him everything.

His laugh was harsh. "Don't worry, love. I'll give you exactly what you need."

When he pushed two fingers inside her channel and pressed his thumb over the tight knot of her sex, moonlight and stars burst behind her eyelids. She let out a high, choking cry as waves of pleasure overtook her. His hands moving over her, inside her, threw Lia into a shimmering void, sending her soaring higher and higher, reaching for those vibrant shards of starlight. Then he caught her as she fell to earth, holding her gently and murmuring soft endearments as she drifted down into her body.

But when she opened her eyes to take in his tight, almost somber expression, Lia couldn't escape one simple fact— while Jack had catapulted her to the heavens, he'd unfortunately decided to send her there alone.

Only the mightiest of efforts had prevented Jack from ripping open the fall of his breeches and thrusting into Lia's glorious body. But she was a virgin, after all, and no girl deserved to be taken in so slipshod a fashion, especially not one as innocent as Lia.

That fact left him no choice in what he must do next.

His mother and sister would be furious, of course, and it would mean that no wealthy bride would be riding to Stonefell's rescue. But with a half-naked and utterly sated Lia sprawled in his arms, those seemed like minor concerns.

Despite all efforts to the contrary, he was beginning to think his life and Lia's had been leading inexorably to this very moment. And to see her at this damnable ball, pursued by scoundrels and rakes, he'd understood with thundering clarity just how vulnerable she was. When she'd had the unmitigated gall to ask him to help her find a protector . . .

Even if it had taken his brain some minutes to catch up, his body had known exactly what to do—to claim Lia as his, now and forevermore.

No one knew Lia better than he did or cared for her as much. If she'd found a good man to marry, he would have accepted that. But for her to lead the life of a courtesan, a plaything passed from one man to another?

Never.

He cradled her in his arms. To finally give in to the magnetic pull between them sent an almost staggering sense of relief flooding through his body and mind. A special license was very much in order. The sooner he married Lia and got her into his bed, the better.

When she tapped him on the nose—rather hard—he blinked with surprise.

"What are you thinking about?" she asked in a voice too wary for a woman emerging from the throes of passion.

Jack resettled her, wincing slightly as her bottom pressed down on his brutally uncomfortable erection. He'd allowed his mind to briefly wander, compiling a list of what needed to be accomplished over the next few days.

Lia's cheeks were flushed with passion, her mouth red and swollen from his kisses. Her full breasts, her slim waist, her lushly curving hips, and the mink-soft curls between rounded thighs all tempted him to throw caution to the wind and take her right now, staking his claim in no uncertain terms.

"Jack, have you gone deaf?"

Dammit. He'd done it again. "Sorry, love," he said. He tipped her upright and went to work wrestling her stays back in place. "Let me help you get dressed."

She batted his hands away. "I don't need you to help me get dressed. I need you to talk to me."

"Yes, of course. But first let's get you safely home."

Ignoring her resistance, he lifted her to her feet. She wobbled and grabbed his shoulders, letting out a little gasp. He kept a firm grip on her hips, intensely aware of how she trembled under his fingertips. Clearly, she'd never experienced this sort of passion before and, primitive brute that he was, he couldn't help feeling inordinately pleased by that knowledge.

"We're not going anywhere until you tell me what happens next," she said, sounding breathless.

"Next, I'm taking you home." He leaned forward and kissed the tip of her nose. For some reason, that made her scowl.

"We don't need to discuss anything tonight, pet," he added. "I'll call on you tomorrow morning and then we can begin making plans."

When she yanked her stays up over her breasts, Jack had to swallow a sigh of regret.

"Unless those plans involve you becoming my protector," she said, impatiently trying to rearrange her mangled shift, "there's no reason to have a discussion about this . . . this incident."

He raised his eyebrows. "Incident?"

"What else would you call it?" Her entire demeanor had become downright chilly.

Jack got to his feet, his temper rising with him, although

he did his best to wrestle it under control. It had been a difficult evening for her and she was likely suffering from some sort of female reaction. But her response was decidedly not what he'd been expecting. Lia loved him and he'd made damn sure before he removed a stitch of her clothing that she'd wanted this as much as he did.

"I understand that tonight has been rather fraught," he said carefully, "and perhaps your thinking is currently rather muddled. But you have entirely misunderstood if you think my actions were in any way offering a carte-blanche. Precisely the opposite."

She flicked her skirts back in place. "Marriage, you mean? It's entirely unnecessary, Jack. You did not despoil me, so you are under no obligation." Her manner was almost cutting.

"Lia, you are hardly an obligation, as I've pointed out to you possibly a thousand times in the last several weeks. And I most certainly did despoil you. I distinctly recall the feel of my hands on your body. *Inside* your body," he said with emphasis.

Her fiery blush was evident even in the dimly lit room. Still, from her expression, he saw she was not going to give up without a fight.

And he knew why. She'd gotten it into her head that the only way he could save Stonefell was by finding a rich wife. While he wouldn't insult her intelligence by pretending that things might not be tricky, and that he wouldn't be forced to make decisions he'd rather avoid, he had no intention of allowing Lia to sacrifice herself on the altar of his family's estate.

Nor, come to think of it, was he willing to sacrifice himself in a marriage of convenience—not when he could have the woman he wanted instead.

She regarded him with a determined air. "I'm the daughter and granddaughter of courtesans. I know exactly what's involved in losing my virginity, and my maidenhead remains firmly intact. No thanks to you," she added in a snippy tone.

"Wait; you're angry with me because I *didn't* have my way with you?"

Her eyebrows went up in a sardonic arch. "Have your way with me? What a quaint expression, especially given the fact that we're at a Cyprians' ball."

"This conversation is incredibly inappropriate," he said rather inanely.

She let out an exasperated sigh. "Jack, I grew up on a country estate, where I spent quite a lot of time dealing with the tenant farmers and your estate manager. I know exactly how the breeding process works."

"Bully for you, but I fail to see what difference that makes."

For a moment, she looked as if she wanted to smack him, but then she snapped her fingers. "I completely forgot to tell you. Mr. Lindsey wrote to me a few days ago about a new breed of hogs he's been reading about in the *Yorkshire Agricultural Report*. Did he mention that in his most recent letter?"

"And we are *not* talking about hogs either," he said as he retrieved her mask from the floor.

"We can't talk about sex, we can't talk about Stonefell, and now we can't even talk about hogs." She waved her arms in an extravagant circle. "What the devil are we to talk about?"

He handed her the mask. "Right now, the only thing we're talking about is getting you safely home. Then, as I said, I will call on you tomorrow and we will discuss plans for our marriage."

"Jack, please get it through your thick skull that we are not getting married."

"Nonsense, and we are not discussing this any further

tonight," he said firmly. "You are clearly in much too volatile a state of mind."

His state of mind wasn't the best either. If this fight continued, God only knew what would happen. He'd probably end up hauling her back to that chair, flipping her skirts up to her waist, and burying his cock deep in her beautiful body. That would bring an abrupt and definitive conclusion to their ridiculous discussion.

She glared at him for a few seconds longer, then slapped on her mask and began tying the ribbons, all while muttering some salty oaths. Jack made a mental note to speak to Lindsey and also his head groom once they returned to Stonefell; she clearly was spending too much time around the stables and barns.

Of course, she could have picked up such language backstage at the theater or even from her own mother, which was an appalling thought. It was time for him to put his foot down and get the poor girl under some semblance of control.

Once Lia finished tying on her mask, she gave one more upward yank on her bodice and marched to the door.

"Wait," he hissed, leaping after her and slapping his palm onto the door. "Let me check first to make sure no one's out there."

She scoffed. "Don't be such an old miss, Jack. Lord Stanley and his friends got bored and wandered off long ago."

"Can you for once try not to be entirely reckless?" he asked, exasperated.

She let out a heavy sigh but stepped back with a look of long-suffering patience, as if she found him singularly lacking.

He cracked open the door and cautiously stuck his head out. Except for one rotund, middle-aged gentleman snoring loudly on a bench, the corridor was empty. He took Lia's hand and drew her out into the hall.

"Told you," she said smugly after a quick glance around.

"Could you please not talk? I would truly love to escape from this godforsaken affair without you being recognized."

"Whatever you say, your lordship," she said in that horrific accent she feigned.

He led her swiftly toward the front entrance hall. Astonishingly, they met very few revelers on the way. It was now well past midnight, so the celebrations in the ballroom had likely reached their debauched peak. They passed two or three late arrivals who cast curious glances, but after retrieving his hat from the footman, Jack shepherded Lia safely down the front steps of the mansion.

Their luck held when he was able to hail a fortuitously passing hackney. Hauling Lia over to the curb, he bundled her inside, gave the direction, and squeezed in after her.

She glared at him. "Was it really necessary for you to shove me in by my backside, you brute?"

"I was just trying to get you the hell away from here, you peagoose."

She whipped a finger up to his nose. "Now, you listen to me, Jack—"

He grabbed her finger. "Do. Not."

She yanked her hand back and subsided with a grumble, then refused to look at or speak to him on the ride back to Upper Wimpole Street. That suited him perfectly because he was convinced neither of them would have anything productive to add to the already gruesome conversation.

When they pulled up in front of the Sir Dominic's town house, Lia waited for him on the walk, fuming, while he paid off the driver.

"Thank you for escorting me home, Lord Lendale," she said in a frigid tone. "I do not, however, need your assistance in climbing over the back wall of the garden, so I will bid you good night." She spun on her heel, clearly intending to head to the back alley.

Jack grabbed her arm and pulled her toward the steps of the house. "I know how much you love to engage in theatrics, but be assured that Sir Dominic and Lady Hunter know you are not asleep in your bed. That being the case, we will use the front door like civilized people."

"I'm not smashing in there like a brazen hussy," she snapped. "You know very well what sort of assumptions they'll make."

"You should have thought of that before tonight's little escapade." He took her by the arm and marched her up the steps, then banged the knocker.

A moment later, Smithwell, looking unusually harried, yanked open the door. "Miss Kincaid, thank goodness," said the butler in relieved tones.

She managed a smile. "No need to worry, Smithwell. I had my faithful sheepdog with me, scaring away all the wolves." Her smile turned ferocious as she turned to Jack. "Good night, Lord Lendale," she said, starting to close the door in his face.

He wedged his foot against the doorframe. "I swear to God, I will take you over my knee and spank you if you try to slam that door on me."

Her eyes went wide with outrage. Even Smithwell made a slight choking noise. Lia spun around and stormed to the staircase in the hall. Jack followed her inside.

She was halfway up the stairs when Chloe rushed out of the drawing room, her husband on her heels.

"Thank God," Chloe exclaimed, staring down at her. "I was so worried."

Lia faltered a bit, then trudged up the last few steps into her aunt's embrace. All the starch seemed to go out of her as she rested her head on the older woman's shoulder. "I'm sorry I caused you concern, Aunt Chloe. But there was never anything to worry about. I'm completely fine."

"That may be the most demented statement I have ever heard," Jack said.

Lia's head reared back, her gaze furious. "Bugger you, Jack Easton."

She pulled out of her aunt's arms and ran up the stairs to the second floor. A few moments later the sound of a slamming door echoed through the stairwell.

"Oh dear," Chloe said with a sigh. "I'd best go try to calm her down." She hurried after her niece, leaving Jack and Sir Dominic to glare at each other.

"I trust you intend to bring this unfortunate situation under control, Lord Lendale," the magistrate said in a soft tone that nonetheless carried a clear threat. "Before I'm forced to do something on my niece's behalf that I might regret."

"What the hell do you think I'm trying to do?" Jack growled. "If you can't see that, bugger you, too."

He turned on his boot heel and stalked down the stairs and out the front door. For once he'd finally gotten the last word.

Chapter Nineteen

"If this is an Italian picnic I'm the man in the moon," Gillian said as she suspiciously inspected the lobster patty on the dainty china plate in her hand. "For one thing, no self-respecting Italian would dine alfresco in such dreary weather."

Lia glanced at the sky. It was rather cool for August and the clouds and sun had capriciously flirted all afternoon. But compared to the average late summer day in Yorkshire, it was positively balmy. "I suppose you're right, but Lord Peckworth's gardens are truly lovely. And it's so delightful here by the Thames, don't you think?"

Gillian cast a jaundiced eye at the beautiful flower beds and the lush, ruthlessly manicured lawns. "It's too damp, but please don't tell the countess I said that. She'd probably drag me on another tour of the house to punish my lamentable manners."

The Levertons, Hunters, and a small group of mutual friends had come to enjoy the day at the Earl of Peckworth's new villa in Chiswick. Lia and Gillian had spent the first hour trailing along in Lady Peckworth's ample wake, oohing and ahhing over the magnificent house. Gillian had clearly been bored out of her skull, although she'd hid it fairly well. But when Lady Peckworth insisted on showing off both the modern kitchen range and the newly installed water closets, Gillian had adopted a comically pained expression suggesting martyrdom.

Despite her cousin's lack of enthusiasm, Lia had enjoyed talking with the older woman about the many thoughtful touches that made the expansive villa a truly comfortable home. But the domestic interlude had also triggered a bout of homesickness. She'd now reached the point at which she would have preferred spending her days tending to Stonefell's kitchen gardens and searching for newly laid eggs in the henhouse, which was a painful comment on her London misadventures. In fact, she'd much rather shoe a horse than be dragged along to yet another musicale or dinner party where the guests snubbed her, ignored her, or, even worse, tried to make polite conversation while pretending she wasn't a Notorious Kincaid.

Although, in her case, it might be more accurate to describe her as the Notoriously Inept Kincaid, for all the success she'd had in launching her career as a courtesan.

She dredged up a smile at her cousin's jest. "You must admit the boat ride on the Thames was delightful."

Gillian deposited her plate with its untouched lobster patty on the little table between their matching wrought-iron chairs. "Yes, that was rather fun, although the boat cushions and upholstery held the oddest musty smell. I began to wonder if I'd forgotten to take a bath this morning. I knew it couldn't be Charles because he always smells divine."

Lia had to laugh. "Poor Gillian. I'm sorry you had to be forced on yet another dreary outing on my behalf. You must be heartily sick of them—and me."

Gillian patted her hand. "I'm just an old grump. And even though Lady Peckworth is probably the most boring woman alive, she has a good heart, as is evidenced by her kindness to you. That house tour obviously made you happy, which makes me happy."

"It did make me happy. I suppose that makes me a boring person, too."

"Not at all. But you do miss your life in the country, don't you, Lia?"

"Yes, I miss Stonefell and Granny very much. Silly of me, I know, because I've gotten to meet you and Aunt Chloe and everyone spoils me rotten."

"There's nothing silly about it. After all, Stonefell is your home."

Lia ignored the pang in her heart. "Not anymore. And the sooner I accommodate myself to my new life, the better."

Gillian crossed her arms and stretched out her legs, stacking her elegantly booted feet, heel to toe. Leverton, who was standing several yards away with Dominic and Lord Peckworth, glanced over at his wife and raised an eloquent eyebrow.

"Oh blast," Gillian muttered, correcting her boyish posture.

"It can't be easy being married to the most sophisticated man in London," Lia said in a humorous tone.

"Try the most sophisticated man in England." A sly grin teased the corners of Gillian's mouth. "But it has its compensations."

As Lia took in the discreet yet smoldering glance the couple exchanged, she had to swallow a tiny sigh. She felt that same intensity of emotion for Jack, although she doubted he returned it. He held her in great affection and he certainly seemed to find her desirable, but it wasn't the all-encompassing love Gillian and Leverton shared.

That kind of love was a dream she and Jack would probably never realize. Their torrid encounter had been memorable, but the aftermath had been less so. In fact, it had been downright disheartening because it was clear he'd only offered marriage out of a sense of duty and honor. What had been the most wonderful moment of Lia's life had quickly become one of the most humiliating. They'd ended up fighting, naturally. And, once home, Dominic and Jack had ended up fighting, too, although both men were in stubborn accord that she and Jack declare their banns or marry by special license immediately.

Fortunately, Chloe had understood her trepidation over forcing Jack's hand. Her aunt had insisted that they needed a little time away from each other to think about their futures. Dominic had grudgingly agreed, although he'd insisted that Lia be closely chaperoned lest she embark on yet another *mad scheme* to launch her career in the demi-monde. Chloe and Gillian had then swung into action, dragging Lia from one social occasion to another so that she might ascertain if she truly wished to marry Jack or preferred to wait for other potential suitors to emerge from the woodwork. It was a demented plan as far as Lia was concerned, and it left them out of sorts and ready to murder each other.

"Yes, I'm sure marriage to Charles Penley has a number of compensations," Lia said, thinking how splendid it would be to have a husband who adored you.

"You could be enjoying the benefits of the wedded state, too," Gillian said. "You and Jack would be very happy together."

Lia scoffed. "Jack has no true desire to marry me, which you must admit is quite an impediment to marital bliss."

Gillian rounded her eyes. "No true desire to marry you? That's a laugh. The man's an absolute beast whenever the two of you are apart. Charles says he expects him to begin rampaging through London if Aunt Chloe keeps barring the door to him. And when you are together, he can barely keep his hands off you."

Lia had to resist the temptation to press her palms to her

rapidly flushing cheeks. "That's not love, Gillian. That's, um . . . well, he admires my form."

"That's certainly true, but there's more to it than that. He adores *you*."

"You're confusing love with affection. Jack has always been more like a brother to me than anything else."

"Not like any brothers I've ever met," Gillian said sardonically.

Lia winced. "Very well, I suppose we've gone past that. But there are other obstacles that make a union impractical if not completely impossible."

Gillian held up a hand. "Please don't start on about your status as a royal by-blow. That's not a real impediment—not with all of us supporting you."

"Perhaps not, but his mother can't stand me, or any Kincaid for that matter. In fact, she might try to slip arsenic into my morning tea if Jack and I were to marry."

"I'll grant you she's a dragon," Gillian said, "but once you're married, she'd have to accept you."

Lia shook her head. "She'd make Jack miserable. And they're close, you know. He would find it very difficult to be up in arms against her."

"You'd be amazed by what mothers-in-law will eventually accept. My husband's dear mama is a veritable Tartar and yet she puts up with me."

"Yes, but—"

Gillian flipped up a restraining hand. "So, we've got that obstacle sorted. What else?"

Lia snorted. "I'll concede the point for now. What I cannot concede is that Jack needs to marry an heiress. Stonefell is crumbling, and it needs a substantial infusion of income or the situation could become truly dire. I bring no value that would benefit the estate."

"Nonsense. From what I hear, no one knows Stonefell

better than you do or keeps the welfare of its people closer to heart."

That was probably true, for all the good it did her.

"I'm sure the new marchioness will come to love Stonefell, too," Lia said, trying to sound serene about the appalling idea of another woman treading the hallways of the beloved old house, occupying the magnificent Tudor bed in the master's suite with Jack lying next to her.

Gillian studied her with some perplexity.

"What?" Lia asked.

"You *do* know about the discovery of iron ore on Stonefell's lands, don't you?"

She shrugged. "I know Mr. Lindsey was conducting some sort of analysis. But Jack had mentioned some weeks ago that he couldn't afford to exploit any findings they might make. I believe he was having trouble securing the appropriate sort of investors."

"He's got the right sort now. Charles and Sir Dominic have made it clear that they're more than willing to invest in a good mining venture in Yorkshire. They'll give Jack what he needs to get started in good style. In fact, from what Charles tells me, the preliminary explorations are promising indeed."

Lia stared at her. "Jack hasn't mentioned anything about that to me. Are you sure?"

"Our dear Lord Lendale is being a bit stubborn about it. According to Charles, he doesn't want to be indebted to his friends," she said with a scoff. "Silly man. But I'm sure my darling husband and Sir Dominic will bring him around." She winked. "Especially in light of recent events."

Lia's face heated again. "If such is the case, I'm very happy for Jack. But it still doesn't—"

"You're as stubborn as he is," Gillian said, cutting her off. "All right, then. Let's say you *don't* marry Jack. That doesn't mean you have to become a courtesan. Something, by the way, you don't seem to be very good at. Truly, Cuz, I don't think it's your cup of tea."

Lia was beginning to come to the same conclusion. "What else am I to do?"

"You could try getting married. To someone other than Jack, I mean."

Lia blew out an exasperated breath. "That's why you and Aunt Chloe have been dragging me from one blasted social event to the other."

Gillian shrugged. "We think you should marry Jack, but it's always nice to have a choice."

"I don't think *your* plan has worked very well either."

Only a few of the men she'd met recently had seemed at all interested. And rather than courtship or marriage, she suspected they desired a relationship of a less respectable nature.

"I don't know," Gillian said. "Sebastian Sinclair seems *quite* interested in you. And he's clearly not intending to offer you a carte-blanche."

Lia was silent for several seconds. "True on both counts, I think." She'd been surprised by Sinclair's attention to her over the past week. He'd made a point of talking with her at every event they'd attended and had asked her to dance several times.

"If not Jack, do you think you might like to marry Sinclair?" her cousin asked. "You have to admit he's a nice man, plus he's handsome and rich, which is always helpful."

Lia kept quiet, not wanting to lie to her cousin.

Gillian chuckled. "I thought not. I think you'd better reconcile yourself to marrying Jack because he is certainly not going to allow you to become a courtesan. Nor will Sir Dominic or my husband, for that matter." She reached over and squeezed Lia's hand. "Or me. It's simply not on, dearest."

Lia gripped her hand. "I don't know what to do." She

felt wretchedly uncertain, and yet she couldn't deny that a fugitive hope had sparked to life.

"If you want my opinion, you should marry Jack and put him out of his misery."

"But if I did, it could cause him more misery," she said, grimacing.

Gillian cocked her head. "But you do love him, don't you?"

"Of course I do," Lia said, feeling rather growly about it at the moment.

She couldn't remember a time when she hadn't loved him, his gangly, adolescent presence and laughing face the brightest part of her world. As a child, she'd worshiped him with girlish adoration, as if he were her own personal deity. And Jack had tolerated her nonsense, even though she must have irritated him immensely. After all, what boy wishes to have a little girl tumbling after him like an eager puppy, constantly begging for notice?

Yet he'd never been anything but the truest of friends, rescuing her from numerous scrapes and defending her against the slights and censures that sometimes came her way. When Jack Easton was about, no one dared to insult Lia Kincaid—not unless they wished to earn a bloody nose or a black eye.

He'd been her champion for as long as she could remember.

"And you love Stonefell," Gillian said, gently squeezing her fingers. "If you ask me, both Jack and the estate need you, so you should fight for them. Be there for them."

Lia sat very still, letting the notion of *yes* sink in. When she let the idea settle deep inside, without thought or botheration, it felt right. Immensely right.

Over the years, her childish affection for Jack had transformed into something quiet and deep, a love as rooted as the ancient oaks gracing the woods around Stonefell. Lia knew she could live without him if she must, going on to fashion some sort of satisfactory life. But without Jack, something essential would be lost, as if she'd taken the wrong turn onto a road leading far from home and away from everything that truly mattered.

Gillian withdrew her hand. "I've made my case and I hope it's enough," she said wryly. "Because I think you're about to take some heavy fire. Stand firm, old girl. Make us proud."

"What are you talking about?"

Her cousin nodded toward the house. Lia followed her gaze and almost fell out of her seat. Approaching them at a sedate pace across the lawn were Jack and his sister, Lady Anne.

"Oh no," Lia groaned. "Did she know I was going to be here?"

Gillian cast her a sideways glance. "I suspect quite strongly she did."

"Did *you* know about this?"

Her cousin held up her hands in a surrendering gesture. "I knew Jack was coming, but I have to admit his sister's arrival is a surprise. But perhaps it won't be such a bad thing."

"Are you insane?" Lia said. "She hates me."

Gillian flicked an assessing look at Lady Anne across the lawn. "I doubt Jack would bring her along simply to allow her to make a scene or be dreadful." She gave Lia a smile before standing up. "Time to fight for what you want, love. Don't forget: You've got the blood of kings running through your veins. That's got to count for something."

"I doubt it," Lia said sarcastically, rising.

Jack and his sister stopped to exchange greetings with their host and Sir Dominic, then made their way to join Lia and Gillian. As much as she hated to admit it, Lia was so anxious that she could barely think straight. She hadn't seen Jack since that exceedingly fraught night at the Cyprians' ball. To have his sister witness their meeting was utterly nerve-racking.

Jack gave her a wink and a smile, but it did nothing to calm her nerves. "Good afternoon, ladies. Your Grace, I'm sure you remember my sister, Lady Anne Kendall."

"Indeed I do," Gillian said dryly. She gave Jack's sister a polite nod.

Lady Anne sank into a respectful curtsy. "Your Grace, I'm grateful to have the opportunity to speak with you. I wish to extend my sincere apologies to you and your husband for the most distressing episode that occurred at your ball. I deeply regret my mother's behavior and the embarrassment it surely caused you."

Gillian gave a casual wave. "I wasn't embarrassed in the least. But I can't say the same for my cousin and your brother."

Lady Anne regarded Lia with a somber expression. "Yes, I know. I'd like to speak to Miss Kincaid about that, if she'll let me."

"Of course she'll talk to you. She's not an ogre, you know," Jack said. He gave his sister a sardonic smile. "But I don't think you two have ever been formally introduced, have you? Miss Kincaid, allow me to introduce you to my sister, Lady Anne Kendall."

Lia dipped into a somewhat shaky curtsy. "It's an honor to meet you, Lady Anne."

At least her voice sounded relatively normal. Feeling awkward, she would have given anything to be back in her cozy bedroom at Bluebell Cottage, safe and secure under its welcoming—if leaky—eaves.

Lady Anne flashed Lia a lopsided smile that was all too familiar. In that moment, she looked very much like her big brother, her dark eyes friendly and surprisingly warm. "I very much doubt you consider it an honor, Miss Kincaid, and no one could blame you in the least." Then she jabbed her brother in the arm. "As for formal introductions, you're being idiotic, Jack. Miss Kincaid and I know exactly who we are. In fact, we've even exchanged a few words on occasion, have we not?"

"Um, yes, I suppose we have," Lia said.

If you counted the stilted *hellos* they'd mumbled on the rare occasions they'd accidentally run into each other in the gardens or in the lane behind Bluebell Cottage. Lia had been under strict instructions from Lord Lendale to stay far away from the Easton family on their yearly visits, and she'd always feared that Lady Anne would report their encounters to her mother. But nothing had ever come of it.

"That's news to me," Jack said.

"We weren't supposed to even acknowledge each other's existence, or have you forgotten that?" his sister said. "And it was rather uncomfortable for both of us, as I recall."

"As is this unfortunate encounter, I have no doubt," he replied. "But you did insist on coming."

"Lord and Lady Peckworth are my godparents," Lady Anne explained to Lia. "They invited me to visit them while I was in London. When Jack told me he was coming here today, I thought I'd take the opportunity to see them and also talk with you."

"It's almost like a family reunion," Gillian said in a droll tone. "What fun."

"If your idea of fun is sticking a needle in your eye," Jack said in blighting tones. "There is no way this is not going to end in disaster, thanks to Anne's pigheadedness." His sister merely grinned, which he obviously found annoying. "And don't ask me to come to your rescue when Mother finds out about this. I'll leave you to your well-deserved fate."

That was a bit much, even if Jack was deservedly out of

sorts. It couldn't have been easy for Lady Anne to come here or to make a public apology to Gillian.

"Jack, stop being so mean to your sister," Lia said.

"You'd be mean, too, if you had to put up with her antics," he said. This time, though, his mouth curved in a smile of rueful affection.

When he tugged on one of the curls escaping from under Lady Anne's dainty frippery of a hat, Lia's stomach took a flop. He'd tugged on her ragtag curls many times over the years, in an intimate gesture she'd thought was reserved for her. How silly to think she was more important to him than his own sister. Jack had a real family, with bonds strengthened by blood, loyalty, and a shared history. Their curiosity of a relationship could never compare with that.

"That's enough out of you, my lord," Lady Anne said sternly. "Now, I would be most grateful if you took the duchess for a little stroll around the gardens so Miss Kincaid and I can have a chat."

Jack's gaze narrowed. "Anne, I really don't think—"

Lia touched his arm. "I'm happy to hear whatever your sister wishes to say to me."

"And to paraphrase you, dear brother, I'm not an ogre," Lady Anne said. "But I do need to make my apologies to Miss Kincaid and I'd prefer to do so in private."

Lia mentally frowned. Her ladyship had easily apologized to Gillian in front of an audience. Why did she need privacy now?

"Very well," Jack said to his sibling. "But you're not to upset her."

When Lady Anne rolled her eyes at him, Lia was again struck by how much alike they were. They'd inherited the same dark good looks from their father, along with his easygoing charm. When Lady Anne stretched up and gave her brother a fleeting kiss on the cheek, it was another unwelcome reminder that Jack already had a family to which he owed his true allegiance and support.

"I know how much Miss Kincaid means to you, Jack," Lady Anne said. "And I also know how fond our uncle was of her. I promise to treat her with the respect she deserves."

He nodded. "Very well. Lia, I'll take Her Grace for one turn around the garden and then I'll be back. All right?"

"You're as bad as Charles," Gillian said. "You men act as if none of us females can possibly take care of ourselves. It's complete nonsense." She ignored Jack's protests and started to drag him off toward her husband.

Lady Anne chuckled. "Brothers can be such a trial, but it seems her ladyship has Jack well in hand."

"I never had a brother, my lady." Until recently, that is. Of course, she had yet to meet Captain Endicott, so he didn't feel very real just then.

"Jack was always like a brother to you, was he not? At least that's what I'd always assumed."

Lia thought about that for a few moments. "Looking back on it, I'm not really sure what sort of relationship we had." She gestured toward the other chair. "Won't you have a seat?"

"You were close, though," Lady Anne said after she'd seated herself and arranged the skirts of her stylish summer gown. "In fact, I confess to feeling a bit jealous when we were young. Even though Jack was careful not to mention your name around my mother—or me, for that matter—it was clear he was very protective of you."

Lia frowned. "Was he not the same with you?"

Lady Anne smiled. "He was a very good brother and still is. But even though we did not discuss you, I could tell you were special to him. I assumed it was because he thought of you as a little sister." She gave Lia an assessing look. "That, however, no longer seems to be the case."

It took some effort for Lia not to squirm under the

woman's perceptive gaze. "I'm not sure how Jack sees me anymore—or did when we were younger, for that matter. It wasn't anything we ever discussed."

Lady Anne raised politely incredulous eyebrows. "Really?"

Lia shrugged. "It was awkward for all of us, you have to admit, and my grandmother and Lord Lendale never encouraged us to talk about it. Better just to pretend that our odd collection of relationships was quite normal. But to me, Jack was my best friend." She was silent for a few seconds. "My only friend really."

Her companion's eyes warmed with understanding. "Yes, I imagine it was difficult for you. And lonely. You and your grandmother could never truly be accepted into local society, and yet you weren't servants at Stonefell either. That left you rather betwixt and between, didn't it?"

It was a surprisingly sympathetic analysis, coming from someone who had every reason to resent her. "I won't pretend it was always easy, but it was harder for my grandmother."

"But you had no female friends, nor were you able to attend school in the village. My uncle provided for you, but you never had what anyone would call a normal life for a young girl."

"No, but there's truly no need to feel sorry for me. I wasn't put into service, nor did I have to work in the fields like the children of the tenant farmers. And I had Stonefell, which was a splendid place to grow up. I also had Jack, whenever he came to visit."

"Was that enough?" Lady Anne asked, sounding genuinely curious.

"I have no complaints," Lia said quietly.

"No one could blame you if you did." She sighed. "We were not well-served by our elders, were we? You, Jack, and me."

Lia shifted uncomfortably against the hard iron seat. "Forgive me, my lady, but I'm not sure what you want from me."

"Please call me Anne. After all, we're practically family, as the duchess suggested," she said with a wry smile.

Now it was Lia's turn to raise a skeptical brow.

Anne laughed. "All right, I suppose that was a bit much. But I do think we might have been friends, if circumstances had allowed for it."

"Probably not," Lia said. "I was too intimidated by you. You were so beautiful and grand, just like your mother."

"I was an awful snob, you mean," Lady Anne dryly replied.

"Your ladyship . . ." Lia stopped, because there was simply no reasonable response to that remark.

The elegant eyebrow, so like Jack's, went up again. Lady Anne was as stubborn as her brother, too.

"Very well. Anne," Lia said with a reluctant smile. "You said you wanted to offer me an apology for that incident at the Leverton ball. But it's not necessary. You have done nothing to injure me."

Anne's mother was another story, but Lia knew better than anyone that the sins of the parent should not be visited upon the child.

"Mama behaved wretchedly, and I regret that I wasn't able to stop her. Still, I do understand why she did it. Life has not been easy for her."

"I know," Lia said. "Your mother was forced to make many sacrifices over the years, as were you. I know it wasn't easy for you either. Especially when you had to leave your family. Leave London."

Anne looked puzzled for a few moments before understanding cleared her brow. "Are you referring to my marriage to Mr. Kendall? That was no sacrifice, I assure you. In fact, it was the best thing to ever happen to me."

"But I was always told that . . ." There was no delicate way to put it.

"That I'd married beneath myself?"

"You were a diamond of the first water when you came out. According to my grandmother, you were expected to make a splendid marriage. Everyone was counting on it, from what I'd been told."

"And I did make a splendid marriage. My husband is an intelligent, kind, and fine-looking man who simply adores me." She flashed Lia a roguish smile. "He's also very rich and generous, which is certainly nothing to sneeze at. I am happily wed, I assure you."

Lia felt as if a bolt that secured something essential had come loose in her head. "I apologize if I gave offense," she said slowly. "I was clearly under a false impression."

And she had been for years. More than once, Lia had heard the story of Anne's failure *to take*, all for lack of an adequate dowry. She'd also heard how resentful Lady John had been that her beautiful, charming daughter had been forced to marry so far beneath herself—to a mere country squire. Lia had always thought it rather unfair that her lady-ship had partly blamed Rebecca Kincaid for that state of affairs. No one had forced the men of the family to spend their money on gambling and mistresses.

And it wasn't as if Granny hadn't made sacrifices, too. Those sacrifices were likely to ruin both her and Lia if they couldn't figure out a solution to their financial dilemma.

Anne gave an understanding nod. "An impression fostered by my mother. She was very angry when I was *forced to marry Mr. Kendall*, as she put it. And I won't pretend I enjoyed being passed over by eligible suitors again and again, simply because I lacked a dowry. That part wasn't pleasant, nor was the gossip about my father's scandalous behavior."

The young woman glanced over her shoulder, as if checking to see if anyone could overhear; then she leaned in closer to Lia. "But I'll tell you a secret. I was thrilled to escape all the gossip and drama. The day I married Mr. Kendall and left Town was one of the happiest days of my life." She let out a short laugh and sat back in her chair. "If you'd had to live with *my* parents, you would know exactly what I mean. That was another reason I was jealous of you when I was a girl. Your life at Stonefell seemed so peaceful. I never blamed Jack for wanting to escape to Yorkshire and stay with Uncle Arthur."

"I . . . I hardly know what to say," Lia stammered. In just a few sentences, her view of the Easton family—at least part of it—had been stood on its head. "I truly didn't know you felt that way."

Anne shrugged. "My mother has constructed a narrative of our family that suits her and nothing I or Jack say seems to be able to change that. Unfortunately, blaming you and your grandmother forms an important part of that narrative. But the real blame rests with my father." She paused for a moment, her gaze searching. "And with your mother."

Lia frowned. "What does my mother have to do with it?"

"Ah, I thought so." Anne let out a sigh that sounded curiously relieved. "You truly don't know what happened."

Oh no. What did you do, Mama?

Everything inside Lia shrank away from the ugliness suddenly roaring down on her, but there was no avoiding it. "What do you mean?"

Anne regarded her with a calm, almost sad expression. "It occurred shortly after you and your grandmother departed for Stonefell with my uncle. I believe you were not yet three at the time, correct?"

Lia nodded. Her heart was caught in her throat, making it impossible to speak.

"Not long after you left Town," Anne said, "my father and your mother had an affair. And *my* mother, I'm sorry to say, found out about it." She gave Lia a sad smile. "And that, my dear, is why Lady John Easton will forever hate anyone who goes by the name of Kincaid."

Chapter Twenty

"Miss Kincaid, are you well?" Anne said, peering at Lia with concern.

"Please call me Lia." It was a silly answer, but all the sense had been knocked out of Lia's head.

"Yes, of course." Jack's sister snatched up a glass of lemonade on the small table and pressed it into Lia's hands. "You suddenly look quite done in, which is hardly odd after the unfortunate revelation I sprang on you. I'm sorry for that."

Lia took the glass in her slightly trembling hand and brought it to her lips. The drink was tepid, but the tartness of the lemons helped to revive her. "There's no need to apologize. As you pointed out, our parents have poorly served us. But this . . ." She shook her head with disgust. "I cannot believe my mother acted with such wanton disregard for the feelings of your family."

Even though it had happened years ago and many sins could be forgiven, Mama could hardly have made a more ignoble and unwise choice of lovers than Lord John Easton.

"No wonder your mother hates us," Lia went on. "First your uncle installs my grandmother as his mistress on the family estate and then my mother embarks on a scandalous affair with yet another Easton man. We truly must seem like a plague."

Anne nodded. "That's a very apt description from my mother's point of view, especially now that Jack seems . . ."

"Involved with me," Lia finished. Lady John's disastrous conduct at the ball now made complete sense. "Does Jack know about the affair?"

"No. Apparently, it was hushed up almost immediately. My mother discovered the affair and demanded that my father put an end to it. Uncle Arthur supported her." Anne grimaced. "Could you imagine the scandal if they'd been discovered? The Easton men and the Kincaid women—the satirists and the gossips would have had a field day. As morally lax as he was, even my uncle wouldn't tolerate that sort of ugliness."

"I'm sure my grandmother wouldn't have been pleased either. She wanted to escape the scandal of her former life—for my sake, as well as hers. That's why she was so eager to retire to Stonefell and fade into obscurity."

Lia wasn't surprised Granny had never mentioned this nasty little chapter in the family's history. It would have been ugly and embarrassing for both the Eastons and the Kincaids.

"My uncle insisted the affair never be mentioned by any of the parties involved," Anne said. "Uncle Arthur even threatened to cut off my father's income if he so much as breathed a word, much less ever took up with your mother again."

"If no one was ever to speak of it, how did you find out?" Lia asked, putting her glass down on the table.

"A few years after it occurred, I overheard my parents fighting over the fact that Uncle Arthur wanted Jack to spend his school holidays with him at Stonefell. My mother wanted Jack at home with her. She feared exposure to your grandmother would be morally harmful, given . . ." Anne hesitated, as if searching for the right words. "The past history with the Kincaids. My father told her that her reaction was overwrought, and that he had no intention of giving in to her ridiculous fears."

Lia felt sick to her stomach. "How awful for her."

"Afterward, I heard her weeping in her room. When I went to console her, she made me swear on the family Bible that I would never breathe a word about the affair to Jack." She shook her head. "Believe me, I have often regretted making that vow."

"But telling Jack would have engaged his sympathy, would it not? He's very close to her."

"You must understand that my mother's dignity had been stripped away over the years and she couldn't abide the notion that Jack might pity her. Or that he would know the full extent of her humiliation at our father's hands." Anne gave Lia a sad smile. "And Mother didn't want Jack to have to choose between his parents. I think she feared he would choose Papa over her, which would have been devastating."

"Jack is nothing like his father," Lia said quietly. "Surely Lady John realizes that."

"Rationally, she does. But her heart is still afraid—even more so now."

"Because of me." It was hard for Lia to speak calmly, given the horrible, heavy lump in the center of her chest.

When Anne nodded, Lia sighed. "What is it you wish me to do, my lady? Should I tell Jack about this, or simply make it clear that I can have no relationship with him beyond casual friendship?"

Surprisingly, Anne shook her head. "My dear, that is not for me to decide. As I told Jack, your lives are your own to do with as you wish. I know how important you are to him and I have no desire to stand in the way of his happiness—if, in fact, being with you would make him happy. But I thought you should know the full extent of the challenges facing you, including the social and financial consequences." Her brows arched in a knowing look. "And aside from whatever form of relationship that might be between you."

Lia mentally winced. It would appear Jack had not expressly told his sister that he'd made her an offer of marriage, which suggested a degree of hesitancy on his part. She didn't blame him. He'd have to be a complete dolt to think he could marry her without significant repercussions.

"I understand," she said, "and I thank you for being so frank with me. I'm sure it wasn't easy for you."

Anne gave her a wry smile, once again displaying the easy charm she shared with her brother. Lia's heart was full of regret at the lost opportunity of friendship as the girls they'd been or the women they'd become.

"No, it wasn't," said Anne. "But I thought you deserved to know the truth, as sorry as I was to have to tell you."

"It's a shock, I admit. But no blame could possibly attach to you or to your mother."

Anne fleetingly reached out a hand, then pulled it back to her lap. "You're very generous, Lia. I wish—" She broke off and shook her head.

"You're not to worry," Lia said. "I know exactly what to do."

A bleak certainty had settled over her. Someone had to atone for all the damage to the Easton family, especially to the women. And that someone was going to be Lia.

After unceremoniously dumping Gillian on her husband, Jack stalked toward the river, where his sister and Lia sat near a pair of large oaks. A stranger would find it a charming scene—two pretty young ladies dressed in pastel summer gowns and frilly, stylish hats, drinking lemonade and chatting in the dappled sunlight. It couldn't possibly be more genteel.

And yet Jack knew better. The carefully blank look on Lia's face signaled distress. Even though Anne had said she'd support whatever decision he made about Lia, she'd told him in no uncertain terms that he'd be a lunatic to throw away his life by marrying her. At that point, he'd bluntly told Anne to mind her own business or risk facing his wrath. That threat had worked as well as one could expect—which was to say not at all. His sister was just as stubborn as he was, a trait inherited from their mother.

Because he wouldn't have put it past Anne to call on Lia directly under the guise of making an apology, he'd finally agreed to allow her to come with him today. By being close by, he could ameliorate whatever damage resulted from the confrontation as best he could.

His sister was a kind and tolerant woman, but she was also fiercely loyal to their mother and understood better than anyone how fraught all their lives would become if Jack took Lia as his bride. Unfortunately, he hadn't yet come up with any good way to placate his mother. Strictly speaking, there were no benefits to marrying Lia—at least of a material or social nature.

No, the benefits were more ephemeral but even more valuable. Lia's calm, clear-eyed understanding and her cheerful support for the challenges that faced him were blessings probably only he could see.

As for telling his mother that he desired Lia with a passion that now kept him awake at night . . . well, the old girl would be more inclined to take down a set of hunting pistols from the wall and shoot him if he dared make that argument.

When he reached them, the ladies glanced up, surprised.

They'd been so engrossed that they'd failed to note his approach.

He directed a brief scowl at his sister, then sat in the empty chair beside Lia and took her hand. "I hope my annoying little sister hasn't been too much of a bother, sweetheart."

Lia's eyes went wide. He'd clearly startled her, but he didn't see the point in pretending there was nothing between them.

"Um, no," she said, "everything's fine." When she tugged her hand, Jack reluctantly let go.

Anne gave him a reassuring smile. "We've just been chatting, that's all."

"About the weather? Or Lady Peckworth's decorating skills?" he asked sarcastically.

His sister had the grace to blush. "All right, we've been talking about the family, but I swear I haven't said anything to scare her off."

"I should hope not or you'll have to answer to me," Jack said.

"How utterly terrifying," Anne said with a cheeky little grin. "I'm shaking in my boots, I am."

"You are an unrepentant brat. Now, would you please go away so I can talk to Lia? Besides, Lady Peckworth wants to see you—she's practically quivering with anticipation at the thought of taking you through the house."

"Ah, very well." Anne stood and brushed a few stray leaves from the skirts of her gown. She smiled at Lia. "Thank you for speaking with me. I hope we have a chance to talk again soon."

Lia came to her feet as well. "Thank you, my lady. Again, I appreciate your honesty."

Alarm bells started clanging in his head.

When Anne gave Lia a quick hug, it surprised the hell

out of Jack—and, from her expression, Lia, too. His sister briefly pressed his arm and then headed across the lawn to meet Lady Peckworth.

"Don't forget to ask her ladyship to show you the kitchens," Lia called after her. "Especially the new range."

Anne waved a hand and was soon out of earshot.

"She upset you, didn't she?" Jack said. After her illness, Lia had yet to recover her healthy country glow, and today she was looking even paler than usual. "I swear I'll throw her into the Thames myself, even if she is my only sibling."

A gleam of humor sparked in her eyes. "Your sister is a very nice woman. In fact, she told me she regretted we were never able to be friends. She also said she'd been jealous of me, if you can believe it."

"Actually, I can. Our mother relied on Anne for support from an early age, and it placed too great a burden on her."

"So she said. I'm so sorry, Jack." She grimaced. "I'm sorry for everything."

He wrapped his hand around her much smaller one. Still, there was strength and sturdiness in her grip, the sign of a girl not afraid to work. "There's nothing to be sorry for, love. You've never hurt anyone in your life."

"Yes, but my family hurt your family very much. I feel awful about that."

"Most of the blame rests with the men in *my* family, not the women in yours," he said dryly. "Given the workings of the world, your mother and grandmother had far fewer choices in life. They did what they had to do to survive and protect their children."

When Lia withdrew her hand and took a step back, it felt as if she'd put a hundred yards between them.

"There were some choices they could have chosen *not* to make," she said in a voice that held a low vibration of sorrow.

"Why don't we sit down and you can tell me all about it," he said gently.

She looked around, almost as if seeing her surroundings for the first time. "I think I'd rather walk. Do you mind? The gardens are quite extensive, and I've hardly seen any of them."

Even better. Jack had already discovered a few very private spots, and if conclusions were drawn about their absence, that would fit nicely into his plans.

"I'm already familiar with Lord Peckworth's gardens," he said. "I can show you the finest spots. Let's start with a stroll along the river."

He offered an arm and she took it without hesitation, tucking herself neatly against his side. They set off along a graveled path, Lia easily matching his pace. The fact that she never dawdled was just another thing he loved about her.

Once they were out of sight, she untied the ribbons of her bonnet and pulled it from her head. A few pins came loose and glossy streamers of hair fluttered around her neck and shoulders. She briefly raised her face to the sun and let out a sigh. As attuned as Jack was to her, he knew it was not one of contentment or relief. While her profile presented an enchanting picture, the set of her mouth was tight and unhappy.

"I'm glad we're friends again," he said, testing the waters.

She flashed him a quick, quizzical smile. "Of course we're friends. We'll always be friends. At least I hope so," she added.

"I hope for rather more than that, Lia," he said.

She threw him a veiled, even wary look. "Really? Have you decided to become my protector, after all?"

He brought her to a halt. "We've already discussed this. I am not turning you into a whore." He deliberately used the ugly term, hoping to shock her into awareness.

"No? Are you a magician? Can you turn me into something more to your own liking?" She snapped her fingers.

"Perhaps a fairy-tale princess? That would be nice, and very apt."

"Very funny," he said. "What I would like to turn you in to, as you should know with thundering clarity, is a wife. *My* wife, to be precise."

She started walking at a fast enough clip that it took a few strides to catch up to her.

"Jack, you know that's not possible and it's time you accepted that," she said.

He steered her in the direction of a beech tree bordering the riverbank. A lovely wrought-iron bench in the shade of the leafy, overhanging limbs offered a sheltered spot far enough away from the house and the main gardens that they should be undisturbed.

"I don't accept anything of the sort." He gave her shoulder a little push and she plunked down on the seat with what he could only describe as an adorable scowl.

Her glare was sharp enough to slice him into slivers, and yet all he could think about was how enchanting she looked even when she was mad at him. He wanted nothing more than to take her down into the soft grass, slowly divest her of her clothing, and devour her gorgeous, naked body from tip to toe. He burned with the need to be inside her, plunging deep, feeling her clench around him until he found his blessed release.

She was truly going to send him straight to the madhouse—or cripple him with thwarted lust.

He propped one booted foot up on the bench and rested an arm on his thigh. "What did my sister tell you that put you off marrying me?"

"You are an utter booby," she said with exasperation. "It seems to have slipped your mind that I have not, in fact, agreed to marry you. Quite the opposite."

"After the events at the Cyprians' ball, I would beg to differ."

"If you mention that blasted ball one more time, I'm going to have to do something desperate."

"Which would be?"

She eyed him with disfavor. "I'm thinking I might shoot you. At least then you'll stop nagging me."

When he laughed, her mouth curled up into a reluctant grin. She settled her bonnet on her lap and let her gaze drift to the river.

Jack was content to hold his fire and allow the scene to work its quiet magic. A gentle breeze set the tall reeds to rustling and dragonflies darted in erratic zigzags across the surface of the water. With only a few smaller boats sailing by, it was the kind of peaceful, bucolic setting that usually bored him. But this time it made him think of Stonefell and wonder how life there was proceeding in his absence. He almost missed it, which was a new sensation. The old estate had always been more of a burden than anything else. Sometimes, it had felt like a millstone around his neck, strangling him.

But now, another feeling was slowly supplanting his resentment, slipping inside so quietly he'd almost missed its arrival. It was a sense of pride in Stonefell, and recognition that it was a beautiful and noble old place very much worth saving. He couldn't help but think that its rescue would be more honor than burden.

Lia's features had now settled into lines of lovely serenity. The country was where she belonged, and when he thought about taking her home to Stonefell as his bride, eagerness surged within him, along with an optimism he hadn't felt in a long time. With her by his side, to help him and to love him, what had previously felt like a burden seemed no sacrifice at all.

"I'm looking forward to going back," he said. "To Stonefell."

It took her a moment to catch up. When she did, her gaze narrowed. "Have you been drinking?"

"Of course not. I'm simply telling you that I'll be happy to return home, especially with you. As my bride," he added with pointed emphasis.

"If you take me back to Stonefell as your bride, it will be more along the order of a forced retreat because we'll be fleeing your mother."

"She'll come around."

"I doubt it."

"Lia—" he began impatiently.

"Very well," she said, cutting him off. "Does this mean you've decided to accept Dominic and Leverton as investors in the mining scheme?"

"Who told you about that?"

"Gillian. She said they're quite keen on it but that you're dragging your heels."

He cursed under his breath, wanting to throttle Gillian, along with his sister and mother for good measure. They were all making what should be a simple situation needlessly difficult.

"While I'm grateful for their support," he said, "it's not yet clear that the mine will yield enough profit to justify their investments. As you can imagine, I do not wish to find myself deeper in debt if it does not."

"Gillian seems to think the mining venture is viable."

"She doesn't know everything," he said.

"I thought she was being too optimistic," she said with grim satisfaction.

Confound it. He'd backed right into that one. "It will likely be very profitable at some point, but these things take time. That's all I'm saying."

She crossed her arms over her chest. "Time Stonefell

does not have, as we both know. You can't possibly afford to marry me, Jack, and what you said just proves it. You need a rich wife and you need one soon."

The determination in her voice raised the hairs on the back of his neck. "It's truly not that bad," he said firmly.

"It is that bad and you know it. We all know it. Marrying me will simply make the situation worse. And I refuse to be the cause of Stonefell's ruin."

. He plunked his foot to the ground. Looming over her, he mustered up his most forbidding scowl. "Because you are no longer on the stage, I would remind you that such dramatic utterances are no longer necessary."

She snorted. "I'll determine what's necessary when it comes to my life, Jack. You cannot force me to marry you. And I feel quite confident that your mother and your sister will support me in my decision."

"Lia—"

"There are only two options here. You either take me as your mistress or you agree to help me find a protector. If you fail to choose either, I will simply proceed as planned and find my own protector."

She'd very ably cornered him again. Lia had always wanted the best for him, and if that meant sacrificing her own happiness, she would do it. She loved him and she also loved Stonefell, possibly more than she loved him. It was a thought he chose not to dwell on at the moment.

In her mind, she'd made the entirely rational decision that marriage wouldn't solve any of his problems. But when it came to Lia, Jack felt anything but rational. She was his. She'd always *been* his, he realized, as he'd always been hers. The notion of not having her in his life was simply unthinkable.

As for taking her as his mistress, that was no option at all. He wasn't his father or his uncle. To take her in that way would dishonor and eventually destroy them both.

So play along and buy some time.

"Very well," he said. "Let's say I agree to your mad scheme. What would that entail exactly?"

Her mouth sagged slightly open. "Uh, are you saying you might actually take me as your mistress?"

"We'll see." He could draw a hard line, too. "I need to know your terms first. And I need time to make a decision. This isn't something a man should rush in to blindly."

"Perhaps, but don't think I'll let you drag this out forever, Jack Easton," she said suspiciously. "I won't let you manage me."

"I wouldn't even try. Now, your terms?"

She eyed him warily before holding up three fingers. "You have three weeks. If you have not made a decision in that time, I will proceed on my own."

It was more than enough time for him, but it was an odd qualification. "What's so special about three weeks?"

She blushed, shifting on her seat. "It's just a nice, round number, that's all," she said.

He decided to let it pass for now. "Very well, I accept that condition. What else?"

"If you decide *not* to become my protector, I want you to help me devise some tests."

His mind went blank. "Tests?"

"Yes, tests," she said defiantly. "For potential protectors."

"What sort of tests?"

She waved a vague hand. "You know."

"I bloody well do not know. Perhaps you could try being more precise."

The gentle blush of a few moments before had now deepened to a blazing rose. "Um, well, a kissing test, for one."

He stared at her, his brain finding it hard to function. "What would be the purpose of such a test?"

"I'm going to have to kiss my protector, obviously, so

I want to make sure I'm doing it right. That and other things," she added.

He couldn't hold back a laugh. "Sweetheart, you had no trouble with kissing the other night, I assure you."

"That was different."

"Why?" He was almost beginning to enjoy himself. Almost.

"Because it was you," she snapped.

Ah.

"I see." He stroked his chin, as if deep in thought. "And did you enjoy kissing me?"

She regarded him with an expression of acute dislike. "You know, I think you're simply too annoying to be my protector. Are you going to help me or aren't you?"

He had to swallow his smile. "Perhaps I'm not clear on the purpose of the kissing test."

"I would assume that one could determine quite a bit from the way a gentleman kisses a woman, correct? Such as whether he's someone who would treat his mistress with consideration and respect." She twirled a hand. "So . . . what sort of kissing behavior should I be alerted to? What would suggest that a man might not be a good candidate for the role of protector?"

"If he tries to force himself on you, as Sir Nathan did, I'd say that might be a fairly good indication," Jack said sarcastically.

She bolted to her feet. "If you're not going to take this seriously—"

"Forgive me, pet," he said, mustering a soothing tone as he gently pressed her back down. "I take this very seriously indeed."

There was no way on God's earth he would ever let another man kiss her, unless it was a friendly peck on the cheek from a relative or friend.

She subsided with a grumble. "Then please get on with

it, Jack. My backside is beginning to feel numb from sitting on all these iron seats."

He had to wrestle his mind off the image of her naked backside, preferably underneath his naked front side. "Very well. Number one—if a man tries to take liberties with you, you must put a stop to it immediately."

Lia frowned. "But he's already taking liberties, because I'm allowing him to kiss me."

"I mean further liberties, of course. Such as if he attempts to insert his tongue into your mouth."

She winced. "Right. But eventually he'll wish to do that, will he not?"

Jack gave her a gentle smile. "He'll insist on it. I know I would."

She fidgeted with the satin ribbons of her bonnet. "I suppose I'll just have to get used to it, then. Although perhaps I could institute a rule that he can only use his tongue when I give him permission."

"That's ridiculous. No man in his right mind would agree to a rule like that from his mistress."

"Oh blast," she muttered. "I'm sure you're right."

"He'll want to do lots of other things, too," he said.

She began to look slightly alarmed. "What sort of things?"

"Like the sort of things we did the other night."

"Hmm. If I'm being honest, I must say I enjoyed that interlude quite a lot. So, that's a good sign, isn't it?"

"Will you enjoy doing it with men who are virtually strangers?"

Her barely suppressed grimace suggested not. "I'll just have to get used to it, won't I?"

"If you don't, you might have trouble with the other physical requirements, too. And some men have very particular tastes. Peculiar might be a better term." Yes, he was laying it on rather thick, but it was the truth. "Ask your mother if you'd like a more detailed explanation."

She'd been leaning against the back of the bench, absently chewing a fingernail, but that comment brought her upright in a flash. "My mother is the last person I'd ask," she said sharply. "So don't suggest it again."

Something was clearly wrong—well, even more wrong than their demented conversation had been up to this point.

"As you wish." He found it interesting—and disturbing—that she was so rattled. Obviously, it had something to do with her mother. But he knew Lia well, and the subject was closed, at least for now.

She came to her feet and slapped the bonnet on her head, tying the bow with brisk efficiency.

"I take it our discussion has concluded," he said.

"Indeed." She gave him a look more suited to a governess or disapproving spinster than a budding courtesan. "I'm sure I'll have more questions in the future. For now, though, please be clear on the basics. You have three weeks to decide whether to accept me as your mistress or help me find a suitable candidate who will. Are we clear?"

"As clear as crystal," he said with a gentle smile.

"Good. Then I suggest we return to the house. The others will be wondering where we are."

He snagged her by the arm. "In a moment. I have a condition, too."

Although she was several inches shorter, Lia still managed to convey the impression that she was glaring down her nose at him. She looked very much like the princess she should have been.

"Which is?" she asked.

"I insist on having veto power."

"Veto power over what exactly?"

"Over your potential protectors, of course. If they don't pass muster with me, you have to reject them."

She looked momentarily flummoxed, but then her gaze narrowed and her brows leveled into an irritated line. "That's ridiculous. Knowing you, you'll never approve of any man."

"That's my only condition. If you want my help, I suggest you accept it. If not, you're on your own. And we both know how well you've done so far."

She glared at him for several long seconds. "You can go straight to perdition, Jack Easton," she finally said. Then she pulled out of his grip and stalked off.

Chapter Twenty-One

"You truly wish to marry me?" Lia blurted out. It seemed impossible. She'd been branded a pariah by the Ton, and yet here was another eminently respectable offer of marriage, her second in as many weeks.

Jack's proposal had been understandable because he felt responsible for her—even though that was nonsense. This one, however, was quite surprising.

Sebastian Sinclair, sitting next to her on the settee in the Hunters' drawing room, seemed taken aback by her astonished response. "Yes, I do, as a matter of fact. I would never jest about something as serious as marriage, Miss Kincaid."

When the baby snuffled a protest, Lia realized she was holding Dom's little body tight to her chest. She loosened her grip and settled him on her shoulder.

"I have to admit to feeling confused," she said. "You were adamant at Mr. Welby's masquerade ball that you neither wished to marry me nor take me as your mistress."

"I would never insult you by proposing a carte-blanche. But as for the other . . ." He shrugged. "You caught me off guard. Young ladies don't usually propose marriage to gentlemen of fairly short acquaintance."

"Or ever," she said wryly. "Especially not at a scandalous masked ball, where the atmosphere isn't generally conducive to clear thinking. I imagine all the scantily clad women would be quite a distraction, for one thing."

A flush colored his tanned skin. "Perhaps it's best we leave that unfortunate occasion in the past, where it belongs."

Lia found it interesting that the men in her life seemed more squeamish when it came to sexual matters than the women. While amusing, it was also annoying because it prevented one from having frank discussions when most needed. "Very well, but I'm still surprised by your offer, sir. Although flattered, naturally," she added.

"You don't sound flattered," he said dryly.

When Dom squirmed, half-awake, she patted his back. "I'll grant that we get along well when we meet at social engagements, but aside from that, I can't imagine one good reason why you should wish to make an offer."

"Can't you?"

His smile was warm enough to make her flush, although more from discomfort than pleasure. True, he was a very handsome man, with his wheat-colored hair and striking green eyes. And as Gillian had pointed out he was terribly rich and came from a good family. A marriage proposal from Sinclair would be a godsend to most women.

"You're very kind," she said, forcing a smile. "But marrying me would not further your position in polite society. The opposite, in fact."

"I don't give a hang what society thinks of me. Besides, you're hardly a cutpurse from the streets. Indeed, you have the support of some very powerful and highborn members of the Ton."

Lia shifted the now-sleeping baby into a more comfortable position on her shoulder as her tired mind scrambled to come up with an adequate response. She wished she could crawl off to some quiet corner and fall sleep, too. Life seemed to be growing more complicated by the minute and a marriage proposal from Sinclair simply added to the pressure.

When she didn't answer, he flashed her a truly enticing, seductive smile. "No, I wish to marry you because I like you," he added. "A lot, as I'm beginning to discover."

If Lia had a brain in her head, she'd leap to accept his proposal, but it would appear she'd been rendered brainless by the events of the last several weeks—and by Jack.

"You're a beautiful woman, Miss Kincaid," he said, "and you're kind, intelligent, and exceedingly practical. You don't prattle on about the latest gossip and fashions and you don't care about the idiocies of the beau monde." He reached out and fleetingly touched the baby's head. "You care about normal, everyday things like children. And from what I can tell, you prefer life in the country, as do I."

While kind, his recitation sounded more like a shopping list than a marriage proposal—dry and rather *too* normal.

"In fact," he added, "I think we share a similar view of the world, one that should stand us in good stead as a wedded couple."

"And what is that view?" she cautiously asked.

"We're both outsiders who forged our own way. We're not dependent on others for our happiness, nor do we allow them to stand in the way of what we wish to achieve. If we have to go it alone, we do it. All that makes us very well matched, and we would have a good, satisfying life together."

His assessment was probably true, but Lia was heartily sick and tired of standing on the outside, looking in on someone else's family and longing to be part of it. Just once, she wanted to belong—truly and completely belong. As nice as he was, she was sure she wouldn't find that belonging with Sebastian Sinclair. There was something about him that seemed almost detached, albeit in a friendly sort of way, as if strong emotion was more a bother than something to be desired.

"Sir, I truly am flattered by your proposal, but—"

"But the answer is no," he said wryly. "I expected as much, but I thought I'd give it a try."

She gaped at him. "You expected me to say no?"

"Your heart belongs to someone else, I believe," he said gently.

She couldn't imagine marrying anyone but Jack and she certainly couldn't marry someone as nice as Sinclair. He deserved more than a gloomy wife who pined for another man.

"I'm sorry," she said helplessly.

"You needn't be. I've enjoyed my time with you and I hope we can continue to be friends."

"Of course."

As much as he liked her, his sanguine expression told her that she hadn't broken his heart. In fact, his fleeting glance toward the door suggested he was now as eager to end their awkward interview as she was.

Cradling the baby close with one arm, she extended him a hand. "Thank you, sir. Please believe me when I say I truly value your friendship."

He held on to her hand, his gaze penetrating and sincere. "You don't have to do it, you know."

She lifted an eyebrow.

"Take a protector," he said. "My offer of marriage will stand. If you ever feel you have no other choice, please remember that you do."

Lia had to blink for a few seconds. "Thank you," she finally whispered.

He was bowing over her hand when the door opened and Jack strode into the room. Smithwell scrambled behind, a pained expression on his features. "The Marquess of Lendale," the butler announced with pointed dignity.

"What the hell are you doing, Sinclair?" Jack all but growled as he stalked up to them.

"I'm bidding Miss Kincaid a good evening," Sinclair said. "Not that it's any of your business."

"It is when my betrothed is having an intimate tête-à-tête with another man."

"You and Lendale are engaged?" Sinclair said to Lia, obviously surprised.

"No, we are not," she said firmly.

"We just haven't announced it yet," Jack said at almost the same time.

When Sinclair studied him for a few moments, Jack's returning glare was so hostile it raised the hairs on the back of Lia's neck.

"I see," Sinclair finally murmured. Then he smiled at Lia. "Well, then, I'll bid you good night. Please remember what I told you, Miss Kincaid. I do mean it."

"I will," she replied.

He gave Jack a brief nod. "You're a lucky fellow, Lendale. I hope you realize it."

Jack's animosity didn't abate a jot. He scowled at Sinclair until the man left the room, followed by Smithwell.

"What was all that about?" Jack asked, his attention swinging back to Lia.

"To paraphrase Mr. Sinclair, none of your business." Dom had started fussing again, so Lia carefully lowered him into the cradle next to the settee, gently patting his little chest. "And please lower your voice. You're disturbing the baby."

"Very well," he said quietly. "But I still want an answer. And why the hell were you alone with him in the first place?"

She was about to scold him when the door opened again. Chloe, dressed in a shimmering gown of wine-red silk, entered the room.

"Good evening, Lord Lendale," she said, giving him a warm smile. "How nice of you to visit. You can sit with Lia while we're at Lady Fernton's party."

Jack gave her a brief bow. "Lady Hunter, I didn't realize you would be going out. I hope you don't mind that I've come to call."

"Goodness, why would I?" she asked.

"Because I'll be without a chaperone?" Lia said in a hopeful tone. She truly didn't want to be alone with Jack right now. He was sure to pester her about Sinclair's visit and start yet another argument over marrying him.

Chloe waved a dismissive hand. "Nonsense. Lord Lendale is like family, is he not? You've said so a hundred times, my love. Besides, I don't want you to become bored or lonely, sitting here all by yourself."

More likely Chloe and Sir Dominic were afraid she would sneak out and do something scandalous, like attending another masked ball or some equally salacious affair. Lia couldn't help wondering if they'd asked Jack to come serve as her watchdog.

"I'm happy to stay home and rest," she said. "In fact, I'll probably go to bed early. I'm still rather worn out from yesterday's, er, delightful excursion to Lord Peckworth's villa."

Jack snorted, making his opinion of her absurd statement crystal clear. Lia glared at him.

"I understand completely." Chloe's eyes twinkled with amused understanding. "And it's very sweet of you to watch Dom while Nanny is feeling a trifle under the weather. But my maid will be happy to put him to bed, so you needn't play nursemaid if you don't wish to."

"He's no trouble at all," Lia said. "I enjoy it, truly."

Chloe peeked into the cradle to examine her son, smoothing a gentle hand over his tumbled curls. "I think he'll sleep for the rest of the evening."

"I'll put him to bed in a little bit," Lia said.

"Yes, *after* we talk," Jack said.

Blast.

There was clearly no escaping the dratted man. Lia didn't know how much longer she could keep resisting him, especially when he looked so handsome in the severe but beautifully tailored coat that set off his broad shoulders to such wonderful effect. No one looked more attractive in evening wear than Jack.

Chloe gave Lia a quick kiss on the cheek. "Enjoy your chat with Lord Lendale, my dear."

"Yes, I'm quite looking forward to it," she replied in a dry tone.

Her aunt nodded to Jack and glided to the door, pausing to give Lia a roguish wink before exiting.

It seemed Lia's entire family conspired against her. If they had their way, she'd be married to Jack before the week was out.

Of course, if they knew what Lady Anne had revealed, they might change their minds. Lia had been too disturbed—and mortified—to tell even Chloe or Gillian.

But she'd have to tell Jack. Nothing she'd tried so far had knocked him off course, including her ridiculous requests for his assistance in finding her a protector. No matter what she threw at him, he feinted. That left one weapon in her arsenal, but she loathed the idea because it would wound him as much as it would her.

Thunderstorms still lingered in his gaze, but above the black clouds lurked sunlight and warmth and so much concern. Lia had to resist the impulse to fling herself into his arms and burst into tears. She was so tired of batting aside one problem only for another to take its place. In the past, Jack had always been there for her, smoothing out the disturbances that had troubled her life. The temptation to let him do so again was so strong it frightened her.

She had to remind herself that *he* was now the cause of

many of her troubles. If Jack would simply get out of her way, she could put into action the plans to support herself and Granny. And then he could get on with his own life, finding a suitable bride and caring for his estate.

"What's wrong, love?" he asked gently.

It took a second before she could answer. "Nothing. I'm just a little weary."

"Then come sit and let me take care of you." His seductive smile pulled her inexorably toward him. "I'll massage your feet, if you like. I know how much you enjoy that."

"You'll do no such thing," she said, trying to sound scandalized. He'd done that more than once when they were children, after they'd tramped through the snow or gone for rides in damp weather. Her feet had always gotten cold because her boots were invariably worn thin and were often downright leaky. And Jack had invariably worried that she would catch a chill.

"Then just come sit and talk to me." He took her hand and coaxed her down to the settee with him.

"There, now, isn't that better?" he murmured as he draped a casual arm over her shoulder. His fingers teased the little puff at the top of her sleeve.

"Not really. In fact, you're behaving very improperly."

"You and Sinclair were also behaving quite improperly, from what I could see. And it's time you answered my question. Why were you alone with that bounder anyway?"

She twisted out of his loose hold. "Sinclair is not a bounder and it's none of your—"

He gently grasped her chin, silencing her. "Yes, sweetheart, it is."

She glared at him, but he was entirely unmoved. "You're so annoying," she said.

"I know, but you love me anyway."

Because she couldn't dispute that, she stuck her tongue out at him instead.

"Do that again and I'll have to kiss you," he said, the seductive gleam back in his eyes.

"If you must know, Sinclair proposed marriage," she said, knowing it would irritate him.

Well, it was rather more than irritation, given the flare of anger in his gaze. His features turned hard as marble. "Bloody hell," he growled. "That bas—"

She slapped a hand on his chest. "I refused him, so don't start blustering."

"I should damn well hope you refused him; you're going to marry me."

"I'm not marrying you either, Jack. We discussed this yesterday. You know very well what my terms are."

"I know you're insane if you think I'm letting you embark on some misguided venture to become a courtesan." He paused for a few seconds. "Or to marry anyone else but me."

"It's simply impossible and you know it," she said, starting to feel desperate.

He caressed her cheek. "Love, it's not. I'll grant you there are a number of inconveniences to manage, but we do have the support of your family. That counts for a lot. The Levertons and Hunters will do everything they can to smooth the way, and I'm sure we can even persuade the Dowager Duchess of Leverton and Gillian's grandmother to come on board."

"But *your* family won't come on board."

"Anne will be fine—she's said as much. As for my mother, she'll grow used to it, especially when she has the chance to truly get to know you."

"No, she won't." Lia pressed her lips tight against the sick feeling welling up in her throat.

"Is that what you and Anne discussed yesterday?"

She nodded, hating that she would be forced to tell him. Her chest constricted, making it hard to suck in a full breath.

He leaned against the back of the settee and crossed his arms, putting a bit of distance between them. While she knew she should be relieved, she missed his warmth and the sense that when he was near, nothing could truly hurt her.

But that was an illusion. Soon Jack would be gone from her life forever.

"Whatever it is, you'd better tell me and get it over with," he said calmly.

"It's . . . it's about my mother."

He nodded encouragingly.

"And your father."

Jack didn't move, but his big body seemed to tense up. "Go on."

As she retold the sordid story, his expression barely changed. A slight frown descended on his brow, but he didn't interrupt her and didn't seem nearly as appalled as she thought he would be.

"So you see," she said in conclusion, "I could never marry you, even if all our other problems were solved. Your mother hates all the Kincaid women, and rightfully so. You could never ask her to accept me into the family after what my grandmother and mother have done to her."

"I understand the point about your dear mama," he said, "but neither you nor Rebecca have ever done anything to hurt my mother. It's nonsense to think otherwise."

She couldn't keep her mouth from dropping open. "But you know how much it hurt Lady John to have Granny installed at Stonefell. It made things very difficult for your entire family for years."

He shrugged. "The relationship my uncle had with Rebecca was their business and theirs alone. As much as my mother disliked it, it really had very little impact on her life."

"How can you say that?" Lia exclaimed. "She hated coming to Stonefell because of it."

His mouth lifted in a sardonic smile. "I'll tell you a secret, my darling. My mother hated going to Stonefell because she loathes the country and always has. To a considerable extent, she used Rebecca's presence as an excuse to avoid visits to the old place."

"Really?" she asked doubtfully.

"Really. And if I'd known you worried about it so much as a child, I would have told you so years ago. As for my mother's resentment of you, I refuse to accept it. You are an innocent party in all of this, Lia, just as my sister is."

"As are you," Lia added softly. "Your sister told me yesterday that we were not well-served by our elders."

"She was correct."

Jack had barely batted an eyelash when she'd told him about the affair. It didn't make sense, unless . . .

"Jack, you didn't seem very surprised by what I told you about my mother and Lord John. Did you already know about their affair? Lady Anne said you didn't."

He sighed. "My father made a few veiled comments over the years, as did my uncle. I suppose I didn't want to think about it, so I never followed up on my suspicions, especially because I knew it would humiliate my mother. So, no, I'm not surprised to hear it confirmed."

She grimaced. "I'm so sorry. It was very poorly done of them."

"It was, but you have no need to apologize for it."

"Well, someone's got to," she said. "Your poor mother has suffered greatly as the result of my family's bad behavior. Asking her to accept me as your wife would poison your relationship with her and I couldn't live with that."

"I wouldn't let that happen."

His blasted self-confidence and arrogance made her want to shake him. "You're not a god, Jack. You can't just order people about willy-nilly, telling them how they must feel about things—or people."

"So you're going to sacrifice your own happiness to make up for something that happened years ago? To atone for the failings of your mother and my father?"

"If that's what it takes. Besides, I don't think I can face Lady John, not after everything she's gone through." In fact, the very notion made her sick to her stomach.

"I never thought you a coward, Lia," he said.

Her anger spiked and she started to jump to her feet. But Jack grabbed her arm and plunked her back down.

"This discussion is over, Lord Lendale," she snapped. "Please leave."

"Lia, I truly regret the indignity my mother suffered, but I will not sacrifice my life—or yours—to make up for it. I've already lived through my parents' unhappy marriage. One relationship of that nature was sufficient; I have no intention of repeating their mistakes. Is that clear?"

"Jack, it's not as if you truly want to marry me. You're just doing it because you have to."

He grimaced. "Where the hell did you get that idea?"

"It's the truth."

She yanked herself out of his grip and clambered awkwardly to her feet, turning her back on him. It *was* the truth, but that didn't make it any easier to say. Yes, he had a great deal of affection for her and wanted to keep her safe, but he only wished to marry her because he'd compromised her. It was a terrible basis on which to begin a marriage, whether he realized it or not. Eventually, he might even come to resent her, which would all but destroy her.

Lia heard him come to his feet.

"It's far from the truth." His big hands came to rest on her shoulders. "I do want to marry you. Very much."

Her eyes started to itch with incipient tears, but she forced herself to remain firm. "It doesn't matter because I have no intention of marrying you."

He gently turned her and tipped up her chin, making her look at him. His gaze was so tender that she could almost believe he truly did love her in the way she wanted to be loved. And that tore her heart into a thousand little shreds of tattered lace.

"Do you know why I came to call tonight?" he asked.

"So you could annoy me?"

His laugh was low and husky, sending flutters of pleasure deep in her belly despite her seesawing emotions.

"No, it's because I couldn't wait days, much less three weeks, to sort this out," he said. "I want you, Lia, more than anything I've ever wanted in my life. We're going to settle this tonight, once and for all."

When he lowered his head to kiss her, Lia's thoughts scattered like dandelion puffs on the breeze. She told herself to move, to shove him away, but her limbs refused to respond.

Just as his lips touched hers, an earsplitting wail came from behind them. They sprang apart as if a giant had thrust his hands between them and tossed them away from each other.

"Bloody hell," Jack muttered. "That probably took ten years off my life."

Lia pressed both hands to her chest, gasping as her heart pounded against her rib cage. "Dom does have a rather healthy cry," she said with a quavering voice.

As she went to retrieve the baby, she told herself it was for the best that he'd woken up and interrupted them.

Kissing Jack would be so dangerous. Once she started, she likely wouldn't be able to stop.

And she knew very well where that would lead.

"There, there, darling," she said in a soothing voice as she picked Dom up. She cradled him against her shoulder, patting his back. He started to settle, gave a little hiccup, and then proceeded to spew up his dinner all over the front of her dress.

Jack took one look at her and burst into laughter.

Chapter Twenty-Two

Lia stared down at her bodice, then looked at Jack, who was practically doubled over with mirth. Sighing, she fumbled for her kerchief and wiped the baby's chin. Dom now seemed as happy as a robin in springtime, despite his little mishap. He chortled as she cleaned him up, waving his fists with glee.

"I don't know why you find this so amusing," she said to Jack in a grumpy tone. "Babies throw up all the time. It's what they do."

"Yes, I know," he said, trying to contain himself. "It's just that I finally had the chance to woo you in an appropriately romantic fashion, only to have young Dominic decide to interrupt us so emphatically. It's rather ridiculous, you must admit."

She grimaced as she dabbed at her bodice. Lia had only worn the lovely primrose gown twice and suspected it would never be the same, even after a thorough cleaning.

"I think it's very mean of you to laugh at my predicament," she said, trying to maintain her dignity. It was a challenge because Dom now had grabbed her hair and was yanking with a fair degree of enthusiasm.

"You're right," Jack said. "But I can't help wondering how many courtesans find themselves in this sort of position. It would be rather off-putting to the average lover, you have to admit."

Lia was beginning to wonder if she did have the necessary skills or even the luck to become a successful courtesan. So far, she'd been an utter failure, and this silly incident seemed to underscore that point.

"Now, darling, don't pull my hair," she said in coaxing voice to Dom. She tried to ease a lock away from him, but he had a tenacious grip for one so small. "You don't want to—ouch!"

The baby yanked so hard it made her eyes water. Or so Lia told herself. Truthfully, though, she was close to succumbing to an inconvenient bout of tears. She rarely cried, but the stresses of the last several weeks were finally catching up to her, and at the worst possible moment. It would make Jack even more convinced she was completely inept and that he needed to take care of her.

"Here, pass me the little imp before he hurts you," he said, reaching for the baby.

"He's a complete mess. He'll ruin your coat."

"He's not as messy as you are." He gently pried the baby's fingers apart. "You're a disaster."

Even though he was joking, tears pricked her eyes. It wasn't just her dress that was a disaster—it was her entire life.

"Come here, scamp," he said, lifting the baby into his arms. Dom went happily enough, transferring his interest from Lia's coiffure to Jack's cravat.

"I told you," she said dolefully as she watched the baby demolish the neckcloth's crisp folds.

Jack gave her an assessing glance. "It's just a cravat, love. Now, sit down and rest for a moment."

"I should go up and get changed."

"Sit," he said in a stern voice.

And she did, likely because she didn't have the strength to argue.

Jack carried Dom out to the hall. She heard him talking to Smithwell, and then he returned without the baby, locking the door behind him. If she'd had her wits in any kind of order she'd no doubt be alarmed by that particular action, but all her energy was currently focused on not covering her face with a pillow and sobbing hysterically.

"You gave the baby to Smithwell?" she asked as he joined her.

"He was appropriately appalled by Dom's unfortunate state, but I have every confidence he'll be able to handle the situation. Besides, there's a houseful of staff to assist him."

"You should have let me take him up. I have to change anyway." She lifted her lace collar and tentatively sniffed. "I smell ghastly and this dress is ruined. It's one of my favorites, too." Her voice wobbled.

He gently arranged her so that her back was facing him. "I'll buy you a new one just like it," he said as he started to unbutton her dress.

"Jack, wh-what are you doing?"

"I'm getting you out of this. You're the one who said you smell ghastly."

"You *cannot* undress me in Aunt Chloe's drawing room. You should just go."

"One, I have no intention of leaving, not until we finish our discussion."

She felt a tear slip down her cheek. "Must we?"

"I'm afraid so," he said, not sounding the least bit regretful. He reached around and pulled her sleeves down her arms, enveloping her in his warmth. Lia had to fight the urge to lean against his broad chest, seeking refuge.

"What's two?" she whispered, as he pulled the dress down to her hips. He urged her up a bit and whisked it from under her. She shivered slightly, more from nerves than from the air hitting her exposed skin.

"Hmm?" he asked as he rolled up the garment and placed it on the floor.

"You already told me number one. What's number two?"

He turned her to face him, his big hands curling around her shoulders. She looked up into his beloved, handsome face. His expression was both amused and tender and she wanted him so much that her entire soul ached with yearning.

"Ah. Number two is that I'm definitely going to undress you in the drawing room. You needn't worry, love. No one will interrupt us."

"It's not that," she said miserably. "I just don't think—"

"Why are you crying, sweet girl?" he murmured, tracing a gentle finger across her damp cheek. "I've told you everything will be fine."

She shrugged. The fact that she truly didn't know Jack's mind made her feel both self-conscious and vulnerable. After all, it wasn't as if he'd laid his heart at her feet or made ardent declarations. Mostly, he delivered well-meaning but irritating lectures, which he seemed to think was enough to settle matters between them.

It wasn't.

"I don't know," she hedged. "I suppose I'm just tired."

He smoothed a hand down her neck and let it rest across the top of her chest, solid and comforting. "And perhaps a bit worried?"

She managed a choking sort of laugh. "A bit? Everything's an absolute fright and you know it."

His slow smile tilted up a corner of his mouth. "Shall I kiss it and make it all better?"

Lia rubbed her cheek as another tear fell. "You can't. It's simply not possible."

"That sounds like a challenge to me, and you know I can never refuse a challenge."

"Jack—"

He swooped down, his mouth devouring the protests that had been about to fall from her lips. She clutched at his shoulders as he took her with a passion she could no longer resist. Her eyes fluttered shut and she sank into the heat and strength of his embrace. It was like coming home after a very long time away and her heart longed to surrender.

Jack explored her mouth with a thoroughness that pulled a whimper from deep in her throat. Desire swept aside every argument, every fear, every barrier she'd erected against him. When he sucked her tongue into his mouth, she finally succumbed, ravished by the wet, delicious slide. It was a dominating kiss, one that said he would take what he wanted, when he wanted—and damn anyone who stood in his way.

But when one of his hands slipped down to her breast, a wisp of sanity penetrated her dazed brain. Her eyes popped open and she jerked back.

Jack's gaze displayed equal parts heat and irritation. "What's wrong now?" His husky growl was laced with masculine ire.

If she weren't feeling breathless, Lia might have laughed at his surly response. As it was, his low, rasping tone sent a dart of sensation between her thighs.

"I . . . I don't think you've thought this through, Jack."

He snorted and went to work on her stays. "Lia, I've been thinking of little else since that day you kissed me in Stonefell's library."

When she tried to bat his hands away, he ignored her ineffectual efforts. "Jack Easton, you cannot make love to me in the drawing room."

"Why not?" he asked as he deftly unlaced her.

"Because . . . because it's reckless and scandalous and . . . and completely inappropriate for a man of your position."

He regarded her with disbelief. "Says the woman who was sauntering about at a Cyprians' ball."

"I was *not* sauntering about," she said as she fumbled to hold up her sagging stays.

He again pushed her hands aside. "I don't know what else you'd call it."

"A complete failure, actually," she said with a sigh.

"Not a complete failure." He eased her stays down to her hips, then stroked the tip of his finger over one of her nipples. It hardened into a little peak, pushing against the soft linen of her chemise. "In fact, I recall that parts of it were very successful." His voice had taken on the low, rumbling quality that made her insides quiver.

"Jack . . ."

"God, you're so beautiful," he whispered as he gently rubbed his palm across the sensitized tip of her breast.

Lia felt as if she was teetering on the edge of the most wonderful experience of her life—or the most miserable, if she had to walk away from him.

When he pushed down the strap of her chemise, exposing one of her breasts, she had to swallow hard to get words out of her throat. "I think this is a mistake. A very large, very dangerous mistake."

His fingers closed possessively around her breast, searing her with heat and sensation. If she hadn't been sitting down, she would have instantly collapsed because it felt so wonderful. It took every ounce of willpower not to lean into him.

"This is the opposite of a mistake," he said. "This is perfect. You're everything I want, Lia. Don't doubt that."

"I must doubt it." Weeks of pent-up emotion forced out

the words. "I would bring so little to a marriage between us. I have absolutely nothing to give you."

For a moment he looked genuinely shocked. Then his gaze took on an expression of such tenderness that it made her want to weep. He cupped her cheek. "You have your own sweet self, love."

She gnawed on her lip, buffeted by conflicting emotions and a desire as strong as a fierce summer storm. When he swooped in, nipping her lower lip before kissing her, Lia shuddered and her body went soft and wet in response.

"Shall I show you all the wealth you would bring to our marriage?" he murmured against her lips.

Lia was too muzzy-headed to fully grasp what he meant. But she managed a jerky nod.

His eyes sparkled with both lust and amusement as he straightened up. "Very well, madam. Let's get started." He surprised her by standing and pulling her up. Her loosened stays fell to the floor.

"What are you doing?" she asked.

"I don't want there to be any misunderstandings, so I'm going to enumerate your good points, one by one."

"That sounds embarrassing and silly," she grumbled as he pulled the pins from her hair and tossed them onto a side table. Then he struggled out of his coat and casually dropped it on the floor.

"You're the one who insists on a strict accounting," he said as he shook out her hair. "You were always better at numbers and keeping accounts than I was, now that I think about it."

"That part *is* true," she admitted. "As your estate manager will tell you."

"Excellent. Then you can handle the books from now on, which is an added bonus for me."

She rolled her eyes. "This is becoming more ridiculous by the minute."

"Patience, love." He turned her to face the chaise. Then he sat down, leaving her standing before him, as if ready for inspection.

"Don't I get to sit down?" she protested.

"No. You're going to stand there like a good girl and let me illustrate the many assets you will bring to our marriage."

Lia blushed, feeling too exposed and yet excited by the heat in his gaze as it roamed over her body.

"Starting with your hair." Jack drew the thick locks over her shoulders. Lia's hair was longer than the current fashion and it tumbled in a silky fall over her breasts. "I love your hair," he said as he stroked it. "It's like satin, and when the sun hits it, it glows like polished amber. I've had many a fantasy about you lying naked in my arms, covered only by your glorious hair."

"Really?" she whispered.

His sensual smile sent butterflies wheeling through her stomach. "I'm happy to say that particular fantasy is about to come to life."

He tugged her closer, positioning her between his spread thighs. Lia couldn't help glancing down to inspect the healthy bulge that pressed against the fall of his trousers.

"So, we have amber, to begin with," he said, combing his fingers through her hair. "The first precious jewel in the box of riches that is Lia Kincaid. Shall we go on to the next set of gemstones?"

She tried to stifle a laugh. "You're talking nonsense."

He gently kneaded her hips through the thin material of her chemise. "No, I'm keeping an accounting of all the riches you will bring to our marriage."

"But—"

He cut her off with another kiss that quickly turned damp and heated, and Lia could do nothing but sigh with pleasure.

When he finally drew back, Jack's eyes were gleaming. "May I now continue with the accounting?"

Lia could hardly breathe, much less articulate sensible arguments to the contrary. "If you insist."

"I do." Gently, he traced a fingertip along her eyebrow. "Your eyes are next and they are infinitely precious. They're sparkling sapphires, Lia, full of brilliance and light."

It took a few seconds for Lia to answer. "Dear me, Lord Lendale, I had no idea you could wax so poetic."

He smiled. "I find the subject matter very inspiring."

"Very well, what's next?" she said gruffly, trying to exert some control over her emotions. He'd barely touched her and she was ready to dissolve into a puddle and give him everything he wanted.

"Your skin." He trailed a hand down her neck before skimming slightly rough fingertips along the top of her chest. It was so light a touch and yet it left delicious fire in its wake.

"Not a gemstone, obviously," he said, "but exceedingly like the most precious porcelain. Chinese, I think, so smooth and delicate." He inched the other strap off her shoulder, then kissed the hollow above her collarbone. "And so pure," he murmured against her skin.

When he took a little nip, a lightning bolt arced to the very center of her core. Her knees wobbled, forcing her to grab his shoulders for balance.

"I'm hardly what anyone would call delicate," she said breathlessly. A sturdy country girl was how people saw her. "Or pure," she added as an afterthought.

Jack had been licking her collarbone, but his head reared up. "You *are* pure, Lia. It's ridiculous of you to think otherwise."

She grimaced, hating that she'd ruined the moment, but there was little point in mincing words. "Aside from my scandalous background, you're forgetting what happened between us at that ball. That was hardly an innocent encounter."

"I've not forgotten one second of that encounter," he said, "but that's not what I'm talking about."

"Then what?"

He placed his palm flat over her heart. "I'm talking about what's in here. It doesn't matter to me what your background is, or even what you've done with me or anyone else. *This* is what is pure, Lia—your heart. It always was and I know it always will be."

At the moment that particular organ was pounding so hard she could have sworn it was reverberating against his hand. "That's . . . that's incredibly kind of you to say."

"I'm simply being truthful. Now, may I continue?"

She smiled and briefly pressed her hand on top of his. "As you wish, my lord."

"Good. Next up, your lips. That one is easy, of course. They're rubies, precious and delightfully red. But unlike gemstones, they're delicious to taste."

He captured her mouth in a kiss that made her head reel. It went from teasing to possessive in an instant, so hot, wet, and stimulating it made Lia squirm and softly moan. When he eased back, she could barely remain upright.

Jack was rather short of breath, too. His sharp cheekbones had flushed under his tan and his eyes glittered with barely leashed desire.

"I must say I do like rubies," she managed.

He laughed softly. "As do I, love. So much so that I want more of them."

Jack lifted her arms, then bunched up the hem of her chemise and whisked it over her head. Lia emerged from the garment clad only in her garters, stockings, and shoes. A fiery blush swept from the crown of her head to her toes. Her dazzled brain put up a brief, incoherent debate as to which part of herself she should attempt to cover first. In a halfhearted compromise, she clamped her thighs together and crossed her arms tightly over her breasts.

"Are you quite certain the door is locked?" she blurted out, casting a nervous look over her shoulder.

"Positive." Gently, he pulled her arms down to her sides. "Besides, Smithwell knows I would murder him if he let anyone in here."

Lia winced. That meant Smithwell knew *exactly* what they were doing.

"That's embarrassing," she said, jerking a hand over to shield her mound.

He covered her fingers with his hand, pressing down and sending a jolt of delicious sensation right into the nub of her sex. He rubbed gently and slipped through her fingers to her soft folds. Lia could feel herself growing hotter and ever more damp.

"He knows we're having a serious discussion," Jack said. He slid a blunt fingertip right to the entrance of her body. "Very serious."

Lia grabbed on to his shoulders, swaying a bit as she met his intent gaze. Jack was right. This was one of the most serious moments of her life. Nothing had ever felt as important as what was happening between them.

"Are you ready to find out what comes next?" he whispered as he continued to tease her. When he pushed two fingers just inside her, she whimpered and went up on her toes.

"Um, what?" She'd entirely lost the thread of the conversation.

"The next set of jewels in your jewel box."

Lia forced herself to concentrate. It seemed impossible because his every touch was a beautiful devastation.

"More rubies, you said," she gasped.

"Correct. These rubies, to be precise."

He withdrew his fingers and reached up to touch a nipple, now flushed as red as a berry. His fingers were slick, and when he rubbed the stiff point, Lia almost fainted from a bolt of lust that turned her knees to water.

"Jack, what are you doing?" she squeaked.

"I'm going to taste you."

Jack sucked her nipple into his mouth, drawing hard. Lia practically had to bite her tongue to keep from shrieking. She felt the tug all through her body, especially low in her belly. A hard shudder racked her, and his hand clamped onto her bottom, holding her firmly.

He went from one breast to the other, licking and teasing. Her nipples burned in a delicious fire that made her squirm. Deep inside, the first tiny contractions were building into a luxurious ache.

Lia pushed her fingers through his thick hair, holding him to her body. To stand before him like this—every part of her exposed to his demanding mouth and his roving hands—was outside the realm of anything she'd ever experienced.

"Jack," she finally moaned when he'd tormented her to unbearable heights of pleasure. "Stop. Please stop."

He gave one last nuzzle, then glanced up with an almost comical grimace. "I'll do so, if you wish, but I'm dead certain it'll kill me."

She choked out a laugh as she stroked his hair back from his damp forehead. "I didn't mean stop completely. Just stop doing that particular thing."

"Did I hurt you?"

"No, it felt wonderful," she confessed. "But it made me want . . . other things."

His tense mouth relaxed into a teasing smile. "Other things? Could you be more specific?"

"No, I cannot. Besides, I'm sure you know exactly what to do next."

"It would be helpful if you could articulate your expectations."

Lia waved a vague hand. "You know. I want you to . . . to touch me."

He wrapped his fingertips around her nipples and gently tugged. "You mean here?"

She whimpered. "Um, no."

When he pinched the stiff tips, she grabbed his arms. "Stop teasing me, Jack Easton," she gasped. "You know very well what I mean."

He raised a sardonic eyebrow that nonetheless managed to look lascivious.

Lia pointed downward. "Down there, you brute."

He huffed out a soft laugh as he softly cupped her mound. Lia had to resist the impulse to push into his hand, seeking immediate relief from the sensual ache at her core.

"Yes, I am a brute," he said, sounding smug. "But I simply assumed a woman of your vast experience would be more precise in expressing her needs."

When Lia grumpily crossed her arms under her breasts, unconsciously pushing them up, she couldn't fail to notice the flare of lust in his eyes. And even though he was being annoying, his teasing made her feel very naughty.

"We both know I'm a complete failure as a courtesan," she said tartly.

"And thank God for that because I want you all to myself."

"Then because you now have me all to yourself, I propose you get on it with." She was all but twitching with frustrated desire. "I believe you were cataloging my, er . . ."

"Ah, yes. I've been saving the best for last."

Finally, *finally*, he rubbed her sex, slicking his fingers

over her tight knot. Lia moaned and leaned into him, closing her eyes and letting herself drift on the tide of exquisite sensations. Jack massaged and teased, murmuring heady, erotic words of praise that drove her need to a white-hot pitch.

When he slowly pushed two fingers deep inside her, Lia choked out a soft cry. Wide-eyed, she stared down into Jack's flushed face. His features were tight with lust and his fierce, dark gaze pierced her soul.

But need lurked behind the lust in his blazing eyes, and she also saw a vulnerability that matched her own. Jack was willing to risk everything for her, even the relationships he held most dear. He'd laid himself open for her, and at great cost to himself.

How could she not love him with every fiber of her being?

He leaned forward and nuzzled her breast as he slowly pumped his fingers inside her. "You *are* riches beyond compare, Lia. More than any man could ask for."

She heard it in his voice—he wasn't playing anymore. He meant every word he said.

For a few torturous, wonderful minutes, they played with each other. Lia stroked and caressed his face and neck, leaning in for languorous kisses that drove them both mad. Jack kept his other hand clamped firmly on her backside, kneading her as she pushed against him.

"And this," he growled, shaping her bottom. "I love this too—your plump, gorgeous arse. And *this*." He slowly inched his fingers even deeper, making her gasp. "I can't wait to feel my cock inside your wet heat."

His bawdy language thrilled her. Lia moaned, clenching in a desperate effort to hold back her climax.

"All right, you've convinced me," she managed, grabbing the edges of his waistcoat. "I'm the bloody crown jewels of England. Now please do something before I go insane."

"What do you want?" he demanded in a harsh voice. "Tell me."

She shook him. "I want you deep inside me. Now."

"God, yes." He ripped at the fall of his breeches to free himself. His shaft was thick and long and so aroused that it sprang tight against his belly. Unable to help herself, Lia reached out to caress the broad, flushed crown, slipping her fingers through the moisture that had collected at the tip.

Jack pulled her hand away.

"You got to play with me," she protested.

"I'll spend if you keep touching me like that. Climb up, darling," he said as he urged her onto the chaise. He lifted her and arranged her body so that her thighs were spread wide and her knees snug against his lean hips.

Bracing her hands on his shoulders, she stared down at him, wide-eyed. "We're going to do it like this?"

His fingers played with the edges of her stockings, slipping up the inside of her thighs. "I think you'll find it easier for your first time. And this way I get to see all of you, too. *All* of you."

She flushed, which she wouldn't have thought possible given the scandalous activities they'd already engaged in. "But you're fully clothed, except for down there."

He waggled his eyebrows. "How naughty of us. It's like I'm the pasha and you're my little harem girl."

Her snort expressed what she thought of that comparison. Still, she found it unbearably exciting to be perched naked on top of him, while only that one vital part of him was exposed.

She glanced down. *Very* vital.

"Now what?" she whispered.

"Now this," he whispered back.

He eased her onto the head of his shaft, then curled his hands around her hips and began to guide her as he slowly pushed up. She was so wet she thought he'd slip right inside, but he was large and thick and she was tight. Lia winced and closed her eyes as he forged into her in a steady, determined slide.

"Look at me, darling," Jack said in a rasping voice.

Sucking in a deep breath, she dragged open her eyelids and met his gaze. His eyes were obsidian black and he looked drugged with pleasure.

He was so handsome and so hers that Lia's heart throbbed with a joy that felt almost like grief. It was too beautiful, too impossible to last in the real world.

Jack pressed a tender kiss on her lips. "Ready?" he murmured.

She frowned. "Aren't we already doing it?"

"Almost. Right after . . ." He gave one firm thrust and Lia felt a stabbing pain, her maidenhead finally and fully breeched.

". . . this," Jack growled.

She grimaced. "Good Lord. That part was not particularly pleasant."

He leaned his forehead against hers, his hands moving in soothing circles on her damp back. "I know, love. I'm truly sorry, but I have to admit I've never felt anything so good in my life. This is better than anything."

She huffed out an amused breath. "Naturally, I'm so pleased for you."

He leaned back and smiled, looking so carefree and happy that her heart filled with joy. For too long he'd been weighed down by worry.

"You are an imp, my girl," he said, "but I promise it will get better."

"I hope so, my lord, or I shall be most disappointed," she said pertly. Who would have thought this would be a moment for teasing? But she was filled with an emotion as bubbly as champagne and it was all she could do not to laugh.

"No pressure there," he said dryly.

She did laugh at that, but then he moved a hand between them, finding her tight bud again. Pleasure drowned out the fading sting, and she instinctively began to move.

She was tentative at first, with Jack's hands guiding her as he whispered lascivious encouragement. Soon she found her rhythm, rocking on his shaft while his fingers stroked her. The shimmering, startling beauty once more glimmered within reach as she felt the first contractions deep in her womb. Jack thrust harder, one hand on her hip to steady her, the other teasing her sex.

All pain had been replaced by the most wonderful, utterly filled sensation. She draped her arms over his shoulders and let herself move in sensual, undulating waves. It was so wrong to be with him like this and so wildly scandalous, sitting on top of him, taking her wicked pleasure.

Lia loved every moment of it.

"That's it, my love," he said in a harsh voice.

He was now thrusting up in sharp strokes that touched an incredible spot deep inside her. His fingers flickered over her sex, driving her higher, making her reach for a sensation akin to an incandescent burst of light and warmth. Lia wrapped herself around him, letting him control the movement, relishing the slippery silk of his waistcoat rubbing over her tight nipples.

Jack growled and tipped her over his arm, leaning down to suck a nipple into his mouth. He gave a hard thrust and everything contracted in one last burst of need, suspending her on the edge. Then her need expanded and burst, flooding her trembling limbs with rapture. Her body clenched around him, inside and out, and she let out a few tight sobs of joy and relief.

They remained locked together for a few minutes, panting, their heated bodies slowly cooling. Jack smoothed a hand up and down her spine, gently pulling her back to sanity. Lia went along reluctantly, letting the perfect moment slide away with a gentle sigh of regret.

"All right, love?" he murmured against her ear.

She pushed up so she could see his face. He stroked her messy hair, regarding her with so much tenderness and concern.

"Yes, I'm fine," she said. "Thank you."

He kissed her nose. "You're welcome, although I do think I should be the one thanking you."

"I suppose we can split the spoils, can we not? We can be mutually grateful."

"Sensible as always, Miss Kincaid, which is another thing I love about you."

Jack eased them around to rest against the arm of the chaise, arranging her on top of him before snatching his coat from the floor. After draping it over them, he cradled her snug in his arms. The delicate entrance to her sex felt sore and tingly, but a delicious lethargy filled the rest of her body. Part of her longed for a hot bath, but she couldn't bear the thought of leaving his comforting embrace.

"I am sorry it hurt," he said. "I promise it won't the next time."

Next time?

That easy expectation on his part brought reality crashing back in. How could she have been so stupid as to let this happen? Their encounter—as spectacular as it was—didn't solve any of their problems.

In fact, it simply created *more* problems.

Lia pushed up, bracing on his chest. He was sprawled casually, with his head propped on one muscular forearm. His hair was disheveled and his cheekbones were still flushed from passion. It took a mighty effort of will not to crawl further up his body and start kissing him all over again.

"Jack, despite what just happened, we do need to stop to think about this . . . about what happens next."

"What happens next is that I'm going to get a special license so we can be married as soon as possible, either here or at Leverton House. I think a quiet wedding makes the most sense, don't you?"

"We will do no—"

When he stroked a finger across her lips, she lost her voice. "I can't wait to get you back to Stonefell," he said. "Everyone will be so pleased to see you, especially your grandmother."

For a moment she imagined them returning home as husband and wife. It made her heart ache with anticipation and longing.

"You know it won't be as easy as you make it sound," she said.

"Of course it will. Besides, who else but you can make a decision about those blasted hogs Lindsey keeps nattering on about? I haven't a clue what to tell him, but you do."

She couldn't help smiling. "I thought we weren't supposed to talk about hogs."

"I believe sex was the topic to avoid, but we seem finally to have put that issue to bed . . . as it were."

It was a terrible joke, but she couldn't help snickering. Lia told herself it was from nerves rather than from the fact that everything he said felt perfectly right. Stonefell *was* home. It was where she truly belonged. "Jack, are you sure about this? Really sure?"

He gently cupped the back of her head. "Lia, do you love me?"

"Of course I do, you booby. How can you even ask?"

He grinned. "I simply wanted to establish the point

conclusively. And since that's the case, I will assure you again that everything will be fine."

She mulled that over for a few seconds. "And do you love *me*?"

He planted a kiss on the top of her head. "Pet, no one in the world could care for you more than I do, of that you can be sure."

Her heart sank; his words were too casually affectionate to evoke joy. So many obstacles loomed before them, starting with Lady John. Only a genuine, ardent love could hope to survive a mother who loathed her would-be daughter-in-law and her entire family. A mother who wished more than anything to see the Kincaids destroyed.

Lia wasn't convinced that sort of love existed between her and Jack, or ever would.

Chapter Twenty-Three

"How could you, Mama?" Lia asked in a reproachful voice. "You must have known it would cause trouble."

Her mother sat at the cluttered chest that served as her dressing table, fidgeting with stage makeup and casting furtive glances toward the door, as if seeking escape. Rehearsals had ended and most of the other actors and crew had gone for dinner. That was why Lia had chosen this quiet time to buttonhole her.

After last night's torrid encounter with Jack, she stood in desperate need of guidance, especially because he was insisting on an immediate marriage. Mama would understand the problem in a way no one other than Granny ever could. Although she would no doubt think marriage to Jack was a grand idea, at least her mother wouldn't pretend it would be a fairy tale.

Despite forging a career of make-believe, Mama lived in the real world. If anyone could give Lia the unvarnished truth, it would be her.

"I'm not going to leave until you say something," she said when her mother didn't answer. "So there's no point in ignoring me and hoping I'll just go away."

Her mother let out a dramatic sigh and finally met her

gaze. "You were always stubborn, even as a little girl. Whenever I would send you to bed, you would plant your little feet and refuse to move. And you always set up a fuss when your nanny tried to take you up to the nursery."

Lia rolled her eyes. According to Granny, she'd been a biddable child with a sunny disposition. Perhaps that was her real problem—she'd always been too accommodating, trying to please everyone else instead of herself.

"That's not how I remember it. And stop avoiding the question, Mama. Yes, it's ancient history, but I want to know why you embarked on an affair with Lord John. It seems an entirely demented decision."

Her mother bristled. "Ancient is hardly the term I would apply to myself, my girl. Goodness, you make me sound like an old crone."

How predictable that her mother would focus on her vanity rather than the pain her actions had caused other people. "Mama . . ." she said in a warning tone.

"Very well. I was lonely, Lia. You and Rebecca had departed for the north with Lord Lendale and I'd recently broken off with my lover. I was out of sorts and . . . and a bit frightened, if you must know the truth. I felt very alone."

"I didn't realize that," Lia said, disconcerted. "I thought you were relieved to see us go."

Her mother's hands fluttered to her lap, her fingers twisting into an anxious knot. "*Relieved* is not precisely the right word. Yes, it was sometimes inconvenient to have a child in the house, but it was more than that. Before I was able to finally make my living as an actress, I needed a paramour to protect and support me. I wished you to be raised in a more . . . a more normal atmosphere. Your grandmother agreed with me."

"So you actually missed me?" Lia asked softly.

"Of course I did. I loved you." She flashed her a misty smile. "I still love you."

Lia's throat tightened. "I missed you, too."

"Thank you, darling, but we mustn't get too sentimental about bygone days. It all worked out for the best, did it not?"

"That remains to be seen. You still haven't told me why you took up with Lord John. Aside from everything else, his pockets were rather moth-ridden, from what I understand. He certainly wasn't a practical choice."

"No, but he was a charming one, and so very handsome. He obviously sensed I was lonely and began courting me. He was very good at that, as I'm sure you've heard." She gave Lia a roguish wink. "*And* he was an excellent lover. I can only hope Jack is as accomplished in that regard as his father."

That was not a comparison Lia wished to think about—ever. "So you're saying Lord John took advantage of your loneliness? That seems caddish of him, given that Granny was already involved with his brother. He had to know how upsetting it would be for everyone, especially his wife."

Mama rolled her lips together and went back to fidgeting with her makeup.

Lia felt disappointment in the pit of her stomach. "You wanted it, too, didn't you?"

"And why not?" her mother asked in a defiant burst. "Wasn't I good enough for him? Aren't any of us good enough for those blasted Lendale men? I gave up my own daughter into Lord Lendale's protection." Her beautiful eyes were hard with resentment. "Lendale was devoted to your grandmother, or so he claimed. Yet she wasn't good enough for him to marry, was she? Rebecca gave up *everything* for him, Lia. So what was wrong with my taking a little of what the Kincaids were due from that bloody, stuck-up family?"

Now *that* made sense. Her mother had always been a canny businesswoman and would never have taken up with a penniless aristocrat simply because he was handsome or an accomplished lover.

"It was revenge you were after," Lia said.

Her mother threw her a scowl. "We were good enough to bed but not good enough to marry. Good enough to dally with but not good enough to bear their children." She fisted a hand and pounded it on the table, causing the little containers of rouge and powder to shake. "No, it was only the pure English roses who were worthy of marriage to the Lendale men, not common whores like the Kincaids."

Her mother's outburst was raw and sour, like bitter garlic, and Lia's heart ached for her. Resentment had festered for too long for both the Kincaid *and* the Easton women. Their men had betrayed them time and again, leaving deep wounds. While Jack had treated them all with true affection and respect, even he couldn't seem to drain the infection.

Lia sighed. "Good Lord, this is worse than *Romeo and Juliet*."

"Ha. I'd like to poison the lot of them. Except Jack, of course," her mother said hastily.

"I understand, Mama, but we weren't the only ones who were hurt. There was Jack and Lady Anne, too, and especially Lady John. She didn't deserve to be humiliated by you and Lord John."

Her mother waved a dismissive hand. "I know you would like to think so for Jack's sake. But she treated your grandmother and me like dirt. Rebecca was never anything but respectful and utterly discreet, and yet Lady John treated her like she was a common whore. That bloody woman deserved a little of her own back and I was glad to give it to her."

Lia pressed thumbs to her throbbing temples. So much

anger had been handed down from one generation to the next. How could she and Jack possibly bridge that divide? The idea of her mother and Lady John even standing in the same room together seemed utterly impossible.

"Do you have a headache?" her mother asked in a puzzled voice.

Lia dropped her hands into her lap. "Yes, I suppose I do."

Both a headache and a heartache that she was beginning to suspect would never go away. Her mother hadn't simply slipped into a foolish, brief affair with Jack's father—it had been a deliberate act intended to cause maximum pain. Lady John would never forgive that, nor would Lia expect her to.

Her mother reached out and touched a fluttering hand to Lia's cheek. "Now, darling, there's no need to be mopey about what happened in the dreary old past, and don't worry about Lady John. You're as good as any girl in the Ton. Better, in fact, because your father is the Duke of York himself. And Jack actually wishes to marry you, which is simply splendid. If you want my advice—"

Lia let out a faint, hollow laugh. She'd wanted plain speaking from her mother and she'd certainly gotten it. "I don't think I do anymore."

"You should give up this silly notion of becoming a courtesan," her mother blithely carried on. "It's not the life for you, Lia. The best thing you can do is marry Jack and return to Stonefell. God knows you've earned the right to be mistress of that blasted place."

Earned it? How did one earn something like that? Love and all that came with it was a gift that must be freely given or it wasn't worth having at all.

"I must say," her mother added with a sly smile, "I wish I could see Lady John's expression when Jack tells her that he's going to marry you. That would be quite delicious."

"None of that, Mama," Lia said in a sharp voice. "There's

been enough pain in our families and I will not have you gloating. Besides, it's far from settled that Jack and I will be marrying at all."

"Oh pish. You'd be a fool not to marry him, and I know very well that your grandmother would never raise a fool." She glanced at the small watch pinned to her waist. "Goodness, look at the time. Your stepfather will be waiting for me." For her, the discussion was clearly over.

Mama stood and made for the door but then paused to look back. "I would advise you not to keep him waiting long. Men are not the most patient creatures on the planet, and you certainly don't want to give his mother any more time to influence his decision. I strongly suggest you take at least that bit of advice from me."

"Mama, wait," she said, getting up and following her out into the hall.

"Yes, dear?"

"If I'm not able to take care of Granny, you will, won't you?"

She smiled and again patted Lia on the cheek. "Of course I will. She's my mother and she gave up everything for me, too."

And with that, her mother turned and bustled off in the direction of the stage. After the sound of her short train swishing over the floorboards faded, the old building seemed to settle into a decrepit silence. With a sigh, Lia made her way toward the dressing rooms of the principal dancers and singers. She had the answers she'd come for, most of them dreadful. She might as well try to salvage a bit of good by stopping in to see how Amy was faring.

As she traversed the dingy corridors of the theater, they made her feel slightly claustrophobic for the first time. The city, with its cramped spaces and high walls, was beginning to wear on her. She missed the country more than she cared to admit and longed for a good, clean breath of brisk Yorkshire air.

"May I come in?" she asked, pausing at one of the dressing room doors.

Amy was sitting on a stool, fiddling with her dancing slippers. She glanced up with an eager smile. "Miss, it's so good to see you." She dropped her slippers and rose to give Lia a fierce hug. "You're looking a bit peaked for someone who's keeping company with such a handsome gent as Lord Lendale. Everything all right?"

Everyone asked Lia that same blasted question. "Don't worry about me, I'm fine. How are you? It's your first day back, is it not?"

Amy nodded. "'Tis, and I'm happy to be here. Your ma and Mr. Lester were grand to take care of me, but I was like to crawl out of my skin being laid up in bed for so long."

Mama and Stephen had been horrified by how Prudhoe had abused Amy and had insisted on bringing her to their town house to recover. Stephen had been so infuriated that he'd been ready to challenge the baronet to a duel, or at least to *mill him down*, as he'd put it. Only Jack's insistence that he was taking care of the matter—and Mama's frantic demands that her husband not tangle with *quality*—had stopped him.

"You'll be dancing in no time," Lia said, pleased to see the bruising had mostly faded from Amy's lovely face. "You've not had any more trouble, have you? With Sir Nathan, I mean."

"Not a peep from that bloody degenerate," Amy said with a sneer. "Lord Lendale said he would see to it that he never bothered me again and so far he hasn't. Mr. Lester even sent a note telling him that he wasn't welcome anymore at the Pan."

"Huzzah. Good for my stepfather."

Amy gave her a rueful smile. "I'm not sure Sir Nathan

would give two hoots about that, or even listen to Mr. Lester. But I think your beau put a real scare into him. Sir Nathan would never have the guts to go up against a marquess."

"I'm happy Lord Lendale has been so supportive, but he's not really my beau," Lia said.

"That's not what the gossips are saying. According to them, Lendale's been sniffing around your skirts like—"

"Yes, well, never mind the gossips," Lia interrupted. "They'll say anything."

Amy looked disappointed. "That's too bad. I was hoping you would marry him. He's such a fine-looking fellow, and if anyone deserves a happy ending, it's you, miss."

"Thank you, but I'll have to find my happy ending some other way," Lia said, trying not to sound depressed by the notion.

Amy cocked her head and studied her, like an inquisitive sparrow. "You love him, don't you, Miss Lia?"

"Is it that obvious?"

"It is to anyone with eyes in her head. You light up when you're around him, even when you're sniping at each other. And it's clear he's mad about you, too."

"Mad *at* me, more like it," Lia said with a false little laugh. "It doesn't matter anyway. We're not suited."

Amy frowned. "Why not?"

"He's an aristocrat and I'm the illegitimate daughter of an actress. Lord Lendale needs a proper lady, a person of his own social standing, not someone whose very existence is a scandal. And other reasons," she added vaguely after a moment.

Amy took her hand. "Lord, miss, you're the daughter of a prince. You don't get more highborn than that."

Lia gave her a rueful smile. "That's not how people see it."

"I'll tell you what I see. I see a bang-up girl who'll do anything for the people she cares about. That's why your man loves you, not because you're some nose-stuck-in-the-air lady of quality. Besides, what truly matters is whether he treats you like a lady, whether you were born one or not."

Lia's throat went tight, so she simply gave Amy's hand a grateful squeeze.

The dancer sighed and shook her head. "You'll do what you think best, but it would be a shame to let such a handsome bloke slip away. Anyway, what will you do with your ma dead set against you acting?"

"My half brother and his wife have invited me to stay with them in Vienna. Perhaps I'll do that."

Lia had toyed with the idea before, although only as a last resort. But now that Mama had promised to look after Granny, it was an option to seriously consider, at least until she had some idea what to do with her life—a life without Jack, which was an idea so dreary it made her chest feel hollow and cold.

"That sounds lovely," Amy said enviously. "I've always wanted to travel."

"Then I'm sure you will someday," Lia managed. "Forgive me, Amy, but I must be off. My cousin is coming for tea and I promised to be home by the time she arrived."

"I'll walk out with you, miss. I'm finished for the day."

Lia waited while Amy fetched her cloak and bonnet, and then they took the stairs down to the back door and to the alley behind the building. Sammy, the boy who watched the stage door on the days the theater was dark, scrambled down from his stool to let them out. He was an engaging scamp, not much more than ten, and had a large mop of curly hair and a grimy but friendly face.

Sammy was also a good deal more reliable than the regular doorman because he was apparently immune to taking bribes from overly bold gentlemen wishing to get backstage. He took his duties very seriously and always responded to requests from company members with alacrity.

"Evenin', Miss Lia, Miss Amy," he said, holding open

the door for them. "It's lookin' stormy out there, so you best trot on home as quick as you can."

Amy gave his cheek an affectionate pat. "Thank you, my lad. We'll be sure to do that."

"Your face is ever so much better," he said in an earnest tone. "I'd like to kill the bastard that done hurt you, I would."

"I wish you could," Amy said. "Lord knows he deserves it."

Lia shot her a quelling glance before addressing the boy. "That's a noble sentiment, Sammy, but I think we'd best leave that sort of thing up to the authorities."

Sammy snorted his disdain. "Then we'll be waitin' forever. The swells never get their due when it comes to hurtin' regular folks like us."

That one so young had such a cynical—and accurate— view of the world made her want to weep. "I'm afraid that's too often true. But in this case, I'm confident the villain received his just due."

Jack had been vague on the details of Prudhoe's punishment after discussing the situation with Dominic and Leverton, but he'd assured Lia that he had everything well in hand and that she was not to worry about it. She'd been annoyed at his well-intentioned but condescending attitude, but she understood that men didn't like to discuss these matters with ladies, thinking them too tenderhearted or softheaded to deal with such unpleasantness. It was a ridiculous assertion for anyone to make, especially if they knew her cousin Gillian.

"I hope they got him good for hurtin' you, Miss Amy," he said. "But you come tell me if he ever bothers you again. *I'll* give him a bit of home-brewed."

"I will be sure to do that." Amy's tone was solemn, but her eyes twinkled with laughter. It was wonderful to see her sunny disposition coming back to life.

"Don't forget to lock the door behind us, Sammy," Lia said as she followed Amy down the steps to the cobblestones.

"No fear, miss. I'll keep everything right and tight."

They set off down the long alley between the theater and the warehouse next door, heading toward the street. Dark clouds roiled overhead, casting a premature dusk. A gust of wind forced their heads down as they clutched their bonnets.

"Goodness, we'll be lucky to get home before it rains," Lia said.

Amy glanced up, but then her gaze darted ahead to the end of the alley, some yards ahead. "Why is that coach parked like that in the alleyway? We'll never get around it."

A large black carriage blocked their way. Two big men—*hulking* might be a better description—lounged against the wheels, both smoking pipes. They affected a casual stance, but their caps were pushed low over their faces and they radiated a strange air of menace. One of them looked up to meet Lia's gaze with a hard stare before knocking his pipe against the wheel of the carriage and shoving it in his pocket. The other man straightened as well, his attention focused on them.

Lia pulled Amy to a halt. "We'd best go back to the theater."

The dancer gave a tense nod and they reversed their steps, only to immediately hear the pounding of heavy footsteps behind them. Not looking back, they picked up their skirts and ran.

They almost made it. Amy had reached the set of stairs at the back of the theater and Lia was just behind her when she felt the rush of movement and a long, burly arm wrapped around her waist. She let out a shriek and started to kick like mad, flailing her arms in a futile attempt to break free. The man ripped off her bonnet and dug his fingers into her topknot, then yanked her head back so hard it felt as if her neck was going to snap.

Amy launched herself back down the steps. "Leave her alone, you brute!"

She started pummeling Lia's captor but was snatched up by the second thug. He grabbed her by the throat and lifted her right off her feet. Amy clawed at his hands, her eyes wide with panic. He plowed a fist into her chin and her eyes rolled back as she collapsed onto the stairs.

"No," Lia gasped out. Fear and rage lent her strength and she slammed her bootheel into her captor's shin. He let out a vile curse and she felt his grasp start to slip. But when she tried to wriggle free, he tightened his grip and pulled her around to face him.

She stared into his flat, pockmarked features. His breath, hot and smelling of sour beer, made her gorge rise in her throat.

"Help," she cried out. She thrashed and managed another strangled shriek, trying to make as much noise as she could.

"Shut up, you silly bitch," the man said in a cold, calm voice. He gave her a vicious slap, so hard that stars burst across her vision. A rank-smelling hood came down over her head, enveloping her in blackness. Lia was barely able to suck in a breath before he lifted her and threw her over his shoulder, knocking the wind from her lungs.

Struggling to breathe, her hold on consciousness slid away.

Chapter Twenty-Four

Lia jerked as the hood was yanked from her head. Blinking frantically, she struggled to focus against the harsh glare of a nearby lamp. Although she'd been hazy for a few minutes, thanks to the nasty blow to her face, she guessed that only a short time had passed since their abduction. Thrown onto the floor of the carriage, she'd huddled against Amy and done her best to fight a choking sense of terror.

At one point she'd nudged her hood up to take in her surroundings, only to earn another slap to the back of her head. After that—and after her ears stopped ringing—she simply listened, straining for clues to their route. Unfortunately, the rumble of the carriage wheels on the cobblestones blunted her hearing.

Their captors had remained silent for the entire ride. Amy had put on a good show of defiance, but that had simply resulted in a kick to her ribs. After that, they'd both held their tongues, even when the men dragged them from the carriage and hauled them to this room.

Her blurred vision finally resolved into hard reality. She and Amy were seated side by side on rickety chairs in some sort of parlor. The furnishings were shabby but respectable enough, and the woman sitting across from Lia was dressed rather like a housekeeper in a neat gray gown and a lace cap. But most housekeepers didn't sport blazing red, elaborately curled hair and heavily rouged cheeks. Nor did they usually participate in kidnappings.

Lia's temper flared when the woman smirked at her. "I don't know who you are, but I demand that you release us this—"

Amy's shocked exclamation cut her off. "Bloody hell. It's *him*, Miss Lia. He's done it, the bastard."

Lia's stomach lurched when she saw who stood on the other side of the room, casually leaning against the doorframe and looking as natty as if he were about to attend a ball. Clamping down hard, she forced back a sickening wave of fear. "Sir Nathan, are you responsible for this outrage?"

The baronet laughed. "Of course I am, you ninny. Although I must admit I didn't expect to catch you in my net. My darling little Amy was the target. But when I saw you in the alley . . . well, how could I resist?"

"And a fine catch they are, my lord," said the woman sitting across from them. "My gentlemen are always looking for something new, even if these dainty morsels are soiled doves."

Prudhoe pointed at Lia. "I would imagine this one is barely touched, even though her mother is one of the greatest whores in London."

Lia bolted out of her chair. "You listen to me, you degenerate—"

A large hand slammed her back down on the seat, almost toppling her. After she righted herself, she glanced over her shoulder. She'd been so surprised to see Prudhoe that she'd failed to notice one of their abductors standing behind them. The brute gave her a taunting grin, as if daring her to make another move. His expression made it abundantly clear he would relish the opportunity to hurt her again.

She subsided, trying to think through her terror and rage. They'd almost made it inside the theater, so perhaps Sammy had noticed the commotion and gone outside to check. It was a faint hope, but the only one she had.

"No point in struggling, love," said the woman. "We don't want to have to damage the goods." Then she glanced at the baronet. "Are you saying this one is a virgin?"

He shrugged. "I think it's quite probable, although one can never be entirely sure until one checks for oneself."

"You leave her alone," Amy cried. "She don't deserve any of this."

Prudhoe pushed away from the door and strolled over to the dancer. She shrank against the back of her chair but maintained her defiant gaze as he took her chin in his hand.

"She deserves exactly what she's going to get, as do you," he said. "Thanks to you and Miss Kincaid's friends, I'm all but ruined. I'll have my revenge for that." He let out an ugly laugh. "And some welcome compensation. Double, now, don't you think, Mrs. Grace?"

The woman looked perplexed, as if she'd forgotten something. "Perhaps. We'll have to see what my customers are willing to pay."

"Who are you?" Lia asked. "And what in God's name are you talking about?"

The woman's full lips parted into a smug grin. "I'm the owner of this little establishment and you and your friend are going to be the evening's entertainment."

"Do you mean a . . . private theatrical?" Lia cautiously asked, vainly hoping that such would be the case. Though it must be one of a salacious nature, perhaps she and Amy could still negotiate some way out of this.

"She's a bawd, Miss Lia," Amy said in a grim tone. "And this is a brothel."

"That's right," said Prudhoe. "And we're going to sell you both to the highest bidders."

Lia couldn't help laughing. "You *must* be joking."

He shoved his face a few inches from hers. "We're going to sell you off as whores to the highest bidders and make a very pretty penny, I assure you."

Her stomach cramped from the stench of his gin-soaked breath and a surge of horror.

"You're a dead man if you go through with this," she said, trying to keep calm. "Lord Lendale will kill you, unless the other men in my family get to you first."

"Lendale. You mean the marquess?" Mrs. Grace asked in a suddenly concerned tone.

Prudhoe straightened. "It's nothing to worry about."

"You have a great deal to worry about," Lia said. She frowned at Mrs. Grace. "Did he not tell you who I am?"

The madam threw a wary glance at the baronet. "You said she was an actress, newly arrived in town." She pointed at Amy. "And this one was a dancer and a whore, so no one would think twice if she went missing."

"Which is exactly true," Prudhoe said through clenched teeth.

"I'm not an actress," Lia said. "Although my mother is. She's Marianne Lester. Surely you've heard of her. She's quite the most popular actress in London—perhaps in all of England."

Mrs. Grace went white under her palette of rouge. "What did you say your name is?"

"Lia Kincaid, of the Notorious Kincaids. So notorious, in fact, that a great many people *will* notice if I go missing."

"Shut your goddamn mouth," Prudhoe shouted.

Lia couldn't entirely suppress a smile as she met the baronet's infuriated gaze. "Did Sir Nathan also neglect to tell you that I'm betrothed to the Marquess of Lendale? The wedding ceremony is to be held later this week at the

Duke of Leverton's house." She transferred her focus to the brothel owner, who looked ready to faint with horror. "The Duchess of Leverton is my cousin. Perhaps you've heard of her, too."

Mrs. Grace seemed to be choking on her own tongue. A few seconds later, she recovered herself, and then all hell broke loose.

Amy touched Lia on the shoulder. "How long do you figure it's been?"

Lia shifted on the unforgiving floorboards, trying to find a more comfortable position. Sighing, she gave up and used the wall to push herself to her feet. Her head throbbed and her body ached, but she worried much more about Amy. Dragging them upstairs to this gruesome little bedroom, one of their captors had banged the poor girl's face on a banister, splitting open the skin above her eyebrow. She was dreadfully pale and had already retched once into a heavy chamber pot Lia found under the bed.

"Not yet an hour, I think." Lia grimaced and stretched, trying to relieve the cramped muscles of her back.

"Miss Lia, you take the chair. You shouldn't be sitting on the floor."

Lia gently pushed her down onto the seat. "I'm fine. Just rest while I try to think of some way out of this mess."

"Good luck with that," Amy said, casting a morose glance around the room.

Lia had already gone over their prison twice, looking for a weapon or means of escape. Aside from the ratty old bed, its linens so wretched that neither Lia nor Amy would sit on it, there was only the chair, a small battered table, one branch of candles, and the chamber pot. The lack of a window meant no means of escape but for the door, which was locked. They had their wits as their weapons, and so far they'd not had much luck with them either.

"What do you suppose is going on down there?" Amy asked.

Lia crouched to peer through the keyhole, seeing only a murky half darkness and a grimy bit of wall opposite their room. She straightened with a sigh. "We can only hope Mrs. Grace is trying to talk some sense into Sir Nathan's extraordinarily thick head."

After Lia had informed everyone that she was Jack's fiancée, Mrs. Grace had launched into a full-throated tirade, berating Prudhoe for kidnapping *quality*. Events had quickly deteriorated after that when the madam boxed his ears, all while yelling they could end up facing the gallows.

In the mayhem Lia had pulled Amy to her feet and tried to escape. They'd made it into the corridor before their guard got his hands on Amy, throwing her face first against the staircase banister. Lia had launched herself at him, but the other thug suddenly had materialized and pulled her away. On the orders of the madam, she and Amy had been hauled off and locked in this room with threats of a beating if they didn't *keep their gobs shut*.

Silence had descended quickly after that. Wherever they were, this section of the building was apparently little used. No one had come near and nothing could be heard through the thick plaster and brick walls of the house. All they could do was wait and pray for a miracle.

Amy closed her eyes. "They're not going to let us go."

"They'd be insane not to," Lia replied, trying to sound confident. "Imagine what will happen when Sir Dominic finds out about this. He's a powerful magistrate, you know. He will see them all hang if they dare to injure us."

When Amy opened her eyes, her gaze was terrifyingly bleak. "Which is exactly why they're going to have to kill us."

Lia's heart jolted. "What?"

"There's no backing away from this, Miss Lia. As soon as Mrs. Grace heard who you were, we were done for. Even if Sir Nathan is too stupid to realize how much danger he courted by kidnapping us, *she* certainly did. She's a nasty piece of work, that one, and she hasn't survived this many years by acting the fool."

"You know her?"

Amy's mouth quivered for a moment before she regained control. "My sister was the prettiest, happiest lass you ever did see. Mrs. Grace lured her into the trade and did everything she could to keep her there, even when my Nancy wanted to leave." She grimaced. "She died of the pox a few years ago."

"I'm so sorry, my dear," Lia said quietly.

"That's why I worked so hard to become a dancer. I didn't want to end up like Nancy." Her gaze was hardening. "I may take a lover now and again to protect myself, but I'd never sell myself to one of these places, Miss Lia. I'd starve before I did that."

Lia hunkered down and took her hands. "You won't have to, I promise. We're going to get out of this."

Amy slumped against the seat back with a weary sigh. "There's no way out of it, miss. You know too many important people and *you're* too important. Lord Lendale and Sir Dominic would go berserk if they found out about this. Mrs. Grace knows that, too. She knows she'd end up hanging at the end of a rope."

Lia sat down on the hard floorboards, aghast at the turn of events. She finally had a big, loyal family that loved her and wished to protect her, and that simple fact was probably going to get her killed. She would never see Aunt Chloe or Gillian again, or meet her half brother, who'd already written Lia the most warm and loving letter.

And Jack. She would give anything to be with him now, to have the chance to tell him that, yes, she would marry him. All the obstacles that had loomed so large were now insignificant. And he would be devastated if she died, blaming himself for not taking care of her, for not being there when she most needed him.

Lia had wanted to disappear from his life, thinking it best for him. Yet now she was about to get her wish and the irony was all but choking her. It was like being trapped at the bottom of a hill watching a landslide hurtling down on her. Already she felt buried, her chest constricting with panic, and she had to force herself to take one slow breath after another.

Amy scrubbed away tears from her cheeks. "What they had planned for us before . . . well, it wouldn't have been pleasant, but at least we would have survived. Now . . ."

Lia sat quietly for a good minute. Now that she'd calmed down, she could think. "I think we were sunk before actually."

"How so?"

"Because Sir Nathan knows exactly who I am and who I'm connected to. He knew as soon as he snatched us that he couldn't allow me to survive. He might have acted on impulse, but the die was cast as soon as he told his thugs to kidnap me as well as you."

Amy came up out of her slump, her fury quickly replacing despair. "That degenerate bastard," she hissed. "He couldn't just hurt me. He had to go after you, too. Which meant the end of both of us as soon as he touched you."

"I'm afraid so. Eventually, he knew he would have to kill us."

The girl let loose a stream of hair-raising curses, ending with a threat to string Prudhoe up herself.

"I hope you get the opportunity," Lia said with a rueful smile. "But what I can't figure out is why the idiot would risk so much on this crazed venture. He obviously wants to punish us very badly."

Amy let out a hollow laugh. "Looks like he'll get the chance."

Lia scrambled up from the floor. "I have no intention of making it easy for him. From what Mrs. Grace said, you're to be, ah, offered to some gentlemen who would bid on you for your services?"

"They hold an auction. Someone like me, who's younger and fresher than most of the girls, could fetch a pretty penny."

"That's revolting, but we might be able to turn it to our advantage."

Amy cocked her head. "How so?"

"Some of the gentlemen might recognize you; you're one of London's premier dancers, after all. See if you can get close enough to one of them to ask for help. Or even tell the man who purchases you that you're being held against your will."

Amy looked grim again. "Most of them won't care. They think forcing a woman makes it more exciting. That's why they come to something like this."

God. How ridiculously sheltered she'd been her entire life. "That's awful."

Amy shrugged. "Men are awful."

"Not all of them, and perhaps we'll get lucky." She took Amy's hands and pulled her out of the chair. "I know the odds aren't good, but you have to try. Do your best to communicate with anyone who might seem at all sympathetic. Tell him to go to Bow Street or fetch a constable. Or ask him to help you escape, if nothing else."

Amy gave a dubious nod. "I'll do my best, miss."

Lia gave her a quick hug. "You're one of the bravest girls I know, Amy. You can do whatever you need to do to save yourself."

When they heard footsteps rapidly ascending the stairs, they glanced at the door.

"Listen," Lia said urgently, "if we are separated and you have a chance to escape, you must take it."

Amy started to tear up. "I can't just leave—"

"You must. Then go for help."

When the key scraped in the lock, they clutched at each other.

"Promise you will," Lia said.

"Bloody hell. All right, miss. I promise."

The door opened and their two thuggish captors barreled into the room, followed by Sir Nathan.

Lia tried to brazen it out. "Ah, Sir Nathan. Have you decided to let us go?"

The baronet gave her a chilling smile. "Quite the opposite. Mrs. Grace insists that I take care of you. Immediately, in fact." His smile turned into a leer. "Well, not quite immediately. I'm determined to enjoy myself before I hand you over to my men for disposal."

"I'm going to see you all hanged," Lia said, glaring at the baronet and his thugs. "Sir Dominic Hunter will make sure of that. And if he doesn't, then my cousin, Griffin Steele, will see the deed done. In fact, he'll probably slit your throats himself."

The men, who were holding on to Amy, exchanged a startled glance. Lia was worried she might be overplaying her hand, but she'd clearly landed a hit.

"You're Steele's cuz?" one of them asked.

"I am. And he's very fond of me, I might add." She had every confidence he would be, once he finally met her.

"Nobody said nothin' about Griffin bloody Steele. He'll gut us like fish." The thug glared at Sir Nathan. "You ain't payin' us enough for this job."

"You have nothing to fear," Sir Nathan said dismissively. "I doubt anyone knows these women were even taken, and they certainly won't know who did it."

Lia kept a steadfast gaze on the other men. "Are you

willing to risk your life on that chance? People inside the theater must have heard all the commotion. I wouldn't be surprised if someone came out and saw you dragging us away."

"Then why haven't they come to your rescue?" Sir Nathan said with a sneer.

"Because they—"

He delivered a slap that made Lia stagger and grab for a bedpost.

"Leave her alone, you bastard," Amy yelled, struggling. But the thugs simply shook her like a rattle until she hung, panting, between them.

Rubbing her jaw, Lia directed a lethal glare at Prudhoe. "You'll be sorry for that."

"I doubt it." The baronet scowled at his men. "You're perfectly safe. Now take Amy downstairs. Mrs. Grace wants to get her ready." He flashed the poor girl a deranged grin. "You're going to be sold to the highest bidder, love, and he gets to do whatever he wants to you. Mrs. Grace has assembled a most interesting group tonight—men with some highly unusual tastes. I'm sure you'll find it . . . eye-opening."

"Don't forget what I told you," Lia called out as the men dragged the protesting Amy from the room.

The door slammed shut, leaving her alone with the most evil-minded man she'd ever met. When he locked the door and stowed the key in his waistcoat pocket, she had to bite down hard on her lip to steady herself.

"You ruined me, you silly bitch." Prudhoe's eyes blazed with hatred. "You and that bloody family of yours. Because of them, I must leave England."

"I don't understand."

"I'm in debt, and some of it is to that devil, Steele. Your cousin," he added with a snarl. "He's called in all my markers. And Dominic Hunter has dripped poison into other ears. I've been booted from my clubs, hounded by creditors, and now I have no choice but to leave for the Continent."

While he talked, Lia continued to inch her way around to the other side of the bed, a vague idea formulating in her head. "That's certainly not Amy's fault. You have no business taking out your vengeance on her."

"If she'd done what I told her, none of this would have happened." A spasm of fury pulled his face into an ugly grimace. "This is all her fault and I hope whoever buys her rips her apart."

"You're an absolute monster," she said hotly. "And I hope my fiancé rips *you* apart."

He snorted as he began to stroll around to her side of the bed. "Lendale will never know what happened to you. You'll disappear like a wisp of smoke, soon forgotten. After all, you're nothing but a whore, just like your mother."

Lia didn't waste energy refuting his assertions. She was too busy bracing herself for what would come next.

As soon as the baronet rounded the bedframe, he launched himself at her. Lia dodged to get around him, but he was surprisingly fast. He crashed into her and sent her flying into the bed. She sprawled half on and half off the mattress, scrambling for purchase. She blocked his attempt to pull her up onto the bed by letting her weight drag both of them down to the floorboards. Lia's backside connected with a painful jolt that shot up her spine.

"Fine with me," Prudhoe said, puffing like a dragon. "The floor it is."

He hooked a fist into the front of her bodice and yanked. The fabric gave way with a loud rip. When he tried to come down on top of her, Lia wriggled partway under the high bedframe, forcing him to flop across her lower body.

"Stay still, goddamn it," he growled.

When he wrapped his right hand around her neck and

started to squeeze, Lia frantically thrashed. His erection pressed against her belly and his face loomed only inches away. His breath was hot and foul, his grin a rictus of cruelty.

Stretching her hand for it, her fingertips hit the chamber pot. She hooked the rim and dragged it until she had a firm grip on the handle. When Prudhoe pulled her out from under the bed and yanked up her skirts, her fear infused her with a desperate strength. She whipped the heavy pot at his head.

It connected with a sickening thud and his body went slack with surprise. When she gave a mighty heave and shoved him off, the baronet rolled to the side, groaning and cursing.

She needed to finish the job.

"You bitch," Prudhoe choked out as he tried to sit up. "I'll slit your goddamn throat."

With a desperate burst of energy, she clawed her way onto the bed, rolled across it, and hit the floor running. She grabbed the rickety chair and dashed back to the baronet.

He'd pushed himself up onto his hands and knees as Lia swung the chair high and hammered it down on his shoulders. When he crashed back to the floor, she grabbed the heavy chamber pot and smashed it against the back of his head. It shattered into jagged pieces, spraying Amy's vomit all over him.

With a whimper, he slumped and fell still.

Lia staggered backward and grabbed the bedpost for support, trying to calm her rebellious stomach and steady her racing heart. She pinched her nose and sucked in several deep breaths through her mouth, willing her body to settle. The baronet seemed to be out cold and probably no longer posed a threat, but she still had to escape and find help.

Gingerly, she nudged him with her foot, but he didn't

respond. She felt rather sick at the notion that she might have killed him, but she'd worry about that later.

She was steeling herself to turn him over and begin searching his pockets for the key when she heard footsteps pounding down the hall. "Lia, where are you?"

Jack's voice jolted energy through her body, like a thousand blazing suns. "I'm here," she cried, running to the door.

The doorknob rattled. "Stand back," he ordered. "I'm going to kick it in."

She barely had a chance to scuttle out of the way before the door half-flew off its hinges. Jack stood in the doorway, his waistcoat askew, his cravat half-ripped off, and his hair standing on end. He looked like a wild man, and Lia had never seen anything more wonderful in her life.

"Jack!" She threw herself into his arms.

He held her tight as a vise, all but pushing the air from her lungs. She didn't care a jot. He could squeeze her like a stuffed toy for the rest of her life and she would never utter a word of complaint.

"Jesus Christ," he growled. "I thought I was too late." He eased her back to study her, his mouth flat and tight, his gaze shadowed with anxiety. "Are you all right? Did he hurt you?"

She managed a wobbly smile. "I'm a little bruised, but he didn't have time to do much damage."

He touched her cheek, then trailed a hand down to her throat. Prudhoe must have left a mark because Jack's gaze turned black with fury.

"Where is he?" he asked in a lethal voice.

"On the other side of the bed."

He eased her out of his embrace and stalked over to the bed, stumbling to a halt as Lia came up beside him. "You did this?" he asked, staring at the heap on the floor.

She nodded, carefully breathing through her mouth. The baronet was exceedingly ripe, and, to be fair, she didn't

smell like a bouquet of posies either. Some of the contents
of the chamber pot had landed on the skirts of her gown—
a small price to pay for her safety.

"Well done, love," Jack said with a ghost of a laugh.

She grimaced. "I'm afraid I may have killed him."

He crouched down and felt for the baronet's pulse. "No
such luck. You just knocked him out." He straightened
and put his hands on her shoulders. "You're sure he didn't
hurt you?"

"Not in any way that matters," she said, mistily smiling
up at him.

She braced her hands on his chest. Now that the worst
was over, she was feeling wobbly and light-headed. And
despite what she'd just told him, her head was starting to
pound—no doubt from those ringing slaps.

"You look like hell," he said, frowning with worry.

Lia was surprised she could still laugh. "Thank you very
much, kind sir."

He pulled her close. "I thought I'd lost you forever," he
said, his voice thick with emotion. "Don't ever do that to
me again."

"I'll try not to." She nestled her cheek against his
wrinkled cravat. "Jack, Amy is in trouble. You brought help,
did you not?"

"I did. In fact, I think our reinforcements have arrived."

They heard quick steps out in the hall and then Gillian
strode through the door. She was hatless but garbed in a
stylish green walking dress that seemed utterly incongru-
ous, given the setting and circumstances.

She also held a knife in her hand.

"Darling, are you all right?" her cousin asked as she
came up to Lia.

"Yes." She waved a vague hand at Gillian's knife. "Is
that . . . blood?"

"I'm afraid so," her cousin said with a shrug. "One of

the louts downstairs wasn't very cooperative, so I was forced to teach him a lesson." Gillian scowled at the baronet, who was finally stirring, then leaned down and casually wiped her blade clean on his coat before slipping it back into her half boot.

"Good God," Jack muttered, shaking his head. "Please tell me you didn't kill someone. Charles will be furious if you did. Come to think of it, he'll be furious anyway, because I allowed you to come along with me."

"As if you could have stopped me," she said with a snort. She nudged Prudhoe in the ribs with her boot. He responded with a moan. "Well done, Jack."

"Sadly, I cannot take credit. Lia is responsible for Prudhoe's sorry state."

"Bully for you, old girl," Gillian said with a grin. Then she sniffed. "What is that dreadful smell? Did someone cast up his accounts?"

"You don't want to know," Lia said, clutching Jack's coat with both hands. She was feeling more light-headed by the moment and a very odd sensation was overtaking her, as if her brain was pressing up against the top of her skull and trying to escape.

Gillian frowned. "You're looking rather grim, Lia. Are you going to faint?"

"Don't be silly," she said, blinking at the swarm of dots drifting across her vision. "I never faint."

Then she proceeded to do exactly that.

Chapter Twenty-Five

"There, you're all set for bed," Chloe said as she finished braiding Lia's hair. "I do wish you'd agreed to see the doctor, though."

Lia turned at her dressing table to smile at her worried-looking aunt. "My headache is gone and I feel fine. Besides, I've been told on a number of occasions that my head is quite hard."

"And who would be so rude as to say that?"

"Jack for one, along with my grandmother, my mother—"

Chloe chuckled. "Very well, I see your point. But it wouldn't hurt to see the doctor, just to be sure."

Having a family who would do anything to protect her was a blessing Lia never thought she'd have. How ironic that she'd almost had to die before she'd recognized that she was loved simply for herself, without judgment or expectation of anything but love in return.

"I'm truly fine, thanks to all of you," she said.

Chloe glanced at the clock on the bedroom mantelpiece. "Goodness, it's almost ten o'clock. Why don't you climb into bed and I'll bring you a cup of tea? Unless you'd rather go right to sleep."

"I'd rather wait for Jack, if you don't mind. I won't be able to rest until I know everything that happened tonight."

"It might be some time before he and Dominic return from Bow Street. There was much to explain to the magistrate, I'm sure."

"I know. I'll wait."

After her embarrassing fainting episode, Lia had regained her senses as Jack carried her from the brothel to Gillian's carriage. Because Mrs. Grace's nefarious establishment was only a few blocks from Covent Garden, the Runners were already arriving from Bow Street by the time Jack loaded her into the coach. She'd barely had a chance to exchange a word with him before the lawmen pulled him away to deal with the aftermath of their rescue. Gillian had then climbed in and taken both Lia and Amy back to Upper Wimpole Street.

Lia stood and hurried to the big four-poster. Shivering a bit, she quickly slid under the heavy, comforting bed linens and propped herself against the headboard. "How is Amy?"

"She's sleeping, thank goodness." Chloe fetched a soft knitted shawl from the wardrobe and draped it around Lia's shoulders. "She did agree to see the doctor, poor thing, but she looked to be in much worse shape than you."

Lia grimaced. "It was awful what they did to her."

"The doctor gave her a sleeping draught and told her that she needs to spend the next few days in bed, but he expects her to make a full recovery."

"Thank goodness." Lia caressed the smooth bedsheet with the flat of her hand. Never again would she take for granted how wonderful it felt to be safely tucked up in her own lovely, clean bed. "But I don't know if anyone can completely recover from an ordeal like that."

Her aunt wrapped an arm around her shoulders, and Lia relaxed into the warmth of her embrace, breathing in the delicate citrus scent of Chloe's perfume. "I know, darling.

But Amy is strong, and so are you. You both kept your wits about you and fought to stay alive until help could come. I can't begin to tell you how proud I am, and how relieved."

When they'd arrived home, Chloe had immediately sent for the doctor for Amy, dosed them both with large brandies, and then seen them deposited in hot baths. Chloe had washed Lia's hair, allowing her to haltingly relay the evening's traumatic events without interruption, listening with calm attention. It had been infinitely soothing for Lia's rattled nerves.

"Thank you," Lia said. "I'm rather proud of us, too, although I know that sounds horribly conceited."

Her aunt laughed. "You have every reason to crow. From what Gillian tells me, you were a true heroine."

"If anyone would know, it would be Gillian." Lia grinned. "She's a warrior princess."

"Indeed she is. Much to her husband's consternation."

"I, for one, am exceedingly grateful she is the way she is."

According to Amy, Gillian, along with Jack and one of her grooms, had taken care of Mrs. Grace and her thugs in short order. To Gillian, it was apparently all in a day's work, but she'd rendered Amy into an almost babbling state of admiration. After all, it wasn't every day one was rescued by a duchess who could disarm a ruthless thug twice her size.

"Did Gillian go home?" Lia asked.

"Yes. She said she needed to explain things to Charles before he heard any *nonsensical gossip*, as she called it, about tonight's events."

"I wish I could have heard that conversation."

"I don't," Chloe said wryly. "Now, do you think you could rest a bit before I bring you a cup of tea?"

"I'll try, but I don't really think I'll be able to sleep until I see Jack."

With every moment that passed, Lia grew more restless

to be with him. She still didn't know precisely what would happen between them, but she needed to feel his arms around her. And she needed another chance to tell him that she loved him. Whether they married or not, she would never view his presence in her life as anything less than the most precious of gifts.

Chloe cocked her head. "Your wait is over, I believe." She glided to the door and opened it. "Ah, Lord Lendale. Lia has been waiting for you."

Jack stuck his head into the room. "Good evening, Lady Hunter. Are you sure she's not too tired to see me?"

"Of course I'm not," Lia said. "Please come in."

He strode quickly to the bed, obviously as eager to see her as she was to see him.

"How are you, love?" His gruff tone—which she knew stemmed from emotion—was offset by how gently he stroked her hair.

"I'm fine," she said, gazing up at him, knowing she looked like a love-besotted fool.

He smiled back, but his gaze was somber and weariness had scored deep lines around his mouth.

"I'm not sure about you, though," she added. "You look exhausted."

He grimaced. "Bow Street is a taxing environment at the best of times, and there was a great deal to be sorted out."

"I suppose my husband is still down there," Chloe said with good-humored resignation.

Jack glanced over his shoulder. "Yes. He expects to finish up there shortly, but then he intends to go on to Carlton House. He asked me to tell you not to wait up for him."

Chloe made an exasperated noise. "He always says that."

"And you always wait up for him, don't you?" Lia said.

"Of course. That's what wives do." She winked. "As I expect you'll find out."

Lia glanced at Jack and could feel herself blushing. "Yes, well, we'll see," she said vaguely.

He narrowed his gaze. "We'll see?"

She wrinkled her nose at him.

"I must check on my son and then I'll wait for Dominic in his study," Chloe said, clearly trying to suppress a smile. "Just ring if you need anything."

"I will," Lia said.

"And do not keep my niece up till all hours, Lord Lendale," Chloe added. "She needs her rest."

"Yes, ma'am," Jack said dryly.

When the door closed, they silently regarded each other. Lia's heart throbbed with a yearning she knew would last a lifetime if she walked away from Jack. But now that he stood before her, she couldn't muster up the right words to navigate through the unresolved issues still looming between them.

"Are you sure you're all right?" he finally said, taking her hand. "God, Lia, you scared the hell out of me when you fainted."

She squeezed his fingers. "It was so silly of me. Even Amy didn't faint, and she was in much worse shape than I."

"Perhaps you were feeling a little woozy from hunger," he said with a gleam of humor. "Perfectly understandable because you missed tea."

She let out a reluctant chuckle. "Wretch. But Jack, are you sure *you're* all right? You look rather battered."

He sighed and rubbed a hand back through his hair. Although still somewhat disheveled, he'd set his clothing to rights as best he could. "I'm fine, although I'll admit that dealing with Prudhoe and his thugs—not to mention Mrs. Grace, who shrieked all the way to Bow Street—did try my patience. Thank God Dominic showed up to take charge of it all."

Lia scooted over and patted the mattress. "Here, sit down

while you tell me about it. I haven't a clue what happened after you sent me home."

"All right, but let me take off these boots. You know how filthy that brothel was. And I saw a great deal more of it than I wanted to."

"As did I," she said wryly.

After he wrestled off his boots, he climbed onto the bed and propped himself against the headboard, stretching out his long legs with a weary sigh. "I hate that you had to see even one inch of that benighted place. The Runners and I made a sweep of the entire building, just to make sure there were no other women being held there against their will."

"I'm so glad you thought of that. Were there any others?"

"No, thank God. In fact, most of the ladies seemed quite annoyed by the disturbance, their customers even more so. I will say, however, that very few of the women were distressed to see the back end of Mrs. Grace. She was clearly not well-liked by her, er, employees."

"I'm not surprised. She's a horrid woman."

When he slung an arm around her shoulders, pulling her close, everything inside her finally settled. As he held her, it felt like the rhythm of their hearts slowed and started to beat as one. For a few precious moments, Lia allowed herself to rest in a place of perfect contentment, as if floating in infinite sunlight.

She was reluctant to reenter the world, but there were too many unanswered questions and too many decisions yet to make. "Why was Dominic going to Carlton House? That seems rather odd."

"He thought it best to report to the Prince Regent on tonight's events before rumors started circulating."

She frowned. "Why would the prince care? Sir Nathan is only a baronet, one without much power, it seems."

He dropped a kiss on the top of her head. "Not because

of him, sweetheart, because of you. You're the daughter of a royal duke, and both the Duke of York and the Regent will certainly want to know about tonight's unfortunate events."

She twisted in his embrace to stare up at him. "That seems unlikely. My father has never even met me." It felt odd to even use the term.

"That doesn't mean he's not interested in your welfare."

"Jack, not once in my entire life has he shown an iota of interest, nor did he ever give Mama any money for support after their affair ended."

"I suspect that's about to change, thanks to your half brother—who *is* quite close to the duke. Captain Endicott is very concerned for your welfare and has written to York about you." Jack smiled. "I'm sure Sir Dominic will have something to say about it, too, as a member of York's inner circle. Don't be surprised if your royal father begins to take an interest in you, especially after tonight."

Apparently she was acquiring family by leaps and bounds. It would take getting used to, but it also felt quite lovely. "Better late than never, I suppose."

He pulled her back into his embrace. "Not that it truly matters, because I'll be taking care of you from now on."

"Jack, about that—"

"Although you're obviously capable of taking care of yourself," he said, sounding a bit disgruntled. "I was all set to charge in, your knight in shining armor, only to discover you'd dispatched the villain quite handily."

She patted his chest. "You'll always be my knight in shining armor. And I cannot tell you how happy I was to see you burst through that door. I must admit I was stunned, though. How did you know we were there?"

"Your little friend Sammy heard your screams in the alley. He rushed out in time to see you being hauled off to Prudhoe's carriage. He bravely followed and managed to keep the carriage in sight, thank God."

"He's a very quick and clever lad." And Lia could never be grateful enough for his courage.

"He is at that and shall be amply rewarded, I assure you."

"So, he followed us to the brothel. Then what did he do?"

"He knew where you lived, so he came here. That showed on uncommon presence of mind, and I now suspect Sir Dominic will take the boy under his wing. Sammy deserves a better future than hanging about the back door of a theater."

"Ah, so that's why Gillian was with you. We'd planned to meet here for tea."

"Yes. In fact, your cousin wanted to storm the barricades with only her groom's assistance. Fortunately, your aunt was able to hold her back until she could send for me. It took a little longer to track down Dominic, though, and we decided not to wait for him. Thank God," he added with a mutter, giving her a squeeze.

She wrapped her arms around his waist and hugged him back. "Yes, poor Amy was in a very bad fix. If you'd been much later, I don't know what would have happened."

"Yes, we had to scramble. Lady Hunter dispatched word to Bow Street, but I had to make sure we had enough men for the job because I had no idea what we would be facing. Charles would have murdered me if anything happened to Gillian." He shook his head. "She was quite annoyed with my *blasted caution*, as she termed it. As if *I* didn't want to go charging straight in there myself, pistols firing."

"Or knives slashing, as the case may be. What an amazing person she is."

"Don't tell her that. You'll just encourage her."

Lia couldn't help laughing. "I have every intention of emulating her from now on. She was truly inspiring. As were you," she hastily added when he lifted a sardonic brow.

"Your enthusiasm overwhelms me, my love," he said.

She poked him in the ribs. "Don't be silly. You were absolutely splendid. All you needed was a white stallion and the heroic picture would have been complete."

"You were the true hero, Lia. You kept your head under the most horrific of circumstances and rescued yourself. Gillian and I merely mopped up after you." He cupped her cheek, his gaze tender and full of emotion. "I'm beginning to think you don't need me at all. I don't like that part very much, which makes me sound like an insufferable coxcomb," he added with a rueful smile.

His praise brought tears to her eyes. "Jack, you'll always be my hero. Just think of all the times you've rescued me over the years."

"Like the time you fell into the pond and I fished you out?"

"You pulled me into the pond, as I recall," she protested. "After I pushed *you* in."

"Oh, right. Well, then, what about that time you stepped on that wasp nest and I carried you to safety?"

"Actually, *you* stepped on it, although I admit you did carry me to safety. But I was only five years old at the time. I couldn't run as fast as you."

He let out a dramatic sigh and nestled her back against his chest. "Clearly, I need to work a little harder at this hero business."

"Perhaps Gillian could give you lessons."

"What a horrifying idea."

She chuckled, then turned serious. "Jack, what will happen to Prudhoe and the others?"

"That will be up to the magistrate and the courts, of course, but they all might hang," he said in a somber tone. "God knows they deserve it."

She couldn't help cringing a bit. As much as Prudhoe and his men—and Mrs. Grace—had earned their fate, she hated that they might find their deaths because of her.

"It's not your fault, love," he said gently. "Only they are responsible for their actions."

She breathed out a trembling sigh. Of course he would know what she was thinking—he always did. "If only I hadn't gone to that stupid Cyprians' ball. That started everything."

He nudged up her chin, making her look at him. "And what would have happened to poor Amy if you hadn't gone? You rescued her that night, too, remember?"

She blinked, startled by his response. He'd been so furious with her that night, and yet now he was praising her for going.

"Not that I want you making a habit of that sort of thing," he added. "Let's be clear on that."

"Yes, my lord," she said meekly, subsiding back on his chest.

His snort told her how little he was fooled by her manner.

"You are giving up on that idea, are you not?" he asked a few moments later, sounding doubtful. "The whole courtesan nonsense. You know it's not the life for you."

She sighed. "It's not the life for most women, Jack. I've come to hate the entire sordid business. No woman should be forced to sell herself to survive. It's disgusting and heart-breaking."

He let out a heavy sigh. "I agree entirely. And I'm greatly relieved that I don't have to spend the rest of my life scaring off potential protectors and keeping you out of trouble. That would be exhausting for both of us."

"Jack, what I'd really like to do is help some of these unfortunate women, perhaps assist Aunt Chloe in her work."

"You don't need to do that in London. There must be charitable organizations who assist such women in Yorkshire and would be happy to have the support of the Marchioness of Lendale. If not, you can start one."

Lia hid her face in his cravat. "About that . . ." she said, her voice muffled.

His big body stiffened beneath her. "About what? About our impending marriage? Because that is not up for debate, Lia. We *are* getting married, and sooner rather than later."

She sat up and tried to pull out of his arms, but he refused to release her. Instead, he cupped her chin and feathered a kiss across her lips that quickly transformed from gentle to demanding, full of heat and hidden promises. She sighed and wrapped her hands around his strong wrists, taking in the sweep of his tongue with an eagerness she wouldn't deny. Too soon, he eased away to trace the curve of her cheek with his lips. Lia couldn't hold back a shiver of pleasure.

"Sweetheart," he murmured between kisses, "I almost lost you tonight. I swear that would have been the end of me."

She reluctantly retreated from his delectable kisses to study his face. His dark gaze burned with hunger, propelling a rush of desire through her body.

"Do you love me, Jack?" she whispered.

His smile was crooked and endearing. "I can't believe you need to ask. My darling, don't you realize how much I need you? You're everything to me."

"You say that now, but—"

He took her firmly by the shoulders, gazing at her with an intensity that made her tremble. "I will *always* say it. Lia Kincaid, I love you more than anyone on God's earth. I want to marry you. Now, is that clear enough?"

Joy unspooled in her heart like colorful strands of silk. "Yes, thank you, and I love you, too. But—"

"No buts. We're getting married."

"Well, perhaps . . ." She wrinkled her nose when he scowled at her. "Very well, but not right away."

His expression lightened. "Ah, do you wish to have the

ceremony at Stonefell?" He cut her a sheepish grin. "You want a proper wedding, with Rebecca and the rest of your family. Of course you should have that, and I'm a brute to suggest otherwise."

"No, I think I need more time than that," she confessed. "More importantly, *you* need more time than that."

"What the hell does that mean?"

Lia pulled out of his embrace, and this time he reluctantly let her go. She folded her legs to sit tailor style facing him. "It means I should visit my half brother and his wife in Vienna before we make any final decisions. Captain Endicott has made it clear he would be delighted if I stayed at least three or four months. I think that's an excellent idea."

Jack crossed his arms over his chest, looking so put out she was tempted to laugh—if she didn't start crying first. She loved him so much it made her heart ache. Leaving him for even a few months was an awful prospect. What if he decided he didn't truly wish to marry her? For his sake, though, she needed to take that risk.

"I think it's a horrific idea," he said.

"This is a momentous decision, Jack, and you need time to think it through without me right in front of you, making you feel guilty."

He rolled his eyes. "You do not make me feel guilty."

"Jack, you feel guilty about everything."

He was about to deny it when she lifted her eyebrows, prompting him to let out a disgruntled laugh. "Very well, I partially concede your point. But we're still getting married, and it's because I love you and want to be with you, not because you make me feel guilty. That's just nonsense."

"Of course you feel guilty. You feel obliged to marry me because you rather precipitously stole my virtue."

"I did not steal it, nor was I precipitous. I took it with

full knowledge of what I was doing." He gave her a smug smile. "That was part of my plan."

"It was not," she exclaimed.

He waggled a hand. "Well, perhaps not right away, but it certainly is now."

"Jack, that's ridiculous."

"I'm joking, sweetheart. Trust me when I tell you that I would never have laid a hand on you if I had doubts about what I was doing." He gave her a wry smile. "Especially considering the consequences of my actions. I'm well aware of the challenges before us, which should convince you of the seriousness of my intentions. This is not a feckless or haphazard decision on my part, Lia. I make it with full understanding. And," he added quietly, "it's one I make with a great deal of gratitude and happiness."

"Oh," she whispered, pressing a hand to her chest. "That's . . . that's rather lovely." When he put it that way, it was hard not to see his logic.

"And because I'm such a wise fellow," he said, "I also understand that I need your help. No one knows Stonefell as you do. If I don't marry me, I'm sure to muck everything up."

She had to smile. "Now, that's plain silly. But what are you going to do about Stonefell's situation? You need to get the money somewhere."

"That's where your family comes in. Sir Dominic and Charles are quite insistent about investing in the mining scheme, and they're confident they can bring in other investors. And believe it or not, Lindsey is feeling better about the way the harvest is shaping up for the fall."

"That's all good news, but is it enough?"

"It will be once I sell the mansion in Bedford Square."

Lia almost fell off the bed. "Jack, no! You can't do that."

He raised an eyebrow. "Why not?"

"Because it's part of your family legacy, that's why.

Besides, your mother will hate it—hate me. And she doesn't need additional reasons to do so," she added morosely.

He leaned forward and kissed the tip of her nose. "I was pondering selling it even before I discovered I wanted to marry you. Honestly, love, I have no attachment to it, and it's simply too big and too expensive to keep."

"But where will your mother live? Where will *you* live when you come to London?"

"You mean, where will *we* live? As to that, I was thinking of buying one of those new terrace houses going up in Belgravia. My mother will be merry as a grig in a stylish new town house, I assure you. As for us, we'll be spending most of our time at Stonefell."

"Jack, your mother will never agree to this."

He took both her hands, cradling them in his warm grip. "I know she won't be happy, but that is her choice, Lia. I cannot live my life for her. I must live it for myself."

She gnawed her lip, wanting to believe they had a chance. "Are you sure?"

He nodded. "Beyond doubt."

"Stonefell has never been your dream," she said. "Can you be happy with such a quiet life?"

"Lia, dreams change. My dream now is *you*. You are the kindest, sweetest person I've ever known. How could I not want to spend my life with you?"

She clutched his hand, blinking back tears. "Thank you, but I'm afraid others won't see me in the same light."

"Then I want no part of them. Now, my darling, all that's left is for you to face down your own fears. Can you do that?"

She stared into his loving gaze and knew he was right. She'd been afraid for most of her life—afraid she would lose the small circle of people she loved and the one place she could call home. And yet she'd spent weeks trying to push all that away, push *him* away, because she'd thought it was best for him. But that was a decision Jack needed to make for himself, and apparently he had.

"Well, it would appear you've figured everything out to everyone's satisfaction, Lord Lendale," she said, emotion making her voice gruff.

A slow, utterly masculine smile turned up the corners of his mouth. "I have, although I do wish to make one other point."

"And that is?"

He clamped his hands around her waist and lifted her into his lap. She gasped at the feel of his erection pressing against her bottom.

"I also have an unquenchable lust for your delectable figure," he said in a husky tone that made her shiver. "And if I don't get you into my bed very soon, I will no doubt go stark-raving mad."

"Dear me, that would be most unfortunate," she said in a breathless voice.

He bent down until his mouth was a mere inch from hers. "I love you, Lia Kincaid," he murmured. "With all my heart. We're getting married and I'm not taking no for an answer."

Lia's throat had gone so tight that all she could do was nod. But for once, she was more than happy to give him the last word.

Epilogue

"My lady, you should let me carry that tea tray," the butler replied in a mildly disapproving tone as he hurried to intercept her. "It's too heavy for you."

Lia paused before the door of the library. "Richard, I've been lugging tea trays around the manor for years. You never objected before."

"That was *before* you were the lady of the house." A twinkle lurked in his eyes. "At least officially."

"It still seems strange, to tell you the truth. Every time one of the servants addresses me as *my lady*, I'm tempted to look behind me."

"You're doing splendidly, my lady. And everyone below-stairs agrees, I might add."

"Especially right before Boxing Day, I would imagine," Lia joked. She had collected quite a pile of gifts and small change purses, ready to distribute to the staff in the morning.

"Especially then."

She smiled. "Very well, Richard, that will be all for the night."

"Very good, my lady," he said, reaching for the door-knob.

"I suppose I shouldn't call you Richard anymore, should I? I keep forgetting."

On their return to Stonefell, Jack had encouraged the old butler to retire. Debbins had never approved of her and he'd been more than happy to be pensioned off rather than suffer the indignity of answering to a Kincaid as lady of the house. Jack had replaced him with Richard, the head foot-man and her old friend. It was just one of the many changes, large and small, her husband had made to ensure her comfort.

"Lady Lendale, you may call me whatever you like." He cracked a slight smile. "Just not in front of the other servants."

She laughed. "Thank you, Betley. Good night and happy Christmas."

Richard pushed the door open. "Happy Christmas, my lady."

Lia started across the spacious room. The tea tray *was* rather heavy, and she'd hate to spill on the new and very beautiful carpet that had been installed only last week.

"Here, let me help you," Jack said, striding around his desk to take it from her. "Why didn't you let one of the servants bring that in?"

"Betley wanted to, but I didn't wish to inconvenience him, and the others are down in the kitchen having a bit of a holiday party. They've been working so hard to get the manor ready for Christmas."

He placed the tray on his desk. "Love, you'll hurt their feelings if you don't ask them to do things. They want to help you."

She smoothed her skirts as she sat in the big leather club chair in front of his desk. "The staff have made it tremendously easy on me, so there's no need to worry."

Ever since their return in October—as husband and wife—the servants had been welcoming and helpful. The tenant farmers had also seemed pleased to see Lia in her new role, as had most of the shopkeepers in the village. There were, of course, a few who disapproved. Some of the local gentry were mortally offended that Jack had picked her instead of one of their own daughters. Jack had taken an exceedingly dim view of anyone having the nerve to snub her, prompting her to suggest that it might be best to ignore the offending party rather than tear a strip off him or her. After all, one couldn't spend the rest of one's life going about insulting neighbors; it was simply too exhausting.

"The servants respect you," he said. "They know how much you love Stonefell and care for the people who live here."

"How could I not love it? It's my home."

"I'm glad you finally realize that," he said wryly as he handed her a cup of tea.

"I always realized it. I just didn't think it was the right place for me to be, for your sake as well as my own."

He sat on the edge of his desk, studying her. "It's exactly where you should be."

She smiled at him over the rim of her teacup. "Wherever *you* are is where I should be."

He grinned. "Then we are in perfect accord."

"As usual."

"I'll remind you of that the next time you contradict me."

Lia affected surprise. "My lord, when do we ever disagree?"

He huffed out a derisive snort.

Hiding a smile, she nodded at the correspondence on his

desk. "You received a letter from your mother, did you not? Is she enjoying herself?"

"I believe she's is in her element. It was a brilliant idea on Gillian's part to invite the old girl to the Leverton family pile in Wiltshire for the Christmas season. It sounds like my mother and the dowager duchess are as thick as thieves, and Mama is most impressed with the distinguished nature of the guests."

Lia set her teacup down on the desk. "It was quite self-less of Gillian to invite her, given that she and your mother are not the best of friends."

"I have a feeling Gillian will talk Mama into accepting the new reality by the end of her stay," Jack said. "Your cousin is a force of nature when she sets her mind to something."

As predicted, Lady John had been infuriated by the news of Jack's betrothal to Lia, and there had been a towering row. Fortunately, Lady Anne had intervened, stoutly coming to Lia's defense. Dominic and Leverton had also made a show of support by calling on Lady John to tell her that they would be assisting the Lendale family and helping to secure Stonefell's future.

Just as importantly, Lia had been able to persuade her mother to send a letter of apology to Lady John, expressing regret for past insults and bad behavior. Of course, Lia had been forced to stand over her mother's shoulder and all but write the letter herself. Lady John had never acknowledged receiving it, but she had grudgingly admitted to Jack that, as a good Christian, she supposed she must try to forgive such a fallen, unfortunate woman.

For now, it was the best they could hope to expect from Jack's mother. Lady John had not attended their small wedding at Leverton House, nor had she yet written to Lia to welcome her into the family. Jack was annoyed, but Lia had counseled patience. There had been too much pain and heartache in the past for her ladyship to suddenly express such generosity of spirit.

"I'm just happy you and your mother are speaking to each other," she said. "I was terrified she'd never forgive you."

"Not to worry, sweetheart. She loves me and she'll come to love you."

Lia doubted that, but she'd be content if Lady John at least deigned to visit Stonefell someday.

"I hope you don't mind that we had such a quiet Christmas," she said. "I know you missed your family and friends."

"Nonsense. This is exactly where I wanted to be. Besides, we had your family."

She smiled. "Yes, it's splendid that Dominic and Chloe are able to spend the holiday season with us. I'd been missing little Dom, too."

"I wasn't," Jack said wryly.

When she poked him in the knee, he laughed. "I'm joking. He's an engaging little scamp."

"He's a darling, although I'm very sorry he cast up his accounts on your new coat. If it's any consolation, he did the same to me only this morning."

Those unfortunate incidents aside, it had been a truly delightful holiday with the Hunters. And for the first time in her life, Lia's grandmother had been able to fully spend Christmas at Stonefell. Granny had gone a bit teary, still missing Uncle Arthur, but she'd also been bursting with pride to see Lia presiding over the festivities as the new Marchioness of Lendale.

"Little Dom is rather like a drunken sailor at this stage, isn't he?" Jack said. "My valet immediately took to his bed when he viewed the extent of the damage."

"Now you're just being foolish."

"I am." He nodded toward the door. "Has everyone else gone up to bed?"

"I think so. Dominic walked Granny back to the cottage and Chloe retired a half hour ago."

"Good, because I have another present. I wanted us to be alone when I gave it to you."

"Jack, you shouldn't be spending so much money on me," she protested. "You've already given me too much."

His gifts included beautiful riding boots, buttery-soft leather gloves, a fur muff, and several books. Rarely a week went by that her husband didn't give her a present—mostly small, intimate gifts like a new kerchief or sweets from the local confectionary. He said he was making up for all the years when he hadn't been able to spoil her.

"Not true, but in any case, you deserve to be spoiled," he said, silencing her protest with a kiss. "For years you took care of everyone else. Now it's time for me to take care of you."

He retrieved a small velvet pouch that had been sitting on his desk, opened it, and tipped a delicate gold bracelet into the palm of his hand. When he took her wrist and fastened the bracelet around it, she saw it had a medallion attached to the chain.

"Is that—" Her throat went tight.

"Happy Christmas, my love," he said, bending down to give her a sweet, lingering kiss. "Thank you for bringing me safely home."

"Oh, Jack," she whispered. "It's the Roman coin I gave you that Christmas, just before you went off to war."

The coin had been polished to a high gleam and set within filigreed gold. It was elegant and beautiful and the most wonderful gift she'd ever received.

"I didn't know you still had it," she said.

"I carried it with me through the entire war. It was my good-luck piece."

"But it brought you luck; are you sure you don't wish to keep it?"

"I'm sure," he said, gently cupping her cheek. "You're my good-luck charm, Lia. I need no other."

"You're going to make me cry and I've already turned into a watering pot too often today."

It had been such a wonderful, emotional day—her first proper Christmas at Stonefell—and she'd found herself choking up more than once.

"We can't have that," he said, pulling her to her feet. "I propose to take you to bed, where I can offer you a very powerful—and large—distraction."

She snickered at his awful joke. "Very well, but do you mind if we step out on the terrace for a few minutes? I'd like to take a look at the stars before we go to bed."

"It's cold out there," he said, apparently a bit puzzled by the request.

"I know, but we did it once before, remember? The night I gave you the coin, we stood on the terrace and listened to the carols."

It was the night she'd wished on a star, hoping to be here someday with Jack, openly and happily in love.

"I remember," he said. "No carols this evening, but we can still look at the stars."

He led her to the French doors, taking a lap blanket off a chair on the way. They stepped out under a clear night sky lit up by a million stars, the universe's jewels scattered across the inky void. Jack wrapped the blanket around them, pulling her into the shelter of his arms. The air was cold enough to tickle her lungs, but his big body kept her warm and safe.

Lia stared up at the glittering celestial arc, drinking in the deep happiness of the moment. "I missed this when we were in London. Most nights you could barely see the moon, much less the stars."

For several moments they gazed upward, taking in the music of the spheres.

"Since we're reminiscing, there's a question I've been meaning to ask you," Jack said.

She wriggled around to face him, enjoying the feel of his erection against her belly. When he sucked in a little breath, she couldn't hold back a smug grin.

"And what is your question, my lord?"

"It's about that demented idea you had to become a courtesan."

She rolled her eyes. "It didn't seem demented at the time. But that point aside, what would you like to know?"

"You gave me three weeks to decide whether to become your lover or help you find a protector, remember? You told me it was simply a nice, round figure, but I think there was more to it than that."

She hid her face against his chest. "Yes, there was," she said, her voice muffled. "But you'll think it's silly."

He nudged her chin up. "I promise not to tease."

"You'd better not, or you'll find yourself sleeping on the chaise in my dressing room."

"Forewarned is forearmed. Now, out with it, lady wife."

"Very well. When I was a girl, I couldn't wait for your visits to Stonefell. I even used to mark them on a little calendar I drew up. You came to visit three times a year and you always stayed for . . ."

"Three weeks," he finished for her.

"Yes. Those were the happiest of times for me, when we were together—even though I'm sure I was a bother to you more than anything else. And I hated it when you left." When he remained silent, she wrinkled her nose. "I told you it was silly."

Silly that a little girl should pine so much for her only friend. Silly that she felt so lonely when he went away. Those three weeks always meant so much.

He bent down to kiss her. Lia melted against him as he

gently brushed her lips, then slipped inside to taste her mouth with a delicious passion.

"It's not silly at all," he said when he finally allowed her to breathe. "In fact, you quite humble me. What did I ever do to deserve you?"

She pretended to consider it. "You made me mistress of Stonefell?"

He laughed. "I got the better end of that bargain, as anyone who works on the estate will tell you. Now, if you've had enough stargazing, perhaps you will allow me to take the mistress of Stonefell to bed?"

"I am happy to comply, my lord." The chill was starting to seep through her gown, despite the blanket and his warm embrace. This was lovely, but bed with Jack would be even better.

He was turning her toward the terrace door when his head jerked up. "Will you look at that?" he exclaimed.

Lia craned back to look and then let out a gasp. Shooting stars were streaking down the sky, one after another.

"It's just like that last Christmas we were together," she exclaimed.

"Quick, make a wish, my love."

She did, keeping it close to her heart. She wasn't certain of it yet—not enough to tell him, anyway. But if her wish came true, in less than eight months, they would welcome a new addition to the Lendale family.

"Did *you* make one, Jack?"

His eyes gleamed with heartfelt emotion. "I don't have to wish on a star because my dreams have come true. You're my dream, Lia. Now and forever."

She smiled as he led her back inside the old manor house, quietly welcoming them on this beautiful winter night.

They were home.

Connect with Us

Visit us online at
KensingtonBooks.com
to read more from your favorite authors, see books
by series, view reading group guides, and more.

Join us on social media

for sneak peeks, chances to win books and prize packs,
and to share your thoughts with other readers.

facebook.com/kensingtonpublishing
twitter.com/kensingtonbooks

Tell us what you think!

To share your thoughts, submit a review,
or sign up for our eNewsletters, please visit:
KensingtonBooks.com/TellUs.

Books by Bestselling Author
Fern Michaels

___The Jury	0-8217-7878-1	$6.99US/$9.99CAN
___Sweet Revenge	0-8217-7879-X	$6.99US/$9.99CAN
___Lethal Justice	0-8217-7880-3	$6.99US/$9.99CAN
___Free Fall	0-8217-7881-1	$6.99US/$9.99CAN
___Fool Me Once	0-8217-8071-9	$7.99US/$10.99CAN
___Vegas Rich	0-8217-8112-X	$7.99US/$10.99CAN
___Hide and Seek	1-4201-0184-6	$6.99US/$9.99CAN
___Hokus Pokus	1-4201-0185-4	$6.99US/$9.99CAN
___Fast Track	1-4201-0186-2	$6.99US/$9.99CAN
___Collateral Damage	1-4201-0187-0	$6.99US/$9.99CAN
___Final Justice	1-4201-0188-9	$6.99US/$9.99CAN
___Up Close and Personal	0-8217-7956-7	$7.99US/$9.99CAN
___Under the Radar	1-4201-0683-X	$6.99US/$9.99CAN
___Razor Sharp	1-4201-0684-8	$7.99US/$10.99CAN
___Yesterday	1-4201-1494-8	$5.99US/$6.99CAN
___Vanishing Act	1-4201-0685-6	$7.99US/$10.99CAN
___Sara's Song	1-4201-1493-X	$5.99US/$6.99CAN
___Deadly Deals	1-4201-0686-4	$7.99US/$10.99CAN
___Game Over	1-4201-0687-2	$7.99US/$10.99CAN
___Sins of Omission	1-4201-1153-1	$7.99US/$10.99CAN
___Sins of the Flesh	1-4201-1154-X	$7.99US/$10.99CAN
___Cross Roads	1-4201-1192-2	$7.99US/$10.99CAN

Available Wherever Books Are Sold!
Check out our website at www.kensingtonbooks.com